Our Dark Duet
Copyright © 2017 by Victoria Schwab

The text of this book is set in 12-point Dante MT Regular.
Book design by Paul Zakris

Library of Congress Control Number: 2017938028

ISBN 978-0-06-238088-3 (hardback)

17 18 19 20 21 PC/LSCH 10 9 8 7 6 5 4 3 2 1
First Edition

 GREENWILLOW BOOKS

Our Dark Duet

A MONSTERS OF VERITY NOVEL

VICTORIA SCHWAB

GREENWILLOW BOOKS
An Imprint of HarperCollins*Publishers*

To those lost inside themselves

He who fights monsters should see to it that
in the process he does not become a monster . . .
if you gaze long into an abyss, the abyss also gazes into you.
—FRIEDRICH NIETZSCHE

Hell is empty,
All the devils are here.
—WILLIAM SHAKESPEARE, *The Tempest*

PRELUDE

Out in the Waste stood a home, abandoned.

A place where a girl had grown up, and a boy had burned
    alive, where a violin had been shattered, and a
    stranger had been shot—

And a new monster had been born.

She stood in the house, the dead man at her feet, stepped
    over his body, wandered out into the yard, drew in
    fresh air as the sun went down.

And started walking.

◈

Out in the Waste stood a warehouse, forgotten.

A place where the air was still full of blood and hunger
    and heat, where the girl had escaped and the boy had
    fallen, and the monsters were defeated—

All except for one.

He lay on the warehouse floor, a steel bar driven through
    his back. It scraped his heart with every beat, and

black blood spread like a shadow beneath his
dark suit.

The monster was dying.

But not dead.

◈

She found him lying there, and pulled the weapon
from his back, watching as he spit black blood onto
the warehouse floor and rose to meet her.

He knew that his maker was dead.

And she knew that hers was not.

Not yet.

VERSE I
MONSTER HUNTER

1

PROSPERITY

Kate Harker hit the ground running.

Blood dripped from a shallow cut on her calf, and her lungs were sore from the blow she'd taken to the chest. Thank God for armor, even if it was makeshift.

"Turn right."

Her boots slid on the slick pavement as she rounded the corner onto a side street. She swore when she saw it was full of people, restaurant canopies up and tables out despite the brewing storm.

Teo's voice rose in her ear. *"It's catching up."*

Kate backtracked and took off down the main road. "If you don't want a mass casualty event, find me somewhere else."

"Half a block, then cut right," said Bea, and Kate felt like the avatar in some multiplayer game where a girl was chased by monsters through a massive city. Only this massive city was real—the capital at the heart of

Prosperity—and so were the monsters. Well, *monster.* She'd taken out one, but a second was heading her way.

The shadows wicked around her as she ran. A chill twisted through the damp night and fat drops of rain dripped under her collar and down her back.

"Left up ahead," instructed Bea, and Kate bolted past a row of shops and down an alley, leaving a trail of fear and blood like bread crumbs in her wake. She reached a narrow lot and a wall, only it wasn't a wall, but a warehouse door, and for a split second she was back in the abandoned building in the Waste, cuffed to a bar in a blacked-out room while somewhere beyond the door, metal struck bone and someone—

"Left."

Kate blinked the memory away as Bea repeated her instruction. But she was sick of running, and the door was ajar, so she went straight, out of the rain and into the vacant space.

There were no windows in the warehouse, no light at all save that from the street behind her, which reached only a few feet—the rest of the steel structure was plunged into solid black. Kate's pulse pounded in her head as she cracked a glorified glow stick—Liam's idea—and tossed it into the shadows, flooding the warehouse with steady white light.

"Kate . . . ," chimed in Riley for the first time. *"Be careful."*

She snorted. Count on Riley to give useless advice. She scanned the warehouse, spotted crates piled within reach of the steel rafters overhead, and started to climb, hauling herself the last of the way up just as the door rattled on its hinges.

Kate froze.

She held her breath as fingers—not flesh and bone, but something else—curled around the door and slid it open.

Static sounded in her good ear.

"Status?" asked Liam nervously.

"Busy," she hissed, balancing on the rafters as the monster filled the doorway, and for an instant, Kate imagined Sloan's red eyes, his shining fangs, his dark suit.

Come out, little Katherine, he'd say. *Let's play a game.*

The sweat on her skin chilled, but it was just her mind playing tricks on her—the creature edging forward into the warehouse wasn't a Malchai. It was something else entirely.

It had a Malchai's red eyes, yes, and a Corsai's sharp claws, but its skin was the bluish black of a rotting corpse, and it wasn't after flesh or blood.

It fed on *hearts.*

Kate didn't know why she'd assumed the monsters would be the same. Verity had its triad, but here she had only come across a single kind. So far.

Then again, Verity boasted the highest crime rate of all ten territories—thanks in large part, she was sure, to her father—while Prosperity's sins were harder to place. On the books, Prosperity was the wealthiest territory by half, but it was a robust economy rotting from the inside out.

If Verity's sins were knives, quick and vicious, then Prosperity's were poison. Slow, insidious, but just as deadly. And when the violence began to coalesce into something tangible, something monstrous, it didn't happen all at once, as in Verity, but in a drip, slow enough that most of the city was still pretending the monsters weren't real.

The thing in the warehouse suggested otherwise.

The monster inhaled, as though trying to *smell* her, a chilling reminder of which of them was the predator and which, for the moment, was prey. Fear scraped along her spine as its head swung from side to side. And then it looked up. At her.

Kate didn't wait.

She dropped down, catching herself on the steel rafter to ease the fall. She landed in a crouch between the monster and the warehouse door, spikes flashing in her hands, each the length of her forearm and filed to a vicious point.

"Looking for me?"

The creature turned, flashing two dozen blue-black teeth in a feral grimace.

"Kate?" pressed Teo. *"You see it?"*

"Yeah," she said dryly. "I see it."

Bea and Liam both started talking, but Kate tapped her ear and the voices dropped out, replaced a second later by a strong beat, a heavy bass. The music filled her head, drowning out her fear and her doubt and her pulse and every other useless thing.

The monster curled its long fingers, and Kate braced herself—the first one had tried to punch right through her chest (she'd have the bruises to prove it). But the attack didn't come.

"What's the matter?" she chided, her voice lost beneath the beat. "Is my heart not good enough?"

She had wondered, briefly, in the beginning, if the crimes written on her soul would somehow make her less appetizing.

Apparently not.

A second later, the monster lunged.

Kate was always surprised to discover that monsters were *fast*.

No matter how big.

No matter how ugly.

She dodged back, quick on her feet.

Five years' and six private schools' worth of

self-defense had given her a head start, but the last six months hunting down things that went bump in Prosperity—that had been the real education.

She danced between blows, trying to avoid the monster's claws and get under its guard.

Nails raked the air above Kate's head as she ducked and slashed the iron spike across the creature's outstretched hand.

It snarled and swung at her, recoiling only after its claws bit into her sleeve and hit copper mesh beneath. The armor absorbed most of the damage, but Kate still hissed as somewhere on her arm the skin parted and blood welled up.

She let out a curse and drove her boot into the creature's chest.

It was twice her size, made of hunger and gore and God knew what else, but the sole of her shoe was plated with iron, and the creature went staggering backward, clawing at itself as the pure metal burned away a stretch of mottled flesh, exposing the thick membrane that shielded its heart.

Bull's-eye.

Kate launched herself forward, aiming for the still-sizzling mark. The spike punched through cartilage and muscle before sinking easily into that vital core.

Funny, she thought, that even monsters had fragile hearts.

Her momentum carried her forward, and the monster fell back, and they went down together, its body collapsing beneath her into a mound of gore and rot. Kate staggered to her feet, holding her breath against the noxious fumes until she reached the warehouse door. She slumped against it, pressing a palm to the gash on her arm.

The song was ending in her ear, and she switched the feed back to Control.

"How long has it been?"

"We have to do something."

"Shut up," she said. "I'm here."

A string of profanity.

A few stock lines of relief.

"Status?" asked Bea.

Kate pulled the cell from her pocket, snapped a photo of the gory slick on the concrete, and hit SEND.

"Jesus," answered Bea.

"Wicked," said Liam.

"Looks fake," offered Teo.

Riley sounded queasy. *"Do they always . . . fall apart?"*

The litany in her ear was just another reminder that these people had no business being on this end of the fight. They had their purpose, but they weren't like her. Weren't hunters.

"How about you, Kate?" asked Riley. *"You okay?"*

Blood soaked her calf and dripped from her fingers, and truth be told, she felt a little dizzy, but Riley was human—she didn't have to tell him the truth.

"Peachy," she said, killing the call before any of them could hear the catch in her breath. The glow stick flickered and faded, plunging her back into the dark.

But she didn't mind.

It was empty now.

II

Kate climbed the stairs, leaving drops of gray water in her wake. The rain had started up again halfway back to the apartment, and she'd relished the soaking despite the cold, letting it wash away the worst of the black blood and gore.

Even so, she still looked like she'd gotten in a fight with a jar of ink—and lost.

She reached the third-floor landing and let herself in.

"Honey, I'm home."

No answer, of course. She was crashing in Riley's apartment—an apartment his parents paid for—while he was off "living in sin" with his boyfriend, Malcolm. She remembered seeing the place for the first time— the exposed brick, the art, the overstuffed furniture designed for comfort—and thinking Riley's parents clearly shopped in a different catalog than Callum Harker.

She'd never lived alone before.

The school dorms had always been two-to-a-room, and back at Harker Hall, she'd had her father, at least in theory. And his shadow, Sloan. She'd always assumed she'd relish the eventual privacy, the freedom, but it turned out that being alone lost some of its charm when you didn't have a choice.

She smothered the wave of self-pity before it could crest and headed for the bathroom, peeling off her armor as she went. *Armor* was a pretty fancy word for the copper mesh stretched over paintball gear, but Liam's combined interests in costume design and war games did the job . . . 90 percent of the time. The other 10, well, that was just sharp claws and bad luck.

She caught her reflection in the bathroom mirror—damp blond hair slicked back, black gore freckling pale cheeks—and met her own gaze.

"Where are you?" she murmured, wondering how other Kates in other lives were spending their night. She'd always liked the idea that there was a different you for every choice you made and every choice you didn't, and somewhere out there were Kates who had never returned to Verity and never begged to leave.

Ones who could still hear out of both ears and had two parents instead of none.

Ones who hadn't run, hadn't killed, hadn't lost everything.

Where are you?

Once upon a time, the first image in her head would have been the house beyond the Waste, with its high grass and its wide-open sky. Now it was the woods behind Colton, an apple in her hand and birdsong overhead, and a boy who wasn't a boy with his back against a tree.

She turned the shower on, wincing as she peeled away the last of the fabric.

Steam bloomed across the glass, and she bit back a groan as hot water struck raw skin. She leaned against the tiles and thought of another city, another house, another shower.

A monster slumped in the bath.

A boy burning from the inside out.

Her hand wrapped around his.

I'm not going to let you fall.

As the scalding water ran gray and rust red and then finally clear, she considered her skin. She was becoming a patchwork of scars. From the teardrop in the corner of her eye and the pale line that ran from temple to jaw—marks of the car crash that had killed her mother—to the curve of a Malchai's teeth along her shoulder and the silvery gash of a Corsai's claws across her ribs.

And then there was the mark she couldn't see.

The one she'd made herself when she raised her father's gun and pulled the trigger and killed a stranger, staining her soul red.

Kate snapped the water off.

As she taped up her latest cuts, she wondered if, somewhere, there was a version of herself having fun. Feet up on the back of a theater seat while movie monsters slunk out of the shadows, and people in the audience screamed because it was fun to be afraid when you knew you were safe.

It shouldn't make her feel better, imagining those other lives, but it did. One of those paths led to happiness, even while Kate's own had led her here.

But here, she told herself, was exactly where she was supposed to be.

She'd spent five years trying to become the daughter her father wanted—strong, hard, monstrous—only to learn that her father didn't want her at all.

But he was dead, and Kate wasn't, and she'd had to find something to do, someone to *be*, some way to put all those skills to use.

And she knew it wasn't enough—no matter how many monsters she slayed, it wouldn't undo the one she'd made, wouldn't erase the red from her soul—but life only moved forward.

And here in Prosperity, Kate had found a purpose, a point, and now when she met her gaze in the mirror, she didn't see a girl who was sad or lonely or lost. She saw a girl who wasn't afraid of the dark.

She saw a girl who hunted monsters.

And she was damn good at it.

III

Hunger gnawed at Kate's bones, but she was too tired to go in search of food. She turned the radio up and slumped onto the couch, sighing at the simple comfort of clean hair and a soft sweatshirt.

She'd never been all that sentimental, but living out of a duffel bag taught you to value the things you had. The sweatshirt was from Leighton, the third of her six boarding schools. She had no fondness for the school itself, but the sweatshirt was worn and warm, a little piece of a past life. She didn't let herself cling to these pieces, holding on just tight enough that they wouldn't slip away. Besides, the Leighton colors were forest green and cool gray, way better than St. Agnes's horror show of red and purple and brown.

She booted up her tablet and logged into the private chat space Bea had carved out in the infinite world of Prosperity's opendrive.

Welcome to the Wardens, said the screen.

That was the name they'd chosen for themselves—Liam and Bea and Teo—before Kate ever showed up. Riley hadn't been a part of it, either—not until she brought him in.

> **LiamonMe**: hahahahahahaha wolves

> **TeoMuchtoHandle**: it's a cover-up. everyone knows what happened in verity.

> **Beatch**: See no evil → hear no evil → tell yourself there's no evil

> **LiamonMe**: dunno I had a mean-ass cat once

For a moment, Kate just stared at the screen and asked herself for the hundredth time what she was doing here, talking to these people. Letting them in. She hated that part of her craved this simple contact, even looked forward to it.

> **RiledUp**: Did you guys catch that headline about the explosion on Broad?

Kate hadn't gone *looking* for friends—she'd never played well with others, never stayed in a school long enough to make any real connections.

RiledUp: Guy walked into his apartment, pulled the gas line straight out of the wall.

Sure, Kate understood the value of friends, the social currency of being part of a group, but she'd never gotten the emotional appeal. Friends wanted you to be honest. Friends wanted you to share. Friends wanted you to listen and care and worry and do a dozen other things Kate had no time for.

All she'd wanted was a lead.

RiledUp: Roommate was home when it happened.

Kate had landed in Prosperity six months ago with that one duffel, five hundred in cash, and a bad feeling that got worse with every piece of news. *Dog attacks. Gang violence. Suspicious activity. Brutal acts. Suspects at large. Crime scenes disturbed. Weapons missing.*

LiamonMe: Creepy.

Beatch: Downer, Riley.

A dozen stories all sporting the telltale signs—the kind made by teeth and claws—and then there were the whispers on the opendrive, referencing the same place, the name scraping over skin: *Verity.*

But short of putting an EAT ME sign on her back and wandering the streets at night, Kate wasn't exactly sure where to start. Finding monsters had never been a problem in Verity, but here, for every actual sighting there were a hundred trolls and conspiracy theorists co-opting the threads. It was a needle in a haystack where a bunch of idiots were shouting, SOMETHING POKED ME.

But there, threaded through the static, she noticed them. The same voices showing up over and over, trying to be heard. They called themselves the Wardens, and they weren't hunters, but hackers—*hacktivists*, according to Liam—convinced that the authorities were either incompetent or determined to bury the news.

The Wardens scoured sites and dug through footage, flagging anything that looked suspicious, then leaked the data to the press and plastered it on the threads, trying to get *someone* to listen.

And Kate had.

She'd taken one of their leads and run with it, and when it had panned out, she'd gone to the source for more. And that's when she'd learned that the Wardens were just a couple of college students and a fourteen-year-old who never slept.

TeoMuchtoHandle: yeah, that's sad. but what does that have to do with Heart Eaters?

Beatch: Since when are we calling them Heart Eaters?

LiamonMe: Since they started *eating hearts* duh.

She still didn't want friends. But despite her best efforts, she was getting to know them. Bea, who was addicted to dark chocolate and wanted to be a research scientist. Teo, who never sat still, even had a treadmill desk in his dorm. Liam, who lived with his grandparents and cared too much for his own good. Riley, whose family would kill him if they knew where he spent his nights.

And what did they know about her?

Nothing but a name, and even that was only half true.

To the Wardens, she was Kate Gallagher, a runaway with a knack for hunting monsters. She kept her first name even though the sound of that one syllable made her jump every time, sure that someone from her past had caught up. But it was all she had left. Her mother was dead. Her father was dead. Sloan was dead. The only one who'd say her name with any sense of knowing was August, and he was hundreds of miles away in Verity, at the center of a city on fire.

Beatch: Makes a hell of a lot more sense than *Corsai, Malchai, Sunai*. Who named *those*?

TeoMuchtoHandle: no idea.

Beatch: Your lack of professional curiosity is maddening.

The Wardens had nagged Kate for months to meet up in person, and when the time came she'd almost bailed. She'd watched them from across the street, all looking so . . . normal. Not that they blended in—Teo had short blue hair and Bea had a full sleeve of tattoos and Liam, in his giant orange glasses, looked like he was twelve—but they didn't look like something spit out of Verity. They weren't Flynn Task Force soldiers. Or coddled Colton kids. They were just—normal. They had lives outside this one. Things to lose.

LiamonMe: Why not just call them what they are, what they do? Body Eaters, Blood Eaters, and Soul Eaters. BAM.

Kate pictured August down in the subway, dark lashes fluttering as he raised his violin, the music pouring out where bow met strings, transfigured into threads of burning light. Calling him a Soul Eater was like calling the sun bright. Technically accurate, but only a fraction of the truth.

RiledUp: Any sign of Kate?

She switched from *incognito* to *public*.

HunterK has joined the chat.

Beatch: Heyo!

TeoMuchToHandle: stalker.

RiledUp: I was getting worried.

LiamOnMe: Not me!

Beatch: Yeah right, Mr. I-know-karate.

Kate's fingers danced over the screen.

HunterK: No need. Still standing.

RiledUp: You really shouldn't go dark without properly signing off.

TeoMuchToHandle: oooh, riley's in dad mode.

Dad mode.

Kate thought of her own father, the cuffs of his suit stained with blood, the sea of monsters at his feet, the smug look on his face right before she put a bullet in his leg.

But she knew what Teo meant—Riley wasn't like the rest of the Wardens. He wouldn't even be there if it wasn't for her. He was a grad student, studying law at the university and interning at the local police department, which was the part that mattered to the Wardens, since it meant access to police surveillance and intel briefings—not that Teo couldn't hack them, as he'd pointed out a dozen times, but why kick down an open door?

(According to Riley, the police were "aware of the attacks and continuing to monitor developments," which as far as Kate could tell was just a long way of describing *denial*.)

RiledUp: *makes dad face* *wags finger*

RiledUp: But seriously. You better not get any blood on my couch.

HunterK: Don't worry.

HunterK: I left most of it on the stairs.

LiamOnMe: O_O.

HunterK: Any new leads?

TeoMuchtoHandle: nothing yet. the streets are quiet.

What a strange idea.

If she could keep this up, knocking out the Heart Eaters as they took shape instead of cleaning up the wreckage, two steps forward instead of back, maybe it wouldn't get worse. Maybe she could keep it from becoming a Phenomenon. Maybe—what a useless word. Maybe was just a way of saying she didn't *know*.

And Kate hated not knowing.

She closed the browser, fingers hesitating over the darkened screen before she opened a new window and started searching for Verity.

Kate had first learned how to tap into foreign signals at her second boarding school, out on the eastern fringe of Verity, an hour from the Temperance border.

All ten territories were *supposed* to transmit openly, but if you wanted to know what was really going on in another territory, you had to slip behind the digital curtain.

That was the idea—but no matter how hard Kate looked, she couldn't find her way home.

True, the quarantine had gone back into effect, the borders that had peeled open so slowly over the last decade slamming shut again. But there was no curtain to slip behind, nothing coming out of Verity at all.

The signal was gone.

There was only one explanation: the tech towers must have gone down.

With the borders closed and the comm grid out, Verity was officially cut off.

And the people in Prosperity didn't *care*. Not even the Wardens—Teo had used the word *inevitable*. Bea thought the borders should never have been opened, that Verity should have been left to consume itself like a fire in a glass jar. Even Riley seemed ambivalent. Only Liam showed the slightest concern, and it was more pity than a vested interest. They didn't know, of course, what Verity meant to Kate.

Hell, Kate didn't know either.

But she couldn't stop searching.

Every night she checked, just in case, clicked through every bread crumb on the opendrive, hoping for some news about Verity, about August Flynn.

It was the weirdest thing—she'd seen August at his worst. Watched him descend through hunger into sickness and madness and shadow. Watched him burn. Watched him kill.

But when she pictured him now, she didn't see the Sunai made of smoke or the figure burning in a cold tub. She saw a sad-eyed boy sitting alone on the bleachers, a violin case at his feet.

Kate shoved the tablet away and slumped back on the couch. She threw an arm over her eyes and let the steady beat of the radio fold around her until she sank down toward sleep.

But then, in the lull between songs, the sound of footsteps echoed in the stairwell. She stilled, turning her good ear toward the door as the steps slowed, stopped.

Kate waited for a knock, but it never came. Instead she heard the sound of a hand on the doorknob, the shudder of the lock as it was tried but held fast. Kate's fingers slipped beneath the couch cushion and produced a gun. The same one she'd used to kill a stranger in her mother's house, the same one she'd used to shoot her father in his office.

A muffled voice sounded beyond the door, followed by the scrape of metal, and Kate leveled the weapon at the door as it swung open.

For a moment, the shape in the doorway was nothing but a shadow, the hall lights tracing the outline of a figure a fraction taller than she was, with round edges and short hair. No red eyes, no sharp teeth, no dark suit. Just Riley, standing there, juggling a box of pizza and a six-pack of soda and a key.

He saw the gun and threw his hands up, dropping the cardboard and the cans and the key ring to the floor. One of the cans exploded, raining soda on the landing.

"Dammit, Kate." His voice was strangled.

Kate sighed and set the weapon on the table. "You should knock."

"This is *my place*," he said, retrieving the pizza box

and the rest of the soda with shaking hands. "Do you pull the gun on everyone, or just me?"

"Everyone," said Kate, "but for you I left the safety on."

"I'm flattered."

"What are you doing here?"

"Oh, you know," he shot back, "checking on the squatter in my apartment, making sure she didn't trash the place."

"You wanted to see if I bled on the couch."

"And the stairs." His gaze flicked from her to the gun on the table and back. "Permission to enter?"

Kate spread her arms along the back of the couch. "Password?"

"I brought pizza."

The smell emanating from the box was heavenly. Her stomach growled. "Oh, all right," she said. "Permission granted."

IIII

Rituals were funny things.

People thought of them as either elaborate formulas, magic spells, or compulsions drilled into the subconscious by months or years of repetition.

But really, *ritual* was just a fancy word for *habit*. A thing that became easier to do than not do. And habits were simple—especially bad ones, like letting people in.

Kate curled up on one side of the couch, Riley on the other, while some late-night talk show host murmured bad jokes on the TV.

He held up one of the cans he'd dropped. "This'll be fun," he said, cracking the tab. He cringed in expectation, then sighed with relief when it didn't explode.

Kate grabbed a second slice of pizza, trying to hide the pain as the bandages tugged on the skin beneath her sleeve.

"You didn't have to do this," she said between bites.

He shrugged. "I know."

She considered him over the crust of her pizza. Riley was slim, with warm brown eyes, the kind of smile that took over his face, and a savior complex. When he wasn't at the university or the police station, he volunteered with at-risk teens.

Was that what she was to him? His latest project?

Kate had been in Prosperity for all of three weeks when their paths crossed. She'd spent her nights squatting in abandoned buildings, her days nursing cups of coffee in café corners as she scoured the opendrive for clues.

It was only a matter of time before the café kicked her out—she hadn't bought anything in hours. Still, she didn't appreciate it when a guy sat down at her table on the pretense of studying, only to ask her if she needed help.

She'd had her first run-in with a monster the night before, and it hadn't gone well. But considering that the extent of her experience—schoolroom self-defense aside—consisted of executing a bound Malchai in her father's basement and nearly getting disemboweled by a Corsai on the subway, she really shouldn't have been surprised.

She'd gotten away with a split lip and a broken nose, but she knew she looked rough.

She told the guy she wasn't interested in God, or whatever he was selling, but he didn't leave. A few minutes later a fresh cup of coffee appeared in front of her.

"How did that happen?" he asked, nodding at her face.

"Hunting monsters," she said, because sometimes the truth was strange enough to make people go away.

"Uh, okay . . . ," he said, clearly skeptical. He got to his feet. "Come on."

She didn't move. "Where?"

"I have a hot shower, an extra bed. There might even be some food in the fridge."

"I don't know you."

He held out his hand. "Riley Winters."

Kate stared at his open palm. She wasn't big on charity, but she was tired and hungry and felt like shit. Besides, if he tried anything unwanted, she was pretty sure she could take him. "Kate," she said. "Kate Gallagher."

Riley didn't try anything—thanks to the aforementioned boyfriend—just gave her a towel and a pillow and, a week later, a key. To this day, she wasn't exactly sure what had happened. Maybe she'd had a concussion. Maybe he was just persuasive.

Kate yawned, tossing the paper plate onto the table beside her gun.

Riley reached for the remote, switching the TV off.

Kate responded by switching the radio on.

Riley shook his head. "What did silence ever do to you?"

He didn't know, of course, about the car wreck that had killed her mother and stripped the hearing from her left ear. Didn't know that when sound was taken from you, you had to find ways to take it back.

"If you want sound," said Riley, "we could always *talk*."

Kate sighed. This was his game.

Ply her with food and sugar until she was blissed out on empty calories, and then, invariably, start prying. And the worst part was some masochistic part of her must want it, must relish the fact someone *cared* enough to ask, because she kept letting him in. Kept ending up here on the couch with empty soda cans and pizza boxes.

Bad habit.

Ritual.

"Okay," she said, and Riley brightened visibly, but if he thought she was going to talk about herself, he was wrong. "Why did you bring up that explosion?"

Confusion streaked his face. "What?"

"On the chat, you mentioned an explosion. Man-made. Why?"

"You saw that?" He sat back. "I don't know. The

Wardens have got me looking for things that don't line up, and it caught my eye. . . . It's the fifth murder-suicide this week. That's really high, even for Prosperity."

Kate frowned. "You think it's some kind of monster?"

Riley shrugged. "Six months ago, I didn't *believe* in monsters. Now I see them everywhere." He shook his head. "It's probably nothing. Let's talk about something else. How are you holding up?"

"Oh, look at the time," she said dryly. "Malcolm's going to get jealous."

"Thanks for your concern," he said, "but I assure you, our relationship is stable enough to allow for time with friends."

Friends.

The word glanced off her ribs, hard enough to leave her winded.

Because she knew a secret: there were *two* kinds of monsters, the kind that hunted the streets and the kind that lived in your head. She could fight the first, but the second was more dangerous. It was always, always, always a step ahead.

It didn't have teeth or claws, didn't feed on flesh or blood or hearts.

It simply reminded you of what happened when you let people in.

Behind her eyes, August Flynn stopped fighting,

because of her. He collapsed into darkness, because of her. He sacrificed a part of himself—his humanity, his light, his soul—because of her.

She could handle her own blood.

She didn't need anyone else's on her hands.

"Rule one," she said, forcing her voice even, light. "Don't make friends. It never ends well."

Riley rolled a soda can between his palms. "But doesn't it get lonely?"

Kate smiled. It was so easy when you could lie.

"No."

꜀꜀꜀꜀꜀ ~~~~~

Violence
has a taste
a smell
but most of all
it has
    a *heat*—
the shadow
stands
in the street
engulfed
in smoke
in fire
in wrath
in rage
    basking
        in the warmth
and for an instant
light glances
off a face
finding—

cheekbones
a chin
the barest
hint
of lips
for an instant—
but it is not enough
          it is never enough
one human holds
so little heat
and it is cold again—
hungry again—
its edges
blurring
back into darkness
the way edges
always do
it wants
more
searches
the night
and finds—
a woman, a pistol, a bed
a couple, a kitchen, a cutting block
a man, a pink slip, an office
the whole city
a book of
matches
just waiting
    to be struck.

‖‖‖ ‖
VERITY

The steel violin shone beneath his fingers.

Its metal body caught the sun, turning the instrument to light as August ran his thumb along the strings, checking them one last time.

"Hey, Alpha, you ready?"

August shut the case and swung it up onto his shoulder. "Yes."

His team stood waiting, huddled in a patch of sun on the north side of the Seam—a three-story barricade that stretched like a dark horizon line between North and South City. Ani was drinking from a canteen, while Jackson studied the magazine on his gun, and Harris, was, well, he was being Harris, chewing gum and throwing knives at a wooden crate on which he'd drawn a very crude, very *rude* picture of a Malchai. He'd even named it *Sloan*.

It was a cool day, and they were dressed in full gear,

but August wore only combat slacks and a black polo, his arms bare save for the rows of short black lines that circled his wrist like a cuff.

"*Checkpoint One,*" said a voice over the comm, "*five minutes.*"

August cringed at the volume, even though he'd pulled the comm piece out of his ear and let it hang around his neck. The voice belonged to Phillip, back at the Compound.

"Hey, Phil," said Harris. "Tell me a joke."

"*That's not what the comms are for.*"

"How about this one?" offered Harris. "A Corsai, a Malchai, and a Sunai walk into a bar—"

Everyone groaned, including August. He didn't really understand most of the FTF's jokes, but he knew enough to recognize that Harris's were awful.

"I hate waiting," muttered Jackson, checking his watch. "Have I mentioned how much I hate waiting?"

"*So much whining,*" radioed their sniper, Rez, from a nearby roof.

"How's it looking up there?" asked Ani.

"*Perimeter's clear. No trouble.*"

"Too bad," said Harris.

"*Idiot,*" radioed Phillip.

August ignored them all, staring across the street at the target.

The Porter Road Symphony Hall.

The building itself was embedded in the Seam, or rather, the Seam had been built up around the building. August squinted at the soldiers patrolling the barricade, and thought he spotted Soro's lean form before remembering that Soro would be at the second checkpoint by now, half a mile east.

At his back, the usual argument was kicking off like clockwork.

"—don't know why we bother, these people wouldn't do the same for—"

"—not the point—"

"Isn't it, though?"

"*We do it, Jackson, because compassion must be louder than pride.*"

The voice came through the comm set crisp and clear, and August instantly pictured the man it belonged to: Tall and slim with surgeon's hands and tired eyes. Henry Flynn. The head of the FTF. August's adopted father.

"Yes, sir," said Jackson, sounding suitably chastised.

Ani stuck out her tongue. Jackson gave her the finger. Harris chuckled and began dislodging his knives.

A watch chirped.

"Showtime," said Harris brightly.

There had always been two kinds of people in the

FTF—those who fought because they believed in Flynn's cause (Ani) and those for whom Flynn's cause was a good excuse to fight (Harris).

Of course, these days there was a third kind: Conscripts. Refugees who'd crossed the Seam, not because they necessarily *wanted* to fight, but because the alternative of staying in North City was worse.

Jackson was one of those, a recruit who'd bartered service for safety and ended up as the squad's medic.

He met August's gaze. "After you, Alpha."

The team had taken up their formal positions on either side, and August realized they were looking at him, looking *to* him, the way they must have looked to his older brother once. Before Leo was killed.

They didn't know, of course, that August had been the one to kill him, that he had reached into Leo's chest, wrapped his fingers around the dark fire of his brother's heart, and snuffed it out, didn't know that sometimes when he closed his eyes the cold heat still ached in his veins, Leo's voice echoing steady and hollow in his head, and he wondered if gone was gone, if energy was ever lost, if—

"August?" It was Ani speaking now, her eyebrows arched, waiting. "It's time."

He dragged his spiraling mind back into order, allowed himself a single, slow blink before he straightened, and said in the voice of a leader, "Fall in line."

They crossed the street with quick, sure steps, August at the front, Jackson and Ani flanking him on either side, and Harris at the rear.

The FTF had stripped the plated copper from inside the hall and nailed it to the doors, creating solid sheets of burnished light. The presence of so much pure metal would burn a lesser monster—even August cringed, the copper turning his stomach—but he didn't slow.

The sun was already past its peak, the shadows beginning to lengthen along the street.

An inscription had been etched into the copper plating on the northern doors.

SOUTH CITY CHECKPOINT ONE
BY THE WILL OF THE FTF,
ACCESS WILL BE GRANTED
TO ALL HUMANS FROM 8AM TO 5PM.
NO WEAPONS ALLOWED BEYOND THIS POINT.
PROCEED TO THE SYMPHONY HALL.

NOTE: BY ENTERING THIS FACILITY,
YOU ARE CONSENTING TO BE SCREENED.

August brought his palm to the door, and the other FTFs twisted out of the way as he pushed it open. Once, early on, he'd come face-to-face with an ambush, taken a round of heavy fire to the chest.

The bullets had done nothing to August—a well-fed Sunai was impervious to harm—but a glancing shot had taken Harris in the arm and, ever since, the team was more than willing to let him serve as a shield.

But as August stepped inside, he was greeted only by silence.

According to a plaque on the wall, the Porter Road Symphony Hall had "been a center of culture in the capital for more than seventy-five years." There was even an image beneath the writing, an etching of the main lobby in all its wood and stone and stained-glass glory, filled with elegant couples in evening attire.

As August moved through the room, he tried to bridge the gap between what it had once been, and what it was now.

The air was stale, the stained glass gone, the windows boarded up and covered over with more stripped copper, the polished stone floor littered with debris, and the warm light traded for Ultraviolet Reinforced bulbs burning high enough for him to hear, loud and clear as a comm signal.

The lobby itself was empty, and for a single, hopeful, foolish second August thought that no one had come, that he wouldn't have to do this, not today. But then he heard the shuffle of feet, the muffled voices of those waiting in the symphony hall, just as they'd been told.

His fingers tightened on the violin strap.

Ani and Jackson branched off to do a quick sweep, and he drifted forward, stopping before the depiction of a woman set into the floor. She was made of glass: hundreds, maybe thousands of small glass squares, something more than the sum of its parts—a *mosaic*, that was the word.

"Left hall, clear."

The figure's arms were stretched out and her head was thrown back as music spilled in gold squares from her lips.

"Right hall, clear."

August knelt and ran his fingers over the tiles at the edge of the mosaic, tracing the purples and blues that formed the night around her, letting his hand rest on a single golden note. She was a siren.

He'd read about sirens, or, rather, Ilsa had read about them. August had always been more interested in reality than myth—reality, existence, that fickle state of being between a whimper and a bang—but his sister had a fondness for fairy tales and legends. She was the one who had told him about the women of the sea, their voices beautiful and dangerous enough to send sailors crashing onto rocks.

Sing you a song, and steal your—

"Ready when you are," said Ani at his side.

His fingers fell away from the cool glass tiles, and he straightened, turning toward the inner doors, the ones that led into the symphony hall itself. The violin hung heavy on his shoulder, every step creating a faint hum of strings only he could hear.

August stopped before the doors and touched his comm. "Count?"

Phillip's voice buzzed across the line. *"On camera, it looks like about forty."*

August's heart sank.

But this was why he was here.

This, he reminded himself, was what he was for.

HHt

II

Once, the symphony hall might have been stunning, but time—the Phenomenon, the territory wars, the creation of the Seam—had clearly taken its toll.

August's gaze trailed across the hall—the copper-less ceiling, the walls scraped bare, the rows devoid of seats—before landing inevitably on the people huddled in the center of the floor.

Forty-three men, women, and children who'd crossed the Seam in search of shelter and safety, their eyes wide from too little sleep and too much terror.

They looked bedraggled, their once-fine clothes beginning to fray, bones showing beneath their skin. It was hard to believe these were the same people August had passed in the streets and on the subways of North City, people who could afford to pretend that the Phenomenon had never happened, who'd scorned South City for so many years and purchased their safety instead of fighting for it, who'd closed their eyes and covered their ears and paid their tithes to Callum Harker.

But Callum Harker was dead. August had reaped that soul himself.

He hung back now, letting Harris take the lead. The soldier marched down the center aisle, leaped up onto the stage and spread his arms with the flare of a natural performer.

"Hello!" he said cheerfully, "and welcome to Checkpoint One. I'm Captain Harris Fordam, here on behalf of the Flynn Task Force . . ."

August had heard Harris give this speech a hundred times.

"You came here of your own choice, so you've clearly got *some* sense. You also waited *six months* to make that choice, so you haven't got much."

He was right; these were the dregs, the ones convinced they could get by without South City's help, too stubborn to admit—or too foolish to realize—what they were in for.

In those first few weeks, when it was obvious that Callum's death rendered his promise of protection void, there had been a massive influx, hundreds of people streaming through the Seam every day (Jackson and Rez had been among them).

But some of them chose to *stay,* locked themselves

in their homes, hunkered down, and waited for help to come to *them*.

And when it didn't, they were left with three options: stay put, brave the Waste—that dangerous place beyond the city where order gave way to anarchy and everyone was out for themselves—or cross the Seam and surrender.

"You made it here," continued Harris, "so you know how to follow directions, but you're also a sorry-looking bunch, so I'm going to make this nice and simple . . ."

Somewhere in the crowd, a man muttered, "Don't have to take this," and turned to go. Jackson blocked his path.

"You can't keep me here," snarled the man.

"Actually," said Jackson, "you should have acquainted yourself with the fine print. Entering a screening facility serves as consent to be screened. You haven't been screened yet, so you're not free to go. Consider it a precaution."

Jackson gave the man a good hard nudge toward the stage as Harris's face turned from cheerful to somber. "Listen to me. Your governor is dead. His monsters see you as food. We are offering you a fighting chance, but safety isn't free. You know that, because you all chose to pay for it with cash. Well, bad news." He shot a dark glance at a woman clutching a roll of paper bills in her ringed hands. "That's not how it works in South City. You want food? You want shelter? You want safety? You have to work for them." He jabbed a finger at the FTF badge on his uniform. "Every day and every night we're out there fighting to take this city back. The FTF used to be optional. Now it's mandatory. And *every* citizen in South City serves."

Ani gestured for him to wrap it up, and just like that, Harris's demeanor flipped back to friendly.

"Now, maybe you're here because you've seen the light. Maybe you're here because you're desperate. Whatever the reason, you've taken the first step, and for that, we commend you. But before you can take the next, we've got to screen you."

That was August's cue.

He pushed off the wall and began the long walk down the center aisle, his boots beating out a steady rhythm amplified by the hall's acoustics. Someone started to cry. The acoustics amplified that, too. He scanned the crowd, searching for the telltale twitch of a person's shadow that only Sunai could see, the movement that marked a sinner, but the light in the hall and the nervous shifting made it difficult to spot.

Whispers moved through the room as he passed.

Even if they hadn't yet realized *what* he was, they seemed to sense he wasn't one of them. He'd worked so hard for so long to blend in, but it didn't matter now.

A little girl, maybe three or four—he'd never been good at telling age—clutched at a woman in green. Her mother, he guessed, based on the steel in those tired eyes. August caught the little girl's gaze and offered what he hoped was a gentle smile, but the girl just buried her face in her mother's leg.

She was afraid.

They were all afraid.

Of *him.*

The urge to retreat rose like bile in his throat, competing with the urge to speak, to assure them that there was no reason to be afraid, that he wasn't there to hurt them.

But monsters couldn't tell lies.

This is your place, said a voice in his head, smooth and hard as stone. A voice that sounded like his dead brother, Leo. *This is your purpose.*

August swallowed.

"This part's simple," Harris was saying. "Spread out, arm's distance apart, there we go. . . ."

As August stepped onto the stage, the room went quiet—so quiet he could hear their held breaths, their frightened hearts. He knelt, opening the clasps on his case—the snap as loud as a gunshot in his ears—and withdrew his violin.

Sunai, Sunai, eyes like coal . . .

The sight of the instrument and the sudden under-standing of what the FTF meant when they said *screening*, sent a ripple of shock through the room.

Sing you a song and steal your soul.

A man in his midthirties lost his nerve and took off at a full sprint toward the doors. He made it three or four strides before Ani and Jackson caught up and forced him to his knees.

"Let me go," begged the man. "Please, let me go."

"Why?" chided Jackson. "Got something to hide?"

Harris clapped his hands to draw the crowd's atten-tion back to the stage. "The screening is about to begin."

August straightened and brought the violin to rest beneath his chin. He stared out at the audience, a sea of faces all marked by emotions so intense they made him realize how his own attempts had paled. He'd spent four years trying to learn—to *mimic*—these human expres-sions, as if that would make him human.

That was all he'd wanted, and he'd wanted it so much he would have given anything, would have sold his very soul. He'd done everything he could, even starved him-self to the edge—and gone over.

But August could never be human.

He knew that now.

It wasn't about *what* he was, but *why*, his purpose, his part. They *all* had parts to play.

And this was his.

August set his bow against the strings and drew the first note.

It hung on the air for a long moment, a single, solitary thread, beautiful and harmless, and only when it began to weaken, waver, did August close his eyes and plunge into the song.

Out it poured, taking shape in the air and twining through the bodies in the room, drawing their souls to surface.

If August's eyes had been open, he would have seen their shoulders slump and their heads bow. Would have seen the fight bleed out of the man on the ground and every other body in the room, the fear and anger and uncertainty washed away as they listened. Would have seen his soldiers go slack and empty eyed, lost in the rapture of the song.

But August kept his eyes closed, relishing the way his own muscles loosened with every note, the pressure in his head and chest easing even as his longing deepened into need, hollow and aching.

He imagined himself in a field beyond the Waste, tall grass moving in rhythm with the music, imagined himself in a soundproof studio at Colton, the notes rippling and refracting against the crisp white walls, imagined himself alone. Not lonely. Just . . . free.

And then the song was done, and for a final moment, while the chords trailed off through the room, he kept his eyes closed, unready to return.

In the end, it was the whisper that drew him back.

It could only mean one thing.

His skin tightened, and his heart sank, and the need rose in him, simple and visceral, the hollow center at his core, that unfillable place, yawning wide.

When he opened his eyes, the first thing he saw was light. Not the harsh UVRs that lined the lobby, but the simple auras of human souls. Forty-two of them were white.

And one was red.

A soul stained by an act of violence, one that had given rise to something monstrous.

It belonged to the woman in green.

The *mother*, with the little girl still beside her, one small arm still wrapped around the woman's leg. Red light beaded on her skin, streaking down her cheeks like tears.

August forced himself down the stairs.

"He broke my heart," confessed the woman, fingers curled into fists. "So I sped up. I saw him in the street and I sped up. I felt his body break beneath my tires. I dragged it off the road. No one knew, no one knew, but I still I hear that sound every night. I'm so tired of hearing that sound. . . ."

August reached for the woman's hands and stopped, his fingers hovering an inch above her skin. It should be simple. She was a sinner, and the FTF harbored no sinners.

It didn't feel simple.

He could let her go.

He could . . .

The light in the hall was beginning to dim, the pale glow of forty-two souls sinking back beneath the surfaces of their skin. The red on hers shone brighter. She met his eyes, looking past him, perhaps through him, but still at him.

"I'm so tired . . . ," she whispered. "But I'd do it again."

Those last words broke the spell; somewhere in the city, a monster lived, hunted, killed, because of what this woman had done. She had made a choice.

And August made his.

He wrapped his hands around hers, snuffing out the light.

‖‖‖
‖‖

August retreated to the lobby as soon as it was done, as far as he could get from the collective sounds of shock, the palpable relief of the spared, the child's piercing scream.

He stood over the siren mosaic, rubbing his hands, the sinner's last words echoing in his head. Her life still sang beneath his skin. It had given him a moment of strength, steadiness, less like hunger sated—he hadn't been *hungry* in months—than the sensation of being made solid, real. A calm that evaporated the moment the little girl began to scream.

He'd moved the mother's corpse, carried it out of the hall, out of the child's sight, for the collection team. Her skin had felt strange beneath his touch, cold and heavy and hollow in a way that made him want to recoil.

He'd spent a lot of time watching the soldiers of the FTF—he no longer tried to mimic their faces, postures, tones, but studying them had become a habit. He had watched the way their hands shook after bad missions, the way they drank and smoked and joked to cover it.

August didn't feel sick, or jittery.

Just empty.

How much does a soul weigh? he wondered.

Less than a body.

The symphony doors swung open.

"This way," said Harris, leading the group through. Ani had the little girl in her arms.

August felt Jackson put a hand on his shoulder. "You did your job."

He swallowed, looked away. "I know."

They ushered the crowd toward the southern doors. They were locked, but August keyed in the code as Ani tapped her comm. "Clear?"

A crackle of static, and Rez's dry voice. *"Clear as it gets."*

The whole group parted around August as he made his way to the front of the group, recoiling as if that small measure of distance would keep them safe.

Outside, North City now rose at their backs, but the sun was continuing its slow descent between the buildings.

There was still safely an hour before day began edging to dusk, which meant that monsters weren't the most pressing concern. The Corsai kept to the dark, and while the Malchai weren't *incapacitated* by daylight, it did weaken them. No, the real danger, as long as the sun was up, were the Fangs—humans who'd sworn allegiance to the Malchai, who worshipped the monsters like gods, or simply decided they'd rather submit than flee. It was Fangs who'd ambushed his team at the symphony hall that time, Fangs who committed most of the daylight crimes, Fangs who ushered new monsters into the world with every sin.

August started forward across the street.

Only six blocks separated the checkpoint from the safety of the Flynn Compound, but forty-two dazed civilians, four FTFs, and a Sunai would be too tempting a target. They had a dozen jeeps, but gas was tight, and the vehicles were in high demand, plus tensions were always high in the wake of a screening, and Henry didn't want the new recruits to feel like prisoners being carted off to jail.

Walk with them, the man had said. *Step for step.*

So August and his squad led the way toward the broad set of stairs on the corner.

Boots sounded nearby, the stride even, casual, and a moment later Rez fell into step beside him.

"Hey, boss."

She always called him that, even though she had ten years on him—more than that. After all, August only *looked* seventeen. He'd risen out of gun smoke and shell casings on a cafeteria floor five years before. Rez was short and slight, one of the first North City recruits to trade their Harker pendant for an FTF badge. She'd been a law student in her past life, as she called the time before, but now she was one of the best on August's team, a sniper by day and his partner on rescue and recon after dark.

He was glad to see her. She never asked how many souls he'd reaped, never tried to make light of what he had done. What he had to do.

Together, they reached the gated stairwell, a steel arch overhead marking it as a subway station. At the sight of it, several people slowed.

August didn't blame them.

The subways were largely the domain of the Corsai— dark tunnels like the one he'd raced through with Kate, full of shadows that twitched and twisted, claws that glistened in the dark, whispers of *beatbreakruinfleshbone-beatbreak* sliding between teeth.

But beyond the gate, *these* stairs blazed with light.

The FTF had spent three painstaking weeks securing the line, sealing up all the cracks and pumping the passage so full of UV rays that Harris and Jackson had nicknamed it "the tanner," since you could pick up a tan between the checkpoint and the Compound.

Rez undid the series of locks, and August flinched a

little at the brightness as they made their way down to the platform and then onto the tracks.

"Stay together!" ordered Ani as Harris locked the gate again behind them.

It was a dead zone down here, and the comm signals guttered out, the tunnels echoing around them as they walked in rows of two and three. Jackson and Harris punctuated the silence by lobbing instructions at the shaken recruits while August focused on the beat of his heart, the tick of his watch, the markers on the walls, counting down the distance until they could come up for air.

When they finally climbed the stairs to the street, the Compound rose like a sentinel before them, lit from tower to curb. A UV-Reinforced strip the width of a road traced the building's base, the technological equivalent of a castle moat, powering up as the daylight began to thin.

The Compound steps were flanked by soldiers, their expressions varying from grim to annoyed at the sight of the newest North City survivors; but when they saw August, their eyes went to the ground.

Rez peeled away with a "later, boss," and the forty-two recruits were marched up the steps, but August lingered at the edge of the light strip, listening.

In the distance, somewhere beyond the Seam, someone cried out. The sound was too far away, too high, too broken for human ears to catch, but August heard it all the same, and the longer he listened, the more sounds he heard, and the more the chords began to untangle, the quiet unraveling into a dozen distinct noises: A rustle in the darkness; a guttural growl; metal dragging against rock; the buzz of electricity; a shuddering sob.

How many citizens, he wondered, were still across the Seam?

How many had fled into South City or escaped into the Waste?

How many had never made it out?

One of the first things Sloan and his monsters had done was round up as many humans as possible and trap them in makeshift prisons fashioned from hotels, apartment buildings, warehouses. Word was that every night they'd let a few of them go. Just for the fun of hunting them down.

August turned back and went inside. He headed straight for the bank of elevators, avoiding the eyes of the soldiers, the new recruits, the little girl being handed off to a member of the FTF.

He leaned against the elevator wall, relishing the moment of solitude—right before a hand caught the closing door. The metal parted, and another Sunai stepped in.

August straightened. "Soro."

"Hello, August," said Soro, eyes brightening. Their fingers brushed the button for the twelfth floor.

The newest Sunai appeared older than either of their siblings, but they treated Ilsa like a ticking bomb and looked at August the way *he* had once looked at Leo, with a mixture of caution and deference.

Soro was tall and lean, pale skin marked with small black X's. They sported a plume of silver hair that worked like a shadow, changing their face depending on how it fell. Today it was swept back, their delicate cheekbones and strong brow on full display.

August had first thought of Soro as a *she*, though in truth, he hadn't been sure, and when he'd worked up the courage to ask whether Soro considered themself male or female, the newest member of the Flynn family had stared at him for a long moment before answering.

"I'm a Sunai."

That was all they said, as if the rest didn't matter, and August supposed it didn't. He never thought of them as anything but Soro after that.

As the doors slid shut and the elevator rose, August cast a short, sideways glance at the other Sunai. The front of their uniform was caked with a mixture of blackish gore and human blood, but Soro didn't seem to notice or, at least, didn't seem to care. They enjoyed hunting—no, *enjoyed* was probably the wrong word.

Soro possessed neither Leo's righteousness, nor Ilsa's whimsy, nor, as far as August could tell, his own complicated desire to feel human. What they *did* possess was an unshakeable resolve, a belief that the Sunai existed solely to destroy monsters and eliminate the sinners responsible for them.

Pride—perhaps that was right word.

Soro *prided* themself on their ability to hunt, and while they lacked Leo's passion, they more than matched his technique.

"Did you have a good day?" asked August, and Soro flashed him the ghost of a smile, so faint others probably wouldn't even see it, so faint August himself might have missed it if he hadn't spent so long learning how to put his own emotions on display just so humans would see.

"You and your strange questions," they mused. "I ended seven lives. Does that count as *good*?"

"Only if they deserved to die."

A slight crease formed in Soro's brow. "Of course they did."

There was no waver, no doubt, and as August stared at Soro's reflection in the steel door, he couldn't help but wonder if their catalyst had anything to do with their resolve. Like all Sunai, they had been born from tragedy, but unlike the massacre that brought August forth, Soro's had been more . . . voluntary.

A month after North City's plunge back into chaos, a group calling themselves the HPC—Human Power Corp—got their hands on a weapons cache and decided to bomb the subway tunnels, home to so many of the city's monsters.

And because killing Corsai was tricky (shadows were easy to disperse, but hard to erase), they lured as many Malchai as they could into the tunnels, using *themselves* as bait. It was a success—if a suicide mission can ever be called a success. A fair number of monsters were killed, along with twenty-nine humans, a stretch of the North City underground collapsed, and the self-named Soro was the only thing to emerge from the wreckage, followed out by a thin, wavering trail of classical music, the kind Harker had piped into the subways for so long.

The elevator came to a stop at the twelfth floor, and Soro stepped out, glancing back before the doors closed.

"Did *you*?"

August blinked. "Did I what?"

"Have a *good* day?"

He thought of the man begging for his life, the little girl clutching her mother's leg. "You're right," he said, as the elevator door slid shut. "It's a strange question."

By the time August reached the Compound roof, his body was aching for air.

It wasn't a physical thing, like hunger or sickness, but he felt it all the same, driving him up, up, up to the top of the Compound.

You could see the whole city from here.

It wasn't the kind of roof you were *supposed* to go onto. It couldn't be reached by the elevators or the main stairs, but August had found an access hatch in an electrical room on the top floor the year before. Now he stepped out into fresh air as the sun touched the horizon and let out a slow, shuddering exhale.

Up here, he could breathe.

Up here, he was alone.

And up here, at last, he came apart.

That's what it felt like, a slow unraveling, first his posture, then his face, every inch of his body stiff from being held in place under the weight of so many searching eyes.

Pull yourself together, muttered Leo in his head.

August smothered the voice and stepped forward until the toes of his boots skimmed the roof's edge. It was a twenty-story drop, nothing but concrete waiting at the bottom. It would hurt, but only for an instant.

He'd always loved Newton's law of gravity, the part about things falling at the same speed, no matter what they were made of. A steel bearing. A book. A human. A monster.

The difference, of course, was what happened when they hit the ground.

The impact would split the concrete beneath his boots. But by the time the dust cleared, he would still be there. On his feet. Unbroken.

All things fall, mused Leo.

August inched back a step, and then two, sinking to the sun-warmed rooftop and wrapping his arms around his knees. The tallies shone against his skin.

He'd spent so long trying to hide them, but now he wore them on display. One for every day since August last went dark.

One for every day since he'd—

Killed me.

He squeezed his eyes shut.

You truly are a monster now.

"Stop," he whispered, but Leo's voice played on in

his head, and the worst part was he didn't know—couldn't tell—if it was just a memory, an echo, or really Leo, some last piece of his brother clinging to August's bones.

He'd killed Leo, reaped his life, or his soul, or whatever it was that Sunai had in them, and now it was *in* him. August pictured their two lives like water and oil, refusing to mix.

He'd often wondered if the humans he reaped stayed with him, if some part of who they were—who they'd been—lingered in his blood, fused with his soul. But the humans never had a voice. And Leo did.

Tell me, August. Are you still hungry?

He dug his nails into the rough surface of the rooftop. He hadn't been hungry in months, and he hated it, hated the fullness, hated the strength, hated the fact that the more often he fed, the emptier he felt.

But most of all, he hated the fact that some small part of him *wanted* to slip again, to feel that feverish prickle, like an oncoming cold, to remember what it felt like to be alive, to be hungry. Every day when he entered the symphony hall, he hoped the souls would all shine white. They almost never did.

The sky began to darken like a bruise and August let his forehead come to rest against his knees and breathed into the sliver of space as dusk thickened. The sun was almost gone when the air shifted at his back and a hand settled in his hair.

"Ilsa," he said softly.

He dragged his head up as his sister sank to the roof beside him. She was barefoot, her strawberry curls loose and rippling in the breeze, everything about her so open, unguarded. It was easy to forget that she was the first Sunai, that she had made the Barren, erased an entire piece of the city and everyone in it.

Our sister has two sides. They do not meet.

But August had never seen Ilsa's shadow self, had only known this one, playful and sweet and sometimes lost.

Now the only thing lost was her voice.

He missed it, that lilting cadence that made everything sound light, but Ilsa didn't speak anymore. Her collar was open, revealing the vicious line that ran like a ribbon around her throat. *Sloan's* work. He'd cut right through her vocal cords, severed her voice and stolen her ability to speak, to *sing.*

And yet, just as Leo's voice had a place in August's head, so did hers, and when she met his gaze, he read the question in her eyes. The constant concern. The gentle pressing.

Talk to me.

As she twined one long arm through his, and let her head fall against his shoulder, he *knew* that he could tell her.

About the girl and her mother, about Leo's voice

scratching away inside his skull, about the way he longed for hunger, and that he was afraid: afraid of his purpose, afraid he couldn't do it, afraid he could, afraid of what he needed to become, and what he was becoming, what he already was, and the truth that underneath it all— quieter than it had been, but there, there all the same— was that vain and useless and impossible longing to be human. A desire he kept trying to drown. A desire that held its breath until his focus slipped, and then surged up again, gasping for air.

He could tell her—confess, as so many damned souls did to him—but what was the point? The words were like dominoes lined up in his head, and if he started speaking, if he toppled that first tile, they would all come crashing down. For what? The selfish urge to feel . . .

Her fingers tightened on his arm.

Talk to me, little brother.

But a Sunai's command carried no weight without words. It was unfair, he knew, that because she couldn't ask, he didn't have to answer.

"Everything went as it should," he said, because that wasn't a lie, even if it didn't feel like the truth.

Ilsa lifted her head and sadness swept across her face like a flush. He looked away, and she pulled free and lay back on the concrete roof, her arms spread wide, as if trying to embrace the sky.

The cloudless day was giving way to a clear and moonless night, and this high up, with most of the northern grid down, he'd be able to make out a handful of stars. Nothing like the paintings of light he'd seen in the sky beyond the city, just a handful of dots flickering overhead, there and gone and there again, like the memory of that night in the Waste when he was with Kate and the sickness was just starting. When the stolen car broke down and they stood on the side of the road, Kate shivering and August burning up, and overhead, the sky was a fabric of light. When he stared, mesmerized by the sheer number of stars, and she said that people were made of stardust, and maybe he was, too.

He'd wanted her to be right.

"Alpha?" Phillip's voice came over the comm.

August straightened. "Present."

"We've got an SOS. Delta team requesting backup."

"North or South?" asked August, rising to his feet.

The slight pause told him the answer before Phillip spoke. *"North."*

August looked out past the Seam, the north half of the city reduced to sharp edges and shadows. He felt his sister's gaze but he didn't look back as his boot brushed the lip of the roof.

"I'm on my way," he said.

And then he stepped off the edge.

卌 卌

The buildings reminded Sloan of jagged teeth, a broken mouth biting into wounded sky. It was dusk, that time when day collapsed into something darker, when even human minds gave way to primal things.

He stood before the tower windows looking out, just the way Callum Harker had done so many times. He could appreciate the elegance, the poetry of *made* replacing *maker*, shadow outlasting source.

The office occupied a corner of the building once called Harker Hall, and two of its walls were comprised of solid glass. Against the darkening backdrop, the floor-to-ceiling windows caught shards of his reflection and swallowed others. His black suit blended with the twilight, while the sharp planes of his face shone white as bone, and his eyes burned twin red holes in the skyline.

As night swept through, his reflection grew solid in the glass.

But as the sun set, artificial light seeped in from the south, streaking the picture, fogging the image like a haze, a *pollution*, the lit spine of the Seam, and the Flynn Compound beyond, rising up against the dark.

He rapped a pointed nail thoughtfully against the glass, tapping out a steady rhythm, the pace of a ticking clock.

It had been six months since he'd risen to his rightful place. Six months since he'd brought half the city to heel. Six months, and the Compound was still standing, the FTF was still *resisting*, as if they couldn't see that it was a doomed endeavor, that predators were *made* to conquer prey. He would show them, of course, that they would not win, *could not* win, that the end was inevitable—the only question was whether they would submit, whether they would die fast or slow.

Sloan's attention drifted to his own half of the city, cast more in darkness than in light. What light there *was* served a purpose—it kept their food alive. The Corsai had never been creatures of temperance—they would feed on anything in reach; if it fell into the shadows, it was theirs. But the Corsai were bound to those shadows, and so the Malchai caged their meals in well-lit buildings and cut high-wattage paths through the dark.

Yet there were *other* lights dotting the city.

The lights of the *hiding*.

Thin ribbons that escaped beneath doors and boarded windows, bulbs of safety turned to beacons, as steady and luring as a heartbeat.

Here I am, they said. *Here I am, here I am, come and get me.*

And he would.

Voices sounded through the open office door, the broken mutterings of a struggle, a body being dragged kicking, screaming against a gag.

Sloan smiled and turned from the glass. He rounded the broad oak desk, his eyes drawn as always to the stain on the hardwood floor, the place where blood had cast a permanent shadow. The last remains of Callum Harker.

Unless, of course, you counted *him.*

He opened the door wide, and a second later a pair of Malchai came crashing in, dragging the girl between them. She had everything he wanted: blond hair, blue eyes, a fighter's spirit.

Katherine, he thought.

The girl, of course, was not Katherine Harker, but there was a moment—there was *always* a moment—before his senses caught up and he registered the dozen differences between Callum's daughter and this imposter.

But in the end, those differences didn't matter. The most important feature wasn't in the face or the shape or the scent. It was in the way they fought.

And she *was* fighting. Even with her mouth taped shut and her hands roped together. Tears had drawn tracks down her face, but her eyes blazed and she kicked out at one of the Malchai but missed as he forced her to her knees.

Sloan's eyes narrowed at the sight of the Malchai's grip on the girl's bare arm, the places where his pointed nails had drawn blood.

"I told you not to hurt her," he said flatly.

"I tried," said the first Malchai. Sloan didn't learn their names. He didn't see the point. "She wasn't an easy catch."

"We did our best," said the second, adjusting his grip.

"You're lucky we didn't eat her ourselves," added the first.

Sloan cocked his head at that.

And then he ripped out the creature's throat.

There was a misconception about Malchai. Most humans seemed to think the only way to kill them was to destroy their hearts. It was certainly the *fastest* way, but severing the muscles in the neck worked, too, if your nails were sharp enough.

The monster clawed uselessly at his ruined throat as black blood spilled down his front, his jaw flapping open and closed. He wouldn't die from the wound, but he'd be too weak to hunt, and Malchai were not a generous lot when it came to blood.

Sloan watched the Malchai thrash. Useless. They were all useless.

He kept waiting for a challenger, someone to rise up and attempt a coup, but no one ever did. They knew, as well as he, that all monsters were not created equal. They knew they were lesser, down to the black hearts beating in their core. Knew it the way any predator knew its betters.

Sloan had always been . . . unique.

All Malchai rose from murder, it was true, but he had risen from a *massacre*. The first night of the territory wars, when Callum Harker claimed North City as his own, he did so by eliminating the competition. An image flickered in Sloan's mind, more dream than memory, of a long table, a dozen bodies in a dozen chairs, blood pooling on the floor beneath them.

What was it Callum said?

The road to the top is paved with bodies.

Sloan often marveled that he could have been a Sunai—that whatever invisible hand cast their shapes had given him this instead. Perhaps because there were no innocents in the room that night.

Or perhaps fate simply had a sense of humor.

The wounded Malchai was losing steam. A rasping

sound escaped his throat, followed by a wet gurgle as the creature collapsed to his knees. His blood dripped in thick clots, staining the floor, and Sloan kicked the Malchai back, out of the path of Callum's mark.

The girl was still on her knees, pinned down by the second monster, who stared at the black blood pulsing from the other Malchai's throat, his skeletal face a mask of shock.

Sloan tugged a dark swatch of cloth from his shirt pocket.

"Go," he said, wiping the gore from his fingers. "And take him with you."

The Malchai obeyed, releasing the girl so he could haul the other monster toward the door.

But the moment her captor's grip was gone, the girl was up, ready to flee.

Sloan smiled and dug the heel of his shoe into the rug, jerking it toward him. She staggered, fighting for balance, and in that beautiful moment before the girl could either fall or find her feet, he was on her, forcing her back against the floor. She fought beneath him, the way Kate had fought in the grass and the gravel. She clawed at him with bound hands, raking too-short nails across too-hard skin, and for a moment he let her fight, as if she hadn't already lost. And then his fingers tangled in her straw-blond hair, forcing her head back, exposing the line of her throat, and Sloan pressed his mouth to the curve of her neck, relishing her rising scream.

"Katherine," he whispered into her skin right before he bit down, pointed teeth sinking easily through flesh and muscle. Blood spilled over his tongue, surging with power, with life, and the scream died in the girl's throat. Some part of her was still trying to fight, but every blow was weaker, her limbs growing sluggish as her body slowly, haltingly surrendered.

She shuddered beneath him, and Sloan savored the perfect seconds when her limbs stopped but her heart struggled on, the blissful stillness when it finally gave up.

His jaw unclenched, teeth releasing with a wet *slick*. He drew his fingers from her hair. Gold strands clung like cobwebs until he shook them free. They settled over her face, as thin and fine as old scars.

"What will you do," said a dry voice in the doorway, "when you run out of blonds?"

Sloan's teeth clicked together. The intruder's shape hovered at the edge of his vision, a ghost of the girl beneath him, a shadow, familiar but distorted.

Alice.

He dragged his gaze toward her.

She was dressed in Katherine's old clothes, scraps Katherine had left behind, black jeans and a fraying shirt. Her hair was more white than blond, chopped at a violent angle along her jaw, and blood—dark arterial sprays—coated her arms from elbows to pointed nails. From those bloody fingers hung a handful of patches, each printed with three letters: *FTF*.

"We each have our tastes," said Sloan, rising from his crouch.

Alice tilted her head, the motion slow, deliberate. Her eyes were ember red, like Sloan's, like *all* Malchais', but every time he looked at her, he expected to find them blue, like her—he almost thought *father*, but that wasn't right. Callum Harker was *Katherine's* father, not Alice's. No, if Alice was born of anyone, it was of Katherine herself, of her crimes, just as Sloan was born of Callum's.

"Did you succeed?" he asked. "Or simply make a mess?"

Alice drew something from her pocket and tossed it toward him. Sloan plucked the object from the air.

"Four caches down," she said. "Three to go."

Sloan considered the soft cube in his palm. A small quantity of plastic explosive. A *very* small quantity.

"Where is the rest?"

Alice shot him a mischievous grin. "Somewhere safe."

Sloan sighed and straightened, the blood settling in his stomach, the high of the kill so woefully brief. In death, the girl at his feet looked nothing like Katherine, which was terribly unsatisfying. As for the body itself, he'd have someone throw it to the Corsai. They weren't picky when it came to a pulse.

Alice followed his gaze down to the corpse, its appearance a vague echo of her own. Her eyes shone, not with anger or disgust, but with fascination.

"Why do you hate her?"

Sloan ran his tongue thoughtfully over his teeth. He didn't *hate* Katherine, he simply loved the thought of killing her. And he resented her for taking the one life that should have been his: her father's. He'd never know what Callum's blood tasted like. But as long as Katherine was out there, somewhere, he could imagine hers.

"Does a predator hate its prey?" he asked, dabbing a stray drop of blood from the corner of his mouth. "Or is it simply hungry?"

Alice's attention remained fixed on the girl. "She's out there, somewhere." Her red eyes flicked up. "I can feel it, in my bones."

Sloan understood. Every day of their shared existence, he had felt the threads of Callum's life, thin, invisible, impossible to be rid of. And he'd felt his maker's death like a sharp pair of scissors cutting him free.

Alice flexed her fingers, and the last clinging beads of blood dripped to the floor.

"One day, I'm going to find her and—"

"Clean yourself up," he cut in, flicking the pocket

square toward her. "You're making a mess." What he didn't say was that Katherine was *his* prey, and when she returned home—and she would return home, was always drawn home—her death would be his.

But Alice made no motion to grab the swatch of fabric, and it fluttered to the floor, landing like a sheet over the dead girl's face. Alice held Sloan's gaze, a slow smile spreading across her face. "Sure thing, *Dad*."

Sloan's teeth clicked together in disgust.

The first time she had called him that, Sloan had hit her so hard that her body cracked the wall. Alice for her part had only straightened and given a little goading laugh and walked out, out of the penthouse, out of the building, and into the night.

When she returned just after dawn, her limbs were slick with blood, but there were no FTF patches in her hands. She'd said hello and gone to her room. It wasn't until he left the penthouse that he discovered what she'd done: Alice had gone out and killed every blond-haired, blue-eyed girl she could find. Left the bodies in a row on the steps of Harker Hall.

He'd thought of killing her, then, had thought of it a hundred times since, but some urges were made sweeter by the waiting. Perhaps when he ran out of Katherines . . . yes, thought Sloan, returning the smile

He would save her for last.

‖‖‖ ‖‖‖ |

Back at her third boarding school, Kate had read a book about serial killers.

According to the first chapter, most isolated acts were crimes of passion, but those who killed repeatedly did it because they were addicted to the high. Kate had always wondered if there was more to it than that—if those people were also trying to escape the *low*, some hollow, unfulfilling aspect of their lives.

It made her wonder what kind of job those people must have had, to need such violent hobbies.

Now she knew.

"Welcome to the Coffee Bean," she said with all the false cheer she could muster. "What can I get started for you?"

The woman on the other side of the counter didn't smile. "Do you have coffee?"

Kate looked from the wall of grinders and machines,

to the patrons clutching cups, to the sign above the door. "Yes."

"Well?" said the woman impatiently. "What kind of coffee do you *have*?"

"There's a board on the wall over there—"

"Isn't it your job? To know?"

Kate took a steadying breath and looked down at her nails, studying the faint stains of black from the blood of the monster she'd slayed the night before, as she reminded herself that this was just a job.

Her fifth job in six months.

"Tell you what," she said with a smile. "Why don't I get you our best-selling blend."

It wasn't a question. Deep down, most people didn't want to make decisions. They liked the illusion of control, without the consequences. She'd learned that from her father.

The woman nodded brusquely and trudged over to stand with the huddled mass waiting for their orders. Kate wondered who was more addicted to their high, serial killers or coffee addicts.

"Next!" she called.

Teo appeared, his blue hair spiked like a flame above his head. "You've got to see this," he said, pushing his tablet across the counter. And where there was Teo . . . her gaze flicked past him to the corner booth and saw

Bea's curly brown hair, Liam's purple beanie.

"I'm sorry, *sir*," she said. "Do you want to place an *order*? Since I'm at *work*," she added, as if the apron and the spot behind the counter and the line of customers didn't make it obvious.

Teo flashed a mischievous grin. "Triple half-sweet, nonfat caramel macchiato—"

"Now you're just being obnoxious—"

"—with sugar-free whipped cream. Put it on my tab."

"You don't *have* a tab."

"*Aw.*" Teo gave an exaggerated sigh as he withdrew a crumpled bill. "I asked you to start one for me."

"And in the interest of not getting fired—*again*—I didn't." As she took the cash, her gaze flicked down to the tablet. She caught the edge of a headline—A NEW CRIME SCENE—and her pulse ticked up. *This*, this was the high that killers and coffee-addicts hunted for. "Go sit down."

Teo obediently withdrew and as soon as the line was clear, she made his damn drink and ducked out from behind the counter.

"I'm going on break," she said, tearing off the apron and heading to the corner booth where the motley crew of Wardens had taken up residence.

She slammed down the macchiato and dropped into an open chair. "What are you doing here?"

"Manners," said Bea, who'd gotten her the job.

"Macchiato!" said Teo cheerfully.

Liam was busy counting out chocolate-covered espresso beans and popping them into his mouth one by one. "Relax," he said, "it's not like anyone's gonna figure out you have an alter ego."

"Please stop talking."

"Bad barista by day," said Teo in a stage whisper, "badass monster hunter by night."

This was why Kate worked alone. Because the only thing worse than having a secret was letting other people in on it. But the Wardens were like quicksand: the harder she fought, the deeper she sank. They took her standoffishness and rolled with it, even seemed to find it endearing. Which only made her prickle more.

Once, just to mix things up, she'd been obnoxiously sweet, called them nicknames, and thrown an arm around Liam's shoulders, returning all that affection.

They'd looked at her in horror, as if someone else was wearing her face.

"I only have ten minutes," she said. "Show me what you've got."

Teo offered up his tablet. "Check it out."

A photo of a smiling businessman was printed below the headline: OWNER FOUND MAULED BEHIND EATERY.

Kate scanned the text.

Police are still trying to determine the cause . . . speculating whether . . . intentional or foul play . . . no witnesses . . . animal attack . . .

"Animal attack—who buys that?" said Bea. "We're in the middle of P-City."

Kate looked to Teo. "Morgue file?"

"Riley said there's no autopsy yet, but there's a pretty decent hole in his chest, and the heart is missing from the organ inventory. *That* part's not public knowledge, of course."

"Wouldn't want to scare anyone," said Kate dryly as she scrolled down, looking for more details.

She passed a brief mention of the explosion on Broad, and then her hand stopped, hovered over the next article, the familiar face staring up at her, blond hair curling into dark blue eyes.

THE VILLAIN OF VERITY

She held her breath, caught by the sudden blow of meeting her father's unflinching gaze. His voice ground through her head.

Katherine Olivia Harker.

"Kate?" pressed Bea.

She forced herself back to the coffee shop, the table, the Wardens' waiting stares, and flicked her fingers so the page scrolled back up, the article vanishing.

"We've been talking," said Teo, "and Bea and I, we want to help."

"You *are* helping."

"You know what he means," said Bea. "We could go *with* you. Provide backup."

"Yeah!" said Liam.

"Not you," said Teo and Bea at the same time.

"Not *any* of you," said Kate.

"Look," said Bea, leaning forward. "When this all started, it was a theory, right? But because of you we know it's real, and it's not going away, so maybe—"

Kate lowered her voice. "You don't know the first thing about hunting monsters."

"You could teach us," said Teo.

But the last thing Kate needed was more people to worry about, more blood on her hands. "Send me the location of the crime," she said, getting to her feet. "I'll check it out tonight."

卌 卌 ‖

The members of the FTF Council stood in the command center, talking over and through one other, their voices tangling in August's ears.

"Every person we take in is another mouth to feed, another body to clothe, another life to shelter." Marcon brought his hand down on the table. "My allegiance is to the people we already have. The ones who *chose* to fight."

"We're not *forcing* any of our troops across that Seam," said Bennett, a younger member, "but the fact remains that what we're doing now, it's not enough."

"It's *too much*," argued another, Shia. "We're running out of resources—"

"This isn't a war, it's a siege—"

"And if you would agree to attack instead of defend then maybe—"

August stood silently against the wall, his head resting back against the map of the city. He might as well have been a picture; he wasn't there to speak or even to listen. As far as he could tell, he was there only to be seen, to serve as a warning, a reminder.

There is power in perception, observed Leo.

Not Leo, he corrected himself. Not real. Only a voice. A memory.

Not-Leo *tsked*.

At the head of the table Henry Flynn said nothing. He looked . . . tired. Shadows permanently stained the hollows under his eyes. He'd always been slim, but recently he'd started edging toward gaunt.

"We tried to take a fridge last night," said Marcon. *Fridge*, that was what they called the buildings where Malchai and Fangs were keeping prisoners. Fridge—a place to store *meat*. "And we lost five soldiers. *Five*. For what? Northerners who didn't give a damn about us until they had no choice. And people like Bennett and Paris who think—"

"I may be blind but my ears work fine," sniped the old woman across the table. The first time he'd met her she'd been dripping cigarette ash into her eggs in a house two blocks north of the Seam, but she looked right at home in her council chair. "And everyone knows my support for those across the Seam. Easy to say what you would have done if you were there, but you can't fault them for wanting to live."

The quarrel started up again, the volume rising. August closed his eyes. The noise was . . . messy. The situation was messy. Humanity was messy. For the majority of his short life, he'd thought of people as either good or bad, clean or stained—the separation stark, the lines drawn in black and white—but the last six months had shown him a multitude of grays.

He'd first caught a glimpse of it in Kate Harker, but he'd always thought of her as the exception, not the rule. Now everywhere he looked, he saw the divisions made by fear and loss, hope and regret, saw proud people asking for help, and those who'd already sacrificed determined to refuse it.

The FTF was divided—not only the Council but the troops themselves. Tens of thousands of soldiers, and only a fraction of them willing to cross to the North.

"We need to protect our own."

"We need to protect everyone."

"We're buying time with lives."

"Have we gained any ground?"

"August. What do you think?"

He blinked, coming back to himself. What did he think? He thought he would rather be reading, rather be fighting, rather be doing *anything* than standing here listening to men and women talk about human lives as if they were nothing but numbers, odds, watching them reduce flesh and blood to marks on paper, X's on a map.

He fought the urge to say exactly that, searching instead for other truths.

"Monsters," he said slowly, "all want the same thing: to feed. They are united by that common goal, while you are all divided by your morals and your pride. What do I think? I think that if you cannot come together, you cannot win."

Silence fell across the room.

Spoken like a leader, said Leo.

A tired smile tugged at Henry's mouth. "Thank you, August." There was a warmth in his face, a warmth August had spent years learning to imitate, and even now his features tugged automatically into that shape, before he stopped himself, forced his face smooth.

Shortly after, Henry gave his marching orders and the room disbanded. Finally free, August slipped out.

Across the hall was the surveillance room where Ilsa stood before a bank of monitors, her strawberry hair haloed by the screens as light and shadow played across her skin, causing the stars on her shoulders to wink in and out.

August slipped past her, and then past the comm center with Phillip at the board. His left arm rested on the table in a way that might have passed for natural if August hadn't seen the damage himself—held Phillip's thrashing body down on the medical counter as Henry tried to suture the shredded skin and muscle where the Corsai's claws had raked down to bone.

Phillip had learned to shoot with his other hand, was one of the too-few FTFs willing to fight across the Seam, but Harris wouldn't let his old partner back onto his squad until he could take his friend in a fight. Today a bruise colored the hollow of his cheek, but he was getting close.

August was nearly to the elevator when he heard Henry's long stride catching up.

"August," said the man, falling in step beside him. "Take a walk with me."

The elevator doors opened and they both stepped in. When Henry punched the button for the second floor, August tensed. It was easy to forget that the Compound had once been an ordinary high-rise. The second floor housed the fitness facilities and ballrooms, all of which had been converted into training spaces for the new recruits.

The doors opened onto a broad hall.

Newly minted FTFs jogged past in rows of two, and August forced himself to straighten under their gaze.

Through a door on his right, a huddle of children sat on the floor while an FTF captain spoke in a calm, even voice. There, in the middle of the group, was the little girl from the symphony hall, her face scrubbed clean, her eyes wide and sad and lost.

"This way," said Henry, holding open the ballroom door.

The massive space beyond had been quartered into training areas, each one crowded with recruits. Some were being taught self-defense, while others knelt over disassembled weapons, and Henry's wife, Emily, led a group of older conscripts through a hand-to-hand combat sequence. Em matched her husband in height, but where he was fair and thin, she had dark skin and a fighter's build. Her voice rang out, crisp and clean, as she called formations.

August followed Henry onto the track that ringed the training space. They kept to the outer edge, but he still felt like he was being put on display.

All around the hall, heads were turning, and he wanted to believe they were looking at Henry Flynn, the legendary head of the FTF, but even if their eyes were drawn first to Henry, it was August they lingered on.

"Why are we doing this?" asked August.

Henry smiled. It was one of those smiles August couldn't parse, neither happy, exactly, nor sad. Neither guarded nor entirely open. One of those smiles that didn't mean *one* thing, and usually meant a bit of

*every*thing. No matter how many hours August prac-
ticed, he would never be able to convey so much with
only the curve of his lips.

"I take it you mean *this* as in taking a lap, and not *this*
as in the battle for North City." Henry walked with his
hands in his pockets, staring at his shoes. "I used to run,"
he said, almost to himself. August could see it—Henry
had the long, lean build that made motion seem natural. "I'd go out at dawn, burn off all that restless energy.
Always felt better on my feet—"

His chest hitched and he trailed off, coughing against
the back of his hand.

A single cough, but the sound was like a gunshot in
August's skull. For four years, he had lived with the static
of distant gunfire in his head, an echo of his catalyst, a
staccato noise filling every silence. But this single sound
was worse. He slowed his step and held his breath, waiting to see if it would come again, counting, the way you
counted seconds between lightning and thunder.

Henry slowed and coughed a second time, softly, but
deeper, as if something had come loose inside him, and
as they reached a bench, he sank onto it, hands clasped
between his knees. The two of them sat in silence, pretending it was natural, instead of an excuse for Henry to
catch his breath.

"Stupid cough," he muttered, as if it were nothing,

a nuisance, the relic of some protracted cold. But they both knew better, even if Henry couldn't bring himself to say it, and August couldn't bring himself to ask.

Denial—that's what it was called.

The idea that if a thing went unsaid, it didn't really exist, because words had power, words gave weight and shape and force, and the withholding of them could keep a thing from being real, could . . .

He watched Henry watch the training hall.

"FTF," he mused when the coughing fit had passed. "I've always hated that name."

"Really?"

"Names are powerful," he said. "But a movement shouldn't be built on, around, or for a single person. What happens when that person is gone? Does the movement stop existing? A legacy shouldn't be a limitation."

August could feel Henry's mind bending toward him, the way a flower bent toward the sun, the way mass bent toward a planet. He didn't feel like a sun or a planet, but the fact was that he exerted more force on the things around him than they did on him. In his presence, people *bent*.

"Why did you bring me here with you, Henry?"

The man sighed, waving a hand at the new recruits. "Sight is an important thing, August. Without it, our minds invent, and the things they invent are almost always worse than the truth. It's important that they see us. See *you*. It's important that they know you're on their side."

August frowned. "The first thing they see me do is *kill*."

Henry nodded. "That's why the *next* thing you do matters so much. And the next, and the next. You're not human, August, and you never will be. But you're not a monster, either. Why do you think I chose *you* to lead the FTF?"

"Because I killed Leo?" he ventured darkly.

A shadow crossed Henry's face. "Because it *haunts* you." He tapped August's chest, right over the heart. "Because you care."

August had nothing to say to that. He was relieved when Henry finally freed him from the track, from the prying eyes, the fearful looks. He slipped back into the hallway, and headed for the elevator.

"Hey, Freddie!"

August turned and saw Colin Stevenson in FTF fatigues. He was struck by a split second of memory— an ill-fitting uniform, a cafeteria table, an arm around his shoulders. The brief illusion of a normal life.

"That's not my real name," he said.

Colin gaped at him. "Are you serious?" He clutched his chest. "I feel so betrayed."

It took August an instant to catch on: sarcasm. "How's training?"

Colin gestured down at himself. "As you can see, it's doing wonders for my physique."

August actually smiled. The last six months had stretched *him* into a new shape, but Colin hadn't grown an inch.

The boy's family had been found on a rescue mission in the yellow zone during those first weeks. They'd been cornered by a pair of Malchai content to wear them down or starve them out. August himself had been on the extraction team, which was quite a shock to Colin, who'd known him only as Frederick Gallagher, quiet sophomore transfer student, but in Colin's words, "I guess the whole saving thing kind of clears the slate."

The weird thing was, Colin didn't treat him differently, now that he knew. He didn't cower or startle whenever August entered a room, didn't look at him as if he were anyone—anything—but who—what—he'd been.

But Colin hadn't seen him fight a Malchai or reap a sinner's soul, hadn't seen him do anything monstrous.

Then again, knowing Colin, he'd probably say it looked "badass" or "cool." Humans were strange and unpredictable.

"Mr. Stevenson," called one of the squad leaders. "Back to your training circle."

Colin gave an exaggerated groan. "They make us do sit-ups, Freddie. I hate sit-ups. Hated them at Colton, hate them here." He started walking backward. "Hey, some of us are meeting in the lobby for cards. You in?"

You in? Two small words that shook something loose in August, that almost made him forget—

But then his comm buzzed, and he remembered who he was.

What he was.

Alpha.

"I can't," he said. "I work Night Squad."

"Cool, cool."

"Mr. Stevenson," called the captain. "I'm adding sit-ups for every second you're late."

Colin started jogging off. "Once they give me the all clear, I'm signing up. Maybe we'll end up on the same team."

August's spirits fell. He tried to imagine Colin— kind, short, bright Colin—hunting monsters beside him in the dark, but instead he saw the boy lying on the pavement, warm eyes open, his throat torn out.

August had never belonged in Colin's world, and Colin didn't belong in his, and he would do whatever it took to keep him out.

$$\cancel{||||}$$
$$\cancel{||||}$$
$$|||$$

Corsai.

Kate's pen scratched across the paper.

Malchai.

Letter by letter, square by square.

Sunai.

She ignored the puzzle's clues—six down, "a spicy pepper," four across, "the largest supercity"—just killing time. Now and then her attention flicked up from the crossword and through the bookstore windows to the crime scene across the street, the alley roped off with yellow tape.

There had been a cop out there earlier, and then a few photographers lurking around to get a shot, but now that dusk had given way to dark, the scene had emptied out. Not much to see with the body carted off and the business closed.

Kate abandoned the crossword and stepped out

into the night, fitting the wireless bud into her ear. She tapped her phone and silence gave way to voices talking over each other.

"Not what I'm saying—"

"—strike you as weird?"

"Mercury in retrograde or something—"

Kate cleared her throat. "Hey guys," she said, "reporting for duty."

She was met by a swell of *"hey"* and *"what's up?"* and *"it sounds cool when she says it."*

"Any updates?" she asked, setting off down the block.

"No new leads," said Teo over the continuous tap of fingers on a keyboard.

Kate crossed the street, heading toward the crime-scene tape. "Square one, then," she said, ducking under the yellow line. She skirted the markers, trying to recreate the scene in her mind. Where had the monster come from? Where would it go next?

"You think it'll come back?" asked Liam.

Kate crouched, fingers hovering over the shadow of a bloodstain. "These monsters aren't all that bright. This one found a meal. No reason it won't come back looking for another."

She pulled a UV light from her back pocket. As she switched it on, the bloodstain beneath her turned vivid blue against the pavement. So did a trail. It led away like bread crumbs, clusters of dry drops where the blood had dripped from the monster's taloned hands. Kate straightened, following the trail down the alley.

"Come out, come out, wherever you are," she whispered. "Nice juicy human heart."

"*Not funny, Kate,*" said Riley.

But the blue dots had already vanished, the trail gone cold. Kate sighed and pocketed the light. It had taken her two weeks to find the last pair of monsters, with three bodies to go on. But the night was young, and she had to start somewhere.

"Time to widen the net," she said.

"*Already on it,*" answered Bea as the furious sound of typing filled Kate's earpiece and the Wardens did what the Wardens did best: hack street cameras across the city.

"*Let's start with a quarter-mile radius.*"

"*I've got eyes on First through Third over to Clement.*"

"*Fourth through Ninth as high as Bradley.*"

"Hey, little lady."

The voice came from behind her, its edges slurred. Kate rolled her eyes and turned to find a man leering, his eyes glassy as they roved across her. Because of course, monsters weren't the only thing she had to worry about. "Excuse me?"

"*Kick his ass,*" offered Bea.

"Kate," warned Riley.

"Shouldn't be out all alone." The man swayed a little. "Not safe."

Kate arched a brow, fingers drifting toward the taser at her belt. "That so?"

He took another step toward her. "Think of all the bad things that could happen."

"You planning to protect me?"

The man gave a weak chuckle and licked his lips. "No."

He lunged for her arm, and when Kate took a single swift step back, he stumbled, losing his balance. She caught him by the throat and slammed him into the wall. He slid down the bricks with a groan, but there was no time to celebrate.

Because just then, someone *screamed*.

The sound hit Kate in the stomach and she spun, already moving toward the source as a second voice joined in, and a third.

She sprinted down the block and skidded around the corner, expecting to find a Heart Eater amid a crowd of people. But the street was empty, and the screams were coming from inside a restaurant. Kate slammed to a stop as a line of blood streaked across the front window. The door hung open and someone was crawling forward on hands and knees, while others slumped on tables. At the back of the room she saw a man, holding what looked like a pair of kitchen knives. The knives were slick with blood, and his eyes shone strangely, and he was *smiling*— not a deranged grin, but something calm, almost *peaceful*, which made the whole scene so much worse.

Kate touched her ear. "Call the police."

"What?" asked Teo. *"What's going—"*

Her voice was shaking. "One Sixteen South Marks."

A body tumbled back into the glass, leaving a red streak in its wake. The man with the knives vanished into the kitchen.

"Kate, are you—"

"Now."

The air smelled like blood and panic as she forced herself toward the restaurant, toward the massacre, toward the chaos.

And there, in the middle of it all, so still she almost didn't see it, stood a monster.

Not a Heart Eater, but something else, something shaped more or less like a person, at least around the edges, but made entirely of shadow. It stood, watching the scene unfold with a serenity that matched the killer's, and as it watched, it seemed to grow more solid, more *real*, details etching themselves across the blank canvas of its skin.

"Hey!" she called out.

The monster twitched at the sound of her voice and turned toward her, revealing the edge of a silver eye just as sirens came blaring down the street. Kate spun around as the red-and-blue strobes of police cars swung around the corner, barreling past her toward the restaurant, where the screams had given way to horrible, blanketing silence.

The monster was gone.

Kate turned, searching the street. She'd looked away only for an instant, a breath; it couldn't have gotten far, but it was nowhere, nowhere—

There.

The shadow reappeared at the mouth of an alley.

"What's going on?" demanded Liam as Kate took off at a sprint.

The shadow vanished again and reappeared farther down the alley as Kate cut into the gap between buildings.

Sirens wailed, and behind her eyes she still saw the streaks of blood, the man's knives, but also his calm resolve, and the creature's own expression, a mirror, an echo.

Her mind raced. What had it done? What did it feed on? Why was it standing there just *watching*—

"Kate, are you there?"

She drew an iron spike as she ran. The alley around her was empty, empty—and then it wasn't.

She slid to a stop on the damp concrete, breathless from the chase and the sudden appearance of the shadow in her path. This time, the monster didn't flee. And neither did Kate. Not because she didn't want to—in that moment, she did—but because she couldn't look away.

She'd thought of the monster as a shadow, but it was more—and less. It was—wrong. It *looked* wrong, it *felt* wrong, like a hole cut in the world, like deep space. Empty and cold. Hollow and hungry.

It drew all the heat out of the air, all the light, all the sound, plunging them both into silence, and she felt suddenly heavy, slow, her limbs weighed down as the darkness, the monster, the nothing, closed the gap between them.

"Kate?" pleaded a voice in her ear, and she tried to speak, tried to pull free, tried to will her limbs to move, to fight, to *run*, but the monster's gaze was like gravity, holding her down, and then its icy hands were on her skin.

Riley's voice in her ear: *"Kate?"*

Somewhere, distantly, she felt the spike slip from her fingers, the far-off sound of metal hitting asphalt as the creature lifted her chin.

Up close, it had no mouth.

Only a pair of silver eyes set like discs into its empty face.

Like mirrors, thought Kate, as she caught sight of herself.

And then she was falling in.

卌
卌
||||

At first
it thinks
she is
another toy
to wind up
and release
another match
to strike
but she is
    already lit
so full
of grief and anger
of guilt and fear
Who deserves to pay?
it asks her heart
and her heart
answers
everyone,
    every one
and it knows

she is
like *it*
a thing
    of limitless
        potential—
she will burn
like a sun
among stars
she will make it solid
she will make it real
she will—
(Kate?)
(Kate!)
and then
—somehow—
she
pulls away
it lets her go
    and it does not
she tears free,
and she does n—

"KATE?"

Riley's voice screamed in her ear and she tore herself free—and it *felt* like tearing, clothes caught on a nail, skin on barbed wire, pieces left behind, something deep inside her ripping.

She was on her knees—when had she fallen?—hands scraping pavement and her head a riot of pain, everything blurred as if she'd taken a blow. But she didn't remember—she couldn't remember—

The voices were shouting in her skull, and she wrenched the earpiece from her ear and cast it into the dark as the alley slid in and out of focus, a second image ghosting her vision in a sickening overlay.

She squeezed her eyes shut, counted to five.

And then she blinked, and saw the red-and-blue lights dancing on the alley wall. Remembered the restaurant, the screams, the man—then the monster, that void with its mirror eyes and a voice that wasn't a voice inside her head.

Who deserves to pay?

She remembered, distantly, a swell of anger, a longing to hurt something, someone. But it was like a dream, quickly fading. The monster was gone, and Kate lurched to her feet, the world rocking violently. She caught herself against the wall. One step at a time, she made her way back toward the flashing lights, stopping at the mouth of the alley as an ambulance sped away.

A crowd had gathered, morbidly curious, but the attack was over. Whatever it was, it had moved from an active scene to a passive one. A row of body bags lined the curb, and police moved in and out, the sirens off, and the scene already growing still, like a corpse.

A cold fear crept through her. She didn't understand what had happened, what she'd *seen*, but the longer she stared, the less she could remember, and the harder she thought, the worse the pain in her head. Something dripped from her chin, and she tasted copper in the back of her throat and realized her nose was bleeding.

She pushed off the wall and nearly fell again, but forced herself to keep moving and didn't stop until she was home.

When she finally stumbled into the apartment, she nearly missed the person on the couch.

Riley was already on his feet, moving as if to catch her.

"Jesus, Kate, what *happened*?"

At least, that's what she thought he said. The words themselves were muffled by a ringing in her ears, a white noise like being underwater, pain lancing through her head, a strobe behind her eyes.

"Kate?"

Her vision blurred, focused, blurred again, and she could feel the bile rising in her throat. She beelined for the bathroom and felt more than heard Riley on her heels but didn't look back.

Why was he here?

Why was he always getting in the way?

Anger rose in her, sudden and irrational. Anger at the look on his face, the worry in his eyes, the fact he was trying so hard to be someone she didn't want, didn't need.

He caught her by the arm. *"Talk to me."* Kate spun, shoving him forcefully back into a spindly table in the hall.

Riley let out a yelp as both he and the table went crashing to the floor, and for an instant, looking at him on the ground, so open, so pathetic, Kate wanted to *hurt* him, wanted it with such simple clarity that she knew it *wasn't real.*

What was happening to her?

She turned and stumbled into the bathroom, locked the door, and retched until her stomach was empty and her throat was raw, brought her forehead to rest against the cold porcelain as the pounding on the door was drowned out by the pounding in her skull.

Something was wrong; she had to get up, had to open the door, had to let Riley in. But then she closed her eyes, and the darkness felt so good.

Somewhere, far away, her body hit the floor, but she kept falling down, down, down into black.

|||| ||||

|||| ||||

|||| ||||

It moves
in the cold
nothing
a shadow
of itself
folded
between
what is
and what could be
the girl's mind
a shard
of heat
within
its own—
in her head
it saw a city
carved in two
a hundred
faceless faces
defined only

by the red
of their eyes
the flash
of their teeth
a place
of blood
and death
vice
and violence
and
      such wondrous
          potential
it saw
and it knew
it *knows*—
this is
the way
together
the girl
and the city
the city
and the girl
and the heat
will be
enough
    to burn
enough to be
made
real.

|||| |||| |||| |

They were on the wrong side of the Seam when the call came in.

There *was* no right and wrong side, according to Henry, no North and South, not anymore, but the fact was that *one* side of the city was being run by monsters. *One* side was a field of land mines, a place of shadows and teeth. On the south side of the Seam, running into trouble was a risk.

On the north, it was a certainty, especially after dark.

August's squad had crossed the Seam to offer backup to another team securing a depot. It had gone off without a hitch, and they were almost done loading the trucks with supplies when the comm on August's collar crackled to life.

"Night Squad One, we've got a problem. Squad Six has gone offline midmission."

A bad feeling brushed his ribs. It wasn't a good sign when whole squads went dark.

"How many soldiers?"

"*Four.*"

"Location?"

"*The Falstead Building on Mathis.*"

He met Rez's gaze over the hood of the truck. "X code?"

The "X code" referred to the the FTF maps in the Compound's control room, the ones covered in small colored crosses. Black marked locations actively held by the enemy. Blue marked ones held by the FTF. Gray was for places cleared or abandoned.

"*Gray,*" said the dispatcher, "*but it hasn't been rechecked in more than a month. Patrol on the Seam caught a light signal from the third floor. Squad Six went to investigate.*"

August was already peeling away.

He would have gone alone, but there were no solo missions—that was the rule in the FTF, even for Sunai—so Rez came with him.

Nothing needed to be said. This was the order of the rank and file—Harris, Jackson, and Ani would stay with the other squad, help them back to the Compound with their supplies.

Rez was his second, had been since the squad was formed.

They moved at a brisk pace, August with his violin out, his bow ready, and Rez cradling her gun. The Falstead

Building was two blocks north and three east, and they kept to the streetlights, wherever they weren't broken, trading exposure for a modicum of safety from the night.

When they rounded the last corner, August's steps slowed, then stopped. There was no sign of the Falstead, no sign of anything; the city just *ended*, replaced by a wall of black.

Rez let out a curse, fingers tightening on her gun.

They were standing at the edge of a blackout zone. Someone—or something—had killed a section of the power grid, plunging several square blocks into solid darkness. There was another name for these blackout zones, among the FTF: *boneyards*.

"Wait here," said August.

It was an empty order, one Rez always disobeyed, but he had to say it.

She snorted, shouldering the gun. "And let you have all the fun?"

They both drew light batons from their pockets. Unlike the HUVs, which issued a single beam, the batons threw light to every side. The result was a diffuse glow, better than shadow, but not as safe as focused light. The techs hadn't found a way to make them brighter.

Together, they crossed the line into the dark. It parted around them like a fog, thrown back a few feet in each direction by the light of their batons, but just beyond, the Corsai's wet white eyes blinked, their voices hissing out like steam.

beatbreakruinfleshbone

August could hear Rez's heart thudding in her chest, but her steps were steady, her breathing even. When they were first paired up, he'd asked her if she was afraid.

"Not anymore," she'd said, and she'd showed him a scar, running down her front.

"Monsters?" he'd asked, and she'd shaken her head and said her own heart had tried to kill her, long before the monsters had, so she'd decided not to be afraid.

"Doesn't do much good," she'd said, "to fear one kind of death and not another."

Their lights caught broken glass on the Falstead's front steps. The doors hung askew, and the place had the eerie feeling of the recently abandoned.

Someone had already set a baton in the center of the lobby floor. The pool of light didn't reach the corners of the room, but it carved a path. Another waited at the base of the stairs.

Bread crumbs, thought August absently. A relic from another one of Ilsa's stories.

As they started up the stairs, a bad feeling began to spread like cold through August's chest.

Feelings again, little brother?

He pushed Leo's voice aside as they climbed.

Around them, the Falstead began to change.

The lobby below had retained its air of luxury, but the second floor was starting to show the rot. By the time they reached the third, wallpaper was peeling back, boards crumbling underfoot. The walls were riddled with bullet holes and flaking drywall, whole sections staved in, as if someone had taken a sledgehammer to them. Through open doors he saw furniture overturned, glass shattered, dark stains coating every surface, stale smoke and old blood, all of it human.

"What the hell is this place?" murmured Rez.

August didn't have an answer.

They found the first body on the stairs. A baton sat in his lap, casting an eerie pool of light around his corpse, shining on the blood spilling down the steps. His combat vest was gone, his head hung at an impossible angle, and the FTF patch had been torn from his sleeve.

"Shit," muttered Rez, her voice laced not with panic, but anger. "Shit, shit . . ."

Beyond the steady beat of her swearing, August caught the far-off sound of something dripping, the faint creak of boards somewhere overhead.

He held a finger to his lips, and she went silent, crouched beside the body. Nothing happened, and after several long seconds, they both started moving again.

Up ahead, a mass coiled and writhed in the middle of the hall.

August caught a glint of silvery talons, a razor jaw, but Rez was a step ahead, lobbing a small light grenade across the floor. August squeezed his eyes shut as it detonated, throwing out a silent blast of UV light. The Corsai scattered with a hiss, fleeing into deeper shadow. Most of the creatures escaped, but one went up in smoke, its teeth and claws raining to the floor like chips of ice.

Two more corpses lay in the hall, their bodies twisted.

But by the looks of it, the Corsai hadn't killed them. Their bodies were still mostly intact, their patches taken like trophies.

What had the voice on the comm said?

Patrol on the Seam caught a light signal . . . went to investigate.

Where was the fourth soldier?

Light danced in a doorway at the other end of the hall, not the steady glow of a dropped baton but the fickle stutter of a candle. August pocketed his light, and gripped the neck of his violin with one hand and the steel bow with the other. He left Rez with the bodies and moved toward the room, drawn by the light and the soft sound of a weight on floorboards, the drip of something against wood.

A single candle burned upright in the middle of the

room—it was more like a cage, slats missing from the ceiling and floor—and against the far wall, beneath a cracked window, sat the last member of Squad Six, gagged and bound. The soldier's head lolled. His vest was gone, and his shirtfront was soaked through with blood.

Dead weight, warned Leo, and real or not, he was right. August could hear the man's heart fighting, losing, but it didn't stop him from calling for Rez or picking his way through the room.

He didn't slow until he was close enough to see the word on the floorboards, scrawled in the soldier's blood.

BOO

August's gaze snapped to the cagelike room, and then to the window. The darkness beyond was studded with a pair of watching red eyes, the sharp corner of a smile.

Alice.

Rez was beside him now, reaching for the soldier's pulse. He caught her wrist.

"Get back," he said, pushing her toward the door, but it was too late.

The ceiling creaked above them and August looked up just in time to see the glint of metal, the flurry of limbs, before the first monster came crashing down.

||||| ||||| ||||| ||

They came from everywhere.

Not monsters, he realized, but humans, *Fangs* with blood on their cheeks and steel collars wrapped around their throats and the manic smiles of the drugged and the mad. Some had knives and some had guns, and one dropped down right behind Rez.

She spun, cracking him across the face as August raised his violin. Bow met strings, but before he could draw a note, a shot exploded through the air, grazing the steel and ripping the instrument from his hand. It went skittering across the floor.

Rez kicked out, trying to send it back while headlocking a man twice her size, but it was lodged between two broken boards, and before August could reach her or the violin, a hulking man slammed him backward into the soldier, the wall, the window. The soldier slumped, lifeless, and the glass gave way. August nearly fell through, catching himself against the jagged edge. Glass bit into his palms, but drew no blood, and he surged back into the room just as an ax caught him in the chest.

The blade cut through mesh and cloth before slamming into his ribs. It didn't break the skin, but it drove all the air from his lungs, and he doubled over, gasping. The Fangs circled him and he slashed out with the sharp spine of his bow as a length of iron chain wrapped around his throat.

The pure metal turned his stomach. His legs went weak, the chain wrenching him to his knees, and for one horrible second he was back in the warehouse in the Waste, heat screaming through his skin as he burned from the inside out and Sloan stood laughing at the edge of the light and—

The blunt side of the ax came down on the back of his neck, and he hit the floor hard, the boards cracking beneath him. His vision doubled, the chain at his throat vising, and then they were on him, kicking and beating, the blows shallow, the pain brief, but disorienting.

". . . Sunai . . ."

". . . just like she said . . ."

". . . truss him up . . ."

August's hands tightened into fists, and he realized he was still holding the bow, the steel pinned beneath someone's boot.

Through the tangle of limbs he saw Rez wrest herself free. She managed a single step toward him, and he tried to tell her to *run,* to get out, but she wouldn't listen. She never listened.

She threw herself at the tangle of bodies, peeling one away from the group. In the instant of distraction, the other Fangs faltered, torn between the two targets. The boot came off his bow and August slashed violently across the man's leg. He went down screaming and clutching his calf as blood, but also light, bloomed across his skin.

Music wasn't the only way to bring a soul to surface— Leo had taught him that. August grabbed the man's ankle, bone cracking beneath his fingers as the soul sang through him, sharp as electricity and just as violent. Ice water and anger and a single, pealing scream.

Embrace it, urged his brother, as the world slowed, every detail in the broken room suddenly vivid, from the warped boards to the candlelight.

The Fang collapsed, his eyes burned black, and August shot to his feet, tugging the chain from his neck as the others scrambled back, clearly torn between whatever they'd been told—given, promised—and simple, physical fear.

They all recoiled, except for one.

A single Fang stood in the doorway, holding Rez

like a shield, one hand clutching her hair and a serrated blade at her throat.

"Put down the bow," he said through bloody teeth.

"Don't you dare," growled Rez.

Dead weight, repeated Leo.

August heard the clank of chain, sensed the other Fangs closing in on him again, the violin still wedged between the cracked boards a yard away.

"Hey, boss . . ." August met Rez's gaze and saw the glint between her fingers, but before he could stop her, she drove the dagger back into the man's leg. He howled and let go, but not before slicing her throat.

A sound left August then, low and animal, and he forced himself to lunge, not for the killer but for the violin. Hands tore at him but he ignored them, grabbing the instrument and slashing the bow across the strings.

The first note came out hard and sharp, and the Fangs recoiled, pressing their hands over their ears as if that would save them, but it was too late. They were too late.

By the second note, the fight went out of them.

By the third, they were falling to their knees.

August left the music echoing on the air and ran for Rez. He dropped the violin and sank to the floor beside her.

"Stay with me," he said, pressing his hands to the wound at her neck. There was so much blood bubbling up between his fingers, too much, and it slicked his skin, made his fingers slip. *So much red*, he thought, *and none of it light.*

Her mouth opened and closed, but no sound came out.

Her chest juddered up, down.

"Stay with me." The words came out pleading.

August had reaped a thousand souls, but it was such a different thing to feel a life bleed out beneath his hands, powerless to staunch the flow. For all the souls he'd reaped, he'd so rarely seen this kind of death, never felt the way it stole beneath his fingers, life spilling across the floor until that horrible cusp, the instant when it ended. When Laura Torrez stopped being a person and became a body. No transition, no ease, gone and there, there and gone, gone, gone.

August's hands slid from the wound at Rez's throat. Her eyes were open and empty, and red light flickered across her face. Not hers, of course, but *theirs*. A room of ruined souls waiting to be reaped.

August eased Rez's body down and rose to his feet. He moved among the Fangs, bloodstained fingers searching out skin.

They whispered their sins, but he didn't listen, didn't care. Their confessions meant nothing to him.

He snuffed their lights, reaped their souls, his whole body humming with the sudden influx of power, his senses sharpened to the point of pain, until there was only one left.

The man who'd killed Rez.

His lips were moving, his soul a sheen of sweat against his skin, but August didn't reach out to reap it. Leo's words swam inside his head, not the stuff of madness, but memory—a memory from the night he'd taught August about pain, and why he so often used it.

"Our purpose is not to bring peace," his brother had said. *"It is to bestow penance."*

August watched the man's soul sink back beneath the surface of his skin, watched his senses return.

"Why shouldn't they suffer for their sins?"

The Fang blinked, straightened, his mouth twisting in a grimace, but before he could speak, before he could say or do *anything*, August slammed his boot into the man's wounded leg, and he buckled, clutching at his thigh before August forced him to the floor, fingers closing around the steel collar at his throat.

"Look at me," he said, squeezing until the metal bent and buckled. "How does it feel?"

The man couldn't answer, couldn't breathe. He scrambled and scratched and gasped as the red light of his soul surfaced again, pouring through August's hands.

It hit him like ice, a cold so sharp it hurt, and it was

the pain that brought August back to himself, to what he was doing, what he had done.

He wrenched backward, but it was too late. The light was gone, and all that was left was the man's contorted body, eyes burned out and mouth open in a silent scream, red and purple welts rising around the crushed collar.

August felt sick.

His body ached with the pressure—the presence—of the souls, and he wished he could retch them up, expel the weight of so many unwanted lives, but it was no use. The souls were a part of him now, fusing to his bones and surging through his veins.

His chest hitched and he brought his hand to his front where the ax had cut through armored vest and uniform but failed to wound.

"Alpha pair, report."

He looked down at his hands, coated in Rez's blood. It was drying on his skin, tacky and cold.

"Alpha pair."

August had always hated blood. It was the same color as a soul, but empty, useless the moment it left a person's veins.

"August."

He forced his mind back.

"I'm here," he said, startled by the calm in his voice,

steady when something deeper wanted to scream. "We were ambushed." His gaze went to the broken window where the red eyes had watched from the dark. "Rez is dead."

"*Shit.*" Phillip, then. Phillip was the only one who swore on the comm. "*And the other squad?*"

"Dead," answered August.

What a simple word that was, not messy at all.

"*We'll send a team at dawn, for the bodies.*" And then Phillip's voice was gone, and others were ricocheting across the comm, none of them directed at him. He picked up his bow, his violin—these small, solid pieces of himself—then busied his hands arranging light batons to keep the corpses safe.

Corpse—another simple word that did so little work, failed to describe something that was once a *person*, and now was simply a shell.

Eventually a familiar voice broke the static in his ear.

"*August,*" said Emily, "*you should return to the Compound.*"

Her voice, as steady as his own. He swallowed back the *no, no, no* and said instead, "I'm waiting. . . . I have to wait."

And Emily didn't make him say why, so she must have understood what he meant. Violence begets violence, and monstrous acts make monsters.

The Malchai in the hall came first, rose up like spirits from the bodies of the soldiers. And he cut them down. Then came the Malchai by the smothered candle, rising up beside the word written in blood, and he dispatched that one, too. And then, it came down to Rez.

Her murder had been the work of an instant, but it felt like forever before the shadows finally began to twitch.

His fingers tightened on his bow as the night took a shuddering breath, and then, standing among the corpses, stood the monster.

It looked down at itself in a gesture so human, so natural, and yet so wrong, and then its head came up, red eyes widening right before August drove his steel bow into its heart.

Half a block from the Falstead, August knew he was being followed.

He could hear the shuffle of steps, not on the street behind him but somewhere overhead. He didn't slow until something floated to the ground at his feet.

It was a patch, three letters—*FTF*—visible through the blood.

As he straightened, another drifted down.

"Hasn't anyone told you?" said a voice on the air. "It's not safe to wander after dark."

He looked up and saw her standing on a nearby roof, moonlight tracing her pale hair.

"Alice."

She smiled, flashing knifepoint teeth, and sank into a crouch at the edge of the roof. August told his hands to move, to lift the violin, but it hung there, dead weight at his side. She *wasn't* Kate, but every time he saw her, his stomach still dropped. Every time, for just a second.

The Malchai didn't *look* like her, not really—all the pieces were wrong—but the whole was more than the sum of its parts. Alice looked like the Kate he'd never met, like the one he'd expected to find at Colton before he met the real girl. The way she'd been described to him—daughter of a monster. All the things Kate wasn't, all the things she pretended to be, Alice *was*.

He had known—hadn't wanted to think about it, but had known all the same—that *something* would walk out of that house beyond the Waste, and yet it had still been a shock, meeting her. It was two weeks—maybe three— after Kate. After Callum. After Sloan. He was responding to a distress call, but when he got there, all he found were corpses. Corpses, and *her,* standing the middle of it all, covered in blood, and *grinning*, the same grin she was wearing now, a grin that was all monster.

"Your trap didn't work," he said.

Alice only shrugged. "The next one will. Or the next. I've got plenty of time, and you've got plenty of people to lose. Such a shame about your friends." She tossed patches like petals over the edge of the roof, far more than the number of soldiers he'd lost that night. "They're all so fragile, aren't they? What do you see in them?"

"Humanity."

Alice laughed softly, a sound like steam escaping

from a pot. "You know, I thought, if I used humans, you might try to spare them." Her red eyes danced over his bloodstained front. "I guess I was wrong."

"I don't spare sinners."

Alice's gaze flicked up. "You spared *Kate*." The name like a barb in the monster's mouth. "You're sparing *me*, right now, with your friend's blood still on your hands. Must not have been a very good friend."

He knew she was baiting him, but the anger still rose like heat on his skin.

As if on cue, red eyes began to flicker around him in the dark.

Alice hadn't come alone, but there was a reason she kept her distance, lobbing taunts down from the rooftop. A Sunai's music was as toxic to a Malchai as a Malchai's soul was to a Sunai. If August started playing, the other monsters would die, but Alice would get away.

She flashed a smile, and there it was again, in the twist of her lips, the shadow of someone else.

"I'm *not her*," sniped the Malchai, and August recoiled at the sudden venom. "You've got that look on your face, poor little lost monster. Do you miss her, our Kate?" Her eyes narrowed. "Do you know where she is?"

"I don't," he said. "But I hope it's far away from here. Far away from *you*. And if she has any sense, she'll never come back."

Alice sneered and, with that, the illusion shattered—what little resemblance she bore to Kate was gone, and all that was left was monstrous. The sight of that true face freed August of any hesitation. He swung the violin up in a fluid arc, the tension collapsing as Alice lunged backward into shadow, and the other Malchai rushed at August in the light, and his bow sliced like a knife across his strings.

As he walked home, it started to rain. A steady curtain of water that soaked August through and left a dark trail, the blood of friends and enemies, of FTFs and Fangs and monsters, mingled in his wake.

Somewhere between slaughtering Alice's Malchai and reaching the Seam, August realized something: it didn't have to hurt this much.

For months he'd been playing a part, instead of *becoming* it, pretending to be strong while all the while harboring a shred of hope that there was still a world where he could feel human.

"Because you care." That's what Henry had said, but Henry was wrong. Henry was human; he didn't understand that in trying to be both, August succeeded at neither. Leo had understood, had sacrificed humanity to be the monster the humans *needed*.

All August had to do was let go. It was time to let go.

"Stop!" ordered a pair of FTFs as he reached the Seam.

The violin should have been enough to ID him, but the bow was slick with gore, the instrument streaked red, and, in the rain-slicked night, he hardly passed for human.

When the soldiers saw his face, they staggered back, apologies caught in their throats as they opened the gate. He continued on, through South City and across the light strip and into the bright warmth of the Compound lobby.

The clash and thrum of conversation died, the steady thud of movement froze, and in the silence, a hundred pairs of eyes turned toward him.

August had avoided his reflection in every pane of glass, every dark puddle, every steel sheet, but he saw it now, not in a mirror, but in the faces of everyone who looked at him, and then quickly looked away.

Could they see the light of the souls he'd reaped, the monsters he'd slain? Could they feel the darkness in the lives he'd taken, the hate and violence wicking off his skin?

He started across the lobby, the heels of his boots leaving damp crescent moons of blood and ash in his wake. No one approached. No one followed.

Even Henry Flynn, surrounded by captains, took one look at him and stilled.

You wanted them to see me, thought August.

So let them see.

The head of the FTF started toward him, but August held up a hand—a command, a gesture of dismissal.

And then his eyes found Colin, and he had the grim satisfaction of seeing the boy inhale sharply, stricken by the sight of him. Some small part of August exhaled with relief. It had only been a matter of time before Colin saw the truth, the monster behind the mask. Until he realized August was not—would never be—like him.

He reached the elevators, the silence heavy on his shoulders. But he felt the shift inside it, the awe as well as the fear. These people looked at him and saw something not less than human, but more. Something strong enough to fight for them. Strong enough to win.

Stand straight, little brother.

And for the first time, August listened.

$$\cancel{||||} \cancel{||||} \cancel{||||} ||||$$

Sloan stood at the kitchen counter, flipping through a book on war.

Alice left them scattered all over the penthouse, a trail of crumbs marking her ceaseless movement and fickle attention. He let the book fall shut as she came in. "Where have you been?"

He didn't trust it when she wandered off—she was the kind of pet one needed to keep on a leash.

Alice hopped up onto the island. "Hunting."

Sloan's eyes narrowed. She'd always relished making a mess when she fed, and tonight there was no blood on her hands or face.

"I take it you failed."

A pile of FTF patches sat beside her hand, and she twisted and began absently building a tower, as if they were cards. "I prefer to think of success as a process," she mused. "He's not an easy catch."

Ah. *August.*

It was indeed hard to catch a Sunai, harder still to kill one. Sloan knew from personal experience. Ilsa had been a lucky turn, but the new Sunai, Soro, was developing a reputation. Sloan's old friend, Leo, had driven a steel pole through his back, and August had slipped through Sloan's grip before he had a chance to break him.

He didn't expect Alice to succeed where he hadn't. He had simply given her the task as a means of distraction, something to do besides feeding her bottomless appetite.

"If I catch him, can I keep him?" she'd asked.

Now her tongue rested between her sharpened teeth as she stacked a second tier. "I did lose a few Fangs."

"How many?"

"Seven, I think? Maybe there were eight."

He was beginning to regret her assignment. "And how, pray tell, did you lose them?"

"I'm not sure it really counts as losing." She continued building her tower. "They did take out five soldiers and, really, isn't that what they're for?"

"Alice—"

"Don't *Alice* me." The mask of humor was suddenly replaced by scorn. "They're pawns, to play with Flynn's little toy soldiers."

"This isn't a game."

"But it *is*." She swung back to face him. "And games are meant to be *won*. Aren't you tired yet, of playing this tug-of-war? Of keeping your pieces on only half the board? Make a move. Change the play. You are supposed to be king of the monsters, Sloan."

She leaped down from the counter, flashing a wide smile full of teeth.

"So *act* like it."

Sloan had held his ground through her whole little speech, but now he moved. In a single motion, he pinned her back against the counter. Alice's shoulders knocked into the makeshift tower, and it collapsed with a soft sound.

She stilled as Sloan drew his fingers through her white-blond hair.

"Careful, Alice," he murmured. "My patience is like that house, precariously balanced." His grip tightened, forcing her head back to expose her throat. "Who knows when it might tip."

Alice swallowed. "Careful, Sloan," she said, eyes flaring bright. "It's one thing to kill a nameless thug. But start killing those close to you, and the others might wonder . . ."

She let the sentence die, but the threat was clear.

"Well then," he said, loosening his grip, "it's a good thing we're on the same team."

One day, he thought, *I will savor your death.*

"As for your concerns"—his eyes danced over the pile of patches that had so briefly been a tower—"I can only promise that your patience will be rewarded."

He took up the nearest patch from the pile and ran a nail across the letters on its front.

FTF.

Three letters that had come to mean a *force*, a *wall*, a *war*. But were, in truth, nothing but a *compound*, stones and mortar assembled by men.

And what goes up, thought Sloan, can always be torn down.

VERSE 2

THE MONSTER IN ME

I

She is
not
she is
not
she is
not
herself
she has no body
and she is falling
    without falling
        down
darkness
rushes past her
through her—
because she is *not* her
and her first thought
is how good it feels
to be *not* her
to be no one
to be nothing at all.

The world came back in pieces.

The pulse in Kate's ears, the couch beneath her back, the voices somewhere overhead.

"You should have called someone."

"I called *you*."

"I'm not a doctor, Riley. I'm not even a medic yet."

Kate dragged her eyes open and saw a ceiling streaked with daylight. Her head ached and her mouth was dry, the salt taste of blood coating the back of her throat. All she wanted was for them to shut up and let her go back to sleep.

"She should go to a hospital."

"What am I supposed to tell them? My friend got hurt fighting monsters? I'm pretty sure she's not even supposed to *be* in Prosperity."

Riley swam in her vision. Over his shoulder, his boyfriend, Malcolm, was pacing.

"How long has she been out?"

"Six hours. Almost seven. I should have called sooner but—"

"Too loud," she groaned, pushing herself upright. She quickly wished she hadn't. The room swayed and her pulse slammed inside her head. "Son of a bitch."

Riley knelt beside her, one hand tight on her shoulder. "Kate? Jesus, you scared me. Are you all right?"

Malcolm leaned in, flashing a penlight in her eyes,

which did nothing for the pain in her head.

"What happened?" she asked.

Riley was pale. "You showed up here, looking like hell, locked yourself in the bathroom, and passed out. I had to break down the door."

Kate remembered cold tile against her skin. "Sorry."

Malcolm checked her pulse against his watch. "What's the last thing you remember?"

She hesitated, her mind filling with fragments—the scream, a man holding knives, a body against glass, sirens and a shadow, the sense of falling, falling into *what*?

Instead of trying to work backward from that, she started at the beginning.

"The restaurant."

Riley nodded. "It's all over the news," he said, holding out her tablet. There it was, splashed across the screen:

ROMANCE RUINED: SHUNNED LOVER KILLS TWELVE

The banner photo was a shot of the restaurant's front, a streamer of bright yellow tape caught in the air. A sheet covered the bodies.

"Good thing you didn't go inside," said Riley. And then, "You *didn't* go inside, right?"

No, she'd stopped in the street, caught by the sudden, unexpected horror of the scene.

"We called it in as soon as you told us, but by the time the police got there—it was over. Did you see anything?"

See anything. Fragments drifted together in her head.

"Apparently the guy just showed up, went into the kitchen, and took the knives."

That man, so calm, like he wasn't even there.

"They're not releasing names yet," said Riley, "but someone leaked it to the press that his ex-wife was inside."

"So he had motive," said Malcolm.

Motive, thought Kate. It could have been an ordinary crime—a gruesome one, yes, but something human—except for the fact it *wasn't*.

"You were right, about the explosion," she said, "the string of murder-suicides. There's nothing normal about this."

"Are you sure?"

She remembered the wrongness in the killer's eyes. A pair of silver discs shining in the dark. She'd seen the shadow, followed it . . .

But there the memory faltered, dissolving into darkness and the press of cold.

"Any survivors?" she asked.

"One," said Malcolm. "She was rushed to the hospital in critical condition."

Kate stilled. "Why do I sense a *but* coming?"

"They got her stabilized, but the moment she

woke up—well, she snapped. Killed a doctor. Attacked two nurses, too. If she hadn't been as bad off as she was, it would have been worse for everyone. They ended up quarantining the wing. Put the nurses under observation, in case whatever she had was contagious."

Kate pressed her palms to her eyes, trying to quell the headache, trying to smother the feeling that rose in her throat at the word *contagious*. She'd been there. She'd seen . . .

"Kate?" pressed Riley in a too-even tone. "How are *you* feeling?"

Like hell, she thought. *Like hell, but like myself.*

"She should to go to a doctor," said Malcolm.

"*She* is fine," snapped Kate. Her phone chirped. "And *she* has to go to work."

She got to her feet, steadied herself a moment, and turned toward the hall.

"Is that such a good idea?" asked Riley.

Her temper flared. "I said I'm *fine*."

"And I'm just supposed to believe you?"

Kate spun. "I don't care if you believe me. You're not my parent and I'm not your pet project."

"That's uncalled for!"

"Hey, hey," cut in Malcolm. "Everyone calm down."

Kate scrubbed at her face. "Look," she said slowly,

"you're right, I don't feel great. But I've got to go to work. I'll bail if I have to. Promise."

Riley opened his mouth, but in the end said nothing.

If there was one sound Kate hated, it was the bell above the café door.

What was the point, when the counter faced the door and she could *see* the people coming in? At this time of day, the line stretched all the way back to the door itself, the constant open and close eliciting a near-continuous chime.

"Next!" she called impatiently.

To take her mind off the bell, she tried to focus on the customers themselves and play a game called "guess the secret." The woman in the purple dress two sizes too small? Sleeping with her handyman. The man on the cell? Embezzling. The one in front of her right now? Addicted to sleeping pills. That was the only thing that explained how long it was taking for him to order.

A vein in Kate's temple twitched.

"Next."

A man shuffled forward without looking up from his phone.

"Sir?"

He was talking softly, and she realized he was taking a call.

"Sir?"

He held up a finger and kept talking.

"Sir."

Annoyance rose inside her, taking a sudden sharp turn into anger, and before Kate realized what she was doing, her hand shot across the counter.

She snatched the cell phone and hurled it against the exposed brick wall installed to give the Coffee Bean that extra homey charm. It smashed, and when the man's head finally came up, veins bulging as he stared, not at her, but at the pieces of his cell raining down the wall, Kate's first thought was of reaching out and snapping his neck. Of how nice that would feel.

The urge stole through her, so simple and quick, she almost didn't notice.

She could *see* it, clear as glass, could feel his flesh beneath her hands, hear the clean snap of bone. And the very idea was like a cold compress on a fevered head, a balm on a burn, so sudden and soothing that her fingers actually started curling—that little voice in her head, the one that said *don't*, suddenly replaced by one that said *do*—before she thought *no, stop*, and came jarringly back to her senses.

It was like being thrown out of a pleasant dream and into a nightmare, the wonderful, certain calm replaced by a wave of sickness and a lancing pain behind her eyes.

What had she just done?

What had she *almost* done?

Kate forced herself backward—away from the counter, away from the stunned line and the man who'd now begun to shout—tore the apron over her head, and fled.

11

She dropped her bag beside the door.

Riley and Malcolm were no longer there—thank God for small mercies.

Her pulse was still a raging beat inside her skull, but whatever had come over her back in the coffee shop was gone, leaving only a headache and a pressure behind her eyes.

A migraine? But Kate had never gotten migraines, and she was pretty sure their side effects didn't include the sudden desire for violence.

Violence—her mind snagged on that word, and the night before came back again: the man and the shadow, both so steady, so calm. The emptiness in the man's face as the monster's own seemed to fill out. And then—the alley. Kate standing face-to-face with the monster, the *nothing* of it, all cold and hollow hunger and those silver discs, like mirrors—

Her vision doubled and she had to close her eyes for a second to keep from losing her balance. She went to the bathroom and ran the tap, splashing handful after handful of cool water on her face and neck. She dragged her gaze to the mirror, surveying her pallid complexion, the scar that traced her jaw, the flat blue of her—

Kate froze.

There was something in her left eye. When she raised her chin, it caught the light, shining like a lens flare, the kind of thing that belonged in a photograph, not a human face. It was a trick of the light, it had to be, but no matter how she turned her head, it stayed. She leaned in, close enough to fog the mirror with her breath, close enough to see the interruption in the dark blue circle of her iris.

It looked like a silver crack. A sliver of light.

A *mirror* shard.

It was so small and yet the longer she stared, the more it seemed to stretch across her vision, blotting out the room and swallowing her sight. Kate squeezed her eyes shut, trying to pull her mind free, to hold herself in the here and now, but she was already falling forward into—

A memory—
the window is open
the fields outside
waving in the breeze
she sits on the floor
with a pile of necklaces
trying to pick apart
the tangled chains
while her mother
hums by the window
her small fingers dance
over the metal links
but the harder
she tries
the more
    tangled
        everything gets
annoyance
rises like a tide
turning to anger
with
each
failed
attempt
every
worsening
knot
the anger spreads
from the tangled chains
to her mother

at the window—
her mother
who doesn't seem to care
what a mess she made
her mother
who isn't even there
to make it right
her mother
who *left* her alone
with monsters—

"Get out of my head," snarled Kate, slamming a soap dish into the mirror.

It struck the glass with a splintering crash as she lurched back to her senses, to herself.

She dropped the dish and retreated a few steps, sinking onto the edge of the tub. Her hands were shaking. A cobweb crack fractured the image in the glass. She'd broken the monster's hold.

But it was still there, inside her head.

And she remembered now, its face from the alley, seeing herself in its eyes and falling down into that dark, violent place, remembered Riley's voice calling her name, pulling her back. But she'd left something behind, or *it* had, this sliver of itself, this crack in her head.

How was she supposed to get it out?

How did you hunt something that had no shape, a shadow that made puppets out of people?

How could you destroy a void?

Kate's head spun, but as her pulse steadied and the panic and confusion cooled, her focus sharpened, the way it always did at the beginning of a hunt.

It was a monster. No matter what form it took. And monsters could always be hunted. Killed. You just had to find them first.

Kate's head came up. They were connected, somehow, she and this *thing*. And connections usually went two ways. She cut a look at the mirror. From this angle she couldn't see her reflection, couldn't see anything but the cracks running down the mirror's surface.

But if the monster could get into her head, could she do the same?

Kate rose to her feet and approached the mirror. She curled her fingers around the sink's edge, anchoring herself, and tried to steady her breathing. She'd never been one for meditation—she would rather hit something than try to find stillness—but she went looking for it now as her gaze drifted up.

The instant the shard caught her eye, she felt the pull, but Kate resisted, charting a course from her chin, along the line of her scar up her jaw, before shifting over lips, up nose—

Show me, she thought, as her gaze finally reached the shard.

The silver blossomed, and then she was falling forward, but not as fast as before—it was more like a slow and steady slide, the ground tipping away beneath her. She gripped the counter hard as the silver spread across her senses, tangled through her head, and something that wasn't a voice whispered a humming cloud of *want* and *hurt* and *change* and *fight* and *make* and *kill* and the ground began to fall away faster and faster until—

She is
trapped
in another memory
the night is black
and she is
in her mother's car
white noise
blaring
through her head
her mother's cheek
against the wheel
Where are you?
she wonders
as red eyes
multiply
beyond
the broken glass
and there
again
is the anger
the pain
the burning
need to—

Stop, she thought, dragging her mind, not back, not out, but through.

Pressure in her head, against her palms as—

—back in the car
her mother's eyes
open wide
marred
by a single
silver
crack
—*Where are you?*—
she asks
and the car
the night
the vision
shudder
and give way
    to cold
    to nothing
and—

It moves
in and out
of shape
of shadows
through a place
singing
with promise
a city
carved in two
so many
dark thoughts
so many
monstrous minds
so much
kindling
just waiting
to catch—

Kate lurched backward, out of the vision.

Her nose was bleeding, and her head pounded, and her hands ached from gripping the sink, but none of it mattered.

Because Kate knew where the monster was going.

Knew where, somehow, it already was.

Verity.

Six months, condensed into a single bag.

The same one she'd first brought with her to Prosperity, the same things inside: cash, clothes, fake ID, a pair of iron spikes, a silver lighter with a hidden switchblade, a handgun.

It should have made leaving easy, but it didn't. She told herself it was just a mission, told herself she was coming back, even as the echoes of a city she had once called home burned against her retinas, and the cold shadow twisted through her head. Kate didn't know how to fight this thing, didn't know how to kill it, but she knew she had to try.

She scooped up her tablet from the coffee table and sank onto the couch. The device booted to reveal the carnage from the restaurant, still on display where Riley had left it.

Twelve dead. A violent thought turned into a violent deed.

And now the monster was in Verity, a place that *thrived* on violence, that fed and nurtured it, and Kate couldn't shake the idea that she had led the shadow there. That she had let it see into her mind, had shown it a place rife with potential.

Moth, meet flame.

But where had it come from? There had been no massive attacks, nothing on the scale she imagined necessary to create something like *this*. Was it the product instead of Prosperity's slow poison? A city's decay?

And what would a thing like this do in a city like *hers*? She'd already seen what it could do—hell, she'd *felt* the effects herself. The darkness stirred in her even now, a *want* whispering through her pulse, telling her to reach for the gun in her bag.

Instead she took a deep breath and opened a new message window. She addressed it to the Wardens and dropped every photo she had of the Heart Eaters into the file, along with a message:

Pure metal only. Aim for heart.

Her finger hovered over the SEND.

It wasn't enough, she knew that. The Wardens weren't hunters—but they would find one. Someone stupid enough to do what she'd been doing. Maybe even someone better.

She told herself she had to go.

Had to warn the FTF. Warn August.

She hit SEND, and rose to her feet, shoving the tablet into her bag. By the time she reached the door, her
phone was ringing.

Riley.

She didn't answer, didn't let herself stray from the
task at hand. It was just like any other hunt, she told
herself, letting her limbs take over, moving with a purpose she wasn't sure she felt. She didn't know *what* she
felt, but she knew how to move. She paused at the door,
scribbled out a note on a pad of paper.

She locked the door behind her, and slid the key
beneath, listening to it skid away across the wooden
floor, out of sight, out of reach.

After that, she didn't let herself look back.

Running was just like every other habit.

It got easier with practice.

Riley's building had a parking garage in the back, and
as Kate scanned the rows of cars, she regretted ditching
her father's sedan when she got to the city.

She could have kept it, but everything about the car
said Verity, said money, said *Callum*, down to the gar-
goyle on the hood, so she'd left it on the side of the road
twenty-five miles from Prosperity's capital in case anyone came looking for her.

In the end, no one did.

And now she was stuck searching for a ride out of town. Thank God the weather was nice, she thought, stumbling across a coupe with the windows halfway down. She didn't even have to break the glass.

She tossed her bag into the passenger seat and climbed in, overwhelmed by sudden déjà vu. Another life, another world, August breathless and Kate wounded, her fingers shaking from the fight with the Malchai as she threw the car into gear.

Her cell buzzed in her pocket.

Kate didn't answer, kept her hands busy prying off the ignition's cover and splicing the wires. The engine sparked, sputtered, sparked, started.

She hit the gas.

III

"Please, please . . ."

　"Our father who art in . . ."

　"What do you want . . ."

　"Get off me . . ."

　"Burn in Hell . . ."

　"I haven't done anything wrong . . ."

　"Let me go . . ."

　"Please . . ."

Humans, thought Sloan. Always *talking*.

There were eight of them, kneeling on the warehouse floor, men and women with bruised faces and hands bound behind their backs. They were filthy, half-starved, dressed in an assortment of suits and dresses and casual attire, as though they'd been snatched right off the street or out of their homes, which, of course, they had.

Late afternoon light streamed through cracks in the

windows and doors, but there was work to be done. Besides, thought Sloan, letting a hand pass into a beam of light, it was important to remind the humans that while the sun may weaken him, a weak Malchai was still more dangerous than a strong human.

The sun turned his skin translucent and his bones dark, and for an instant, the prisoners stilled and stared, as if hoping he might burst into flame. They were quickly disappointed.

When he did not burn, did not so much as wince, the whining started up again.

"Please . . ."

"Don't hurt me . . ."

"We haven't done—"

Sloan let his hand slip back into shadow. "Be quiet."

Behind the kneeling forms stood four more humans, unbound save for the metal collars circling their throats. The Fangs met Sloan's gaze, hungry for approval, while those on their knees shivered in fear.

He rapped a nail thoughtfully against his teeth. "This is all of them?"

"Yes, sir," said one of the Fangs, quick as a dog. "Engineers from the fridges, just like you asked."

Sloan nodded, turning his attention to the quivering shapes on the concrete floor.

"The brightest minds . . . ," he mused. A man began

to sob. Sloan brought the tip of his boot to the man's knee. "You. What did you do before?"

When the man didn't answer, a Fang kicked him in the side. One of the other prisoners let out a short, terrified sound that only made Sloan hungry.

"S-software," stammered the man. "Opendrive, internal access . . ."

Sloan clicked his tongue and moved on. "What about you? Come now, don't be shy."

"E-electrical," answered the second.

"Plumbing," said the third.

One by one they shared their expertise. Technical. Biological. Mechanics. Computers.

Sloan paced, his agitation growing.

And then the final captive answered, "Civil."

Sloan slowed, coming to a stop before her. "What does that mean?"

She hesitated. "I . . . worked on buildings, construction, demolition . . ." Sloan's mouth drew into a smile. He brought a sharpened nail to her chin.

"You," he said. "And you," he added to the one who knew mechanics. "And you," he said, to the electrician. "Congratulations. You've all found new employment."

The Fangs hauled the three engineers to their feet, and Sloan turned his attention to the rest of the captives, who clearly didn't know whether to be distraught or relieved.

"The rest of you," he said with a sweep of his hand, "are free to go."

They looked at him, wide-eyed. He pointed at the warehouse door, fifty feet away. "Go on. Before I change my mind."

That was enough to jog them loose. All five scrambled to their feet, hands still bound before them. Sloan rolled his head on his shoulders and watched them rise, stumble, run, racing for the door.

Three of them made it.

But then Sloan was moving, letting that simple, animal self take over as he slipped between shadows. He caught the fourth by her throat and snapped it cleanly before spinning to grab the fifth, catching the man just as his fingers skimmed the warehouse door.

So close, thought Sloan, sinking his fangs deep into the man's throat. Somewhere, someone screamed, but for a beautiful moment, Sloan's world was nothing but a dying heartbeat and a wave of red.

He let the body fall with a thud to the concrete.

"Changed my mind," he said, drawing a square from his pocket and wiping his mouth.

The surviving engineers were sobbing into their hands or holding their heads. Even the Fangs had the good sense to go pale.

"Clean this place up," he ordered the Fangs, turning

away, "and bring my new pets to the tower. And if anything happens to them in your care, I will pull the teeth from your skulls and make you swallow them."

He threw open the doors and stepped outside.

IIII

The Crossroads was a massive center, part shopping mall, part truck stop, part cafeteria, a palace of polished white linoleum. It was the first place you hit on your way into Prosperity, and the last place on your way out, and Kate hadn't been there since the day she left Verity.

She found a pair of sunglasses in the car's center console and put them on, hiding the silver crack as she went inside. She bypassed the food halls for a line of vending machines, and caught her reflection in a dispenser's steel surface, her face distorted by the warp of the metal. She looked away and punched in the code for a cup of coffee.

When the machine jammed, Kate took a few slow breaths.

She hadn't lost her temper at any of the drivers, hadn't so much as sworn when someone cut her off, despite the whisper in her head, the longing—stealing over her like a blanket—to speed up and up and up until someone crashed.

She punched in her order again, and when the coffee finally came out, she downed the drink in a single long gulp, ignoring the way it burned her throat. Two hallways down she found the vast wall of rentable square lockers. The hall was empty, and she knelt in front of a cubby on the bottom row and reached into the narrow gap between the bottom of the locker and the linoleum floor.

Six months earlier Kate had stopped at the Crossroads, not knowing when or if she'd ever come back. But her father had been a strategist as well as a dictator, and one of his few bloodless sayings was this: *only fools get cornered.*

In Callum Harker's decade-long rise to the top, he *always* had a way out. Cars across the city, safe houses and stashed weapons, the home beyond the Waste and the box under the floor filled with fake papers.

The only kind of trail you were supposed to leave was one you yourself could follow home. After several maddening seconds, Kate's fingers snagged the corner of the packet, and she drew out a single padded envelope.

Inside were the last remnants of another life. A few folded bills and a bundle of IDs—school card, driver's license, two credit cards—all under the name *Katherine*

Olivia Harker. A whole life reduced to the contents of an envelope.

Kate emptied it into her bag, then began shedding the last six months of her identity, shoving papers and ID into the envelope, until all that was left of her time in Prosperity was her cell phone. Kate weighed it in her palm. It was still off, and she knew she should leave it that way, put it in the envelope with the rest, and walk away, but some traitorous thing inside her—not the monster, but something all too human—held down the power button.

A few seconds later, the screen filled with missed calls and messages. She should never have hesitated, should never have turned the phone on, but she had, and she couldn't unsee the latest text.

Riley: Not like this.

Kate swore softly to herself, and called him.

Riley picked up on the second ring.

"Where are you?" He sounded breathless. She'd spent half the drive planning what she'd say, but now nothing came out. "I mean what the hell, Kate? First Bea hears you lost your shit at work and then you just up and leave? No word?"

Kate ran a hand through her hair, swallowed. "I left a note."

"Oh, you mean, *sorry, duty calls*? That's your definition

of a note? What the *fuck* is going on?" Kate winced. Riley never swore. "Is this about what you saw? At the restaurant? What are we dealing with here?"

"*We* aren't dealing with anything," she said. "I'm working this one myself."

"Why?" He cracked his shin audibly against something and swore again under his breath. "What's going on?"

Kate leaned back against the cold metal of the lockers, and tried to keep her voice light. "It's complicated. I've got a lead, but it's not in Prosperity, and I don't know how long it will take; that's why I sent the files, just in case . . ." She couldn't finish that sentence, so she changed course. "I'll be back. As soon as it's done. Tell the Wardens."

"Will I be lying?"

"I hope not."

"Where are you going?"

"Home." The word scraped her throat. And then, because Riley had given her so much, and she had given him so little, she added, "To Verity."

Riley let out a long, shaky breath, but there was no surprise in his silence, as if he'd known all along. When he spoke, his voice was urgent.

"Listen to me, whatever's going on, whatever you're running away from, or toward, I just want you to know—"

Kate swiped a tear from her cheek and killed the call.

Before he could call back, she switched the phone off and dropped it in the envelope, sliding the contents beneath the lockers for safekeeping.

The bathrooms were as clean as the rest of the Crossroads, pristine in an industrial sort of way. A mirror ran the length of one wall above a bank of sinks, and Kate set her sunglasses on the counter and washed her face, wishing she could scrub away the call with Riley, the doubt he'd kicked up like dust inside her head.

She was doing the right thing—wasn't she?

She knew the city in the vision, knew she was headed in the right direction.

Unless she was wrong. The shadow was in her head, weaving through her memories, her darkest thoughts and fears. What if she was only seeing what it wanted? What if she'd left Prosperity for nothing? What if what if what if—

Enough.

She knew the difference between truth and lie, between vision and dream, between her mind and the monster's. Didn't she?

She looked up and found her gaze in the mirror.

Her stomach turned. The crack in her left eye was larger, stealing across the blue. Was it spreading on its own, or was she worrying it like a wound? She hesitated, weighing the potential damage against the need for certainty, all the while losing ground against the shard's strange pull.

The need won out—Kate held her gaze.

"Where are you?" she whispered. It was the same question she'd asked herself a thousand times over the years, whenever she wanted to imagine herself somewhere else, some*one* else, but the darkness answered by pulling her forward, down into—

The hallway
of the house
beyond the Waste
dead flowers
on the sill
a broken picture
on the floor
a coat of dust
as thick as paint
on everything
and she has
    never felt
so alone
it buries her
that sadness
swallows her
    whole
the only sound
    a voice
        her voice
echoing
through
an empty house
—*Where are you?*—
she goes looking
for a pair
of silver eyes
but the rooms
are all empty
and then

she sees it
the body in the hall
the bullet hole
a singed circle
in its throat
she crouches
as his eyes
drift open
wide as moons
holds
its gaze
as the house
shudders
shatters
into—

—blood
everywhere
splashed like paint
over the ground
up the walls
the bodies
strewn
like shadows
their fire
all burned out
nothing now
but shells
    in gray and green
and letters stamped
on bloody sleeves
F
T
F.

Kate pulled free.

She was back at the counter, gasping for air. The harsh white light blurred her vision, and blood dripped from her nose, and she could almost *hear* the shard throwing out fresh cracks, like the sound of splitting ice inside her skull.

It took her an instant to realize she wasn't alone.

An older woman was at her side, one hand tight on her sleeve and a wet wad of paper towels in the other. Her lips were moving, but Kate's good ear was ringing and the words came through broken and studded with static.

"I'm fine," she said, painfully aware of the sunglasses sitting on the sink and the splinter of silver in her eye.

The white noise died just as the woman put a hand on Kate's cheek. "Let me see, darling. I used to be a nurse—"

"No," she gasped, jerking her head away.

Contagious. That was the word Malcolm had used. Kate was already sick—the last thing she needed was to infect anyone else, but when she tried to pull free, the woman caught her face in both hands and angled her chin up, tutting as if Kate were some disobedient child.

And then the woman stilled, her eyes going wide, and Kate's chest lurched, because she'd obviously seen the silver.

But all she said was, "You've got a pair of eyes on you," and pressed the damp towels to Kate's nose, as if that was all there was to it.

"Thank you," murmured Kate, trying to hide the tremor in her voice, the surprise, the relief. But the moment the woman was gone, she slumped against the counter, hands shaking.

Well, thought Kate grimly.

At least she wasn't contagious.

NOW LEAVING PROSPERITY, announced the sign.

There was no guard tower, no armed checkpoint—no penalty for trying to get out—just an open gate. And then she was in the buffer zone, the mile-long stretch of neutral land between territories.

She came to the four-way stop, the same one she'd passed through before, and was hit by another moment of déjà vu. The base of her skull prickled as she pulled forward, taking the road toward Verity.

The signal on the radio failed.

The road ahead was empty.

Turn around, said a voice in her head. *Turn around while you still can.* But it was already being drowned out by the thought of her iron spikes, of her gun, of her bare hands sinking into—

Dammit, she thought, gripping the wheel. Keeping

that voice out, it was like trying to keep your eyes open on the road at night, fatigue wearing you down a little more with every yawn, the slippery slope between a blink and something deadly.

She slowed as the Verity border came into sight.

The barricade was down and a soldier emerged from the patrol building as Kate adjusted her sunglasses and slowed to a stop. She shifted the car into neutral but didn't turn the engine off, letting her fingers rest on the gearshift.

The guard wasn't that old, maybe in his early twenties, a little on the squat side. A patch on his uniform marked him as a Prosperity citizen—the surrounding territories of Temperance, Fortune, and Prosperity took turns manning the Verity border. He had an assault rifle slung on a strap, but at the sight of Kate, he swung the weapon back over his shoulder. Oh, the perks of being perpetually underestimated.

Kate rolled the window down. "Hi there."

"I'm sorry, miss. You've got to turn around."

She opted for naive innocence, raising her eyebrows behind her glasses. "Why?"

The guard looked at her like she was missing a vital piece. "The Verity border's been closed for months."

"I thought it was open again."

He shook his head apologetically.

"Huh," she said, pretending to squint into the sun as she scanned the crossing for other signs of life. "Well, that's a drag. How long have you been at this post"—she scanned his gear for a name tag—"Benson?"

"Two years."

"And who did you piss off to get landed here?"

He chuckled, leaning his elbow on the hood. "Every now and then, someone tries to cross. I don't know what makes them do it, if they've got friends egging them on or a death wish or they think the stories are just stories— I don't know, and I don't care. Protocol is protocol. It's for your own good, miss—"

"Harker," cut in Kate.

He twitched.

"Does that name mean anything to you?" she pressed, the cheerfulness bleeding from her voice as her left hand closed around the gun tucked into the driver's side door. The darkness in her rushed forward at the touch, a current washing over her, trying to sweep her away.

"It should. My father was Callum Harker. You know, the man who kept monsters like pets inside that hellhole. Look around, Benson. All your cameras, all your weapons, all your *everything* is facing the other way. Do you know why that is? Because your job is to keep anyone and anything from getting *out*. It doesn't matter who goes *in*. Don't believe me? Just look."

He actually took his eyes off her, just for a second, and in that second, she raised her gun. Benson looked back and actually jumped, lifting his hands in an automatic plea.

Do it, whispered the thing in her head, in her hand, in her blood. *It will be so easy. It will feel so good.*

Her finger drifted toward the trigger. "I am crossing that border today."

Doubt swept across the soldier's face. "Like you'd actually—"

She fired.

The desire had closed around her hand like a second grip, squeezed the trigger for her, but she'd felt it coming, just in time, and shifted the barrel several inches wide.

Benson stared in horror. "You crazy bitch."

"Open the gate," she said through clenched teeth. "I honestly don't think I'll miss a second time."

The soldier backed away and punched a code into the box by the patrol door. The barricade began to lift. "We're just trying to keep you safe!"

Kate cocked her head. "Haven't you heard?" she said, shifting the car into gear. "There's no such thing." She gunned the engine and the car shot forward into the Waste. "Not anymore."

‖‖‖

The face in the mirror was covered in blood.

It dotted August's cheek, splashed across the front of his fatigues. Red and black, black and red.

He turned the shower on, spun the tap until the hot water was all the way up, and stripped off his clothes, shivering as the air met the tallies on his skin.

He hadn't slept, hadn't been able to settle down long enough, so he'd gone back out again and again, trying to scrub Rez and Alice from his mind, taking on any and every mission. When his own team retired, he joined another, and another, made himself a shield and a weapon, let the trouble come to him. The night was a blur of violence behind his eyes, but the restlessness was gone, excised by action, leaving only an absence in its place.

He stepped into the scalding stream and bit back a gasp. The water burned, each drop a prick of fire on his

skin. The pain was shallow, but he found himself clinging to it the way he'd once clung to hunger.

A way of taking control, of reminding himself that he
could feel, that he wasn't—

A monster? taunted Leo in his patronizing way.

At his feet, blood and grime swirled down the drain,
and August leaned his head against the tile wall, his
vision blurring as fatigue washed up against him. He
wasn't *sore*—that was the wrong word—soreness was
a physical thing, the product of tired muscles, strained
bodies. But there was an ache all the way down to his
core. He was *empty*, like the bodies he'd left behind,
hollow without that spark of life, humans and monsters
both reduced to empty shells, stardust to stardust, and—

He turned the shower off and stepped out, slicking his
wet hair back off his face. The room was full of steam—
when he wiped the fog from the mirror and saw his gray
eyes reflected in the glass, he couldn't shake the feeling
they had gotten darker. Leo's eyes had been black—the
black of piano keys and starless skies—darkened by all
the times he'd shed his human form for the one that
waited beneath the surface.

August turned away from the mirror.

He pulled on fresh fatigues and stepped into the hall.
Allegro was there, chasing a piece of lint, but when the
cat saw him, he shied back, and when August reached

to pet him, the cat recoiled from his touch, black ears going flat against his head. He let out a small hiss and scurried away.

August frowned, following Allegro into the kitchen where the cat darted between Ilsa's legs. She crouched, hauling the creature up into her arms and planting a kiss on his nose before lobbing a questioning look at August.

He took another step toward her, toward the cat, but Allegro hissed in warning.

What was it Ilsa said about animals?

They could sense the difference between good and bad, human and monster.

For a second, only a second, that other piece of himself—the piece he'd put away—tried to surface, stunned and hurt by the cat's rebuff, by what it meant. But August forced it under.

It will weaken, promised Leo. *It will fade.*

Ilsa's eyes narrowed. *What have you done?*

August stiffened. "What I had to."

Her mouth turned down as she folded her arms protectively around the cat and shook her head. There were no words to that, none that August could read.

"What is it?" he demanded.

But she just kept shaking her head, as if unable to stop, and August prickled. He didn't understand what she was trying to say, what she *wanted* from him.

He pushed a pad of paper across the counter. "Dammit, Ilsa, just *write it down*."

His sister pulled back from the paper, from him, as if struck. And then she turned on her heel and swept out.

Soro walked in just as Ilsa rushed past. The two nearly collided, but Ilsa had a way of parting the world around her, and the other Sunai leaped gracefully out of her path. A second later, Ilsa's door closed, a single punctuating note—the loudest sound she'd made in months—and August let out a low, hard breath.

Soro considered him. Their silver hair was swept forward, falling into gray eyes, but August could still tell they were raising an eyebrow.

"Don't ask," he said.

Soro shrugged. "I wasn't planning on it."

August leaned back, shoulders resting against the shelves.

"You are tense," they said.

He closed his eyes and muttered, "I'm tired."

Another beat of silence. "I heard . . . about the ambush."

But Soro had never been one to stand around, had certainly never gone searching for small talk. He dragged his eyes open. "What do you want?"

Soro straightened, visibly relieved by the end of such an unpleasant task. "Want has nothing to do with it," they said, already turning toward the door. "There's something you need to see."

August circled the bodies, trying to understand what he was looking at. It was like a riddle, a puzzle, a what's-wrong-in-this-picture, only *everything* was wrong. In five years, he'd seen a lot of death, but he'd never seen anything like this.

It wasn't the *what* that bothered him.

It wasn't even the *how*.

It was the *why*.

A full FTF squad was made up of eight soldiers. A leader. A medic. A tech. A sniper. And crew. It was a rare thing these days to have a full squad. Too often soldiers were picked off, and casualties usually weren't replaced until a group numbered less than four, and then they were folded into another unit.

That morning, Squad Nine had been made up of seven soldiers.

By midday, all of them were dead.

"What happened here?" asked August, half to himself and half to Soro.

"According to Control," said the other Sunai, "they were on their way back from a recon mission. Their comms were off, and there's no surveillance on this block."

The bodies lay scattered in the street, a grisly tableau.

They hadn't died at night, hadn't been fed on by Corsai. August looked around, then squinted up at the sun.

Judging by the angle of the light, this part of the street would have been in shadow all morning.

But that didn't explain the seven corpses.

The sudden and simultaneous turn of violence.

Bullet casings littered the ground, and a knife lay several feet away, stained to the hilt, but as far as August could tell, Squad Nine hadn't been ambushed, hadn't been attacked by any outside force, human or monstrous.

They'd attacked *their own team*.

Not one on six—this wasn't a matter of one soldier going mad—every one of them had a weapon in hand and a fatal wound. It made no sense.

His gaze trailed across their faces, faces he knew and didn't know, faces that had once been people and were now just husks. Like Rez, he thought, fighting down the sense of loss before it could surface.

"What a waste." Soro stood to the side, absently twirling their flute, as if they were standing in a garden instead of a crime scene. The bodies on the ground wore FTF badges, but in Soro's eyes, he knew, they were no longer soldiers.

They were *sinners*.

And sinners deserved whatever gruesome ends they met.

But still—what could possibly drive an entire squad to do this?

Was it a symptom of the rift within the Compound?

No, there was tension, but verbal sparring was one thing, and this—this was something else entirely. It was too broad a leap between annoyance and this level of aggression.

Some kind of foul play, then?

A Malchai?

He wondered, for a moment, if the dead soldiers were a message from Alice, some kind of morbid gift laid out like a feast. But the patches weren't missing, and none of the wounds had been made by teeth.

No, as gruesome as the deaths were, they were done by men, not monsters.

"Does Henry know?" he asked.

"Of course." Soro paired the words with a flat look, as if the thought of *not* reporting this had never occurred to them. August imagined it hadn't—Henry was human, but he was also the head of the FTF, the general in their makeshift army.

"And the Council?" he asked.

At that, Soro shook their head. "Henry wanted *you* to see it first."

August frowned. "Why?"

The Sunai shifted their weight. "He said you've always had a . . . sensitivity. A way of thinking like a human. He said you study them." The words seemed to make Soro uncomfortable. "That you've always wanted to be one of—"

"I'm a Sunai," said August, bristling. "And I don't have a clue what happened here. If Henry wants a human's take, he should send someone else."

Soro looked relieved.

August turned away from the corpses and started back toward the Compound.

卌 I

Sloan wiped the blood from his hands as he climbed the tower steps.

There was something foul about it—in a human's veins, it was warm, vital. Outside, it was nothing but a *mess*.

In the darkened lobby, Malchai lounged on every surface, leaning on stairs and draping themselves over railings. A dozen Fangs dotted the dark stone floor, steel collars glinting as they knelt beside their masters.

Blood leaked from bite marks on their skin, but Sloan's hunger barely rose at the sight of it, of them. He'd never had a taste for willing prey.

At the sound of his steps, the Malchai stirred, red eyes going to the floor as he passed.

Inside the elevator, Sloan let his eyes slide closed. He dreamed of many things, of blood and power and a broken city, of Henry Flynn brought low and the task force on its knees, of August's burning heart in his hand and Katherine's neck beneath his teeth.

But as the elevator rose, Sloan longed only for sleep. A few quiet hours before the frenzy of the night.

He stepped out of the elevator and into the penthouse, and stopped.

Alice had set the place on fire.

That was his first thought. Heat radiated off the steel coffee table where she had dumped what looked like a bucket of hot coals. A variety of tools and kitchen utensils protruded from the burning mess, and four Malchai crouched on the floor in front of her, feasting on a young man.

"Before you ask," said Alice, "It wasn't like the Falstead. I didn't have anything to do with it this time. I've moved on."

"What are you talking about?" asked Sloan.

Alice gave an impatient flick of her fingers. "Oh, a handful of Fangs—they must have snapped—who knows why. Went and killed each other—so it seems. The Corsai didn't leave much behind. A petty squabble, if I had to guess. Humans are so"—she blew on the coals—"*temperamental.*"

"And what about *them?*" asked Sloan, nodding toward the Malchai.

"Oh, they volunteered."

"For *what*?"

Alice didn't answer. Instead she took one of the Malchai by the chin, raising his red eyes to hers. Her voice, when she spoke, was different, lower, smoother, almost hypnotic.

"Do you want to make me proud?"

"Yes," whispered the Malchai.

She drew a thin metal bar from the fire, its end a burning red tip.

"Alice," pressed Sloan.

"Here's a riddle," she said, her voice threading with manic cheer. "You can banish a Corsai with light, defang a Malchai's bite, but how do you do stop a Sunai's song?"

Sloan thought of Ilsa, the last sound she made before he tore out her throat.

"You don't have to," said Alice with a smile. "You just stop listening."

With that she drove the burning spike into the Malchai's ear.

||||| ||

It didn't feel real until Kate hit the Waste.

Until she saw the open land, the sprawling noth-ing, and remembered dragging August's fevered body through the fields to the house, remembered her mother's room, the man at the door, and the gun in her hand. A single bang, the division between before and after. Innocence and guilt. Human and monster.

She didn't like to think about that.

Didn't like to remember that somewhere, out there, was the monster *she'd* made.

With any luck it had starved to death in the Waste.

With any luck—

The car shuddered, spluttered, and began to smoke. She swore and guided the dying vehicle onto the empty shoulder.

She was eight miles from the outskirts of V-City.

Eight miles, and less than two hours until dark.

Kate got out, and rounded the car. The gun sat on the passenger-side floor where she'd dropped it as soon as the barricade was out of sight. She took it up, savoring the weight in her hand, remembering the sweet recoil and—

She ejected the clip from the gun and put both pieces in her bag, hitched it up on her shoulder, and began to run. Her own shadow stretched out in front of her, cast by the sinking sun at her back, and her shoes beat out a steady rhythm on the asphalt.

Track had been a mandatory activity back at Leighton, and Kate had quickly discovered two things:

She loved running.

And she hated running in circles.

She tried to remember that love now, with nothing but an open road, a straight line ahead, but two miles in, she was pretty sure she'd made it all up.

Four miles in, she wished she had a cigarette.

Five miles in, she regretted ever smoking.

Seven miles in, she staggered to a jog and then a walk, a limp and then a stop, retching on the side of the road. Her head had started aching again, and she wanted to lie down, to close her eyes, but the sun was hovering over the horizon, and the last thing she needed was to be caught out in the Waste after dark.

She had to keep moving, so she did.

Funny, how simple things became when you didn't have a choice.

Her legs and lungs were on fire by the time she finally reached the green zone.

Once upon a time it had been the richest section of the capital, a place reserved for those who could afford not only to purchase Harker's protection but to carry on with their lives as if nothing was wrong. Once upon a time—but now it was *empty*.

It would have been easy to assume that everyone in the green had up and left, some kind of mass exodus.

It would have been . . . except for the number of cars in the driveways. And the blood.

Long-dry brown stains worn thin by weather and sun. But it was everywhere. Splashed like rust against car doors and curbs, garages and steps. An echo of violence.

"What happened here?" she murmured to the empty streets, even though she knew the answer.

Corsai, Corsai, tooth and claw,

Shadow and bone will eat you raw.

The sun dipped below the horizon and Kate perched her sunglasses on her head. The light was quickly thinning—soon it would be gone. She had to get inside.

She unzipped her bag and forced her fingers to gloss over the gun and take up the switchblade and an iron spike instead before starting down the street. She made her way to house after house, but the doors were all bolted. At the third one, she stood on her toes, peered into a window, and stilled.

It looked like a crime-scene photo, minus the bodies, dark stains streaking the walls and floor and toppled furniture. She imagined the people in the green locking themselves inside, waiting, until the power went out and the shadows slipped under their doors.

A low hiss sounded on the air, and Kate tensed, fingers tightening on her weapons before she realized the sound was *human*.

"*Psst*," came the voice. "Over here."

Kate turned and caught a flash of light on metal. No, not metal. A *mirror*. One of the front doors across the street was cracked open and a man was twisting a compact back and forth to signal her.

"Hello?" she called out, moving toward him.

"*Shh*," he hissed, eyes darting nervously around the street. He had a flashlight in one hand, even though it wasn't yet dark, and over his shoulder she could see the glow of more lights inside the hall.

"Get in, get in," he said, opening the door just enough to let her through.

She crossed the yard, but hesitated at the base of the stairs. Her shadow had vanished, swallowed up by the dusk, and she could feel something twitch behind her, but every other house was quiet, empty, except for his. It set her nerves on edge.

"Well?" pressed the man. He didn't *look* very dangerous—beanpole thin, with a receding hairline and the constant twitch of frayed nerves—but Kate knew from experience that men could be monsters, too, especially in Verity. "Those other houses, they got nothing, and we got maybe ten minutes until the light's all gone," he huffed, "so get in or get left out."

"I'm armed," she said. "And I intend to stay that way."

His head bobbed, as if he understood, or didn't care, and Kate blew out a breath and ducked inside. The moment she was through, he shut the door and threw the deadbolt into place. Her stomach clenched at the sound of it, sharp and final as a gunshot.

He brushed past her, turning on more lights and angling them toward the door. As her eyes adjusted, she realized that underneath his coat, the man was draped in metal, had fashioned a kind of chain mail from discs of patterned iron. *Medallions.* The same ones Callum Harker used to sell his citizens as protection from the monsters who hunted at his whim.

But Kate's father had never given anyone more than a single disk. She thought of the blood in the street, the missing bodies. She didn't have to ask where the rest of the medals had come from.

"What were you doing out there?"

"Just passing through," she said. "Seemed like a nice day for a stroll." He stared at her blankly. No ear for sarcasm, then. Up close, his eyes were bloodshot, as if he hadn't slept in days. "Is this your house?"

He looked around nervously. "Is now," he said, still bustling, as if unable to stop. "Living room's through there." He nodded across the hall, then ducked into a kitchen. Kate heard the clank of a pot, the crack of a match as she made her way through a pair of open doors into a sitting room.

A narrow sliver between the curtains showed the dusk quickly giving way to dark. The curtains themselves were made of copper wire threaded together into a delicate version of the same chain mail the man was wearing. In the center of a coffee table was a display of batteries, flashlights, and light bulbs.

An altarpiece to artificial light.

"You got a name?"

Kate jumped. He'd come up on her bad side, and she hadn't heard him, not until he was too close. He was holding two cups.

"Jenny," she lied. "You?"

"Rick. Well, Richard. But I always liked Rick." He offered her one of the cups. She still had the iron spike in one hand, the silver lighter with its hidden switchblade in the other. She set the spike aside to take the cup and lift it to her mouth. It smelled vaguely like coffee and her body cramped with hunger and thirst, but she knew better than to drink it.

Rick shuffled around, adjusting more lights, and Kate lowered herself into a chair, her limbs stiff and her body clumsy with fatigue. She nodded at the curtain, the world beyond the house. "What happened out there?"

"What *happened*?" His voice tightened. "They came. Corsai, Malchai, everything with teeth."

She could see it. First the Malchai had come through, tearing out throats, and then the Corsai, feeding in their wake. No wonder there was nothing left.

"I wasn't even supposed to be here," murmured Rick. "I was on my way into the Waste, thought the green would be a safe place to camp out for the night." A nervous laugh.

"How did you survive?" asked Kate.

"At first I hid. And then I, uh, well, there were all these abandoned houses." The fidgeting grew worse. He moved like an addict, strung out on fear. "I did what I could. What I had to."

Kate turned the silver lighter between her fingers. "Why didn't you leave? Head for South City or go out into the Waste?"

"Thought about it a hundred times. I'd walk outside

in the light of day, try to get myself to go, but who knows what's going on out there? There's no cell signal, and hell, after what happened here, I wouldn't be surprised if the whole world's gone dark. Man came through, a few months back, running from North City, and he said the Malchai had rounded the humans up, keep 'em like meals in a fridge.

"No," Rick went on, "no, I've got everything I need here, and I'm gonna wait it out. Those bastards can't live forever."

Silence fell over the room, and then Kate's stomach growled audibly.

"Hold on," said Rick, getting to his feet. "I'll get you some food."

"What about South City?" she called after him.

"No idea," he called back.

She leaned forward, fingers drifting over the collection of batteries, just as something sounded in the hall. If Kate's head hadn't been turned the right way, she might not have heard it. If she hadn't been her father's daughter, she might not have known what it was: a shotgun shell being locked into the chamber of a gun.

And that, thought Kate, *is why I'm not an optimist.*

Her own gun sat unloaded in the bag at her feet, but the lighter was still in her hand, and with a small snick, the switchblade came free, the sudden shine of its edge stirring the darkness in her head as she rose to her feet.

Rick was in the doorway, shotgun raised. He flicked the barrel toward the blade. "Put it down."

Kate's grip tightened on the knife, and instead of her heart racing, she could feel it to start to slow, to steady. It would be so easy. She could already see the switchblade buried in his throat, could—

No.

That wasn't how it would happen. Rick had a shotgun, and even with addled nerves, it would be nearly impossible for him to miss from this close, not when there were more than a hundred pellets in a shell. He might die, but so would she, and even if the darkness in her head didn't seem to care about that, the rest of Kate sure did.

She set the blade carefully on the back of the couch. "What now, Rick?"

His nervousness hadn't stopped, but it had quieted, pressed down beneath a new resolve. "Hands on your head."

Kate's mind turned over and over—but between the eight-mile run from the Waste and the shotgun leveled at her head, she was coming up blank, every thought drifting back toward blind violence instead of logic, strategy, reason.

"Go on," he ordered, hoisting the shotgun for

emphasis. "Back toward the door." She did what she was told, slowly, trying to buy time. "It's nothing personal, Jenny," he muttered. "It's really not. I'm just so tired. They won't let me sleep."

"Who?"

They were at the front door.

"Slide the bolt."

She did.

"Open the door."

She did.

It was no longer dusk, but full night. The light from the doorway spilled out two or three feet, carving a narrow block of safety, but beyond that, the street was dark.

"I know you're out there!" Rick's voice echoed through the streets, ricocheting off empty houses and abandoned cars.

For a second, nothing happened.

Then the shadows began to stir. White eyes dotted the darkness, teeth gleaming like knives, and Kate's stomach turned with the memory of music and running, of empty subway cars and breaking strings and claws slashing flesh.

The Corsai whispered their awful chorus.

beatbreakruinfleshbonebeatbreak

And then the words began to shift . . .

beatbreakruinrendlittlelostharker

. . . spacing themselves into coherent order.

little lost harker

Fear rose in her, sudden and visceral, and she knew the monsters could smell it on her skin.

"Look here!" called Rick. "I brought you something to eat."

eat little harker little lost

"Just leave me alone for one night," he begged. "Just one night. Let me sleep."

give us the harker

Kate's head spun, an irrational desire brushing up against her fear, the urge to throw herself into the dark, to claw at the things with claws, to tear them apart as they tore into her.

The steel barrel of Rick's shotgun jabbed between her shoulders, and Kate took a halting step forward.

Do something, she thought.

Kill them all, whispered the thing in her skull.

Not that.

"Have you ever killed anyone?" she asked.

"I'm sorry," he said, and the miserable edge in his voice told her all she needed to know. He didn't want to shoot her. "I'm just so tired."

"It's all right, Rick. I'm going." Kate shuffled a half step forward, and felt him sag a little with relief, shifting the shotgun away from the center of her back and up, over her shoulder.

She rocked backward into Rick's chest, one elbow slamming into his face as she twisted around, taking the shotgun with her. Two breaths—that's all it had taken— but Rick was on one knee, clutching his bloody nose, and Kate was in the open doorway, holding the gun.

Shoot, said the voice in her head as he got to his feet, but his heel skimmed the first stair and he lost his balance, tripping down the three short steps and out of the safety of the light.

Shoot, said the monster, but she didn't know if it would be a mercy to Rick or a gift to the madness inside her, so she threw the weapon into the grass. Rick staggered toward it as Kate backed into the house, and the last thing she saw was the glint of the shotgun as he swung it clublike at the shadows before she slammed the door and drove the bolt home.

The house was empty.

Kate knew because she had checked the whole thing, top to bottom, back to front. Rick had done a solid job of securing the windows and doors, but if she listened she could hear the scrape of nails on wood, on brick, on glass, the trail of the Corsai's claws outside, scratching to get in. Reminding her that she was trapped.

"Where are you, Kate?" she wondered aloud, and when her first thought was of Riley and Prosperity and the coffee shop table with the Wardens, she decided she didn't want to play the stupid game anymore.

She had passed the mirror in the hall three times—now she stopped in front of it, a pair of scissors in her hand. Avoiding her own gaze—she didn't want to see the silver spreading, didn't need to be reminded, could feel the thing like a weight, leaning against her thoughts—she loosened her hair, combed it before her eyes, and began to trim.

Strips of blond fell to the floor, and Kate didn't stop until her hair carved a path across her face, sweeping over her left eye. Just another scar.

Torn between the desire to collapse and the fear of letting her guard down enough to sleep, she raided the kitchen cabinets (she ended up with powdered coffee, a liter of water, and a protein bar processed enough to last an apocalypse), switched on every flashlight she could find, and finally retreated to the living room.

Slumping down onto the couch, she dug the tablet out of her bag and booted a message window.

Riley, she started, then stopped when she remembered there was no connection, no signal to tap into.

Her fingers hovered over the blank screen. The cursor blinked, waiting, and she knew it was useless, but the house was too quiet and the monsters too loud, so she started typing anyway.

My real name is Katherine Olivia Harker.

Her fingers moved haltingly across the screen.

My mother's name was Alice. My father's was Callum. I didn't want to lie, but sometimes it's so much easier than the truth. Shorter. I just wanted to start over.

Have you ever done that?

It's freeing, at first, like shedding a heavy coat. And then you get cold, and you realize life's not a coat at all. It's skin. It's something you can't take off without losing yourself, too.

Kate stopped, pressing her palms against her eyes. Why was she writing about Verity as if she'd missed it, as if she'd been looking for an excuse to go home?

She set the tablet aside, the message unfinished, and stretched out, pulling a blanket around her shoulders. Outside the house, the Corsai grew restless, the grinding of their claws and teeth now paired with whispers that whistled through the cracks like wind.

come out little harker come out come outcomeoutcomeout

It sounded as if they were right beyond the windows.

Kate tensed as nails scraped over glass, her nerves tightening with every hiss and scratch and taunt. The iron spike sat on the table, and her fingers drifted toward it as Rick's tired eyes and desperate words came back to her.

Just one night. Let me sleep.

Kate dug through her bag and came up with the music player, skimming through the songs until she found something with a heavy beat. It filled her good ear, blocking out the Corsai's relentless calls, and she turned the volume up and up and up until it drowned out the monster in her head as well.

####### ‖‖‖ ‖‖

The Malchai fell to the ground at August's feet, a hole torn through its chest.

"That was close," said Harris, stepping over another body.

"Too close," said Ani, breathless, a shallow cut along her cheek.

It had been a careless attack: a pair of Malchai and a Fang had thought to catch them by surprise, as if two monsters and a human stood a chance against a squad of FTFs, especially one with a Sunai at the helm.

"What should we do with this one?" asked Jackson. The Fang was trussed up at his feet, one eye swelling shut and blood running into rotting teeth.

It would be easy enough to reap his soul, but August had already taken a half dozen lives, and the thought of taking on another made his bones ache.

"Call a jeep," he said. "We'll take him alive. See if Soro can get anything useful out of him."

They started back, covering the short distance to the Seam, but as the barricade drew nearer, August's steps slowed.

The thought of returning to the Compound, of standing still with all these souls inside him—no wonder Leo never stopped.

The night was full of monsters, and he needed to hunt.

So hunt, said his brother.

And why shouldn't he?

They reached the Seam's gate. Harris signaled on the comm and the doors ground open, the jeep waiting for them on the other side. The squad passed through, but August stopped.

Harris glanced back at him. "What's up?"

"I'll meet you back at the Compound."

"No way," said Ani.

"If you're going back out," added Jackson, "we'll go with you."

"That's not necessary," said August. He was already turning to go when Harris caught him by the arm.

"No solo missions, sir," said Harris. That was the Night Squad's first and most important rule. If you had to work the dark, you did it in teams.

That rule is for them.

Leo was right. August didn't need a team.

"Let go of me," he warned, and when Harris didn't, he shoved the soldier back into Ani, hard enough to send both of them stumbling. Something crossed their faces, but August turned away without trying to read it.

"Take the Fang to the cells," he said. "That's an order."

And this time, when he walked away, no one tried to stop him.

It was a strange thing, to walk alone.

He had grown so used to the echo of other footfalls, the need to think about other bodies, other lives. Without them, he was free.

The lights of South City faded with every step, and August kept his violin out and ready, the neck in one hand and the bow in the other, as he followed the whisper of shadows.

But something was off. The night was too still, the streets too empty, and he could feel the monsters drawing back into the dark.

His comm crackled. *"August,"* said Henry sternly. *"What are you doing?"*

"My job," he said simply, switching off the device just before the streetlights to every side flickered and went out, plunging him into darkness.

A moment later, a sound cut the night—not a scream, but a laugh, high and gritty and full of venom.

"Sunai, Sunai, eyes like coal, play me a song and steal my soul."

Alice. He turned in a slow circle, trying to find her, but the voice echoed off buildings, and eyes began to dot the dark, red and white against the curtain of black.

He lifted the violin, bow resting on the strings as her voice drifted forward.

"What are you waiting for?" she taunted.

The darkness stirred, and four Malchai stepped out of shadow.

"Won't you play us a song?"

As if on cue, they attacked.

The Malchai were fast, but for once, August was faster.

He drew the first note, the sound crisp and clear enough to cut the night. It should have cut the monsters, too, stopped them in their tracks.

But it didn't.

They kept coming, and August retreated one step, two, his bow slicing over the strings, song pouring into the space between them, taking shape, drawing ribbons of light, but the monsters didn't slow, didn't stop, didn't even seem to *hear*—

Too late, he saw their mutilated ears, and realized they *couldn't* hear him.

August swore, dropping the violin and twisting the bow in his hand to reveal the razored edge of its spine as the Malchai fell on him. He slashed a throat, black blood misting the air, noxious as death, as nails dug into his arms, and a hand snarled in his hair.

But they were no match for him, no match at all. For once, August didn't have to worry about humans, didn't have to hold any lives but his own. The freedom was so shocking that he lost himself in the violence.

He became an instrument of *ending*, a piece of music, the notes drawing out as darkness wrapped up around his hands, and smoke swallowed his fingers and climbed his wrists, that other self peeling him away, shedding him inch by inch. The Malchai screamed and thrashed, and heat flared in his chest, his pulse rising, urging him to *let go, let go, let go.*

But it was already over. His violin lay several feet away, the bow in his hand slick with gore, and August stood, panting from the fight, the broken bodies of the monsters strewn at his feet.

Well done, little brother.

He looked down at his hands, the skin still engulfed in shadow and smoke. The darkness lapped at the tallies on his forearms, threatening to erase the writing on his skin, to erase *him*, but there was no need, the fight was done, and as he watched, the shadows receded.

August flexed his hands and tipped his head back to the night.

"You'll have to try harder than that," he called to Alice, his voice echoing through the dark.

Henry was waiting at the Compound doors. At the sight of August, he marched forward onto the light strip. "What were you thinking?"

He doesn't understand.

"How could you be so reckless?"

He can't.

"You could have been taken."

He's only human.

But August had never seen Henry so visibly distraught. The light made him pale and gaunt, and he was breathing hard enough for August to hear the hitch in the man's chest. Concern rose up, but he forced it down.

"What's gotten into you?" demanded Henry.

"Nothing," said August. "I'm fulfilling my purpose. And it feels right," he added, even though the high had already faded, and the blood had gone tacky on his skin, the sick scent of it hitting the back of his throat.

Henry's face filled with dismay, and August was left clawing for the calm that had surrounded him so easily during the fight, grasping at the dregs of the freedom he'd felt in the dark.

"You abandoned your team."

"I sent them home. I didn't need them anymore."

Henry rubbed at his brow. "I know you're upset about Rez—"

"This isn't about Rez," countered August. "This isn't about any one human. I'm just tired of losing. What good is my strength if you don't let me *use* it?"

Henry's hands came to rest on his shoulders. "What good is your strength if we lose you to Sloan? Look at Ilsa. Think of Leo. You may think you're invincible, but you're not."

"I don't have to be invincible," said August, shrugging him off. "I just have to be stronger than everyone else."

~~IIII~~ IIII

Sloan ran his hand along the office shelves, nails trailing over the cloth and leather spines of Harker's collection until he found what he was looking for.

"Here we are," he said, returning to the penthouse's main room.

The three engineers were sitting at the table, a broad plane of slate on a steel frame. A length of chain ran from their ankles to the table legs, which were bolted to the floor. The table was already littered with tablets, but he cleared a space and let the book thud onto the stone top, relishing the way they startled at the sound.

"What do you want?" asked one of the men.

Sloan turned through the pages until he reached a photo of the city, taken from before the territory wars, before Sloan himself. When Flynn's fortress was just another tower in a sea of steel.

"What I want," he said, running his nail down the

page, letting it come to rest on the Compound, "is to bring this building down."

The engineers stilled.

It was the woman who spoke. "No."

"No?" echoed Sloan softly.

"We won't do it," said the other man.

"We *can't*," amended the woman. "It's not possible. A building of that size, it's not as if you could ever destroy it from a distance, and even if you had the materials—"

"Ah." Sloan took the small cube from his pocket, set the explosive on the table. The engineers drew back.

"My predecessor believed in preparation. He cached his arsenals in various places around the city, stored all manner of things, from guns to precious metals to a fair quantity of *this*. Do not worry about materials," he said, returning the cube to his pocket. "Just find a way to plant them."

He started to walk away and heard the rattle of chains, the sound of the book rustling. He turned back in time to see the second man, tome raised, as if to strike Sloan with it. What a pain, he thought, catching the man by the throat. The book tumbled uselessly from his hands.

Sloan sighed, and tightened his grip, lifting the man off the floor. That's what he got for giving these new pets a measure of freedom. He looked past the struggling, gasping form to the other two engineers.

"Perhaps I wasn't clear . . . ," he said, snapping the man's neck.

The woman gasped. The other man shuddered. But neither rose from their seats. That was progress, he thought, letting the body fall to the floor beside the book.

Just then Alice came storming in, her hands clenched and her eyes blazing, no sign of her mutilated Malchai or August Flynn.

"Another failed attempt?" cooed Sloan, picking up the book as she barreled past toward her room.

"Practice makes perfect," she growled, slamming the bedroom door.

||||| |||||

She is alone
in a place
with no light
no space
no sound
and then
the darkness
asks *who*
    deserves
        to pay
and a voice
    —*her* voice—
answers
    everyone
and the word
echoes
over and over
    and over
    and over
and the nothing

fills with bodies
packed in as tightly
as the crowd
in the basement
of Harker Hall
when Callum
stood on stage
and passed his judgment
every human
is her father
every monster
is his shadow
and there is a knife
    in her hand
and all she wants
is to cut them down
one by one
all she wants
all she wants—
but if she starts
she will never stop
so she lets go
and the knife
falls from her fingers
and the monsters
    tear her
        apart.

Kate lurched forward out of sleep, heart racing.

For one terrible, disorienting moment she didn't know where she was—and then it came rushing back.

The house in the green, the man with the shotgun, the Corsai in the street.

She was lying on the couch beside the altar of batteries and bulbs, dawn slicing through the makeshift metal curtains. The ghost of the nightmare lingered as she got to her feet. She'd slept in her boots, unable to shake the fear that something would come, that she'd have to be ready to fight, to run. Her music player had died in the night, but the Corsai, they had never stopped.

No wonder Rick had gone mad.

She washed her face with the last of the water, ate numbly, then spread her weapons on the table, drawn to, and repulsed by, them in equal measure. She strapped an iron spike to her calf, returned the switchblade to her back pocket. The click of the clip sliding into the handgun sent an almost pleasant shiver through her. She thumbed the safety on and tucked the weapon into the back of her jeans. Out of sight, out of mind, she told herself, even as the metal kissed her spine. She hauled her bag back onto her shoulder, then threw the bolt and stepped out into the early morning light.

In daylight, the quiet was even worse, the green's emptiness more unnerving than any number of people.

Rick's shotgun lay on the sidewalk near the street, the only sign of the man save for a thin line of dried blood on the pavement. If there were any others in the neighborhood, they didn't show themselves, and Kate didn't go looking.

She needed to keep moving.

There were plenty of cars on the street, but cars made noise, and the last thing she wanted to do was let all of V-City know she was coming. Especially since she had no idea who—or what—would be there to greet her. Instead she trudged across several dew-wet lawns until she found a bicycle lying on its side in the grass, abandoned like everything else in the green.

Kate righted the bike, trying not to think about whoever it belonged to, or what had happened to the owner, as she swung her leg over the seat and pushed off, toward the yellow, and the red, and the waiting city.

The violin was a mess.

August sat on the edge of his bed, his fingers moving deftly over the steel as he loosened the pegs and pried the strings free. Next came the neck, the fingerboard, the tailpiece, the bridge.

Piece by piece, he dismantled the instrument, the way FTF soldiers dismantled their guns, scrubbing the blood and gore from every curve and crevice, cleaning and drying every piece before putting the violin back together.

He worked in silence, unable to shake the feeling he was rubbing the blood *in*, instead of getting it out, but when he was done, the weapon was whole again, ready for its next fight.

Like you, little brother.

He tucked the gleaming instrument back into its case beside the bow, and rose, stepping out into the hall.

He heard movement in the kitchen, the soft shuffle of steps, the whisper of something like sand, and when he rounded the corner he saw the cupboards open, a sack of sugar spilling across the counter and onto the floor.

None of the lights were on, but his sister stood at the island, hands dancing over piles of sugar, separating it into hills and valleys with her fingers while Allegro padded around her legs, leaving tiny paw prints in the white dust.

August took a cautious step forward, careful not to startle her. He kept his voice low.

"Ilsa?"

She didn't look up, didn't even register his presence. Ilsa lost herself sometimes, got stuck inside her head. Once, during these episodes, her thoughts had poured out in tangled ribbons of speech. Now she unraveled in silence, her lips pressed into a thin line as she swept her fingers through the sugar, and as August drew close, he realized what she was making. It was a shallow model— the loose sugar couldn't form anything tall without losing its shape—but he recognized the snaking line of the Seam running down the center, the grid of streets and buildings to either side.

Ilsa had sculpted V-City.

Her hands slid to the island's edge and she bent forward, bringing her face to the counter as if to peer between the walls of her creation.

And then she drew a deep breath, and *blew.*

The entire city scattered, the only sound the *whoosh* of Ilsa's breath and the rain of sugar as it spilled onto the floor. She looked at him then, at last, her eyes wide, but not empty, not lost at all. No, she looked straight at August, and swept her hand above the counter as if to say, *Do you see?*

But August only saw one thing. "You're making a mess."

Ilsa's brow furrowed. She smoothed the sugar beneath her palm and drew her finger in slow, looping curls. It took August a few seconds to realize she was writing a word.

Coming

August stared at the mess, at the message. "*What's* coming?"

Ilsa let out an exasperated breath and swept her arm across the counter, scattering the remains of the city and sending a cloud of sugar into the air. It dusted August's hair, settled on his skin. To a human, it might have tasted sweet, but to him, it tasted like one thing:

Ash.

||||| ||||| |

Growing up, Kate had plenty of nightmares, but only one of them recurring.

In the dream, she was standing in the middle of Birch Street, one of the busiest roads in North City, but there were no cars. No commuters on the sidewalk. No movement in the shop windows. It was as if the city had been tipped on its side and shaken until every sign of life had fallen out. It was just . . . empty, and no people meant no sound, and the silence seemed to grow and grow and grow around her, the white noise weighing her down until she realized it wasn't the world, it was her ears, the last of her hearing stolen away, plunging her into an eternal silence, and she started to scream and scream until she finally woke up.

As Kate rode through the red zone, that same horrible silence swept around her, that old, irrational fear, and she strained, trying to catch something—anything—besides her own pulse and the hush of tires over pavement.

But there was nothing, nothing, and then—

Kate slowed. Were those voices? They reached her in pieces, highs and lows fragmented by the stone and steel buildings, the sounds brightening in her good ear only to fall away again before she could find the source, or figure out if they were getting closer or farther away. She dismounted as carefully as possible, leaning the bicycle against a wall just as someone *whistled* behind her.

Kate spun, and saw a man perched on a fire escape. He was dressed in dark jeans and a T-shirt, but the first thing she noticed was the band of steel around his throat. It looked like a *collar*.

"Well, well," he said, rising to his feet.

A door swung open nearby, and as two more figures—a man and a woman—stepped through, she realized the first one hadn't been whistling *at her*. He'd been whistling *for them*. They were rougher, their skin weathered and stained by old tattoos, but they wore the same metal circles around their throats.

Like *pets*, she thought, and between the pallor of blood loss and the puncture wounds that ran like needle scars up the inside of their arms, it was obvious whom they belonged to.

"Oh, this is *perfect*," cooed the woman.

The man on the fire escape broke into a grin. "Just his type, isn't she?" *Type?* "Down to the blue eyes."

"It's uncanny. Sloan will be . . ."

If he said anything else, Kate didn't hear it. The name caught like barbed wire in her head, bringing with it red eyes and a black suit, a shadow at her father's back, a voice in her head whispering, *Katherine.*

But Sloan wasn't here in Verity, because he was *dead.* She'd seen him lying on a warehouse floor, a steel bar through his back and—

Kate's attention snapped back to the alley. One of the thugs was coming close—too close—his hands raised as if she were a child or a dog, something easily spooked.

"Careful, Joe, you know he likes them fresh."

Kate shifted up against the wall and felt the familiar weight of the handgun at her back. She drew it out, and the moment the gun was in her hand, her pulse began to slow, and there it was again, that wonderful, terrifying calm, the whole messy world narrowing to a single, even road. *Shoot.*

Her finger came to rest against the trigger, the safety still on.

"Stay back," she said, infusing her voice with all the cold precision she'd learned from Callum Harker.

One of the men actually flinched, but the other let

out a delighted laugh, and the woman kept her eyes on Kate, as if daring her to try it:

"I don't think you have it in you."

Her grip tightened on the gun. "The last person who said that didn't live very long."

It would be so easy, whispered the darkness. *It would feel so good.* She wanted to, she wanted to more than anything wanted to hurt wanted to kill and these people deserved to pay they deserved—

She tried to picture August, stepping between her father and the barrel of the gun.

Not like this.

Even as her thumb clicked the safety off, she forced herself to breathe, to think. The wall behind her was nothing but brick, but to the right there was a dumpster and a low wall leading to God-knows-where.

"See?" taunted the woman, drawing a pair of cuffs from her back pocket. "All bark and no—"

Kate pulled the trigger.

The bullet struck the fire escape with a deafening crack, and the three thugs jumped, twisting reflexively toward the sound as Kate took off. The shock gained her a second's head start, nothing more. She mounted the dumpster half an instant before the woman reached it, fingers clutching at her ankle. Kate kicked her away, swung herself up over the low wall, and dropped to the other side.

She hit the ground running and beelined south toward the Seam, hoping they wouldn't follow.

But the too-quiet streets behind her filled with shouts and echoing steps. Kate was still sore from her run in the Waste, but imminent danger had a way of silencing pain. At last the Seam came into sight, three stories of wood and metal carving a line between North and South City.

She was surprised to see figures along its top, but she didn't have time to wonder who they were. She charged toward the nearest gate, only to realize it was bolted shut. A call went up behind her and Kate skidded, changing direction as she ran for the next gate. Locked. But there *had* to be a way through.

Turn and fight, said the darkness, but she kept running, and there, at last, a way out—or in. A building, one of the structures consumed by the wall. The doors were plated with copper and there was a sign posted on them, something about a checkpoint, but she didn't have time to stop and read, stop and think—

The doors swung open, and she burst through into a derelict lobby. There were voices nearby, the shuffle of feet, but Kate kept running—across the cavernous space toward a second set of doors, a mirror to the first.

Locked.

Of course, they were locked. Kate threw her shoulder

against the wood once, twice, then reared back and slammed her reinforced heel into the digital lock. It cracked and gave just as the northern doors swung open behind her. A voice echoed through the hall.

"Get back here you bit—"

But Kate was already through the doors and out onto the southern side of the city.

Shouts went up from the Seam overhead but she kept running, taking a zigzag course through alleys and around corners, before finally slowing to a jog and then a walk and then, at last, limping to a stop. She clutched her side and realized she was still gripping the gun, knuckles white, and she had no idea where she was, but at least she was on the right side of the Seam.

That was a start.

The bag slid from her shoulder, and Kate sank to one knee and started rummaging through it right before she felt the rush of air, the weight of a mass falling toward her. She jumped back, narrowly avoiding the body that crashed to the ground.

Only it didn't *crash* at all.

The shape landed in an elegant crouch and then rose, revealing long, lean limbs, and a plume of silver hair. Kate swung the gun up on instinct, but the creature was already closing the gap, fingers vising around Kate's wrist before she could think to aim. The gun tumbled from her grip, even as the urge to fight washed through her, but it broke against a wall of shock at the creature's eyes, which were not a burning red, but a flat, colorless gray. Kate couldn't tell if the monster was a man or a woman, but she knew one thing: it was a Sunai.

A short steel blade appeared in the Sunai's free hand, long fingers twirling the weapon, but what Kate had first taken for an ornamented hilt was in fact a kind of flute.

And the Sunai was lifting the instrument, as if to play.

"Wait," said Kate—what a useless word—as the instrument brushed the Sunai's lips. "I'm not—your enemy—" She tried to twist free, but the Sunai's grip was steel.

"Only the guilty fight. Are you guilty, then?"

The answer rose in Kate's throat, and when she swallowed, trying to hold it at bay, the Sunai's hand tightened to the point of pain around her wrist, and the first beads of bloody light began to shine on the surface of her skin.

Disgust darkened the Sunai's face and Kate's head swam, her senses already slipping, but she kicked out, twisting sideways as she did, and managed to wrench herself free, free of the Sunai's hold and the pain and the nearness of her own death. She staggered back a step, two, shoulders colliding with a wall as she clutched her wrist, the pricks of light already gone beneath her skin.

"I'm on your side!" she snapped, even as her fingers ached for the gun, the knife, the iron spike.

"You are a *sinner*," snarled the Sunai with sudden force. "You will never be on our—"

"Caught you!" One of the thugs from North City came crashing around the corner, brandishing a pair of knives. "Thought you could—"

He saw the Sunai, and froze, while the Sunai's own look darkened, their cold gray eyes taking in the collar around his throat. "What a foolish Fang you are."

The thug was already scrambling away, but it was too late. The Sunai was on him in an instant, pulling him into an embrace that might have passed for tender, if not for the blade protruding from his side, the red light flooding to the surface of his skin, the way his mouth opened in a strangled scream.

Kate saw her chance and took off running.

She made it five steps and then an arm marked with black *X*'s snaked around her shoulders, pulling her close before she even registered the sound of the man's body hitting the pavement.

"Be still," said the monster in Kate's ear. "The fight is over. You have already lost." Long fingers slid through Kate's hair and tightened, forcing her head back. "Try to flee, and you will die in pain. Kneel, and I will make it quick."

"I know August."

The Sunai paused at that. "How?"

What were they? Friends? Allies? "He saved my life," she said at last, "and I saved his."

"I see." The Sunai hummed thoughtfully. And then the iron grip was back. "Then you are even."

Panic shuddered through her. "Wait," she pleaded, fighting to keep her voice steady. "I have information."

A boot caught her behind the knees and her legs buckled, forcing her down. "I will hear your confession soon enough."

"If you just let me see August."

"Enough."

Callum Harker once told Kate that only fools shouted when they wanted others to listen. Smart men spoke softly, expecting to be heard.

Now, Kate raised her voice, as loud as she possibly could.

"AUGUST FLYNN!" she called out, right before the Sunai's blade came up beneath her chin. Blood—bright, red, human—coated its length, the tang of copper tickling her throat as her own voice echoed through the city streets.

"I warned you," growled the Sunai.

Kate's heart hammered in her ears.

Not like this.

Her bag sat several feet away. The gun glinted at the

base of the wall. The iron spike traced a cool line against her shin. She hadn't come this far just to be reaped. If she was going to die, she'd be damned if she did it on her knees.

"There is a new monster in your city," she said.

The blade's edge grazed her throat.

"It's turning humans on each other."

At that, the Sunai hesitated, the blade drew back a fraction, and Kate saw her only chance.

"What did you—"

But Kate was already up, spinning as she rose. She caught the flute with the spike, and the instrument went skidding away down the street before the Sunai's fist cracked across her face.

She went down hard, vision going black and then white, head still ringing as she scrambled up. She never made it. The Sunai dragged her to her feet, and threw her like a scrap against the wall. The air left her lungs, and the shadow in her head called for blood even as the Sunai wrapped a hand around Kate's throat—

"Soro, *stop*."

The command echoed, metal on stone.

The Sunai's hand fell away from Kate's throat and she sank to her knees on the pavement. The world tilted and swam, but she dragged her head up and saw him standing at the mouth of the alley.

August.

He was dressed in FTF fatigues, a steel violin hanging from his fingers. The last six months had changed Kate in small ways, but the changes to August Flynn were bigger. He was still lean, but he'd grown into his height, broad shoulders filling out his uniform. The lines of his face were sharp and strong, black curls sweeping over gray eyes—once pale, now the color of iron. But it was more than that, more than the sum of so many pieces. It was the way he held himself, not like the boy she'd met at Colton, hunched against some invisible wind, or the one she'd fled with through the Waste, arms wrapped around his ribs as if he could hold himself together.

This August took up space.

The Sunai—Soro—glared down at her, but didn't attack again.

Kate forced herself to her feet. "Hey there, stranger."

"Kate," answered August.

He didn't seem happy to see her. He didn't seem *anything* to see her, his face arranged into a mask of total neutrality, as if she were nothing, no one. When Kate took a step toward him, Soro blocked her way.

"Soro. This is Katherine Harker. She's—" His gaze cut toward her, then away, and Kate realized he didn't know what to call *her* either, "an ally."

"The FTF does not consort with criminals."

"She said she has information."

Of course he'd heard. He was Sunai. He could hear a pin drop a block away. "Henry will want to speak with her."

"But her soul is *red*."

"Call it in," snapped August. "Let the Compound know we're coming. That's an *order*."

Kate stared at him. Since when did August Flynn give orders?

But the other Sunai didn't question him further, only obeyed, speaking briskly into a comm. The words were lost as the Sunai turned away and August stepped in front of Kate.

"What are you doing here?" he asked, voice low. "You shouldn't have come back."

"Nice to see you, too," she snapped.

His gaze tracked over her, taking in the bruise rising on her cheekbone, the five purple lines around her wrist.

His voice softened a fraction. "Are you all right?"

Four small words, but in that question she glimpsed the August she'd known, the one who cared so much more than he should.

She ached, but at least the red light—that terrible, unnatural reminder of what she'd done—was gone.

"I'm alive. Thanks," she added, "for stepping in."

But the softness had already vanished, leaving his

features smooth and cold. Somewhere nearby, the familiar drone of a car's engine was rising. He produced a zip tie and looped the plastic around her hands as the vehicle came whipping around the corner.

"Don't thank me yet," he said, right before a sack came down over her head.

‖‖‖‖
‖‖‖‖
‖‖

It had been five years since the car crash.

Five years since the force of Kate's head against the glass had shattered her right eardrum and robbed her of half her hearing. Five years, and most days, she got by. She still had one good ear and four other senses all firing to make up the difference.

But as the hood came down over her head, the loss of a second sense left her disoriented.

Disembodied noise—voices, car doors, comm units— reached her good ear in fragments through the suffo- cating cloth. No one spoke—at least, not to her. One second August's hand was on her arm, and the next it was gone, replaced by other, rougher hands, forcing her body forward, head down, off the street and into a vehicle. Her wrist ached against the plastic zip tie, her cheek throbbing from the Sunai's punch.

There was a thin line of light at the bottom of the

hood, but everything else was reduced to shades of black, the jostle of tires, the hum of the engine. They drove for three minutes, nearly four, and when they stopped, Kate had to resist the simple, animal urge to fight back as she was pulled from the car.

She didn't say anything, didn't trust herself to speak. Besides, she had a feeling the time would come when she'd have to. Breathe, she told her lungs. In, one two. Out, one two.

The ground changed subtly beneath her feet— asphalt, concrete, rubber, concrete again—the atmospheric shifts of outdoor and indoor, the echo that came with walled space. She tried to keep track, but somewhere she stumbled and in that dizzying moment, she lost the thread.

Then—a hallway, a threshold, a metal chair.

The momentary kiss of a knife against her wrists, cold on warm, a flicker of panic before the zip tie broke, and then, just as quick, the weight of the cuffs, the clank and pull of metal threaded through metal, fastening her hands to a metal table.

Steps, the door falling closed.

Then, silence.

Kate hated silence, but she held on to it now, used the lack of information to steady her spinning head and focus on the task at hand. She splayed her fingers against the cold metal and tried to decide which would be less suspicious, panic or calm.

The door opened.

Footsteps moved toward her, and then the hood came off.

Kate squinted in the sudden light—stripes of harsh, artificial white embedded in the ceiling—as Soro rounded the table, the shining hilt of the flute-knife jutting from the Sunai's pocket. There was no sign of August. No sign of anyone else. The room was small and square, bare save for the table, two chairs, and the red light of a surveillance camera in the corner. She kept her gaze down.

The wraithlike Sunai, meanwhile, was looking at Kate as though *she* were the monster in the room. Soro said nothing as the bag—*her* bag—was upended on the table. When the first metal spike hit the table, Kate's pulse rose, longing to lunge for it, even though the chain wouldn't reach, even though it wouldn't do a damn bit of good if it did. She kept her eyes on the cuffs themselves instead, studying the intricacies of each steel loop.

But as Soro began to methodically arrange the contents of Kate's bag, displaying them as if they were tools in a torturer's kit, another force began to pull at her— the Sunai's presence, like a hand at her back, a subtle, insistent urge to speak. Kate kept her mouth shut as Soro sank into the opposite chair.

"Well, then," said the Sunai. "Let's begin."

The surveillance feed hummed with static.

It was low enough that humans probably didn't notice, but the sound filled August's head, a background of white noise behind the video.

Kate Harker sat unmoving in one of the two chairs, while the shadow beneath her feet twitched and tangled around the table legs.

Her hair was different—bangs falling into her eyes—but other than that, she looked the same, as if the last six months hadn't touched her.

Do you know where she is? Alice had goaded him.

Far away from here. Far away from you.

Only she wasn't, she was right here.

Why had she come *back*?

Ilsa's gaze flicked toward him, featherlight, as if she'd heard the question in his head. August kept his eyes on Kate.

She looked almost bored, but he knew it was an act, because everything about Kate had always been an act—the bravado, the cold air, all the aspects of her father arranged into a shield, a mask.

Henry stepped up beside them. On the screen, the

door at Kate's back swung open and Soro strode in. When the Sunai glanced up at the camera lens, their gray eyes registered as a smudge of black. Kate's voice echoed through his head. He'd been two blocks away when she'd screamed his name. If he'd been any later . . .

"I should have been the one to question her," said August.

Henry brought a hand to his shoulder. "You're not objective."

He shrugged off the touch. "Soro nearly killed her."

"If you didn't know Kate, would you have spared her?"

August stiffened. "That isn't fair."

Fair? chided the voice in his head. *A sinner is a sinner.*

But it wasn't that simple. Not when it came to Kate. She was his past. A reminder of who he'd been, who he'd *wanted* to be. Of school uniforms, and fevers, of starving and stardust and—

"Well then. Let's begin."

He dragged his spiraling mind to a stop as the mic flared to life and Soro's voice filtered through.

"What is your name?"

Kate tipped her head a fraction. To everyone else, it might have registered as boredom, but August knew she was turning her good ear *away* from the Sunai.

"Katherine Olivia Harker," she answered. If she was afraid, she was doing a good job of keeping it off her face. She tapped the cuffs with a nail. "Are these *pure* metal or alloy?"

"How old are you?"

"Do you really need to establish a baseline, when you know I can't lie?"

"Answer the question."

"Eighteen. I was born at three in the morning on a Wednesday in Jan—"

"Are you the daughter of Callum Harker?"

"Yes."

"Are you afraid?" asked Soro.

"Should I be?"

"You are a sinner," said Soro.

"If that's a question," said Kate, "then you need to work on your inflection." August shook his head—some things really *hadn't* changed—but Kate only straightened in her seat. "You're new. What's your name? *Sorrow?* That's what August called you, right? Not very uplifting is it? Are these too many questions? I know you have to tell the truth."

"As do you," countered Soro. "Why did you leave Verity six months ago?"

Kate paused a moment before answering—a display of will. "Call me crazy," she said slowly, "but I just didn't feel very welcome anymore. Not after my father tried to kill me."

"And why did you return?"

That question struck a chord. "I tried to tell you," said Kate. "I'm hunting a monster."

At August's side, Henry tensed.

On the screen, Soro inclined their head. "What kind of monster?"

Kate shifted in her seat. "I don't know."

"What does it feed on?"

"Violence? Chaos? Death? I'm not sure. It doesn't kill with its own hands. As far as I can tell, it convinces its victims to do the job. It turns people against each other."

August started. Squad Six. He looked at Henry, but Henry had already taken up his comm, issuing a low and steady stream of orders.

On the screen, Soro continued their interrogation.

"Describe this monster."

"I *can't*," she snapped, shaking her head. "It's a shadow. An outline of something you can't see. It doesn't feel— real. It's a nothing, an absence—"

"You are not making sense," said Soro.

"You'd understand if you saw it."

"And you have?"

"Yes."

"And you know it's here?"

"I tracked it from Prosperity."

Soro's eyes narrowed. "There are no monsters in Prosperity."

"There are now."

"How does it hunt?"

"I'm not sure," said Kate, "but it seems drawn to violence. It amplifies it."

Soro crossed their arms. "How did you track it?"

Kate's poise faltered. "What?"

"You said this monster 'doesn't have a real body,' so how did you track it?"

August watched Kate take a breath—buying seconds to bend the truth?—before she answered. "It left a trail."

On the feed, Soro sounded skeptical. "And you followed it all the way back to Verity. How valiant."

Kate's expression darkened. "I guess I have a vested interest. Or maybe I was homesick. Or *maybe* I could tell, from a territory away, that things were going to absolute shit." Her temper was rising. "This thing, whatever it is, I've seen what it can do. It gets into people's heads, and it brings out something dark. Something *violent*. It turns *them* into the monster. And then it *spreads*. Like a virus." She rose to her feet, leaning forward across the table. "So yes, I came back, to help you kill it. But by all means, leave me chained up here instead." She sat back down. "Happy hunting."

Kate's chest was rising and falling, as if the words

had left her winded. Soro's poise didn't waver. They said nothing, and August knew they were waiting to see if their influence would draw out anything else. At August's back, people were talking, comms were buzzing, the rise and fall of voices and feeds. But his attention was leveled on the screen, on Kate's face.

Which was the only reason he saw it.

She tipped her head back, and the blond hair tumbled out of her eyes and for an instant, they met the camera, and there was a single flare, like light reflected back, a streak obscuring her face. The lens couldn't seem to focus. It blurred, steadied, blurred again—the way it did with monsters.

It could have been a glitch, he told himself. An instant later her head was back down, the flare gone. It could have been a glitch—

But Ilsa had seen it, too. Her breath caught, a small but audible sound, and her fingers splayed across the table, her pale gaze darting toward him. Henry's back was still turned, and they stared at each other in silence, each wondering what the other would do.

It gets into people's heads, Kate had said.

I've seen what it can do.

August wasn't sure what he'd just seen, or what it meant, but he knew it was only a matter of time before someone else noticed it, too, and when they did—

You owe her nothing, chided Leo.

She is a sinner, echoed Soro.

What will you do, brother? said Ilsa with a look.

"Henry," he said, turning his back to the screen. The head of the FTF was talking rapidly into a comm. He raised a hand and August held his breath, forcing himself to wait patiently, as if nothing was wrong.

At last, Henry lowered the comm. "What is it?"

This is wrong. Something's wrong. Everything's wrong.

"Kate isn't our enemy," he said, "but you're treating her like one. If you leave her in there with Soro, she'll tell us the truth, but nothing more. She'll give you only what she has to, and it probably won't be enough."

"What do you suggest?"

"Let me talk to her. No cuffs. No cameras."

Henry was already shaking his head. "August—"

"She saved my life."

"And you spared hers. I'm sorry to tell you that good deeds don't prevent bad ones, and until we know exactly—"

"If Kate Harker poses a threat to any of our soldiers, to any of our missions, I will reap her soul myself."

August was surprised to hear himself say it. Apparently, so was Henry. His eyes widened, but he didn't look comforted by the truth in the words.

"Please," added August. "I'm the only one here she'll trust."

Henry looked at the screen, where Kate had her fists clenched on the table and her head up in a posture of defiance. August could feel himself striking the same pose.

But it was Ilsa who decided it. She rose up onto her toes and wrapped her arms around August's chest, resting her chin on his shoulder. He couldn't see the look she gave Henry, the silent message that passed between them, but a moment later, Henry told Soro to terminate the interview.

HHHH
HHHH
III

The girl staggered down the hallway, barefoot and
bleeding.

Her wrists were bound in front of her and she fought
with the rope as she stumbled toward the elevator. Sloan
let her get there before he caught up. Fear—delicious,
defiant fear—dusted the air like sugar as he pinned her
to the wall beside the stainless-steel doors and wrenched
her head back.

"Katherine," he whispered, teeth skimming the pulse
at her throat and—

The elevator doors chimed and slid open.

Sloan hesitated, fangs poised against the girl's skin.
The tower's penthouse was invitation-only. It belonged
to Sloan, and Sloan alone—the engineers chained to the
table and the hateful little thing perched on his kitchen
counter were there because *he* allowed it. No one came
here without being summoned.

Which was why he bristled at the sight of the Malchai hurrying forward into his home. His red eyes were wide with panic, blood speckled his face, and gore leaked down one arm. At the sight of Sloan and the human girl trembling against the wall, the Malchai lurched to a stop, but didn't retreat.

"This had better be important," snarled Sloan.

"Apologies, sir, but it is."

"Speak."

The Malchai hesitated, and in Sloan's moment of distraction, the girl almost slipped free.

Almost.

"Hold on," he muttered, pulling her back and sinking his fangs into her throat. Blood spilled over his tongue and he could feel the other Malchai's nerves, feel his hunger, too, and just for that, he took his time, drinking every drop.

When he was done, Sloan let the body slide to the floor and drew a fresh black square from his pocket. He wiped his mouth and started into the main room, hooking one finger for the Malchai to follow. "You've intruded on my hospitality and interrupted my meal. This better be worth it."

The engineers' eyes were trained on their work, as if they hadn't heard the girl's screams. But the color was high in the woman's face, while the man had gone pale.

Alice meanwhile was sitting on the counter, skimming a chemistry book.

"Forgive me," said the Malchai. "I thought you would want to know"—he glanced at Alice—"in private."

Alice waved her fingers. "Oh, don't worry," she said cheerfully. "Sloan and I are *family*."

Sloan's teeth clicked together. "Yes. Go on."

The Malchai bowed his head. "More Fangs are dead."

Sloan shot Alice a look. "This is the third time in two nights."

Alice shrugged. "Wasn't me."

"I was there," said the Malchai. "There was a monster. Wasn't Corsai. Wasn't one of us either."

Sloan frowned. "A Sunai? On our side of the city?"

Alice glanced up, curiosity piqued, but the Malchai was already shaking his head. "No. Something else."

"Something *else*," echoed Sloan. "And how did it kill them?"

The Malchai's eyes burned with a frantic light. "That's the thing, it *didn't* kill them. The Fangs took one look at it and just started killing *each other*."

Alice snorted. "Sounds like humans being humans."

Sloan held up a hand. "And what did you do?"

"I tried to stop the Fangs, and one actually *went for me*." He sounded indignant. "I killed that one, but the rest killed each other, I swear."

"And the *something else?*"

"It just *watched.*"

Sloan unfastened his cuffs, and began to roll up his sleeves. "Where did this happen?"

"That old warehouse on Tenth."

"And who else was there?"

"Only me," said the Malchai, gesturing to his stained self.

Sloan nodded thoughtfully. "I appreciate your discretion. Thank you for coming to me."

The Malchai's eyes brightened. "You're welcome, s—"

He never finished: Sloan tore out his heart.

He had to reach through the Malchai's stomach to get it, up around the bone plating on his chest, and by the time he pulled the offending organ free, his arm was slick with gore.

Sloan grimaced at the rot of death, the black blood dripping to the floor.

Alice rolled her eyes. "And you say *I'm* the messy one."

Sloan unbuttoned the soiled shirt as a sound came from the table.

The female engineer had her hands over her mouth.

"Something to say?" asked Sloan lightly. "Have you found an answer to my problem yet?"

The woman shook her head.

The man's voice was barely a whisper. "Not yet."

Sloan sighed, turning to Alice. "Keep an eye on these two," he said, shrugging out of the ruined shirt. He dropped it onto the body. "And clean this up."

The Malchai's corpse was already beginning to dissolve on the floor. Alice wrinkled her nose. "Where are *you* going?"

Sloan stepped over the mess and went to change his clothes.

"You heard our dear, departed friend," he said. "We seem to have a pest problem."

HHH
HHH
IIII

The hood went on again, and for several long minutes Kate's world was plunged back into black. The door was opened, her cuffs freed from the table, and then she was hoisted up from her chair and onto unsteady feet.

She was shaking.

She hated that she was shaking.

This was why she'd started smoking.

A single strong hand—Soro's, she could tell by the viselike grip—led her from the room, and down a hall. She could feel the knife holstered at Soro's side.

"You know," said Kate, "I think we got off on the wrong foot."

The Sunai scoffed.

"You don't know me," pressed Kate.

"I know who you are," said Soro, "and I know *what* you are, and that is enough."

"You monsters," muttered Kate, "you think every-thing is black and white." Her shoes skimmed a gap, the narrow line between floor and elevator. "Maybe it is, for you, but for the rest of us—"

The hood came off, and Kate blinked. Soro loomed before her, long as a shadow, their silver hair like metal in the artificial light.

The Sunai was blocking Kate's view of the control panel. "Where are we going?"

Soro's gaze was cold, their voice even. "Up."

Her heart fluttered. She'd gotten through the inter-rogation, white-knuckled it, and for the most part man-aged to keep a grip on the words coming out of her mouth. She'd told the truth, if not all of it.

Maybe she was being released.

Maybe . . . but the absence of the hood worried her—wherever she was being taken next, it didn't matter if she could see, and with every passing second, her nerves tightened, the desire to *do* something wearing away at the knowledge of its uselessness. *Don't, don't, don't,* became the echo in her head.

Soro broke the silence. "Humans have free will," they said, picking up the thread of the earlier argument. "You *chose* to err. You *chose* to sin."

If only you knew, thought Kate, fighting her own muscles, her own mind.

"People make mistakes," said Kate. "Not everyone deserves to die."

A ghost of amusement crossed the Sunai's lips. "You died the day you took another life. I am simply here to clear your corpse."

A cold chill ran through her at Soro's words, at their hand drifting toward the flute-knife, at the echo of pain in her wrist.

But the elevator stopped and Soro didn't draw the weapon. The doors slid open and Kate braced herself for whatever was beyond, for prison cells, or a firing squad, or a plank at the edge of a roof.

But there was only August.

No troops, no cells, nothing but August Flynn, looking so staggeringly normal, hands in his pockets, the tallies peaking out from his sleeves, that for a second, Kate felt her composure slip. The exhaustion and the fear laid bare. The swell of relief.

But something was off. He didn't look at Kate, only at Soro. "I'll take it from here."

Kate tried to step toward him, but Soro caught her arm. "Explain to me, August, why she is—"

"No," he cut in, an edge in his voice. It was the same edge Kate had heard in her father's tone a dozen times, one she herself had mimicked, an edge meant to silence, to quell. It sounded wrong coming from him. "We both have orders. Follow yours, and let me follow mine."

A shadow crossed Soro's face, but the Sunai complied and Kate was shoved forward into the apartment. August caught her elbow, steadying her as the elevator doors slid closed.

"I don't think that one likes me," she muttered.

August said nothing, releasing the handcuffs with brisk, sure movements. The metal clicked free and fell away, and she rubbed her wrists, wincing slightly. "Where are we?"

"The Flynn apartment."

Kate's eyes widened. She'd known South City didn't enjoy the same kind of luxury as the North, hadn't expected Henry Flynn's place to look like Callum Harker's, but she was still struck by the difference, the utter *normalcy* of it. The penthouse at Harker Hall was a thing of steel and wood and glass, all edges, but this place looked . . . well, it looked like a home. Something lived in.

August led her down an entry hall and into the main room, a kitchen opening onto a sitting area, a blanket thrown over the couch. Down a short hall she saw an open door, a violin case leaning against the edge of a bed.

"What are we doing here?"

"I pleaded your case," said August. "Convinced Henry

to release you into my custody, at least for the night, so try not to do anything rash."

"But it suits me so well."

She was trying to defuse the tension, but August didn't smile. Everything about him was stiff, as if they'd never met.

"What's with the act?"

The slightest furrow formed between his eyes. "What act?"

"The steely, dark-eyed soldier act." She crossed her arms. "Don't get me wrong, it's a nice look—I just don't know why you're still wearing it."

August straightened. "I'm the captain of the task force."

"Okay, so that explains the clothing. What about the rest?"

"What do you mean?"

"You *know* what I mean." What had he once said about going dark? That every time he did, he lost a piece of what made him human. Kate refused to believe he'd lost this much. "What happened to you?"

"Things change," he said. "I've changed with them. And so have *you*." He took a sudden step toward her, and the hairs on her arms stood on end. His gray eyes tracked across her face, his intensity uncomfortable. "Why did you come back?"

"Gee thanks, I missed you, too."

"Stop deflecting."

"I already told Soro—"

"I watched the feed," he cut in. "I heard your answers. But I also *saw* . . ." He hesitated, as if looking for the words.

Kate's chest tightened. The camera. There had been a moment—a fraction of a breath—when she'd forgotten about the camera and looked up, desperate to escape Soro's gaze. She thought she'd caught herself in time.

"What happened to you in Prosperity, Kate?"

She fought to keep the words down. "Look, it's been a hell of a day and—"

"This is important."

"Just give me a minute—"

"So you can think of another way to bend the truth, to tell me something that's not entirely a lie? No. What *happened* to you?"

Kate fought for air, for thought, the words rising in her throat.

August caught her by the shoulders. *"Answer me."*

The order was like a blow against a breaking dam. The last of her resolve faltered, failed. She tried to clench her teeth, but it was no use—the truth came pouring out. She heard the words leave her lips, felt them slide across her tongue, traitorous and smooth. A confession.

"It was like falling . . . ," she began.

She told him about the shadow in the dark, the monster she'd faced and fought, the one she was *still* fighting, the truth of how she'd tracked the thing here to Verity.

And then it was out, filling the air between them like smoke.

Kate drew in a shaky breath as his hands fell away, shock scrawled across his face.

"I'm sorry," he said. "I shouldn't have—"

Her fist cracked against his jaw.

It was like hitting a brick wall, but she had the satisfaction of watching his head snap sideways before the pain tore up her hand. She recoiled, clutching her fist as August touched his face, obviously more surprised than hurt.

"No," she snarled. "You shouldn't have."

But the blow had done something, dislodged some small fragment of the August she knew—he looked wounded.

Kate took a step back and then another, and another, until her shoulders met the wall. Blood wept between her knuckles, and the silence between them was so thick that she could hear it.

August probably could, too. He went to the sink, picking up a towel and filling it with ice before holding it out, like an offering. Kate took it and held the cloth to her throbbing hand.

"When did it happen?" he asked.

She had to think. The hours had run together. "Two nights ago. I was hunting something else when I saw it. There was a stabbing in a restaurant, and it was standing in the middle of it all, just *watching*, growing more solid with every scream. I chased it down an alley and then . . ." She trailed off, recalling the cold, dark, chilling fear before she saw its eyes, saw herself, and fell in.

"I got away. For the most part." Kate swept the hair out of her eyes to show him the streak of silver cutting through her left iris. "I said it left a trail."

August tensed, his face unreadable.

"How did you get away?"

Kate shrugged. "I don't know, maybe I'm just resilient when it comes to having monsters in my head. I guess you were good practice."

She didn't tell him the silver was spreading, didn't want to think about what would happen if it took over the remaining blue before she killed the source.

"It's not just for looks," she said. "This shard, it's some kind of link. I can use it to see this . . ." She didn't know what to call it. A Shadow? A Void? Liam's voice echoed through her head. *Call it what it is. Call it what it does.*

"Chaos Eater," she said.

"How does it work?" asked August.

Kate chewed her lip, trying to find the words. "Have

you ever stood between two mirrors? They reflect, back and forth, until you see yourself a hundred times. When I look at myself, at this"—she touched her cheek—"it's like the opposite of that. Instead of multiplying, I disappear into the gap. Does that make sense?"

"No," said August. "But you saw the monster here?"

She nodded. "It's not always easy or clear"—*understatement*—"but it's something."

August hesitated. "You compared it to a virus . . ."

Kate knew what he was trying to ask, even without the words. "I'm not contagious."

"How do you know?"

Kate thought of the older woman in the rest stop, tipping up her chin. "Consider the theory tested." August paled. "Relax," she said. "No one got hurt."

She let her gaze escape to the window.

The walls in her father's penthouse were made entirely of glass, the city laid out on display. The walls here were solid, studded with small windows, but even still, she could tell which wall faced north. The Seam was traced with light—a thin band cutting through the city—and somewhere beyond it, Callum Harker's tower was shrouded in darkness.

"Is it true?" she asked after a moment. "About Sloan?"

His name tasted vile in her mouth.

August's eyes widened. "How did you hear?"

"When Soro caught me, I was running from a group of humans in North City. They all had these metal collars around their necks—"

"Fangs," he said.

"When they cornered me, one of them said Sloan's name. He said, 'She's just his type.'" Kate wrapped her arms around herself. "What the hell did that mean? And how is Sloan even *alive*?"

"We're not sure. Things were messy after Callum's death. Everyone knew it was Harker the monsters followed, Harker they obeyed, but without him, no one knew what they might do, if they'd rise up or scatter." August ran a hand through his hair, a shadow of fatigue crossing his face. "A few citizens tried to step up, impose curfews, maintain some sense of order. It looked like it might work—and then Sloan came back."

A shiver ran through her.

"By the time we knew what was happening . . ." August trailed off, dark lashes shadowing his eyes. "Three solid nights and three days. That's all it took."

She wasn't surprised. Sloan had always wanted to be king.

"If I'd known," she said, "I would have come back sooner."

August's head swung up. "Then I'm glad you didn't know."

"That happy to see me?"

He fumbled—she could tell he wanted to lie and couldn't. "Look around, Kate. Only a cruel person would be glad to see you here."

"You invited me to stay, once."

"Things have changed."

"So you've said." She shook her head, exasperated, exhausted. "Anything else I should know?" Something flickered in his face, too fast to read. "What is it?"

He hesitated. The pause was too long, the answer, when it came, too rushed. "Ilsa survived."

Kate brightened. "That's *wonderful*," she said.

But there was something else—something he wasn't telling her.

"She has no voice," he added darkly.

"But she's *alive*."

August's head bobbed once, and Kate wondered why he had veered toward this particular truth, and what he'd swerved away from. What was he hiding?

"You must be tired," he said, the formality back in his voice, and Kate *was*—too tired to pry, to fight, to grab him by the shoulders and shake him until the real August, the one she remembered, came free.

So she nodded and let him lead her down the hall to the room with the open door.

Unlike her bedroom at Harker Hall, the sterile

surfaces she tried to make hers, this place was August to a T, from the precarious stacks of philosophy and astronomy books, to the music player discarded among the tangled sheets, and the violin case propped against the footboard.

Standing in this place, the August in front of her made even less sense. Kate had spent enough time hiding behind her own walls to know a barricade when she saw one.

His sleeves were rolled up, and she gestured to the marks circling his forearm.

"How many days?"

He looked down, hesitating, as if he wasn't sure. That uncertainty, at least, seemed to bother him. Instead of answering, he reached for the instrument case and turned to leave. "You can have the bed."

"Where will you sleep?"

"There's a couch in the living room."

"So why don't I sleep there?"

It was a challenge. She knew the answer—she just wanted to see if he would say it. Her eyes went to the doorknob under his hand, the locking mechanism on the other side.

August didn't take the bait. "Get some rest, Kate."

She still had a dozen questions—about the FTF, about him, about her own uncertain future—but fatigue was wrapping itself around her, dragging her down. She sank onto the bed. It was softer than she'd expected and smelled of cool linen. August started to close the door.

"One hundred and eighty-four," she said.

He paused. "What?"

"That's how many days since I left Verity. The same number since you fell. In case you couldn't remember."

August didn't say anything, only pulled the door shut behind him.

And Kate was left wondering if she was wrong, if August had gone dark since she left.

It would explain the coldness.

But the August she'd known had fought so hard to hold on.

Kate heard the lock click and rolled her eyes but didn't get up. If she'd traded one cell for another, at least this one had a bed. There were no mirrors, and for that small mercy, she was thankful.

Her bag was sitting at the foot of the bed, and Kate rummaged through it, turning out its contents on the bed. She knew what she would find—her weapons were gone. Confiscated. So was her tablet.

Frustration prickled through her—but it wasn't like she would get a signal, and even if she could write to the Wardens, to Riley, what would she say?

Alive for now. Hope you are, too?

Kate fell back on the bed and tried to find calm, sur-rounded by the familiar scent of August and the unfa-miliar room, by the strange bed and the light beneath the door and the thoughts spinning through her head.

Where are you? she asked herself, and the answer came rushing up: She was on Riley's couch, splitting a pizza, while the TV droned on and she told him about the shadow in her head, about Rick and the green, about the Fangs, and Soro, the race through the red, and the con-crete room, and Riley listened and nodded; but before he could answer, he dissolved, giving way to August, his cold gaze and his voice echoing through her head:

You should never have come back.

And Kate lay there in the dark, wondering, for the first time, if maybe he was right.

卌

卌

卌

August stared down at the tallies on his skin.

One hundred and eighty-four.

All this time, Kate had been counting.

When had he stopped?

Things change.

He returned to the kitchen, trying to clear his head.

I've changed with them.

He tapped his comm. "Command, this is Alpha."

Three short beats of silence. *"Alpha."* Phillip's voice was uncertain. *"Logs show you're off tonight."*

"Since when do monsters take nights off?" said August. "Find me a job."

"I can't do that."

"What do you mean?"

"You've been grounded."

Henry.

The tension in his chest grew. "Let me speak to him."

"He's overseeing a convoy from the southern Waste."

"Patch me through."

There was a short sequence of beeps, and then Henry's voice. *"August?"*

"Since when am I *grounded*?"

"You already have a task. When I get back, you can tell me what you learned. In the meantime, Kate Harker is in your custody."

"Kate is asleep," countered August, temper rising.

"And when is the last time you slept?"

August took a deep breath. "I'm not—"

"Consider it an order."

"Henry—"

But he could tell by the static, the man was gone.

August slammed his fist on the counter, igniting a brief spark of pain, there and then gone. He slid his hands through his hair. Maybe Henry was right. He *was* tired, in a bone-deep way. He shoved off the counter and crossed into the living room, leaving the lights off as he sank onto the couch. If he listened, he could hear Kate moving beyond the bedroom door, rolling over on his bed. Six months, and she was still made of restless limbs and shallow breaths.

Why did you come back?

He tried to focus instead on the patter of Allegro's steps somewhere in Ilsa's room, the distant sound of movement from the floors below. He closed his eyes and felt his body sinking deeper into the cushions, but the quieter the room became, the louder Kate's voice in his head.

What happened to you?

The look on her face when he forced the truth from her, that horrible mixture of betrayal and disgust.

That isn't me, he wanted to say.

Yes it is, insisted Leo.

What happened to you? demanded Kate.

You were weak, said his brother.

What happened to you?

Now you are strong.

What happened to you?

He forced himself up, slinging the violin case over his shoulder. He didn't need a mission. There was plenty of trouble waiting in the dark.

The doors to the private elevator stood open, and he stepped in, punching the button for the lobby. The doors slid shut, and he was met with a rippling reflection, distorted steel twisting his features, erasing everything but the broadest planes of his face.

He waited for the feeling of slow descent, but the elevator didn't move. He punched the lobby again. Still nothing. He hit the button to make the doors open. They didn't.

August sighed and looked up, straight into the surveillance lens mounted in the corner, even though he knew looking straight at it would blur the feed.

"Ilsa," he said evenly. "Let me go."

The elevator didn't move.

"I have a job to do."

Nothing.

He'd never thought of himself as claustrophobic, but the elevator walls were starting to feel close.

"Please," he said tightly. "Let me go. I won't stay out long but I need . . ." He faltered. What was the truth? What did he need? To move? To think? To hunt? To reap? To kill? How was he supposed to find the words to tell his sister that he couldn't stand to sit still, to be alone with the voices in his head, with himself.

"I need *this*," he said at last, voice tight with frustration.

Nothing.

"Ilsa?"

After a few long seconds, the elevator started down.

||||| ||||| ||||| |

The first time Sloan heard that humans feared the dark, he laughed.

What passed for dark was, to him, simply layers of shadow, a hundred varying degrees of gray. Dim, perhaps, but Sloan's eyes were sharp. He could see by the light of the streetlight four blocks over, by the glow of the moon behind clouds.

As for the things that *lurked* in that dark, that lived and hunted and *fed* in that dark—well.

That was another matter.

As he reached the warehouse on Tenth, he could smell the traces of blood, but the space itself was empty, at least of corpses. Which was fine—Sloan wasn't there to speak to the dead. He stepped into the hollow drum of a building, the floor littered with bullet casings and shreds of cloth. Light poured in from a streetlight outside, casting a triangle of safety near the open doors and there, where it gave way to shadow, were the Fangs' steel collars, stacked like bones after a meal.

Sloan stared into the shadows. "Did you see it?"

The shadows rippled, shifted, and after a moment, they stared back, white eyes flickering against the dark.

wesawwesawwesaw

The words echoed around him, taken up by countless mouths. The Corsai were bottom-feeders, half-formed things with no vision, no ambition, only the simple desire to eat. But they could be useful, when they chose.

"*What* did you see?"

The darkness shifted, snickered.

beatbreakruinfleshbonebeatbreak

Sloan tried again.

"What did the *creature* look like?"

The Corsai chittered, uncertain, their voices dissipating, but then, as if reaching a consensus, they began to draw themselves together. A hundred shadowy forms became one, their eyes crowding into two circles and their claws gathering into hands and their teeth tracing an outline of something vaguely human. A grotesque mockery of a monster.

"Can you bring it to me?"

The Corsai shook its collective head.

nonono no not real

"What do you *mean* it's not real?"

The Corsai shivered and fell apart, one form scattering back into many. They went silent then, and Sloan began to wonder if the conversation was over—the Corsai were fickle things, distracted by a scent, a passing whim—but after a few moments they came shuddering back to life, drawing themselves once more into a single form.

Like that, they hissed over and over, *like that likethat-likethat . . .*

Sloan let out a low, exasperated sigh. "What does it *eat?*" he demanded.

But the Corsai had lost interest.

beatbreakruinfleshbonebeatbreak

Their voices rose louder and louder until the walls of the warehouse shook. Sloan turned to go, their violent chorus following him out.

VERSE 3
A MONSTER AT HEART

1

She is standing
in her father's office
alone
the gun
in her hand
when cold air
kisses her neck
and a voice
    whispers
        Katherine
red eyes
reflected
in the window
she turns
lifts the gun
but she is not
fast enough
the monster
in the black suit
forces her

back
against the glass
the gun is gone
her hands are empty
she tears at him
but her fingers
go right through
as the window
cracks
splinters
breaks
     and she begins
         to fall.

Kate jolted forward, fingers knotted in her shirt. Her heart was pounding, but she couldn't remember why. The nightmare was already gone, leaving only a sick feeling and a racing pulse in its wake.

The room was empty, the world beyond August's window still dark, save for the muted glow of the light strip at the Compound's base and the first touches of dawn. She got up, padding barefoot to the door, turning the handle before she remembered it was locked.

Kate sighed and dug around in her bag until she found a couple of hairpins. She knelt before the lock, then paused, running her fingers over the plate that held the doorknob to the door. She fetched her silver lighter instead, thumbing the hidden catch. The switchblade snicked out, and she fit the narrow tip into the first screw and began to turn.

When she was done, the door whispered open.

A faint noise issued from the room to her right. August's violin case was propped against the wall, and when she pressed her ear to the wood, she heard the steady hum of a shower.

The smell of coffee wafted from the kitchen. The lights were on, but the room was empty, and she poured herself a cup, stifling a yawn. Sleep had come quick, but it had been thin, restless.

And the dream . . .

Her gaze drifted absently across the kitchen and landed on a knife block. Five wooden handles jutted from the block, while a sixth knife lay on the counter, blade shining. There was something lovely about knives—the gleam of light on polished metal, the satin smoothness of the handle, the razor-sharp edge. Her fingers drifted toward it, a strange ache in her palm at the thought of—

Something brushed against Kate's leg, and she recoiled, jarred from the pull of the shadow in her head. It had stolen over her so smoothly, and she swore at herself as a dark shape vanished around the corner of the island.

She frowned and peered over, but the other side was empty. And then, out of nowhere, a small black-and-white thing leaped onto the counter.

The Flynns had a *cat*.

It stared at Kate and she stared back. She had never owned a pet—the closest she'd come was walking the school mascot at her third prep school—but she'd always liked animals more than people. Then again, that might have been a reflection on people more than on her.

She wiggled her fingers, watching the cat paw absently at her hand.

"Who are you?" she whispered.

"Allegro."

Kate spun, a kitchen knife in her hand before she even thought to reach for it.

A man was standing in the doorway, tall and slim, his graying hair cut short. She recognized him at once as the founder of the FTF, the man who had held half the city against Callum Harker and his monsters. Her father's greatest rival.

And he was wearing a bathrobe.

"Miss Harker," said Henry Flynn in a steady voice. "I didn't mean to startle you. But you are standing in my kitchen. And that is my favorite knife."

"Sorry," she said, lowering the weapon. "Old habit."

He flashed a wan smile and drew his hand from the pocket of his robe, revealing a small gun. "New habit."

He held the gun by the barrel with only two fingers, as if he hated touching it—then put it back in his pocket. Kate slotted the knife into the block, trying to ignore the way her fingers resisted letting go. She took a step back from the counter, to be safe, as Henry rounded the island and poured himself a mug of coffee. "Did you sleep?"

He didn't ask if she'd slept *well*.

"Yes." She gave him a once-over, saw the slight stoop, as if it hurt to straighten, the shadows under his eyes and cheekbones. Flynn laughed at the scrutiny, a soft, empty sound. "No rest for the wicked." He looked around the apartment. "Are you enjoying our small piece of home? It's no penthouse"—his gaze returned to her—"but it's no prison, either."

His voice was pleasant enough, but his message was clear. Her presence here was predicated on her cooperation.

"Since we're both awake," he went on, "perhaps we could talk about this new monster, this—"

"Chaos Eater," she offered. "What about it?"

"Two days ago, one of my squads turned their weapons on one another without cause or warning, for no apparent reason."

The air caught in Kate's throat—it wasn't shock, or horror, but a strange and unsettling relief. She'd seen the creature, of course, but it was one thing to have visions and another to have facts. She wasn't losing her mind—at least, not entirely.

"At the time, we couldn't explain it, but it sounds as if it fits your monster's pattern." Flynn drew a small tablet from the other pocket of his robe and began typing. Kate's eyes widened.

"You have a connection?" she asked.

Again, the grim smile. "Internal only. The interterritory towers were among the first things to fail. We don't know if the damage was a casualty in the midst of another attack or—"

"I'm willing to bet it was intentional," said Kate, taking up her coffee. "It's a siege break tactic."

Flynn's brows rose. "Excuse me?"

She took a long sip. "Well, which is scarier?" she said. "Being locked in a house, or being locked in a house with no way of calling for help? No way of telling someone you're in trouble? It fosters fear. Discord. All the things a growing monster needs."

Flynn stared at her. "That's quite a mercenary observation."

"What can I say," she said. "I am my father's daughter."

"I hope not."

Silence formed, sudden and uncomfortable. Flynn nodded at her wrist, still bruised from Soro's grip, the knuckles split from hitting August. "Let me see."

"It's fine."

He waited patiently until she finally held out her hand. He prodded the skin and flexed her wrist and then her fingers forward and back with a doctor's care. It hurt, but nothing was broken. Flynn rummaged beneath the counter and came up with a medkit, and she watched in silence as he wrapped and taped her hand.

"The question now," he said while he worked, "is how to hunt this monster. Perhaps you have some insight."

Kate hesitated, wondering if this was simply another kind of interrogation, but the words didn't feel leading or weighted. She drew back her hand, searching for something to say.

"Have you noticed anything?" prompted Flynn.

Kate considered this. She'd seen it—or rather, seen through its eyes—during the day, but the vision had been fractured, insubstantial.

"I believe it hunts at night."

"That makes sense," said Flynn thoughtfully.

"It does?"

"Night has a way of blurring lines in the psyche. It makes us feel free. Studies show people are generally less inhibited after dark, more open to influence and"— he stifled a cough, then continued—"primal behaviors. If this creature is preying on dark thoughts, turning them into actions, then yes, night would be its optimal time to hunt."

"And there's also a camouflage aspect," added Kate. "This thing is like a walking black hole. Easier to blend into the dark."

Flynn nodded.

Kate's stomach growled, loud enough for both to hear.

"You must be hungry," he said.

And she was. Ravenously. But her father's words rose unbidden.

Every weakness is a place to slide a knife.

She hadn't answered, but Henry was already at the fridge. "Omelet?"

"You cook?"

"Two of the five people who live here *do* enjoy food."

She perched on a stool, watching as he set a carton of eggs and a few vegetables on the counter.

"Where does it come from, the food?"

"The task force stores what it can," said Flynn. "We raid depots on both sides of the city. As for fresh food, we hold a grid of farms on the south side of the Waste, but resources aren't endless and scavengers are plenty."

Just one more reason this conflict couldn't last, thought Kate.

Flynn started dicing vegetables with quick, deft motions. He had been a *surgeon*, she remembered not simply a doctor. It was clear from the way he held the knife. Its edge winked at her, and she turned her attention to the cat instead, now asleep in a fruit bowl. Her fingers crept cautiously toward its tail.

"He belongs to August," said Flynn. "Though Ilsa is quite fond of him."

"And Soro?"

Flynn's brow furrowed. "Soro spends most of their time in the barracks." He paused over his work. "The Sunai are not like other monsters. They are like us. Every one of them is as unique as a human."

"And yet, August never struck me as a cat person."

Flynn chuckled softly. "Perhaps not," he said, cracking

eggs into a bowl, "but my son has always been the kind
of person willing to rescue something lost."

Vegetables sizzled in the pan, their scent twisting her
stomach.

"You really think of him that way. As your son."

"I do."

A shadow crossed Kate's mind. The memory of her
own father in his office, and the words he used like
weapons: *I never wanted a daughter.*

Flynn split the omelet onto two plates and slid hers
forward. Kate dug in, ravenous, but Flynn didn't seem
interested in his own portion. "August believes you
want to help."

"I wouldn't have come back if I didn't."

"If that's true, then you'll tell me what you know—"

"I already have," she said between bites.

"—about Sloan," he finished.

She stilled. "What?"

"If anyone can pick apart that monster's logic, figure
out what he *wants* . . ."

Kate set down her fork as revulsion rose in her throat.
She didn't want to get inside Sloan's head, didn't want to
resurrect the specter of her father.

But Henry Flynn was right—if anyone could predict
that monster's motions, it would be her.

She swallowed hard. "If I had to guess," she said,

picking up her fork again, "he wants what all monsters want."

"And what's that?"

"More," said Kate. "More violence. More death." She pictured the crimson light of the Malchai's eyes dancing with pleasure, with menace. "Sloan is like the cat that plays with the mouse before eating it, just because it can. Only this time, the mouse is Verity."

She could feel Flynn's gaze on her, but she focused on the fork in his hand, the way he nudged the omelet on his plate.

Kate had grown up reading people, the smallest tells in her father's mouth, her mother's eyes. She thought of the photos she'd seen of Henry Flynn—the last six months had clearly taken a toll. There was a gauntness to his face, a gray undertone to his pallor, and then there was the shallow way he breathed, as if trying to stave off a coughing fit.

"How long have you been sick?" she asked.

Flynn stilled. He could lie to her, if he wanted to— they both knew that—but in the end he didn't.

"It's hard to know. Our medical facilities have never been as strong as those north of the Seam."

"Have you told—"

"Some things don't need to be *said* to be *known*." His voice stayed steady, calm. "It won't change anything.

I used to think that if we took back the city in time, perhaps . . . but life doesn't always honor plans . . ." His attention drifted to the windows, where dawn was starting to sweep across the city. "A man is not a cause, and a cause is not a man. Control is already being shifted to the Council. With any luck, I'll make—"

He stopped as footsteps sounded in the hall. A moment later Emily Flynn strode into the kitchen dressed in full fatigues. She was as tall as her husband, with short black hair and smooth dark skin, and if she thought it odd that Kate Harker was having breakfast at their kitchen counter, she didn't say so.

"Something smells wonderful."

"Emily," said Henry, a new sweetness infusing his voice.

"I've got three hours before my next shift. Are those eggs for me?"

Flynn held out his fork and Emily swept it from his fingers. He wrapped an arm loosely around her as she ate, and Kate's chest tightened. There was such a simple ease to the gesture, a comfort to the way they moved in and out of each other's space. Even when her parents had been together, it had never been like this.

"Don't let me interrupt," said Emily.

"You're not," said Flynn, kissing her shoulder. "Katherine and I—"

"Kate," she corrected curtly.

"*Kate* and I were just finishing up."

Emily gave a brisk nod, her gaze leveled straight at Kate, clearly the kind of woman used to making eye contact. She was glad she'd opted for the bangs.

"August has work to do, so you'll be confined to the apartment."

Kate's muscles twitched. "Is that necessary?"

"Not at all," she said cheerfully. "If you'd prefer a cell downstairs—"

"Em," said Flynn. "Kate is proving a very cooperative guest . . ."

"Ilsa can monitor remotely and I've already arranged for a soldier to be on comms in case."

But Kate wasn't listening. She couldn't stay here, couldn't lose another day, not with the Chaos Eater out there, stealing more of her mind with every cycle of the sun.

"I want to train with the FTF."

The lie came out so easily without August there to stop it. She had no intention of becoming Flynn's latest foot soldier, but she needed her weapons back, needed a way out of the Compound.

Emily shook her head. "That's not a good idea."

"Why not?" challenged Kate.

The woman gave her a long, hard look. "Miss Harker,

the FTF don't harbor kind feelings toward your family. Word is already spreading that you're here inside the Compound. Some will see your presence as an insult. Others might take it as a challenge. It would be better if you stayed—"

"I can hold my own."

"That's not actually what I'm worried about. We try to avoid discord—"

"You mean violence—"

"I mean discord," said Emily, "in *all* its forms."

"With all due respect," said Kate, "keeping me out of reach will only make it worse. You want to prevent discord? Treat me like I belong, not like I don't."

Emily looked to her husband. "She's persuasive, isn't she?"

"Is that a yes?" pressed Kate, trying to keep the urgency out of her voice.

Emily took the coffee cup from Flynn's hand and considered the contents. "You will be placed under the watch of another cadet. If you disobey orders, or cause any trouble, or if I simply change my mind, you will be returned to your confinement."

Kate's spirits wavered at the mention of another cadet, but it was a minor hurdle compared to being kept at the top of a tower. "Sounds like a plan," she said, carrying her plate to the sink.

August came charging into the kitchen, holding the doorknob she'd removed. His black hair was still wet, and his shirt was open, revealing a lean body newly corded with muscle.

"Was this necessary?"

"Sorry." She shrugged. "I've never been a fan of locks."

August actually *scowled*—or what passed for scowling with him, a deep crease between his eyebrows.

She turned her attention back to Emily. "I'll need a uniform."

August straightened in surprise. "Why?"

Kate cracked a smile, but she let Flynn say the words: "Miss Harker has offered to join the Force."

11

"This is a bad idea," called August.

He was down on one knee, trying to reattach the doorknob to his bedroom door while Kate finished dressing on the other side.

"So you've said," she called back. "Three times."

"It bears repeating."

She rapped her knuckles on the wood—the signal that he could enter. August straightened and nudged the door open. Kate stood there, dressed in FTF gear, her eyes shielded by that pale sweep of hair, the rest of it pulled back into a ponytail, revealing the scar that traced the left line of her face, temple to jaw.

She gestured down at the fatigues. "How do I look?"

The uniform suited her more than it had ever suited him. But it wasn't just the clothes, it was the way she wore them. Commanding. Kate Harker had always had a kind of presence, and seeing her like this, it made him think of that game she played, imagining a different version of her life, herself. For a second he glimpsed the version where she'd stayed.

"August?" she prompted.

He couldn't lie. He didn't need to. "You look like you belong."

Kate flicked him a smile and sank onto his bed to lace up her boots.

"But why would you even want to join the FTF?"

"Oh, I don't," said Kate briskly, "but if I stay in this apartment, I'm going to lose my mind, and that wouldn't be much good to *anyone* now, would it?"

"This is a—"

"So help me God if you say *bad idea*."

"You're Callum Harker's daughter."

She gasped. "Really?"

"Half the FTF would probably like to see you hanged."

She looked up. "Only half?"

He stepped closer, lowering his voice. He wasn't worried about Henry or Em, but Ilsa might be in her room. "What about your . . . bond with the Chaos Eater?"

Kate's attention snapped toward the door, even as her tone went flat. "What about it?"

"Does Henry know?"

"*I* didn't tell him," she said coolly. "Did *you*?"

He'd thought about it. August had never been good

at keeping secrets. But if Henry found out—if *Soro* found out—there would be no protecting her.

Should he be protecting her?

Yes, she was a criminal, but this—this hadn't been a crime; she hadn't brought it on herself. She was the victim, one who'd managed to get away, if not entirely. She was their best connection—their only connection—to the monster, if it was really in their midst.

He wouldn't—*couldn't*—lie for her.

But he wouldn't expose her either.

"Not yet."

He swept the violin onto his shoulder and led Kate to the elevator.

"You're not going to shadow me all day, are you?" she asked. "I'm already persona non grata, and I doubt I'll earn any points by traveling with a bodyguard, especially a Sunai."

"No."

"Great, so just point me in the right direction. I promise not to run off or get in any fights—"

"Kate—"

"Okay, I promise not to *start* any fights—"

"I've enlisted someone else."

The elevator came and they stepped inside, the world collapsing to the space of a five-foot square.

As the metal doors slid shut, he found Kate staring at him—or at least, at his warped reflection—studying him as if she could see the blood he'd scrubbed from his skin. "What?"

"I'm just trying to figure out what happened to you."

He tensed. "Not this again."

"What am I missing? Where did you go?"

He closed his eyes and saw two versions of himself, the first surrounded by bodies, blood and shadow climbing his wrists, the second sitting on the roof, hoping to see stars; and as he watched, that second self began dissolving, like a dream, a memory unraveling moment by moment, slipping through his grip.

"I'm right here."

"No, you're not. I don't know who *this* is, but the August I knew—"

"Doesn't exist anymore."

She twisted toward him. *"Bullshit,"* she snapped.

"Stop."

But she didn't. Even pitched low, her voice had a way of filling the narrow space. "What happened to him? Tell me. What happened to the August who wanted to feel human? The one would rather burn alive than let himself go dark?"

He kept his own gaze forward. "I'm willing to walk in darkness if it keeps humans in the light."

Kate snorted. "Okay, Leo. How many times did you practice that line? How many times did you stand in front of the mirror and recite it, waiting for it to sink in and—"

He spun on her.

"*Enough.*"

Kate flinched but didn't back down. "This new you—"

"—is none of your business," he snapped. "You don't get to stand here and judge me, Kate. You left. You ran away, and I stayed and fought for this city, for these people. I'm sorry you don't like the new me, but I did what I had to. I *became* what this world needed me to be." By the time he finished, he was breathless.

Kate stared, her expression carved in ice. And then she came close, close enough for him to see the glint of silver through her bangs. "You're lying."

"I *can't* lie."

"You're wrong," said Kate, turning her back on him. "There's one kind of lie even *you* can tell. Do you know what it is?" She met his gaze in the steel doors. "The kind you tell yourself."

August clenched his teeth.

Don't listen to her, warned Leo. *She doesn't understand. She can't.*

The elevator came to a stop. The doors opened, and

Kate strode out, and nearly collided with Colin.

He went white at the sight of her, then looked to August with all the desperation of a drowning man. "You've got to be kidding me."

Kate raised a brow. "Am I supposed to know you?"

"Kate," said August, "this is Colin Stevenson."

Colin managed a nervous smile that did nothing to hide his discomfort. "We both went to Colton."

"Sorry," she said blandly. "It was a brief and tumultuous enrollment."

Colin shifted from foot to foot. "It's cool, I don't expect you to remember me. I tried to stay off your radar."

"Probably smart."

August cleared his throat. "You'll be joining Colin's squad for the day." She shot him a mischievous look that said *will I?* And August narrowed his eyes. *Yes.*

"Yeah, I'll be, uh, showing you the ropes."

Kate kept her gaze on August as she flashed a cool smile. "Lead on."

He fell in step behind them as Colin gave Kate the tour. Listened to her punctuate the speech with *mm-hmm*s and *I see*s, even though she clearly wasn't listening.

"The training rooms are all located on the first and

second floors and down that way's the cafeteria, which is like the cafeteria at Colton except for the fact the food is awful. . . ."

As they moved through the halls, August felt the familiar shift of eyes, the weight of attention, but for once it wasn't all on him. The soldiers were looking at Kate, murmuring under their breath, and he could hear, too clearly, the tension in their voices, the anger in their words.

He glanced up and realized Colin was looking at him expectantly.

"What?"

"Did I miss anything?"

"Don't worry," cut in Kate. "I'm a quick learner."

Colin's watch gave a sudden chirp. "Five minutes: we better get to the training hall. Any questions?"

Kate brightened. "Where do they keep the weapons?"

Colin laughed nervously, as if he couldn't tell whether or not she was serious. August knew she was.

"All tech is stored on Sublevel 1—" started Colin.

"But to take any of the weapons *out*," added August, "you have to be approved. Which you won't be."

Kate shrugged. "Good to know," she said, shoving Colin toward the training hall.

"Come on. We don't want to be late."

August caught Kate's shoulder and leaned in, his voice

low, close: "There are security cameras everywhere," he said, "so keep your head down."

She shot him a dry smile. "Thanks for the tip," she said.

And then she was gone.

III

Six months in Prosperity, and Kate had *almost* forgotten what it felt like to be hated.

To be always on display—that strange imbalance of being recognized, judged by your face, your name.

Six months of being no one, and now, as Colin led her into the training hall—putting space between them with every stride—she felt the news travel like a current, felt the heads turn. They looked at her and saw not a girl but a symbol, an idea, a stand-in for all their resentment and blame. Her skin prickled under the scrutiny, and she forced herself to focus on the room itself instead of the discomfort or the dark voice in her head.

Hundreds were packed into what looked like it might once have been a ballroom. A narrow running track edged the wall, the space within broken into training stations. The youngest soldiers looked twelve or thirteen. The oldest were white haired. They were a mix of North and South City—they wore their differences on their faces (the difference between shock and anger, curiosity and fear, caution and contempt), but in every single pair of eyes, in every twitch of lip and brow, a single commonality: distrust.

I don't trust you either, thought Kate.

Six months—and it came back, like riding a bike. Her spine straightened. Her chin went up. It had always been an act of sorts, a part, but it was one she knew how to play.

"You'll be in Team Twenty-Four with me," said Colin, leading her toward a group of fifteen or so cadets standing just inside the track.

"Thank you so much for joining us, Mr. Stevenson." The instructor was a stocky woman with a square jaw and cold blue eyes that landed on Kate for a long moment before returning to the eight crates sitting on the floor.

"This," said the woman holding up a modified rifle, "is an AL-9. Who can tell me why our Night Squads carry them?"

"They can be modified to hold shatter shells."

The words were out before Kate realized she'd spoken. Again, those blue eyes found her, as did every other pair. Kate cursed herself—why couldn't she keep her mouth shut?

"Continue, Miss . . ."

The instructor was obviously going to make her say it.

"Harker," offered Kate. And then, pressing ahead, "Shatter shells are designed to break apart on contact. They'd have to be dipped in silver, iron, or some other pure metal to do any real damage, but within say, fifty yards, they might have enough force to penetrate a Malchai's bone plate. A spike driven up behind the shield would be a better bet, but that method does require close contact."

The rest of the training hall kept buzzing with noise, but Team Twenty-Four was a pocket of silence. The instructor didn't need to raise her voice to break it.

"Indeed," she said curtly. "Each crate contains the parts for an AL-9. You'll spend the next hour assembling and disassembling them. Pair off."

A guy tapped Colin's sleeve, and he shot Kate a questioning look, visibly relieved when she shooed him away.

She didn't bother waiting for a partner—she went to the nearest case and knelt over it, sliding back the clasps—so she was surprised when a shadow suddenly loomed overhead, and a second later another girl knelt across from her. She looked a year older than Kate, maybe two, with curly black hair and a glare that said South City.

"Mony," she said, by way of introduction.

"Kate."

"I know."

"I figured." She nodded at the crate. "You first."

The girl raised a brow. "Eyes open or closed?"

"Suit yourself," said Kate, "but when you use it out there, I'd suggest keeping your eyes open." That earned her the barest smile.

She watched as the girl assembled the weapon with swift, sure movements, humming under her breath.

Monsters, monsters, big and small . . .

"Have you ever actually fired one of these?" asked Kate.

Mony's hands kept moving. "Only active squads are armed. Team Twenty-Four is still in training."

"So we don't actually fight?"

Kate chose *we* on purpose, one of those simple psychological cues that turned *you* vs. *me* into *us* vs. *them.*

Mony checked the barrel. "Occasionally we get tapped for day patrols, or guard shift, but most of our work is onsite until we're cleared for active duty."

"I'm going out for the Night Squad," said Colin, one row over.

Mony rolled her eyes at him. "As what? A stepstool?"

Colin colored, and made an effort to sit up straighter, as if his height deficiency was just a matter of posture.

"So you never go out?" asked Kate.

"We're lucky to be here." Mony set the assembled weapon on the crate. "Your turn."

Kate reached for the gun, but the moment it was in her hands, the thing in her head began to stir. It was like a cold, or a pulled muscle, something you *almost* forgot about until you coughed, or moved the wrong way, and then it flared. For just a few minutes, she'd forgotten, and now her pulse sounded loud and steady in her ears, muting the world beyond, and she felt suddenly calm—the kind of calm that comes with realizing you're in a dream, knowing nothing can hurt you.

"Hey," said Mony, the word muffled, distant, but there. "You good?"

Kate blinked. She looked down at the gun.

It's empty, she told her hands. *Put it down.*

"Yeah," she said slowly, setting the weapon back on the crate. "Guns just aren't my thing."

Mony snatched the weapon back and started breaking it down.

"Good luck with that."

The instructor blew a whistle, and Team Twenty-Four let out a collective sigh, slumping onto the mats. They'd moved from firearms to formations, cardio to crunches.

"I hate sit-ups," moaned Colin, clutching his stomach.

"I don't see what strong abs have to do with hunting monsters . . ."

But Kate felt better than she had in days. Her muscles burned in a pleasant way from the simple physical exertion, and it left her feeling in control of her body, her mind. She got to her feet, ready for the next exercise, but the team was moving toward the doors.

"Lunch break," explained Mony.

They took a left and hit a broad corridor teeming with people in the dark grays and greens of the FTF. She expected the crowd to part around her, the way it had back at Colton, but the difference between Colton and the Compound was that, for every five people who swung wide, one went out of their way to knock into her.

"Watch it," warned someone after they checked her in the side.

Kate's pulse rose. Her fingers curled into a fist.

But Colin was the worst, not because he went out of his way to be cruel—just the opposite, he tried to *comfort* her.

"When I first got here," he said, "half the cadets wouldn't even talk to me because I was from North City, and my dad isn't even . . ."

Mony shot him a look—bless her—and Colin trailed off as they reached the cafeteria.

The place was packed.

With this many people, it should have been easy to disappear by degrees, lose a step here and there, fall to the back of the pack and then just slip away. But every time Colin's attention drifted, Mony was there to pick up the slack.

"This is nothing," she said as they wove through the crowd.

"Yeah," said Colin. "There are nearly ten million people under the FTF's protection just in South City, and fifty thousand of them are active soldiers—"

"Oh God," muttered Mony, "he's like a wind-up toy."

Colin didn't seem to care. "Everyone has to be willing to serve, but there are different ways to do that. There's recon, supply, management, but everyone goes through training, first . . ."

Kate's attention slid toward the polished steel of the utensils—she took a sandwich instead. "How many people live here?" she asked.

Mony groaned. "Don't encourage him."

"Only about fifteen hundred people live in the Compound. The rest of the soldiers are spread out across two square blocks. It's high-density living, but it allows them to keep the power on."

Kate frowned. "Where does it come from?"

Colin opened his mouth to answer, but Mony cut him off.

"Solar generators," she said. "Now dear God, before I die of boredom, let me eat."

The whole team moved toward a table with the automatic flow of routine, and Kate followed. It was clear she was expected to sit with them—and equally clear they didn't want her there. Bodies twisted away. Conversations lowered to a buzz in her good ear. Even Colin and Mony were growing tense under the scrutiny.

She was picking at her food, appetite fading, when Colin lowered his voice and leaned toward her.

"Can I ask you something?" he said, and Kate didn't answer, because it was obvious he was going to ask either way. "Where have you *been?*" Mony raised a brow. "Sorry, I know it's none of my business, it's just—there's kind of a pool going. I don't normally bet, but there's a candy bar in the pot and, like, half the squads thought you were dead but I've got five that you were hiding in the Waste and—"

"Prosperity."

His eyes widened. "Seriously? Why would you come *back?*"

"Oh, you know," she said, "monsters, mayhem, revenge."

She got to her feet. "Look," she said, "playing soldier seems fun, but I have work to do."

Colin's head shot up. "Where are you going?"

"The bathroom," she said, and then, when Colin made a move to rise. "I think I can find my way."

His attention twitched between his food and her, clearly torn.

But it was Mony who spoke up. "Fifteen minutes," she said, tapping her watch. "If you're not back in the training hall, the whole team pays for it."

Kate nodded. "I'll be there."

❙❙❙❙

Kate headed for Sublevel 1.

Nobody stopped her, not when she passed the bathrooms or the bank of elevators, not when she slipped into the stairwell and started down.

The benefits of walking with purpose, she thought. People didn't just assume you knew where you were going—they assumed you were supposed to be going there.

At least until she pushed open the door and stepped into the weapons cache. A man sat at a desk, the wide corridor beyond him lined with armored vests and helmets. She glimpsed weapons through several open doors.

He was skimming something on his tablet, but his head snapped up when she walked in. His eyes instantly narrowed.

Kate forced a lightness into her voice. "Is this the lost and found?"

"Does this *look* like a lost and found?"

"Hey, I'm just following orders. My captain lost some equipment and it's my job to find it."

"What *kind* of equipment?"

"A pair of spikes. Iron. About the length of my forearm."

"That's not something we issue."

Your loss, thought Kate, but she only shrugged. "She's from North City. Must have been a relic."

"Squad?"

"Twenty-Four."

"Name?"

"The instructor's?"

"Yours."

"Mony," said Kate, instantly regretting it. He was clearly waiting for a last name, but she hadn't learned it. "Look, never mind, I'm sure the spikes will turn up—"

Something lit up on the man's screen, and Kate didn't know if it was a red flag or an ordinary message, but his expression went stony and her pulse rose. She took a step back.

"Stay put," he said, two words that made Kate want to do the opposite. Her gaze flicked from the weapons on the walls to the one holstered at the man's hip, but the elevator doors were already opening behind her. And Ilsa stepped out.

She was barefoot in a sundress, her hair a cloud of wild red curls and her shoulders speckled with stars, but it was the brutal red scar across her throat that Kate saw first.

The man at the desk stood and bowed his head, a gesture halfway between deference and fear, but Kate's spirits lifted at the sight of the Sunai.

The first—and only—time they'd met, Kate had woken in a strange motel to find the Sunai's face inches from her own. She'd heard the stories of Ilsa Flynn. The ones that painted the first Sunai as the worst of the monsters, a walking massacre who'd once shed her human form and reduced two hundred lives and a downtown block to charred remains. But the Ilsa in that hotel—the one here now—was someone else. Someone gentle, kind.

She gave Kate a look, lightly scolding, and even without a voice, Kate could imagine her saying, *You shouldn't be down here and you know it.*

Ilsa flicked her fingers toward the soldier, as if shaking off water, took Kate's hand, and drew her back into the elevator.

"It was worth a shot," murmured Kate as the doors closed, but Ilsa's expression was already twisting, a shadow crossing the delicate planes of her face. The air itself seemed to change, laced with a sudden new chill, as if Ilsa's mood were a tangible thing.

"What is it?"

Ilsa reached up, thin fingers hovering over Kate's eyes—no, just the one. Her stomach dropped. Ilsa *knew*—about the shard, the sickness. A dozen different thoughts rose to Kate's mind, but it was a question that crossed her lips.

"What happened to August?"

Ilsa's hands fell away.

She shook her head, but Kate had the feeling that Ilsa wasn't saying *no*, so much as expressing some great sadnesss.

The elevator stopped on the training floor, and the doors slid open. As Kate stepped out, Ilsa brightened, holding up one hand. The other vanished into the deep pockets of her sundress, and a second later she produced Kate's tablet. The one Soro had taken.

Ilsa held the device up, as if in answer, before pushing it into Kate's hands. Kate stared down at the tablet, then slipped it into her vest pocket as her watch chimed a warning. She was out of time.

At one end of the corridor stood an exit, unguarded.

At the other, the door to the training hall.

Kate swore under her breath and took off running.

She was late.

Team Twenty-Four was already gathered, two of the

older soldiers squaring off, one with a red kerchief knotted at his throat.

"Your objective," the instructor was saying, "is to *subdue* the Fang as quickly as possible." The woman saw
Kate jogging up and a malicious little glee sparked on
her face.

"Ten laps."

Kate opened her mouth to say something, but the rest
of the team was already heading for the track. Nobody
argued or groaned, but she knew the moment they
started running that whatever traction she'd earned
that morning was officially gone. Boots appeared out of
nowhere, clipping her ankles or heels.

Kate stumbled once or twice, but didn't fall, and soon
the team gave up trying to trip her and focused on leaving her behind.

"You came back."

It was Mony, her stride easy, as if she could do this
all day.

"I'm starting to regret it," said Kate.

As they circled the hall, Kate watched a dozen other
teams practice the same maneuvers, watched as a pair
toward the center scuffled, and went down in a tangle
of limbs that ended with the "Fang" pinned, one arm
behind his back. The soldier started to let him up when
the "Fang" threw an elbow. It was a dirty move—but

the message was clear. The Fangs wouldn't fight fair.

"What happens if you can't subdue them?"

"We don't have a choice. It's a crime to kill another person."

"Sure, but has it ever happened?"

"Tanner," said Colin, a stride or two behind them.

"Alex Tanner," said Mony, picking up speed. Colin yelped, but Kate lengthened her stride to keep up.

"Go on."

"Alex was a North City guy in the first batch of converts. Never should have had a gun. The kind of man just looking for an excuse to shoot something, you know? Which is fine if all you've got to shoot are monsters."

Their shoes found a steady rhythm.

"But his first time out, he empties his weapon into a group of Fangs. Didn't even try to bring them in."

"What happened?"

"His squad tried to cover for him," called Colin, breathless.

"Idiots," muttered Mony. "Like that kind of thing just washes off. Sunai can *smell* it. So, the Council decided to make an example. They gathered all the squads here in the hall, and brought Tanner out, and made us watch while that one"—at this, she flicked her head toward the doors and Kate twisted to see Soro, straight-backed and chin high, surveying the hall—"reaped him. An object lesson in what happens to sinners."

Kate's chest tightened. "Did it work?"

"I'm telling you the story, aren't I? Every now and then, someone messes up. Tensions get high, mistakes are made. They don't make an example of those. When it happens, the soldier just disappears. There's a saying in the ranks: Soro comes for the bad, but Ilsa comes for the sorry."

They ran a full lap before Kate spoke again.

"What about August?"

Colin panted. "What about him?"

"Well, if Soro reaps the bad and Ilsa reaps the sorry, who does August reap?"

Mony snorted. "Everyone else."

||||

August made his way to the stage.

The crowd parted, staggering out of his way as if he were a live coal.

I'm willing to walk in darkness . . .

He drew the violin from its case, kept his focus on the bow and the strings instead of the people beyond.

I'm willing . . .

He began to play.

The song spiraled out, but for once, his limbs didn't loosen, his mind didn't clear. August wanted to lose himself in the music, to relish these rare moments of peace, but Kate's words were lodged like a splinter in his skull.

What happened to the August I knew?

What happened?

Things change.

I've changed.

He *had* changed.

It was just—his brother wanted him to be like his violin, the one made of steel, but August felt like the first one, the one left shattered on the bathroom floor in Kate's house beyond the Waste. An instrument of music reduced to slivers and sharp fragments.

There was Leo, telling him to be the thing the monsters feared, and Soro, who made him feel selfish for wanting to want to be human, and Ilsa, who made him feel like a monster for not wanting it enough, and Henry who seemed to think he could be everything to everyone, and Kate, who wanted him to be someone he couldn't be anymore.

You're lying.

His fingers tightened on the bow.

Focus, brother, chided Leo.

You even sound like him.

His song quickened.

The August I knew—

The bow slipped, and the note came out too sharp. He stopped playing, let the violin fall back to his side. He hadn't finished the song, but it was enough. The crowd stared up at him, wide-eyed, complacent, souls shining on their skin.

A sea of white, and in the center, a single bloom of red. A man, squat and unassuming, with a woman at his side, the two pressed together despite the space around them. Her soul shone white, but his burned red, and as August approached, he heard the man's confession.

". . . but fear makes us do stupid things, doesn't it? He could have been after me. I didn't know . . ." His head was up, his eyes on August, but his gaze went straight through him. "I wasn't a bad person, you know. It's just a bad world. I was young, and I didn't know any better."

Red light rose off the man's skin like steam.

"Can you blame me? Can you?"

August didn't blame him—it *was* a bad world—but that didn't change anything. He pressed his palm to the man's skin, and the confession faltered, the words trailing off as the man's life rolled through him.

The corpse crumpled to the floor, and August turned away as souls sank beneath skin, and the symphony hall twitched back into life around him.

He heard the woman sob, but didn't turn back. Harris and Ani tried to calm her as he forced himself to keep walking.

Your job is done here.

He was nearly to the door when the gun went off.

August spun back as plaster rained from the ceiling, and people cowered, shielding their heads. The woman had Harris's pistol in both hands, knuckles white as she leveled it at August. Ani and Jackson were already reaching for their tasers as he started down the aisle, hands raised. "Put it down."

"Crazy bitch," growled Harris.

"Drop the gun," demanded Ani.

But the woman had eyes only for August. "He didn't deserve to die."

He took another step toward her. "I'm sorry."

"You didn't know him," she sobbed. "You didn't know him at all."

"I know his soul was stained." Another step, past Ani and Jackson. "He made his fate."

"He made a *mistake*," she spat. "You can stand there, all righteous, but you don't understand. You *can't* understand. You're not even human."

The blow landed, not sharp, but dull and aching and heavy.

August was level with Harris now.

"He chose—"

"He *changed*. People *change*." Tears streamed down her face. "Why doesn't it *matter*?"

Maybe it should, thought August, just before she shot him.

The hall echoed with the deafening cracks as she emptied the gun into August's chest. It hurt, the way everything hurt, but only for an instant. She continued squeezing the trigger long after the magazine was empty and all that left was the impotent *click click click*.

He let her do it, because it didn't change anything. Her husband was still gone and August was still standing, and when the chamber was empty, the last of the strength went out of her limbs and she sank to the floor beside his body, the gun falling from her fingers. August knelt in front of her, one hand resting on the empty weapon, the gun smoke still rising off his skin.

"You're very lucky I'm *not* human."

He jerked his head, and Ani and Jackson swept behind the woman, hauling her to her feet.

╫╫╫
I

The tower lobby hummed with energy.

Corsai pooled in the corners, whispering to themselves, while the Malchai shifted and stirred, restless at being gathered together in one place.

Sloan stood on the lowest landing and looked down at the sea of red eyes, reminding himself that this teeming mass, these filthy, feral things were nothing more than shades, foot soldiers, subjects.

And he, their king.

"There is an intruder in our midst," he said. "A monster has seen fit to come into our city, and feast upon our food. It is a thing of darkness," continued Sloan. "But we are *all* things of darkness. The Corsai claim they cannot catch it"—here the shadows chittered—"but we are not all Corsai."

A low growl, a snarl of agreement.

"Sloan is right." This came from Alice.

She was perched on the rail of a balcony above. It looked as though she were wearing dark gloves—in truth, she simply hadn't washed her hands after her latest feast. The sight repulsed him, but the other monsters stared at her in rapture, as she knew they would.

"We are *Malchai*," she said. "There is nothing we cannot hunt, no one we cannot kill." She flashed a smile at Sloan, all teeth. "What would you have us do, Father?"

He gripped the railing, but did not rise to that last bait. Instead, he looked down at the Malchai.

"The intruder is drawn to live bait. Raid the fridges, take your prey into the streets. The first monster who kills this pest and brings me its corpse will find a place with Alice at my side."

"That is, of course," Alice added, "if *I* don't kill it first."

Sloan spread his hands, the picture of munificence. "Let the hunt begin."

||||| ||

The Compound changed after dark.

Kate didn't *see* the sun go down, but she could feel the shift all the same, the nervous energy coalescing, the tension drawing tight around her. The stream of soldiers thinned as some retreated to off-site barracks and others went on watch or on missions, and the number of guards on each door multiplied.

The cafeteria was still full, but she sat at Twenty-Four's table alone. Whatever invisible thread had bound the teams together during the day, it dissolved by dinner, freeing the soldiers to choose their own company. New divisions were drawn, between North and South, young and old, her exclusion yet another reminder that she didn't belong.

A huddle of twentysomethings played cards a few rows over, and Mony was perched on a tabletop, chatting with friends, while Colin sat against a wall, telling a story. He seemed engrossed, but every time Kate so much as glanced at the door, his face gave a nervous twitch, so she decided to wait him out. Make a game of it. And at some point, outlasting Colin became outlasting every other nervous glance or whispered word, each one designed to chip away at her.

She drew the tablet from her pocket and booted it, surprised to discover *someone* had connected the device to the network.

Her fingers danced over the screen as she booted the server, and typed in the address for the Wardens' chat room.

Page not found.

She tried again.

Page not found.

Frustration welled inside her and she clicked over to the message drive and started a new email. She typed in Riley's address, and wrote a single word—*alive*—before hitting SEND.

It went nowhere.

The message hung suspended, a grayed-out line in a sea of black text. Flynn had been telling the truth about the internal server. There was nothing here but memos, notices transmitted to everyone in the system.

Kate tapped through the various drive folders and found mission logs, registers of targets, captures, casualties.

The files were ordered by month, and Kate was skimming the most recent one when the tablet chimed, and a new message popped up.

The subject line was AUGUST.

The sender was ILSA FLYNN.

There was no note, only a set of attachments. Kate knew exactly what they were. She'd seen her fair share of security footage in Prosperity, and a lifetime ago she'd sat in her room at Harker Hall and scoured her father's database, watching every clip she could find of the monsters that lurked in her city.

Callum had a wealth of footage on Leo, but when but when it came to August Flynn, there'd been nothing.

Now she stared down at the footage Ilsa had sent her.

One was shot from what looked like a symphony hall. Another from a cam on top of the Seam. A third, somewhere in the street. Six months' worth of files, every one of them titled BROTHER.

What happened to August? she'd asked his sister.

And Ilsa had sent her an answer.

Kate braced herself and hit PLAY.

August's hand kept drifting to the six small holes in the front of his shirt.

"I should change," he said as they walked down the hall.

"Nah," said Harris, cuffing him around the shoulders. August tensed—he'd never gotten used to being touched. "Show them you're a man of steel."

Ani shook her head. "I can't believe you let her go."

"She was upset," said August.

"She shot you six times!" said Harris.

"With *your* gun," snapped Jackson.

"It wasn't a crime," said August.

Only because you can't be killed, said Leo.

Or because I don't count.

"Way to let your guard down, Harris," snorted Ani.

"I didn't expect a middle-aged lady to snatch a sidearm."

"Sexist."

Jackson raked a hand through his short hair. "I'm starving."

"Me too," chimed Ani. "Canteen?"

"Think they'll have beef?" said Harris. "I dream of beef."

"Keep dreaming," said Ani.

Jackson shoved open the cafeteria doors and August was met by the din of metal and plastic, scraping chairs and rattling trays and a hundred layered voices. Between the noise, and the stuffy air, he didn't understand why so many soldiers ate together instead of escaping to their rooms. Rez had been the one to explain it to him.

"Sometimes it's not about the food," she'd said. "It's about finding normal."

Harris was holding the door. "You coming?"

This was a well-worn path—Harris always offered, and August usually said no, but the voices in his head were too loud tonight, so he headed into the crush of bodies and noise, hoping to smother them.

And saw Kate.

She was sitting alone near the edge of the room, head bowed over a tablet, and August didn't know if it was déjà vu from their first day at Colton, or that she was the only spot of stillness at the center of a storm, or that she was Kate Harker, and everywhere she went, she brought her own gravity with her.

Whatever the reason, he started toward her.

Harris shot him a questioning look, and Ani's gaze followed, but it was Jackson who spoke. "She shouldn't be here."

"Now, now," started Ani. "The FTF takes in—"

"No," snapped Jackson. "I don't care if she's got intel—she's still a *Harker*."

"She saved my life," said August, his voice low. His team went silent. Here it was, the chill, the spot of cold, right here. The Sunai were supposed to be invulnerable, but they weren't. Unkillable, but they weren't. The fact she'd saved his life meant he'd *needed* saving.

Jackson crossed his arms. "She's not one of us."

"Neither am I," said August simply.

He heard them stomp off toward the food line as he made his way to Kate's table. She had looked up from her screen at some point and was watching him through her veil of blond hair.

"Standing up for my honor?"

August frowned. "You heard?"

She shook her head. "Educated guess."

"What did you do with Colin?"

"Oh, I set him free." She nodded at the far corner. "Sheep and wolves have never been a good fit." Her gaze flitted over the holes in his shirt. "Bad day?"

"It could have gone worse." He sank onto the bench opposite. "How was yours?"

"I'm holding my own," she said. "Not big in the friend department yet, but the enemies are keeping their distance."

"Give it time, and they'll—"

"Stop," she cut him off. "This isn't one of those stories."

Silence fell between them, and August could hear the whispers under the din, the rise and fall of low voices, still all too clear to him.

"Anything good?" Kate was staring at him intently. "I only have one decent ear, and you have two stellar ones.

The least you can do is share."

His gaze fell to the tablet on the table, a vid file open on the screen. "What were you watching?"

Kate slid the tablet toward him. "You tell me."

August looked down and saw the line of a steel bow streaked with blood. His stomach twisted. It was him. Walking back to the Compound the night he'd slaughtered Alice's Malchai. The black tally marks stood out against his skin—at least, the patches of skin not covered in gore.

He didn't recognize the thing on that screen, and he *did*, and he didn't know which was worse. He could feel Kate's eyes on him. He'd never understood how some people had such heavy gazes.

"August—"

"Don't," he warned.

"This isn't you."

"It is now. Why is it so hard to understand, Kate? I'm doing what I *have* to. I . . ."

You owe her nothing, warned his brother. In truth, part of him *wanted* to talk to Kate, to exorcise the voices in his head, make sense of the confusion, but he didn't have the strength to argue. Not about this. His sleeves were rolled up, and he focused on the thin black marks that etched his skin.

"I hated you," she said out of nowhere.

August's head snapped up. "What?"

"When we first met. I hated you. Do you know why?"

"Because I was a monster?"

"No. Because you wanted to be human. You had all this power, all this strength, and you wanted to throw it away—for what? A chance to be weak, helpless. I thought you were an idiot. But then I watched you burn alive for that dream. I watched you tear yourself apart to hold on to it, and I realized something. It's not about *what* you are, August, it's about *who*, and that stupid, dreaming boy—that wasn't a mistake, or a delusion, or a waste of energy. It was *you*."

She leaned forward. "So where did you go?"

August started to answer, but a tray came crashing down onto the table, loud enough that they both jumped. Harris swung a leg over the bench. Ani and Jackson, too. Kate sat very still, and for a long moment, no one spoke, the tension drawing out like a note, warbling and brittle. In the end, Jackson was the one who broke it.

"No beef," he muttered sullenly.

"Told you," said Ani, spearing a piece of wilted broccoli as Kate rose to leave.

"Where are you going?" asked August, but she was already walking away. He swore under his breath and followed, hundreds of eyes following them out. "Kate."

"Fine." She reached the hall and headed straight for the nearest exit. "You're doing what you have to, but so am I. I've been playing boot camp all day, but I'm not going to sit around any longer. You go on having your existential crisis, playing the big bad monster, but there's a real demon out there, in our city, and I'm going to find it, with or without you."

"I can't let you go out there—"

"Then *come with me*. Help me hunt this thing down. Or stay out of my way."

August caught her arm. "What will you do when you find it, Kate? How will you kill it? Are you sure you *can* kill it, with its claws in your head?"

He watched her try to say yes, saw the words catch in her throat. When she finally answered, her voice was brittle. "I don't know," she said, meeting his gaze, "but I'll be damned if I let it kill *me*. You might not want to fight your monsters, August. But I'm fighting mine."

He sighed, slung the violin over his shoulder, and took her hand.

"Come on."

||||| |||

Fresh air flooded Kate's lungs, crisp and cool, and for an instant she was dizzy from the sheer relief of being outside, even at night.

What had Henry Flynn said about the dark?

It makes us feel free.

A ribbon of UVR light surrounded the Compound, tracing a band of safety against the dark beyond. It stretched like a broad sheet, the width of a road. Like a moat. Thinner versions traced the bases of several nearby buildings—barracks, she guessed, extensions of the FTF's main compound—but the rest of the city was dark in a way she'd never seen it.

It was unnerving, that darkness.

Thicker than the lack of light.

The night beyond the moat twisted and writhed, the shadows whispering to her.

hello little harker

She could feel it rising in her, that longing for a fight. All her life she'd clung to it like the grip on a knife, but now she put all her strength into setting it down.

In the distance, the Seam traced a thin line, and beyond that, the looming shape of her father's tower. Sloan's tower.

She thought of him standing in the penthouse with his ember-red eyes, his sickly sweet voice, his tongue running over sharpened teeth.

I will kill him, she thought. *And I will take my time.*

Her focus narrowed, thoughts condensing to a clear and perfect point—a vision of herself drawing a silver blade over Sloan's skin, peeling him open one slice at a time, revealing those dark bones and—

August caught her sleeve.

Her boots were skimming the edge of the light strip.

"Here," said August, drawing a tablet from his pocket. He tapped the screen, and a second later the surface turned reflective. A mirror. "You said this is how you see into its head. So look."

Her eyes were instantly drawn to the glass, but she resisted.

"I'm not your private scrying board. If I see where it is, we go together."

August nodded. His grip tightened on his violin case, and she told herself this would work. It had to. She would hunt the monster down, and August would slay it, and the nightmare in her head would end, and she would kill Sloan, and then she would go back to Prosperity, and the Wardens, and Riley.

That wasn't another life, another Kate, it was this one, it was hers, it was now.

She blew out a breath and turned toward the mirror, bracing herself.

Where are you? she asked the glass, just before she fell in.

She is back
in her father's office
with the monster
in the black suit
and the shadows
whispering
weak
    weak
        weak
in the window
a pair of silver eyes
round as moons
—*Where are you?*—
and for the first time
the darkness
pushes back
the vision
shudders
holds
she forces
her way
to the glass
and when
she reaches
the window
the image
finally cracks
shatters
into—

—red eyes
everywhere
people
screaming
sobbing
begging
for mercy
the taste
of fear
like ash
in its mouth
it moves
away
there
     and gone
         and there again
now
a group
of soldiers
on an overpass
guns
and badges
catching
the light
a tangle
of voices
it reaches
out
from the dark
all hollow hunger

and cold delight
because
they do not see
it coming—

Kate wrenched back, as if struck.

The tablet tumbled from her fingers and August caught it as she doubled over, pain jabbing like a cold knife behind her eyes. For an instant she was still trapped between the mirrors, caught somewhere outside herself, the ground eroding beneath her feet.

She blinked away the blinding white of the light strip.

Three bright red drops of blood hit the ground, and then August's hand was on her arm, his voice lost in the noise as he lifted her face.

She saw the too-even planes of his brow and cheeks fold with worry, and she wanted to tell him she was okay, but she didn't feel okay, so instead she wiped her nose and said, "Sixteen."

August stared at her. "What?"

"I saw a patch. It had a number—"

Understanding lit his face and he reached for the comm.

"Squad Sixteen, are they on mission?"

"Affirmative."

He scanned the dark. "Where?"

By the time the controller read the address, August was already running, Kate close behind. He kept up a stream of orders on his comm, and sections of the grid came up around them. They were getting close—Kate's vision kept doubling, two places overlaid before her eyes. And then they rounded a corner, and she saw the overpass and the Seam, and the stretch of street, and it was empty.

"No," she gasped, first in frustration and then in horror as gunfire shattered the night, lighting up the arch beneath the overpass as a squad of soldiers turned their weapons on one another, and in the staccato bursts of light, she saw it, like a shadow thrown in their wake.

The Chaos Eater.

August saw it.

Only for an instant, when the short, bright flashes of gunfire lit the underpass. It stood there, a spot of stillness amid the violence, its silver eyes glinting. August saw it and felt—*empty*, a numbing cold, as if the burning coal at the center of his chest had turned to ice.

His limbs grew heavy and his mind slowed, and Kate's voice was distant in his ears, a single echoing word that took too long to form.

"Play."

She pulled his face toward hers. "August, *play*."

The world stuttered back into motion, and he got the violin up, the bow on the strings, but the monster was already gone, the killing done, the underpass plunged back into terrible, too-still shadow. He drew a light baton and lobbed it into the dark, throwing the whole gruesome scene into sudden relief as the first Corsai scattered from the bodies.

"Dammit," muttered Kate.

And then, to August's horror, one of corpses staggered to its feet.

The soldier looked down at his hands, covered in blood, and began to sob and rage and then, just as quickly, he went quiet and calm, and smiled, and the smile became a laugh and the laugh became a groan. It was like a flickering image, two selves warring, both losing.

"We're all going to die," he murmured, and then, voice rising: "It's a mercy. I'll make it fast—"

"Soldier," called August, and the man spun toward them, eyes wide.

"Don't look!" said Kate, but it was too late. August met the soldier's eyes and saw the silver streaked across the man's wild gaze, and his first irrational thought was of moonlight. He braced for monster's poisonous power to reach out and wrap around him, the way the coldness had—but nothing happened.

To August, the man's eyes were just eyes, the madness contained by its new host.

"It's a mercy," said the soldier again.

And then he saw Kate, and something in him snapped at the sight of another human, another target. He lunged for the nearest gun. Kate dropped to the ground and August stepped in front of her, drawing his bow across the strings.

The soldier staggered, as if struck, the weapon falling from his hands as August's music warred with the monster's hold. The man gripped his skull and screamed, anguish on his face as he looked down at what he'd done, and then the anguish was gone too, wiped away by the spell of August's song.

When the man's soul surfaced, it wasn't red or white, but *both*, one streaked with the other, guilt and innocence twined together, vying for his life.

August stopped playing.

He didn't know what to do.

Kate was on her knees, gaze empty and crimson light wicking off her skin.

He reached for his comm.

"Soro."

A moment later, they responded. *"August. What is it?"*

He looked from Kate to the soldier, the tangled light to the bodies of the murdered FTFs. "I need your help."

卌
IIII

Four walls, a ceiling, and a floor.

That's all there was in the cell. The door was steel and the walls were concrete, except for the one interrupted by a single strip of glass, that wasn't even glass, but shatter-proof plastic.

Kate stood in the viewing room on the other side, Soro and August and Flynn at her back. Flynn sat in a chair while Soro twirled their flute and August leaned in the doorway, but Kate didn't take her eyes from the soldier.

He was on his knees in the center of the cell, blindfolded and cuffed to a steel loop embedded in the concrete floor. Soro had bandaged the gunshot wounds in his shoulder and leg, but if he was in any pain, it seemed lost beneath the madness.

This is me, she thought. *This is what happens to me.*

She'd come back to herself, somewhere between

the end of August's song and Soro's arrival, in time to see August cinching the strip of cloth over the soldier's eyes.

"He shouldn't be in the building," said Soro, arms crossed. "He's infected."

"That," said Flynn, sitting forward, "is why he's isolated."

Isolated was a kind word for it. Kate wasn't even the one in the concrete cube, and she still felt like she'd been entombed. The cell was one of several on the Compound's lowest level, and no other humans had been allowed even a modicum of contact with the prisoner. The Sunai were, apparently, immune to the soldier's sickness. August, with Flynn's guidance, had tried to sedate the man, but it hadn't worked. Some vital thing was severed between his body and his mind, and no matter what they pumped into his veins, he didn't slow, didn't sleep, didn't do anything but rave.

"He should have been executed," said Soro.

"I overruled," said August, affecting that cold, formal tone.

Soro tipped their head. "Which is why he's still alive."

Flynn rose to his feet. "August was right. He's one of ours. And he's the first survivor we've seen."

Not exactly, thought Kate, but she kept it to herself.

"If there is a cure for this condition—"

"If there is a cure," she cut in, "it will be killing the Chaos Eater."

The silver-haired Sunai shot her a look. "What were you doing outside the Compound?"

Kate kept her gaze on the cell. "Hunting."

"With whose permission?"

"Mine," said August firmly. "And without her, the *entire* squad would be dead."

"The entire squad might as well be," said Soro.

"Enough," said Flynn wearily.

"We're all going to die," murmured the prisoner. "I'll make it fast."

Flynn tapped a microphone. "Do you know who you are?"

The soldier twitched, shuddered at the voice, and shook his head, as if trying to dislodge something. "Myer. Squad Sixteen."

"Do you know what you've done?"

"I didn't mean to but it felt so good so good I want to—*no no no.*" His breath hitched, and then he mouthed something, too low to hear. Kate read his lips.

Kill me.

And then, just as quickly, he was back again, promising mercy, mercy—that he would make it quick—and Kate wrapped her arms around her ribs.

This is me.

A hand settled on her shoulder. "Come on," said August, and she let him lead her away from the soldier and his screams.

As soon as they were in the elevator, Kate slumped against the wall and bowed her head, eyes lost behind the shadow of her bangs. August couldn't read her face like that, and it made him think of the way she'd looked out on the light grid—when she'd looked into the mirror and all of her features had gone eerily blank, like she wasn't even there. And then she'd come crashing back, all the color and life rushing into her face before the force of it—whatever it was—hit her.

"You're staring," said Kate without looking up.

"Out there," he said slowly. "When you were searching for it—"

"Everything has a cost."

"You should have told me."

"Why?" Her head drifted up. "You said yourself, August. We do what we have to. We become what we have to." They reached the top floor, and Kate stepped out. "I thought you of all people would approve."

August trailed her down the hall. "It's not the same."

Kate gave him an exasperated look. "No," she said, "You're right. It's not." She cocked her head, bangs sliding aside to reveal the silver in her eye. It had spread, thrown out cracks and stolen more of the blue. "This thing in my head, it's not going away. It's there, every moment, trying to tip that balance, and turn me into that *thing* parading as a soldier in your basement. But at least I'm fighting it."

With that she turned and vanished down the hall.

Let her go, said Leo.

But August didn't.

He found her sitting on his bed, her knees drawn up.

He set the violin case against the door and sank onto the bed beside her, suddenly exhausted. For a few long moments they sat there, neither speaking, even though he knew how much Kate hated silence. And, even though his presence should make her want to speak, it was his own voice that rose out of the quiet.

"I didn't stop fighting," he said, the words so low he worried Kate wouldn't hear them, but she did. "I just got tired of losing. It's easier this way."

"Of course it's *easier*," said Kate. "That doesn't mean it's right."

Right. The world broke down into right and wrong, innocence and guilt. It was supposed to be a simple line, a clean divide, but it wasn't.

"You asked me where I went," he said, pressing his palms together. "I don't know." And that small confession, it was like stepping off a cliff, and he was falling.

"I don't know who I am, and who I'm not, I don't know who I'm supposed to be, and I miss who I was; I miss it every day, Kate, but there's no place for that August anymore. No place for the version of me who wanted to go to school, and have a life, and feel human, because this world doesn't need that August. It needs someone else."

Kate's shoulder came to rest against his, warm, solid.

"I spent a long time playing that game," she said. "Pretending there were other versions of this world, where other versions of me got to live, and be happy, even if I didn't, and you know what? It's lonely as hell. Maybe there *are* other versions, other lives, but this one's ours. It's all we've got."

"I can't protect this world *and* care about it."

Kate met his gaze. "That's the *only* way to do it."

He folded forward. "I can't."

"Why not?"

"Because it hurts too much." He shuddered. "Every day, every loss, it *hurts.*"

"I know." Kate's hand threaded through his, and for an instant he was curled against the bottom of a bathtub, fever tearing over his skin with Kate's grip and her voice his only anchors.

I'm not letting go.

Her grip tightened.

"Look at me," she said, and he dragged his head up.

Her face was inches from his own, her eyes midnight blue, save for the violent silver crack.

"I know it hurts," she said. "So make it worth the pain."

"How?"

"By not letting go," she said softly. "By holding on, to anger, or hope, or whatever it is that keeps you fighting."

You, he thought.

And for once, a word felt simple, because Kate was the one who kept him fighting, who looked at him and saw him, and saw through him at the same time, and who never let go.

He didn't *decide* to kiss her. One second her mouth was an inch from his, and the next, his lips were on hers, and the next, she was kissing him back, and the next, they were a tangle of limbs, and the next, Kate was on top of him, pressing him down into the sheets.

August had felt fear and pain, the ache of hunger and the steady calm after taking a soul, but he'd never felt anything like this. He'd lost himself before in his music, fallen into the notes, the world dissolving briefly, and even that was not like this. For once there was no Leo in his head, no Ilsa or Soro, just the warmth of Kate's skin and the memory of stardust and open fields, of bleachers and black-and-white cats and apples in the woods, of tally marks and music, of running and burning, and the desperate, hopeless desire to feel human.

And then her mouth was on his again, and the version of himself, the one he tried so hard to drown, came gasping up for air.

For a moment, everything was simple.

Kate forgot the sight of the soldier in the cell and the ticking time bomb in her head, and the violent voice inside her was drowned out by August—by his cool skin and the music of his body against hers. The room seemed to dance with sudden light, a soft and lovely red—

Kate gasped, lurching backward as she realized the light was coming from *her*. August saw it too and half-stumbled, half-fell back off the bed, landing amid a pile of books.

She sagged against the headboard, breathless, the first washes of red light already fading back beneath her skin. She stared at August.

And then, she started to laugh.

It rose up suddenly, like madness, and left her close to tears, and August looked at her, flushed with embarrassment, as if she were laughing at *him* or at *them* or at *this* instead of at *everything*, at the absurdity of their lives and the fact that nothing would ever be easy, or simple, or normal.

She shook her head, one hand pressed to her mouth until the laughter died enough that she could hear August telling her he was sorry.

"Why? Did you know that would happen?"

August stared at her, aghast. "Did I know that kissing you would bring your soul to surface? That—*that*—would have the same effect as pain or music? No, I must have missed that lesson."

She stared at him, agape. "August, was that *sarcasm*?"

He shrugged, toppling another short stack of books somewhere behind him. Kate shifted back, making room. "Come here."

He looked miserable. "I think it's better if I stay down here."

"I'll try to keep my hands off you," she said dryly. "Come on."

He rose awkwardly out of the heap, running a hand through his hair, the color still high in his face as he picked his way toward her. August lowered himself onto the edge of the bed, shooting her a wary look, as if he were afraid of her, or thought she should be afraid of him, but Kate only stretched against the far side, and when he finally sank down beside her, she rolled toward him and he rolled toward her.

His eyes drifted closed, and she studied the dark lashes, the hollows in his cheeks, the short black lines around his wrist. Quiet settled over them, and she wanted to sleep, but every time she closed her eyes, she saw the soldier in the cell.

And then she admitted something, a confession so low she thought—hoped—August wouldn't hear, two words she'd vowed never to say aloud in a world filled with monsters.

"I'm scared."

August stayed with Kate until she fell asleep.

He didn't reach out, didn't take her hand, didn't trust himself to touch her again, not after the . . . He flushed at the thought of it. If Kate hadn't noticed the red light, if his mouth had lingered on hers any longer, if his hands had been pressed to skin instead of cloth—

It could have been so much worse.

Midnight came, marked only by the burn of a new tally on his skin.

One hundred and eighty-six days without falling.

The marks mean nothing, chided Leo. *You have already let go.*

But his brother was wrong. Even when August thought he wanted to let go, some part of him had held on, and he had the marks to prove it.

A soft weight landed on the bed. Allegro. The cat shot August a wary look, but didn't flee, only curled up near his feet, green eyes vanishing behind his tail, and that felt as much a victory as the latest tally. August closed his eyes, and let the low static of the cat's purr fold over him. . . .

The sudden staccato of a cough jolted August awake.

He didn't remember falling asleep, but it was almost dawn, and the cough came again, the sound ricocheting through his head.

Henry.

August held his breath and listened, bracing for the fit to worsen, but mercifully, it trailed off, replaced by Emily's voice, low and stern, and Henry's, short of breath, but there.

"It's all right. I'm all right."

"Jesus, Henry, just because you *can* lie to me . . ."

They kept their voices low, but whispering did no good when August could hear the mutterings of soldiers four floors down. Those he could tune out, but when it came to Henry, to Emily, he couldn't stop himself from listening.

"There has to be *something*."

"We've been through this, Em."

"Henry, please." Emily Flynn had always been made of stone, but her voice, when she uttered that word, was cracking under the weight. "If you would just let the medics—"

"What are they going to tell me? I already know—"

"You can't just let it—"

"I'm not." The sound of space collapsing between bodies, of hands on hair. "I'm still here."

And there, in the dark, August heard the next words, even though they were never said aloud. *For now.*

He didn't sleep again after that.

He tried to focus on the other sounds in the building— on the footsteps, the water lines, the far-off music of Soro's flute—but somewhere beneath it all, he heard the soldier in the cell. It was so far below, it must have been his mind playing tricks, but it didn't matter.

August slipped from the bed, took up the violin, and went downstairs.

He expected to find the viewing room empty, the prisoner alone, but Ilsa was there, her face pressed to the window. In the cell beyond the soldier knelt on the concrete, rambling on about mercy and wrenching against his restraints until blood ran down his skin.

There had to be something they could do.

August looked around. Sublevel 3 was the lowest floor in the Compound, cut off from the world above, below, and to every side by steel and concrete. It was the closest thing to soundproof in the building. A console sat on the table, a red button marking a microphone, and when August tapped it, the soldier's voice poured out of the cell, filling the room with madness and anguish.

He set his case on the table, and Ilsa watched him, a question in her eyes, as he drew out the violin. Leo had always believed that their sole purpose was to cleanse the world of sinners. That music was simply the kindest way to do that. But what if there were other uses? Ways to help instead of harm?

He took a deep breath and began to play.

The first note cut the air like a knife. The second was high and sweet, the third low and somber. The steel strings added their own low thrum, tense under his fingers as the music echoed through the concrete room. Every time a note reached the walls, it doubled back, both less and more as it trailed off beneath the newer notes.

He had never done this, never played to *soothe* a soul instead of to reap it.

But in the cell, the soldier stopped fighting. His shoulders slumped, as if in relief, the darkness inside him subdued by the song.

And August kept playing.

The air smelled of blood and fear.

Sloan inhaled it from the tower steps, but everywhere he looked, he saw Malchai, only Malchai, their mouths red and their hands empty.

"I am so very disappointed," he said, his voice carrying through the night.

They had brought him nothing. They had witnessed nothing. They had played with their prey, dangled it in front of every living, breathing, hunting inch of the city night, and for it all they had gained *nothing.*

Even Alice, small, bloodthirsty thing that she was, had come back empty-handed, brandishing only stained lips and a careless shrug.

"Perhaps," she said, climbing the steps, "we're using the wrong bait."

But humans were humans. The Corsai fed on flesh and bone, the Malchai on blood, the Sunai on souls, each and every part contained in the body of a human. What else was could he use?

"Sloan!"

A group of Malchai were coming toward him.

"What is it?"

"The shadow," growled one.

His hopes rose. "Did you find it?"

But the Malchai were already shaking their heads.

"Then *what*?" snarled Sloan.

The Malchai looked at one another like fools, and Sloan sighed.

"*Show* me."

He wove between the bodies on the station floor.

To call them dead would have been an understatement.

Perhaps if they'd had weapons, it would have been quick. But as far as Sloan could tell, the prisoners had used whatever they could find—chairs, batons, bare hands.

In short, they had torn each other apart.

And yet, Sloan had no doubt this was the *intruder's* doing.

Sloan had made an offering, and been refused. He'd given up a city full of easy prey, and instead the creature had come *here*.

Why?

His shoes echoed on the linoleum, and Alice trailed a few steps behind. She dragged her nails against the wall, whistling softly. The other three Malchai sniffed the air, and when Sloan drew in a breath, he noted a scent like cold steel, faint and strange and out of place. But something else was missing.

Fear.

The taste that coated the streets, painted itself across the night, that most common of human traits—it wasn't here. The station was awash in other things—anger, bloodlust, death, but no fear.

Artificial light buzzed harshly overhead, blurring Sloan's vision. He flicked the nearest switch and the world was plunged mercifully back into muted grays. His eyes brightened, focused, drawing the room into sharp relief.

Bodies sprawled across the ground.

Slumped in halls.

Fell out of open cells.

The Crawford Street Station was a relic of the days before the war, before the Phenomenon, back when V-City had such mundane things as police, men and women enlisted to uphold the peace.

Harker had used the North City's four stations for their onsite holding cells, and Sloan had turned those same cells into pens for some of the city's most violent resisters. Men and women who had no desire to fight for their fellow humans in South City *or* serve as Fangs. Loners with their own taste for blood, for death, for power.

"What a waste," mused Alice, stepping over a broad red pool. "It didn't even *eat* them."

She was right. What was the point of so much death if not to feed? Unless, of course, it had fed on something he couldn't see. After all, the Sunai devoured *souls*. If the act didn't burn out their victims' eyes, there would be no way of telling what was taken, what was gone.

"You," he said, pointing to the tallest Malchai. "Show me."

The Malchai dragged a pointed nail across a tablet, pulling up the footage. Four feeds: two of the cell halls, one of the main room, and one of the front doors.

Two Fangs wandered the cell halls, while a third lounged in the main room.

Nothing out of the ordinary. Sloan rolled the time-stamp forward, watching the seconds, minutes, tick by and—

The lights on the footage suddenly guttered and went out.

They came on again an instant later, flickering and low, and in the half dark, Sloan saw the shadow. It stood a step or two behind the Fang, nothing but a streak of black across the screen. The light itself seemed to weaken around it, a halo of darkness tracing its edges. The camera blurred as if struggling to catch the creature's shape.

"Is that it?" whispered Alice.

Sloan didn't answer. He watched, expecting the human in the room to startle, to scream, to fight, and instead, the Fang *stared*, as if entranced. The shadow advanced, and the human rose to his feet and stepped *toward* the creature. For a long moment the human disappeared from view, swallowed by the shadow on the screen. When it withdrew, the man looked unchanged in every way but one.

His eyes.

They blurred the camera, streaks of light that cut across his face as he turned, took up a set of keys, and headed for the cell halls. He appeared on the next screen, another Fang moving toward him, and Sloan watched, mesmerized, as both men slowed, pausing for the barest second and in that second, something passed between them, spread from one to two. And then they were moving again.

One went to find the third Fang while the other unlocked the first cell door.

And began beating the prisoner to death.

Or at least, he tried. But the man was twice his

size, and in seconds the Fang lay on the floor, his neck snapped, and the prisoner was in the hall, his own eyes shining with that monstrous light.

The other cells were open now.

The slaughter started.

All the while the shadow stood, almost peaceful, in the center of the station. But as Sloan watched, the creature began to *harden*, details etching themselves across its surface. Its arms tapered into long, thin fingers, its chest rose and fell, and the flat plane of its face took shape, cheeks hollowing and jaw growing sharp. And when blood splashed across its front, it did not pass through, as matter through shadow, but landed and stained, having met a solid surface.

So, it *was* feeding on the prisoners.

Not on their bodies or their souls, but on their actions, their violence. Sloan was suddenly glad that his Malchai had failed to kill the shadow. A monster that turned humans against each other—that was a pet worth having.

On the screen, the shadow started moving through the station, fingers trailing along the tables and walls. It brushed up against iron bars and recoiled slightly. So it wasn't invulnerable.

And whatever it had gained from the humans' deaths, the effects did not last long.

By the time it reached the front doors, it was thinning again, edges smudging. By the time it crossed onto the fourth screen and stepped into the street, it folded into mist and simply disappeared.

Sloan stared at the screen, which remained picture-still despite the passing seconds. No Malchai rose from the corpses. No Corsai stretched out of shadows. No Sunai shuddered into life.

Monsters were born from monstrous acts. But here were monstrous acts without the monstrous aftermath. The only aftermath, in fact, appeared to be the creature itself, the violence fed back into its source, leaving nothing but bodies in its wake.

"What do we do?" asked one of the Malchai.

Sloan looked up. "Let the Corsai have the corpses."

"And what about the shadow?" asked Alice, drawing patterns in a pool of tacky blood. "We can't let it run loose."

"No," said Sloan. "We can't."

Her red eyes narrowed. Alice had a way of reading others, reading *him*, that usually made him want to tear out those eyes. But for once, he only smiled.

||||- ||||- |

She is standing
before a mirror
staring
at her own
reflection
and it has
silver eyes
and talks of mercy
with a smile
while blood drips
from its fingers
and the bodies
pile
at its feet
and the reflection
reaches out
a nail
against the glass
tap-tap-tapping
        until it cracks.

Kate woke alone.

The sun was up, and August was gone, nothing but a ghost of space, an indentation on the other side of the bed.

A weight landed on the blankets, and a pair of green eyes peered over her shoulder.

Allegro.

He regarded her uncertainly, as if he didn't know what to make of her.

"You and me both," murmured Kate.

She knew she'd had another dream, but it was already gone, and she forced herself up and into the bathroom, running the shower as hot as she could bear. The pressure in her head was worse, matched now by a vise around her chest.

Steam filled the small room as she knelt and searched the bathroom drawers until she found something that looked like it might ease a headache. She took three before stepping into the scalding spray.

Everything ached, and she had to sing to herself to keep her thoughts from drifting toward the razor on the shelf.

When she got out, the mirror had fogged over.

Kate stepped cautiously toward it and swept her hand across the glass. She let her gaze stray for just an instant, only long enough to see the way the silver had spread, engulfing most of her left eye and throwing lines like roots across her right.

Her heart faltered, panic running like a tremor through fragile ground, and she had to fight to keep her footing, to stay calm.

"You are in control," she told herself, the words like weights in her pockets, anchoring her down.

You are in control, she thought as she dressed in a pair of fatigues. The clothes made her think of Team Twenty-Four downstairs, and she almost felt guilty for not joining them, before she remembered that it had been only a ruse, a failed attempt at freedom. Besides, she didn't think proximity to weapons or people who tested her patience was a very good idea right now.

Another reason to be far from the Wardens and the rest of Prosperity.

Still, as she sank into a chair at the kitchen table, a cup of coffee in one hand and her tablet in the other, she found herself composing another message to Riley. There was a freedom to writing a letter you couldn't send, and she told him about her father and her mother and the house in the Waste, about the Flynns and August and the cat named Allegro.

She wrote until the headache faded and her mind finally cleared, and then she closed out of the message, and got to work, setting a trap for the Chaos Eater.

✦

"What are you doing?"

The bow skipped on the strings and August opened his eyes. The clock on the wall read 9:45 AM. Ilsa was gone and Soro stood in the doorway, their silver hair slicked back, confusion tingeing the steady planes of their face.

"Playing," he said simply.

His limbs ached and if his fingers could have cracked and bled, they would have hours ago. As it was, the steel strings were hot from so much use, the notes wobbling. If they had been made of anything else, they would have snapped.

"Why?" asked Soro.

That question—a single word—with so many answers. "Do you ever wonder why *music* brings a soul to surface? What makes beauty work as well as pain?"

"No."

"Maybe it is a kind of mercy," he went on, "but maybe there's more to it than that." The violin was heavy in his grip, but he didn't stop playing. "Maybe there is more to us than murder."

"You are behaving strangely," said Soro. "Is it the sinner?"

"Her name is Kate."

The Sunai shrugged, as if the information were

meaningless, and turned their attention to the soldier in the cell, the red and white light like oil and water on his skin.

"How odd."

"He is not guilty," said August.

"He is not innocent, either," said Soro. "And your playing will not save him."

Soro is right, sneered Leo in his head. *How many hours have you wasted?* August's grip faltered.

His hands were beginning to shake.

"You are tired, brother. Let me help."

Soro turned toward the door without drawing their flute.

"Wait," said August, but it was too late—Soro marched into the cell and broke the soldier's neck.

August stopped playing, the violin slipping from numb fingers as the soldier collapsed to the ground, the light gone from his skin.

August folded against the wall.

"Why?" he asked when Soro returned. "Why did you do that?"

The other Sunai looked at him with something like *pity.*

"Because," they said, "we must focus on the living. He was already dead. Come on," they said, holding open the door. "Our work is waiting."

◈

Kate stared down at the tablet and tried not to scream.

The need to stay calm was warring with the ticking clock in her head and the fact she didn't know how to trap a shadow, how to catch a monster she was always a step behind.

She had nothing, and the longer she wracked her brain, the more her anger mounted, the more helpless she felt, the more she wanted to take her frustration out on something, anything. It left her feeling brittle, which made her mad, which made her pulse climb all over again, the shadow whispering all the while in her skull.

You are hunter.

You are a killer.

You are running out of time.

Do something.

Do something.

DO SOMETHING.

A sound tore itself free from Kate's throat, and she swept her arm across the table, sending the coffee cup and the tablet crashing to the floor. She put her head in her hands, took a long breath, then stood and picked up the pieces.

There were answers—she just had to find them.

She started clicking through every folder on the FTF server.

She found food logs, census data, a registry of recent deaths, subfolders marked with either an *M* or an *F* (for Malchai or Fang, if she had to guess). There was a third folder, marked by another letter—*A*. There was no telling what that stood for, but the deaths in that one were the most gruesome.

And then, somewhere between her third and fourth coffee, something caught her eye: a map of V-City, marked with *X*'s in blue and gray and black, the month stamped at the top.

The *X*'s, she soon discovered, marked gains and losses on both sides of the Seam.

She backed out of the search until she found the rest of the maps, month by month, going back to Callum's death and Sloan's rise.

Kate straightened in her chair. The images were all the same.

Sure, the *X*'s shifted back and forth, but never strayed from the few blocks on either side of the Seam.

And the more files she studied, the stranger the picture became.

The FTF acted like it was in control, like it was winning, but it *wasn't*. Six months, and the Flynn Task Force hadn't planned or executed a single large-scale attack. Why not?

It made no sense.

Kate got to her feet and went looking for Flynn.

Of course, she quickly realized she didn't know where to find him.

The command center was the first logical place to look, and a quick survey of the elevator buttons showed that one and only one floor—three—required key-card access. Which, of course, Kate didn't have.

She dug the silver lighter from her back pocket and knelt in front of the panel, and she was halfway through prying off the metal plate when the elevator hummed to life. Kate shot to her feet but the doors were already closing. The 3 on the panel lit up, and the elevator started down.

Sloan watched the monster come.

He watched it go.

He sat on the penthouse's gray sofa, his long legs stretched across the glass coffee table, and studied the footage, watching as, over and over, the creature drew itself together, and as, over and over, it fell apart again, waxing and waning as if it were a moon.

He drew a pointed nail across the screen, and the clip began again, an idea coalescing in his head the way the shadow coalesced in the station.

But unlike the shadow, Sloan's idea held firm.

Alice swung her legs over the back of the sofa.

"Seven for seven," she said, rolling a bit of explosive between her fingers. "The caches are clear. And I left the little soldier boys a present, in case they come looking."

She leaped up again, and Sloan sank back and closed his eyes—

And noticed a change in the room.

A new tension.

The two engineers were still at their table, but they were muttering under their breath.

". . . don't . . ."

". . . we have to . . ."

". . . he'll kill us both . . ."

Sloan rose to his feet, but Alice was already there.

"Secrets, secrets, are no fun," she said, ruffling the man's hair. He flinched away from her touch, and her grip tightened, forcing his head back. "Do you have something to say?"

The man's eyes darted nervously as Sloan approached.

"Well?" he asked. "Have you found a solution to my quandary?"

The man glared at the woman, but after a moment, she nodded. "The subway," she said under her breath.

Sloan's eyes narrowed. "There are no subways under the Flynn Compound."

"No," said the woman, "not anymore." She showed him a screen with the underground grid. "This is the most recent map of the subway system, and—"

"D-d-don't," stammered the other engineer, but his protests died when Sloan brought his nails to rest against the man's throat.

"Hush," he said, his attention leveled on the female engineer. "Go on."

The woman tapped through several pages on a second screen. "I dug through the old records and found this: the original grid." She set the tablets side by side. "And here," she said, indicating a place where old tunnels intersected, "is the Compound."

Sloan's gaze ticked back and forth between the two images. In one, the Compound seemed impenetrable. In the other, its fatal flaw was laid bare.

"It wouldn't be hard," she continued slowly, "to access the old subway system from the newer line—for example, from the tunnel that passes beneath this tower. Then, with enough explosives, the damage would be catastrophic. . . ."

Catastrophic.

Sloan smiled.

"And what if," he said, "I no longer wanted to destroy the Compound? What if I only wanted to make a way *in?*"

"That wasn't the plan," growled Alice.

"Plans change," said Sloan. "They evolve." He lifted the woman's chin. "Well?"

"It wouldn't be hard," she said. "You'd need to rig a set of charges. Smaller, controlled blasts. But even minor detonations will draw attention."

"Well then," said Sloan, turning his gaze on the male engineer. "I suggest you also devise a distraction."

He crossed the penthouse, throwing open the doors to what had once been Callum's room, Alice on his heels. He opened the closet and knelt, searching the boxes on the floor.

"Does this change of plans have anything to do with our intruder?" asked Alice.

"It does," said Sloan, drawing out a crate.

She sulked. "I thought we were going to kill it."

"Why kill a thing that can be *used*?"

"How do you plan to *use* a thing you can't even *catch*?"

Alice had a point.

Sloan had been wrong, he realized now, in baiting his first trap, wrong to offer fear when his prey fed on stronger fare. On violence. On chaos. On *potential*.

He knew just the bait he'd need.

But how to *contain* a shadow?

He lifted the lid from the crate. Folded inside was a sheet of gold, a curtain spun from that most precious metal. Once upon a time, Callum Harker had slept beneath the sheet as protection from monsters.

Of course, it hadn't saved him in the end.

But still, a human's shield was a monster's prison.

Alice recoiled at the sight of the gold, and the taste

on the air burned Sloan's throat. He put the lid back on.

"Gather the Fangs."

Alice cocked her head. "How many?"

"*All* of them."

┼┼┼┼
┼┼┼┼
|||

Kate wasn't entirely sure how she'd gotten there.

The Compound's command center was buzzing with activity, the air around her humming with voices and the constant crack and buzz of comms, all blurring into a kind of white noise in her good ear.

She clutched her tablet as she wove through the crowded hall, trying to stay out of the way of the men and women rushing from room to room, some in plain clothes and others in uniform. A trio of soldiers sat before a bank of consoles, sending out orders, and through a glass door, she saw a familiar halo of red curls sitting before a massive bank of screens, each with a sur-veillance feed.

Kate knocked once, so softly that she *felt* the sound more than heard it, but Ilsa turned in her chair. Not fast, as though startled, but calmly, as though she knew exactly who she'd find.

Over Ilsa's shoulder, cameras rotated past, flicking from shot to shot, lingering only a second or two on each angle. Within moments Kate was getting dizzy, but before she looked away she saw a sequence of frames taken from inside elevators and smiled.

"Thanks for the ride," she said, and Ilsa gave an amenable shrug.

The glow from the screens traced an outline around her, casting most of her in shadow, but the small stars across her shoulders and down her arms danced with bluish light.

One hundred and eighty-six.

The same number as August—and Kate, though she didn't bear the same marks. All three of them joined by the actions of a single night.

Her attention drifted from the stars to the scar at Ilsa's throat. She could almost make out the taper of a Malchai's nails.

Sloan.

Anger flashed through her, quick and hot, met by the sudden desire to march across the Seam, to find her father's monster and tear him apart. The urge swept over her like madness, and for a second, it was all she could think of, all she could see—

Ilsa's hand came to rest like a cool weight on Kate's cheek. She hadn't seen the Sunai rise, or cross the room, and she marveled that August could seem so solid, and his sister so insubstantial.

What did that make Soro? she wondered. *Something else entirely.*

Ilsa's eyes were wide with worry, but Kate pulled away.

"It's okay," she said, relieved that she could still *say* those words, which meant they must be true. For now.

Ilsa cocked her head, and swept her fingers across the air, a gesture clearly meant to encompass the entire command center. The question was wordless, but clear:

What are you looking for?

"Henry Flynn," she answered. "Is he around?"

Ilsa's head bobbed once. She pointed to the hall, and Kate was about to leave when she caught Ilsa glancing at the tablet still in Kate's hand, her pale eyes suddenly focused, intent.

Did you see?

Kate started to answer when she heard a familiar word issue from across the hall.

"*Alpha.*"

August's call sign.

Kate started toward the sound and found a door ajar, several people gathered around a speaker.

"*We've reached Fifth and Taylor.*"

Something turned over in Kate's mind. Why did that sound so familiar?

"No signs of trouble."

She closed her eyes, trying to draw a map in her mind.

It was in North City, but there was something else, something more.

"We're going in the front."

"Wait," she said, stepping into the room. Five faces swiveled toward her, only one of them familiar. Henry Flynn leaned against the wall, as if for support. The other four had only one thing in common: scorn.

"Kate?" August's voice sounded over the comm.

She stepped up to the table. "Don't go in yet."

"Miss Harker," said Flynn wearily.

"Never let a Harker loose, Henry," said an older woman. She had an acerbic smile and milky eyes that stared into the middle distance, unseeing.

"What are you doing on this level?" demanded a soldier with a trim beard.

"And in the Council's chamber," added a middle-aged soldier with two black braids.

Kate shook her head. "Fifth and Taylor—I know that building, what is that?"

"You really shouldn't eavesdrop," said Flynn.

"It's a depot," offered the youngest soldier. "Our intel indicates it holds a supply of dry grains."

But that wasn't it. "No," she said, remembering. "It's a subway stop."

Flynn straightened a little, wincing as he did. "It *was*, a while back. Harker built a warehouse over it."

"And you're taking your squad in through the front door?" challenged Kate.

Flynn's jaw tightened. "You think it's a trap."

"You assume it's not?" she countered.

"There's no evidence—" started the female soldier.

"No, August said there were *no signs of trouble*. I'm guessing he means Fangs, or Malchai. Something with a pulse." She looked to Flynn. "You want me to think like Sloan. I can't. But I can think like my *father*, and I can tell you, he would never leave supplies unguarded. "

That, at last, made them hesitate.

"What do you suggest?" asked Flynn.

Kate chewed her lip. "August," she said after a moment, "do you have lights on you?"

"*Yes.*"

"Good," she said. "Then go through the subway."

A muffled curse issued from another comm. Whoever it was, she didn't blame them. Dark spaces were the Corsai's territory. Static filled the line for half a minute, followed by a splash, the shuffle of legs wading through shallow water, a few colorful words, and then the muted sound of hands on bars, and August telling the rest of his team to stay back. The whole room seemed to hold its breath at the scrape of the metal cover. And then, static again, broken only by short sharp intake of breath.

"Alpha?" prompted Flynn.

"*We're inside,*" said August. "*Intel was right: there's a large supply of grain . . .*"

The bearded man shot Kate a withering look.

"*But the whole place is rigged to blow.*"

Kate felt a momentary swell of triumph, but had the decency not to say *I told you so*, given the precarious nature of the situation.

"Well," she said. "Good thing you took the tunnel."

A new voice came on the comm. "*Alpha Squad Tech, Ani, here. I can deactivate it.*"

"All right, Alpha Squad," said Flynn. "Be careful."

The comm static vanished, replaced by a steady quiet, and Kate realized that the whole room had gone silent, all eyes turned toward her. If they expected her to leave, they were disappointed. She held her ground.

"Is there something else you'd like to say?" asked Flynn.

"I've been studying the files on your drive."

"Who gave you access to that information?" demanded the bearded soldier.

"You've been fighting for six months," she went on, "but it looks like a stalemate, not a battle. You're not making any sustainable forward progress; you're just trying to hold your ground."

"Why the hell are we listening to a teenage girl?"

"Oh, am I just a teenage girl now? I thought I was the daughter of your enemy or the soldier who just saved your squad." She could feel her temper rising. "Am I dead weight or a danger to your cause or an asset with information? Make up your mind."

The blind woman gave a short, humorless laugh.

"Miss Harker—" warned Flynn.

"Why haven't you attacked the tower?"

"We don't have enough people," said the female soldier.

Kate scoffed at that. "The FTF has tens of thousands."

"Less than a thousand," countered the young man, "are skilled enough to make the Night Squads."

"If we sent even half," said the bearded soldier, "the loss we could sustain—"

"—would be worth it," countered the blind woman.

So this was the problem, thought Kate. The reason for half measures, stalemates, slow deaths. How could they fight Sloan? They were too busy fighting among themselves.

She looked to Henry Flynn, who had said nothing, only listened.

"Why should they risk their lives for North City?" asked the female soldier.

"This isn't about North and South," snapped Kate.

"It's about *Verity*. You're bleeding soldiers, and Sloan's letting you, because he can. He doesn't care how many pieces he sacrifices in this game."

"War is not a game," said the bearded soldier.

"Not to *you*, but it is to him, and you're never going to end this until you end *Sloan*, and in order to end Sloan, you have to take risks, you have to think like him, play like him—"

The Council started speaking over her.

"We cannot afford—"

"—A coordinated attack on the tower—"

"—you mean a *suicide mission*—"

"You cannot win unless you're willing to *fight*." Kate slammed her fist on the table, and heard the sound of metal burying itself in wood.

The Council recoiled, and she looked down and saw her hand wrapped around the switchblade. She didn't remember drawing the lighter, didn't remember freeing the knife, but there it was, embedded in the table.

The Council stared at the shining metal, and Kate almost reached out to free the blade. Instead she backed away. Putting space between her hand and the knife and the people in the room.

"Kate, are you all—" started Flynn, but she was already out the door.

︱︱︱︱ ︱︱︱︱ ︱︱︱︱

Kate punched the elevator button, pressing her forehead to the cold steel. She listened to the low, slow crank of the machinery, and took the stairs instead.

She hit the lobby and wove through the crowded hall toward the nearest outer door. She needed air. The question was how to get out. She scanned the soldiers congesting the hall and saw one tuck a pack of cigarettes into the fold of his sleeve. That would do. Kate sped up right as he turned toward her.

The collision was brief, and just hard enough to set them both off balance. By the time he righted himself, the cigarettes were in her pocket. He muttered something under his breath, but she didn't wait around to hear it.

Kate was ten feet from the Compound door when a guard stepped into her path. "You're not cleared to leave."

She flashed the pack of cigarettes. He didn't move. "Come on." She gestured down at herself, trying to keep the urgency from her voice. "No gear, no weapons. I'm not going far."

"Not my problem."

She saw herself grabbing the knife from his thigh, imagined the clean line it would make across his throat. She even took a step forward, closing the distance between them as—

"Let her go," muttered another guard. "She's not worth it."

The first one scowled, but shoved the door aside, and just like that, without any blood or bodies, Kate was free.

A shiver ran down her spine as the Compound door slammed shut behind her. It was an unsettling thing, to be on the wrong side of a locked door, even with the last shreds of daylight clinging to the sky and the UVR strip starting to brighten beneath her feet, but Kate filled her lungs with cold air and took a few steps onto the stream of light.

You are still in control.

She looked down at the pack of cigarettes. It had been months since she'd last smoked—she'd half expected the urge to resurface with the city, as if returning to this old life meant returning to her old self, too. But she didn't even crave it.

The pack hung from her fingers as she took a step, and then another, and another, putting distance between herself and the Compound. Beyond the strip of light, dusk was slipping in like fog, and she could almost feel the Chaos Eater stirring in the shadows.

Kate spread her arms.

Come and get me.

The Fangs gathered in the tower basement.

The same basement where Callum Harker had once held court, where a man with a homemade bomb had killed twenty-nine and ushered the first Sunai into the world, where blood still stained the floor and death still ghosted the walls, and Corsai whispered hungrily from the darkest corners.

Sloan stood on the platform, watching them jostle for space—more than a hundred men and women from across North City, united only by those bands of steel around their throats.

They had always been a violent bunch. The kind of humans who found power by taking it from others, who tolerated their own submission only because it placed them higher than the rest of the prey, and who believed, on some level, that they were better than their own kind, stronger than one other, and oh-so-eager to prove that strength.

Bravado. That was the word for it.

They had been gathered for less than an hour and already they were at one another's throats. Posturing, lobbing insults, their bodies coiled with energy and their eyes shining with drink.

Sloan had studied enough humans to know the way their minds weakened and their tempers flared under its effects. The liquor had been a welcome present, a reward, proof that they'd been *chosen*.

He cleared his throat and called for silence.

"I've summoned you because you have proven yourselves worthy of my attention." He shaped his words carefully. "I've summoned you because you are among the fiercest, the strongest, and the most bloodthirsty humans in my employ."

Laughter, low and feral, rippled through the crowd. Sloan's gaze wandered up to the gold-shrouded cage hanging overhead, its shape too dark for human eyes.

"I've summoned you," he said, "because I know you are willing, but I do not know if you are able."

"Come now, Sloan. They are only *humans*." Alice came slinking forward from the shadows behind him, her voice dripping with scorn. "Do any humans really possess the strength to rise above their mediocrity? To become monstrous? To become *more*?" Her face was a perfect mask of disdain.

Collars rattled and voices rose, the basement a riot of hunger and noise, of drunken humans gunning for a fight.

"You are all the same," Alice continued to taunt the Fangs. "Meat. Blood. Soul. No human will ever prove *my* equal."

"Give us a chance!" came a voice from the crowd.

"We'll show you!" shouted another.

Sloan stepped to the edge of the platform. "Who thinks themselves worthy?"

Hands went up, and bodies jostled, and the whole crowd churned, the bloodlust thick enough to taste.

A slow smile spread across Sloan's lips. "Who will prove it?"

"Hey, *you*."

The voice came from behind her, gruff and male.

Kate's arms fell back to her sides as she turned and recognized the soldier from the hall, the one whose cigarettes she'd lifted. He was flanked by a stocky girl and a squat young man.

"The fuck you think you're doing?" he demanded. "You gonna give me my shit back?"

Kate looked down at the pack of cigarettes in her hand and started to apologize, then stopped. She had an idea. It was, admittedly, a very bad idea. But Kate was running out of time inside her own head and if she couldn't hunt the Chaos Eater, then maybe she could *bait* it.

Make it come to *her*.

What was it Emily Flynn had said?

Some will see your presence as an insult.

Others might take it as a challenge.

Right now, she could practically feel the violence wicking off the FTFs.

Would it be enough?

Could she keep herself from hurting them?

"I know who you are," snarled the first soldier. "Harker." He spat the name, as if it were a curse.

He was still coming toward her, and she could feel the smooth resolve spreading through her head, the longing to fight, to hurt, to kill. At least she'd left the switchblade embedded in the table. That ought to give them a fighting chance.

She knew it was a bad idea.

But it was the only one she had.

"You want your cigarettes?" Kate crushed the pack in her hand. "Go fetch," she said, lobbing it into the dark.

And just like that, the soldier *lunged*, not for the cigarettes but for *her*, and they went down on the strip.

Kate rolled, landing on top of him, but before she

could get any leverage, an arm hooked around her neck and wrenched her off.

"You don't deserve to wear that badge," snarled the woman.

Kate glanced at the FTF stitched onto her sleeve. "It came with the clothes," she said, dropping her knee and rolling the soldier over her shoulder. But the moment she was free, someone hit her sidelong and she went down hard, the monster surging up within her.

No, she thought, forcing it back even as she straightened. She fought to keep her breathing even, her pulse steady, as she stared past the soldiers into the shadows of the city.

Where are you?

Kate licked a drop of blood from her lip as the soldiers circled. "You'll have to do better than that."

"I'll show you!" called a Fang, forcing his way toward the stage.

He tried to climb up, but Alice slammed her shoe into his face and he went toppling backward, nose gushing blood.

The taste of copper stained the air and Sloan felt his own hunger stir as laughter rustled through the crowd, low and cruel.

"I didn't say go!" said Alice. "If you want to play,

there are rules. When I say go, bring me a piece of—"
She waved a sharp nail back and forth through the air
before pointing at a man: "*him.*"

The Fang's eyes widened. He was broad-shouldered
and covered in ink, but in that moment, Sloan saw the
bravado falter, fall away.

Alice did have a way with people.

She flashed a vicious smile. "The largest piece wins!"

The crowd's unfocused energy shifted, narrowing to
a point.

"Ready?"

"Wait," begged the man, but it was too late.

"*Go.*"

The Fangs turned, and in a single wave, they surged
toward him. The first scream left his throat just as the
lights overhead flickered and went out.

Kate collapsed to her hands and knees on the light strip,
her vision blurring white.

"Not so cocky now, are you?"

The pain kept her grounded, even as the monster in
head told her to *fight back.*

Make me, she thought, forcing herself to her feet.

They weren't the best fighters, these three, but it was
taking half Kate's strength just to keep the dark at bay,
to keep that horrible, wonderful calm from stealing

through her head, to keep her hands from freeing a soldier's knife and—

She threw an elbow back and up, a dirty move, but the FTFs had trained to fight Fangs, who fought dirty, too, and suddenly her arm was trapped behind her back.

Kate struggled for balance, and for a second, as they grappled, she had a glimpse of the light strip, and the Compound, and a shadow leaning back against the wall.

Not the Chaos Eater, but *Soro*, polishing their flute.

Soro, watching, as if it were a sport, and then Kate's arm was twisted up, viciously, and she was being hauled toward the place where the light strip met the spreading dark.

"Stop." The word came out a whisper. A plea. She refused to shout, refused to scream, but she could see the shadows moving beyond the safety of the Compound's light, the telltale glint of Corsai's eyes and teeth, and panic rippled through her as they forced her toward the edge.

"What's the matter?" sneered the soldier. "I thought Harkers weren't afraid of the dark."

She squeezed her eyes shut and tried to reach across whatever thread bound her mind to the monster's, as if she could *summon* it to her.

"This is the part where you beg," said the soldier as Kate's boots skidded over the last few feet of the light strip, and she felt herself starting to slip. Her vision narrowed and her heart slowed. The urge was there, so simple, so clear.

"Taylor," warned the second soldier.

"Enough," called the third.

But Taylor's mouth was close, his breath hot on her skin. "Beg," he snarled, "the way my uncle did when your father—"

Kate drove her boot back into his knee, and heard the satisfying crack of bone right before he screamed, and in that moment of pain, his grip failed and she was behind him, forcing him to his knees, his face inches from the dark.

It would be so easy to pitch him forward across the line of light, into that place where real monsters waited.

"Stay back," she warned as the other two soldiers started toward her.

Kate bowed her head. "This is the part," she said, "where *you* beg."

Her vision slid in and out of focus, as if she were in a dream, and the soldier began to whimper softly, and everything in her wanted to just—let go. But the Chaos Eater hadn't come—it was still out there, still free.

Kate sighed, and hauled the soldier back into the safety of the light.

For an instant, the tower basement went *dark*.

A dark unlike Sloan had ever seen. True black—a total, unnatural absence of light—and then, just as quickly, the lights were back, flickering and only half as bright.

The Fangs looked around in confusion.

And there, in their midst, stood the shadow.

It smudged the air, just as it had in the footage. It had no face, no mouth, nothing but a pair of silver eyes, round as mirrors. The sight of it left Sloan cold. And hungry. As if he hadn't eaten in nights.

A few Fangs noticed it too, turning on the monster with raised fists and bloodshot eyes, only to stop, to still. Something passed between them, a flicker of motion, the flash of silver, and it was like watching dominoes tip. The Fangs turned away from the shadow, and toward one another—

And the killing began.

Sloan stood on the stage, mesmerized by the frenzy, by the way the Fangs began tearing at one another, their motions vicious but deliberate, moving with a strange mixture of urgency and calm, but what unnerved him most was the quiet. There should have been screams, pleas, terror and pain echoing through the concrete chamber, but the humans slaughtered one other in such perfect silence, while the shadow began to drift through the mass, growing more solid with every step.

Alice was across the stage, a cable in her hand, and when the creature reached the center of the floor, she let go.

The cage came whistling down, the gold veil billowing before it landed with a crash atop the shadow. That crash was so much louder than the killing, and yet the humans didn't waver from their slaughter, not even when Sloan leaped down from the stage and made his way toward the shrouded cell.

The sheet had slipped in the fall, a slice of darkness visible through the gap in the gold, and when Sloan peered through, he half expected the cage to be empty, the shadow gone. But there it was, a solid black shape in the center of the cell, and as he stopped before it, the shadow's silver eyes drifted up until Sloan saw himself reflected in them.

"Hello, my pet."

The soldier was on the ground, clutching his knee.

The other two hurried to his side as Kate stepped around his moaning form and started back toward the Compound.

She was halfway there when it happened.

Between one step and the next, her vision doubled and the world plunged away and she was falling. Not *down*—she was still on her feet, still on the light strip, but she was also somewhere else, somewhere cold and dark, damp and concrete—

—senses filling
with the acrid taste
of blood and ash
a gold cage
that burns
like smoke
and there
beyond the cage
a pair of red eyes
float in the dark
a skeleton
in a black suit
and the world
narrows
to the point
of a single shape
the name rising
like smoke—
    Sloan.

Sloan studied the shadow while the remaining Fangs grappled and strangled and fought among the bodies on the floor. Movement stirred at the edge of his sight as a man covered in blood started toward the stairs, his motions steady, purposeful.

"No one leaves," ordered Sloan, the words directed at Alice, who beamed before launching herself in a blur, snapping one man's neck before tearing out another's heart. She could be efficient when given the right task.

Sloan turned his attention back to the creature in the cage.

The footage had not done it justice.

It had shown Sloan the shadow's appearance, yes, revealed the way its influence spread from victim to victim, the violence like a disease, contagious. But on the tablet screen, the creature had been merely a shape, flat and featureless.

Now, standing in its presence, Sloan felt hollow, cold. His skin prickled and his teeth ached, and something as simple and primal as *fear* began to well inside him, until it met with something stronger.

Victory.

Here was a thing of darkness, like the Corsai; a lone hunter, like a Malchai; a creature that bristled Sloan's edges like a Sunai; but it was none of those things. It was a weapon, a thing of absolute destruction.

And now it belonged to him.

VERSE 4
A MONSTER UNLEASHED

1

Kate didn't remember falling, but she was on her hands and knees, blood dripping from her nose onto the glaring white light of the strip beneath her. Somewhere, beyond the ringing in her head, she heard the sound of steps, brisk and even, and she knew she had to get up, but the pain was tearing through her skull, and her thoughts were rattling around inside her head, shaken loose by the sudden change in who, in what, in where.

Sloan.

Sloan had the Chaos Eater.

Her vision doubled again, and for a flickering instant the Malchai was there, hovering in front of her on the strip, his sallow skin stretched over dark bones, and his red eyes looking right at her, *through* her—but Kate forced herself to her feet as he dissolved, replaced by cold gray eyes and short silver hair.

Soro.

Kate staggered back, or tried to, but the Sunai caught her by the collar.

"What happened just now?"

Kate's head was still spinning, but she managed to find a truth. "Your soldiers jumped me."

Soro wasn't having it. Their grip tightened, hauling Kate closer. "I saw you go down. *What happened?*"

Kate fought the pull of Soro's question, but the truth slid between clenched teeth. "The Chaos Eater," she said. "Sloan has it."

The Sunai's expression darkened. "How do you know?"

The words spilled out. "I saw it."

Soro's other hand grabbed Kate's hair and forced her head up. Her bangs fell to the side, revealing the silver in her eyes.

Soro hissed.

"It's not what you think," said Kate, but Soro wasn't listening. Their grip vanished from her hair, and she tried to twist free, but the Sunai still had a hand on her collar, and it was stone.

They tapped their comm. "This is Omega calling Flynn."

"Listen to me—" started Kate.

"Be quiet."

"Sloan has the Chaos—"

Soro's fist slammed into Kate's ribs. She doubled over, gasping for air, as red light flickered across her skin. One knee buckled beneath her, and before she could get up again, a strip of cloth was cinched tight over her eyes, plunging everything into black.

Alice rose to her feet, spitting blood on the floor.

"They taste off," she said with a grimace, but it hadn't stopped her from slaughtering the remaining Fangs, staining her clothes and limbs red.

Sloan drew on a pair of gloves.

Death was fresh on the air, the corpses still warm, but already the shadow in the cage was losing its substance. Soon it would be smoke again, thin enough to slip through the gap in the gold curtain, and Sloan couldn't let that happen.

He reached out and took hold of the shroud.

Even through the gloves, the gold *burned*—his skin began to blister and his blood to began to boil as he drew the sheet tight over the monster's cage.

He pulled back, hands singed.

Alice glanced at the cage, then looked pointedly away, and Sloan realized with a measure of delight that she was *frightened*.

She turned to go, but he caught her by the shoulder,

and he twisted her back toward the cage. "What do you think of my new pet?"

"I think," she said, "you should have killed it."

His nails dug in. "Are we ready for tonight?"

Alice wrenched free of his grip. "You stay here and play with your new *pet*," she sneered. "Leave tonight to me."

August got back to the Compound just after dark.

There was an energy to the building that night—there was always an energy, with so many people—but the usual rhythm had shifted, fallen out of sync, and for once, the feeling hadn't followed him in—it was already there. In the whispers, he heard Kate's name.

He went straight to the command center in search of her, but as soon as he stepped out of the elevator, he knew something was wrong.

Emily was waiting for him. "August."

And when he asked about Kate, a shadow crossed Em's face. "What is it?"

"Come with me."

"What happened?"

"There's been an incident."

His mind flashed across a dozen possible scenarios but instead of dwelling on any of them, he turned and marched toward the surveillance room.

"August," said Em on his heels. "She was infected."

And he almost said *I know,* but caught himself.

"Ilsa," he called. "Show me where Kate is."

But his sister was already waiting, knees drawn up before the wall of screens. She shot him a look but he didn't stop to read it, looking straight past her at the screens—eleven of the twelve were cycling, but there, in the center of the grid, a single camera held its shot.

The first thing he saw, the only thing he saw, was Kate.

Kate, on her knees in the center of the cell, hands cuffed to the floor and a swatch of black over her eyes. Just like the soldier.

Ilsa's fingers tightened on his sleeve in a wordless apology.

"What happened?" he asked, when what he really meant was *how did they find out?*

Ilsa tapped the keys, and Henry and Soro appeared on a second screen—the viewing chamber.

Another tap and sound streamed into the room.

". . . wasting time," Kate was saying. "I told you, Sloan has the Chaos Eater."

August's heart lurched, but no one else seemed to react to the news. Soro stood silent, arms crossed, while Henry paced.

"And you know this," he said, "because you *saw* it."

August thought he heard a hitch in the man's breath, but it might have been static. "And you saw it, because you have been infected."

Kate was shaking her head. "I'm still in control."

"You attacked an FTF soldier," said Soro.

"He attacked *me*," snapped Kate.

"You told us what this monster does," said Henry. "That it infects human minds. And you have brought that infection into my house, into my ranks."

"No," protested Kate.

"You put this entire Compound in danger—"

"*No.*"

But Henry's voice was cold. "Do you even know what it is, this connection between you? Do you know how far it goes? If you can see through this monster's eyes, what's to stop it from seeing through yours?"

Kate opened her mouth, but said nothing. August had heard enough. He turned toward the door, but Emily barred his path.

"Did you know?" she asked.

He swallowed. "She wanted to help."

Emily's face hardened. "August—"

"She's our best chance of hunting that thing."

On the screen, Henry began to cough. Soro took a step toward him, but he waved the Sunai away. "Tell me again," he said to Kate, "what you saw—"

But he was cut off by a sudden, blaring siren.

The noise tore through August's head as the wall of screens went dark, and the lights around them flickered, and a second later, all the power in the Compound went out.

11

Kate's head snapped up.

Even with one bad ear and the blindfold over her eyes, she knew that something was *very* wrong.

Alarms crashed through the concrete room, rebounding on every wall. Henry's voice was there, somewhere underneath all the noise, and so was Soro's, but the shapes of their words were lost.

And then they were gone, and Kate was alone in the cell, painfully aware that she was still chained to the floor. She bowed her head toward her hands and dragged the blindfold down. No one ordered her to stop. That was the first sign of trouble. The second was that the world beyond the cloth was just as black.

For ten long seconds there was nothing but sirens and darkness, and then, just as suddenly as the alarms started, they switched off, leaving only black space and the ringing in her head.

An emergency power source kicked in, rendering the cell in a bluish half-light.

"Hey," she called to the plastic insert in the wall, but no one answered.

Kate tried to stay calm as she bowed her head, fingers sliding around to the back of her neck. Along the collar of her uniform, she'd slipped two pins. The first bit of metal came free in her hand and she set to work on the cuffs.

The ground shook, a tremor running through the concrete. The power faltered again, and the pin slipped from her fingers, skidding out of reach. Kate swore viciously and freed the second pin, forcing herself to slow, and her fingers to stay steady.

After a few seconds, the cuffs released, and Kate shot up from the ground, but the cell door was locked. From the outside. There wasn't even a handle, only a plate drilled into the steel.

She turned, looking for another way out, which was ridiculous considering the room was six slabs of concrete and a strip of shatter-proof plastic. She had no weapons, nothing but a pair of pins and the clothes on her back. Her boots. They had metal in the soles, maybe with enough force she could—

The power guttered a third time, and the lock inside the door clicked off. Kate threw herself against it, the steel falling open before the generators came back up. She was out.

The hall beyond was empty, lit by the same bluish glow, and the ground trembled again beneath her feet, like the faint aftershocks of an earthquake, as Kate surged up the stairs.

There was too much noise.

The sirens echoed through August's head even after they were shut off, and the command center was a wall of soldiers talking over the buzz of the emergency power and the voices on the comms as reports came in and orders went out.

Someone had attacked the transformers.

The metal towers that routed power to the Compound and the surrounding barracks. The metal towers located *south* of the FTF's buildings, far from the Seam. In six months, the Malchai had never ventured that far, hadn't made a concerted strike—

Until now.

"Squads One through Eight report to the power block," ordered Phillip.

"Ten through Twelve report to the Seam," said Marcon.

"Thirteen through Twenty take the UVR strip," added Shia.

"Twenty-one through Thirty, evacuate the barracks," instructed Bennet.

August was already moving toward the stairs, already issuing orders to his own squad. They had a plan for this. They had a plan for almost *everything*. But plans and realities were different things. Plans were crisp, clean— the stuff of paper and drill—and realities, August had learned, were always, always, always messy.

Soro appeared, supporting Henry, who was white as a sheet and still coughing. This time he couldn't seem to stop. The cough became a retch, and then a spasm, and Henry was fighting for air—and then Emily was there, calling for a medic, and Soro was pulling August away.

"We have work to do, brother."

And August knew that they were right.

"I'll be okay," gasped Henry. "*Go.*"

So August went, plunging down the stairs with Soro at his side. Leo's voice was a stream in the back of his head, a smooth and steady current of orders, and August let himself lean into the efficiency of his brother's thinking. He hit the ground floor and for an instant he thought of going down instead of out, but Kate was safer in a locked room than up here, whether or not she would agree.

Harris, Jackson, and Ani were already in formation by the main doors.

"Alpha team."

They saluted him, Harris grinning as if they were on their way to a party. Harris was always happy about a fight. Ani looked grim but determined. Jackson looked like he'd been caught in the middle of a shower, his wet hair plastered back.

A line of jeeps idled on the strip, their high beams up. The grid was only three blocks away, but with the power being diverted to the main facilities, it would be three blocks of solid black.

"Let's go."

Kate took the stairs two at a time, trying to scrub the last of the dried blood from her face as she reached Sublevel 1.

The armory was an exercise in organized chaos. In the low light, soldiers bustled, suiting up while team leaders issued orders and subordinates talked around and under each other.

"—an attack on the central grid—"

"Transformers one through four are down—"

So they'd gone after the power. Darkness was a dangerous thing in a place like Verity, which made power the most important resource, the only thing that kept the monsters at bay. Sloan was upping the stakes. Bringing the fight to them.

"The first wave is en route—"

"—some kind of explosive—"

Was that what she'd felt?

"—reports of Malchai on the scene—"

Kate's mind reeled as she fell in with the current of soldiers.

She was still dressed like an FTF, and the half-light of the emergency generators cast the same muted glow over everyone, erasing details and reducing the soldiers to shadows in FTF suits.

The corridor was lined with armored vests and—not helmets, exactly, more like modified sparring gear with visors that shielded the eyes and left the bottom half of the face exposed. They made her think of the Wardens, of Liam's attempts to design a proper suit, something that would protect her.

She was reaching for a vest when she realized—this was her chance. She could take advantage of the chaos, suit up, and slip out.

They knew about the sickness now, and when this was over, they'd probably throw her right back in that cell. She should run. But she thought of Ilsa, helping her at every turn. Of August, almost certainly on his way to the grid.

She could go.

Or she could stay and fight.

Show them she wasn't a monster.

Someone pushed a gun into her hands, and her blood sang, vision narrowing as her thumb slid over the safety. Her finger drifted toward the trigger.

Kate ejected the clip and holstered the weapon and ammo separately.

She longed for her spikes, but settled for a baton coated in iron, a pair of knives, and an HUV beam, and followed the stream of FTFs up to the lobby, pulling her helmet on as she went. She knocked the visor down over her eyes and trailed the soldiers out, past the doors and onto the dim stretch that had, hours before, been a vivid line of light.

Jeeps were peeling away toward the site of the attack—marked against the dark skyline by gray smoke and the flicker of fire. Her father's tower loomed in the opposite direction, a beacon of shadow.

Sloan, whispered the darkness in her head.

He had the Chaos Eater, and the urge to go after them both sang through her like madness. But that's just what it was. Madness. Because she knew she couldn't kill them both, not alone.

Kate took off toward the last of the jeeps.

The convoy tore a strip of light through the dark streets as it made its way to the transformer grid, Jackson at the wheel.

August didn't have his violin—not when there were so many soldiers involved—and the absence felt wrong. He took a baton from the utility kit, just to have something to hold, even though its surface made his skin prickle and his stomach turn.

Jackson swore when they rounded the corner and the FTF's central power structure came into sight.

It was on fire.

A blast had taken out a chunk of the transformers, the remnants hissing and sparking in the dark. The FTFs set to guard the station lay scattered at the base of the nearest support building, their bodies—what was left of them—twisted, broken, Corsai already swarming the remains. August leaped out of the jeep before it stopped, and Soro jumped down from the next with inhuman grace, flute-knife out and ready.

"Get the lights up!" ordered August.

The vehicles circled, spinning their high beams toward the wreckage, and the Corsai scattered as technicians hurried to isolate and resequence the remaining power.

Severed lines hissed and skated across the ground, and one of the support buildings looked like it was about to collapse.

And then it did.

It took out another transformer as it crumbled, and a block away, a line of buildings went dark.

❖

Kate leaped down from the jeep and found a world on fire, the air electric and the whole block plunged into chaos. The FTFs were clearly used to fighting small battles—and so was she—but whatever was happening at the power station, it wasn't a fight. It was a set of dominoes being knocked down.

But Kate's first thought wasn't about the power—it was about the number of FTFs standing in the road.

We're exposed, she thought. She craned her neck, scanning the rooftops, and caught sight of a pair of burning red eyes right before a blast went off, not on the transformers, but on the *street.*

The ground shook violently, and nearby the pavement cracked and gave way, plunging a cluster of soldiers down into the dark. Shouts went up as another blast went off.

And another.

And another.

All around her, the road was crumbling.

Kate sprinted for cover, drawing her baton as the ground shuddered and split under her boots. She got her back to a wall just in time to see another section of the street collapse, swallowing two more soldiers.

The blasts were coming from the tunnels below.

"Get off the ground!" she called, her voice lost in the

fray before she remembered the comm hooked to her vest. She punched the button and shouted into the mic.

A few of the soldiers straightened, but too many were still weaving through the wreckage, trying to help the wounded. Idiots.

The night was filling with smoke and dust and debris, and Kate hauled herself a few rungs up a fire escape and squinted through the haze, searching for August. Instead she saw a shock of silver hair moving through the fray. Soro.

A massive blast rocked the night and the Sunai staggered, covering their ears, as the ground nearby split, cracks racing toward them along the street. Soro couldn't see them, but Kate could.

She called out to the Sunai, and Soro's head shot up, eyes narrowing.

"Move!" shouted Kate, an instant before the road beneath the Sunai gave way. Soro moved just in time, lunging out of the path.

Kate climbed another rung, scanning the chaos. She saw August down the block, covered in dust and holding up a wounded FTF.

At the same moment, he looked up and saw her, raising a hand just before the ground exploded at his feet.

|||

The world went white.

One second August was standing on the street and the next, he was engulfed—he couldn't see, couldn't hear, couldn't feel anything but force of the explosion.

Is this what it feels like, he wondered, *to be unmade?*

But then he hit the ground.

He landed hard, the fall knocking the air from his lungs. His head rang from the blast, his hearing swallowed by the high white noise.

The world was dark around him, but at least the darkness seemed to be a shallow thing, somewhere in *front* of his eyes, instead of behind them. High overhead there was a hole and, beyond that, the smoky night, the far-off haze of headlights. Judging by the vaulted ceiling, the long echo, and the metal bars beneath his back, he'd landed in a subway tunnel.

The wounded FTF lay nearby, his body twisted

unnaturally atop the rubble. When August tried to move, he realized he might not be hurt or broken, but he was *stuck*, one leg pinned beneath concrete and rebar.

Slowly, the tinny ringing in his ears subsided, and he could make out a different kind of noise. The steady rush of water.

His chest tightened in panic but the sound wasn't getting any closer. The subway—it was built over a river. When he shifted, bits of rubble tumbled down through the gaps in the floor and dropped the long way to the water below.

August threw all his weight into freeing himself from the debris, but none of it yielded.

The Corsai in the shadows snickered.

sunaisunaistucksunai

August looked around for something, anything, to use as a lever, and as he scanned the tunnel, two burning red dots, like the ends of cigarettes, danced in the dark.

"Alice."

"Hello, August."

There was something in her hand. A remote.

She nudged an object with her foot and it rolled toward him, stopping against a chunk of concrete by his knee. It looked like a lopsided ball, a lumpy package all tied up with tape.

It took him too long to realize what it was.

Alice perched on the farthest piece of rubble and turned the detonator between her fingers. "How long can Sunai hold their breath?"

"August!" Kate's voice echoed through the tunnel.

She was above him, crouched at the edge of the hole, tying a cable to a piece of rebar.

No, thought August. *Run.*

But it was too late.

Alice looked up.

Her red eyes flared wide, and Kate stared back in shock, and August tried to say something—anything— just as the Malchai hit the remote.

The blast went off, and the ground gave way, and he was falling again, still tangled up in the concrete and steel and taking half the subway floor down with him.

And this time, the ground didn't stop his fall.

How long can Sunai hold their breath?

He hit the surface of the water and sank like a stone.

Kate stared down at the Malchai and for a strange, disorienting instant she didn't—couldn't—grasp what she was seeing. It was like a reflection, distorted by smoke and shadow. And then she understood.

She was staring at a ghost, a shade, a monster made in her own image.

And it looked up at her and smiled just before the blast.

The explosion rocked the tunnel, and Kate nearly lost her balance as August crashed into the river.

"Soro!" she called out, grabbing the cable and leaping into the dark. The cord burned her palms as she descended too fast and hit the ground hard, rolling up with an HUV in one hand and the gun in the other.

The shadows hissed around her, rebuffed by the beam of light and the metal tracery on her gear.

A second later Soro landed in a graceful crouch several feet away, no rope, nothing but six feet of long limbs and the inability to break on impact.

All Kate said was "August," but Soro was already moving, fastening a cable to their belt as they dove through the jagged hole in the subway floor and into the shadowed water below.

Kate swung her HUV around, cutting through the clouds of dust and the deeper shadows, but there was no sign of the Malchai. She set the light on the ground and drew the gun's clip from her belt just as something moved behind her—she heard the shift of rock on her good side, the tumble of rubble through slats, and turned.

The Malchai stood waiting at the limit of the light, a nightmarish version of Kate herself, the shape right and the details all wrong.

Red eyes instead of blue.

White hair instead of blond.

The monster was thinner than Kate, gaunt in the way all Malchai were, but she *looked* like her, distorted, an echo, just as Sloan had been an echo of Harker, him and not him, neither and both and something in between.

Had her father felt the same disgust, looking at Sloan?

Or had he seen only proof of his own power?

The monster pursed its lips—*her* lips—and when she spoke, her voice had an echo of Sloan's melodic rise, but also an edge of grit. "Hello, Kate."

Soro swung a wet arm out of the hole, and the Malchai glanced sideways. Kate didn't hesitate. She drove the clip into the gun, swung it up, and fired. It felt good, felt right, the shock of the recoil, the satisfying *bang-bang-bang* as she fired three quick rounds at the Malchai's chest.

Kate had always been fast.

But her shadow was faster, dodging out of the way before the first shot echoed through the tunnel. The Malchai spun with that horrible, monstrous grace and slammed a boot into Kate's chest. She hit the subway floor, all the wind rushing out of her lungs.

The armor absorbed the worst of the blow, but it still left her breathless and wincing as she staggered to her feet.

The Malchai was already gone, swallowed up by the tunnel's impenetrable dark, nothing but a trail of laughter in her wake. Everything in Kate said *run*—not *away*, but *after*. She made it one stride, two, before Soro dragged themself out of the pit, hauling August onto the subway floor.

He coughed and retched, chest heaving.

Kate crossed to his side. "August—"

"He'll be all right," said Soro, slicking back their hair.

"Easy for you—to say—" he gasped, spitting brackish water onto the ground.

But as Kate knelt beside him, as she helped him to his feet, as they climbed back out of the tunnel, her gaze drifted again and again and again to the dark that had swallowed her shadow, wishing she had gone after it.

||||

August sat on the hall floor, his ears still ringing from the blast.

He had gone straight to the Compound's infirmary, expecting to find Henry on one of the cots. Instead he'd found the head of the FTF on his feet, seeing to the wounded as if he himself hadn't just collapsed.

"He's stronger than he looks," Em had said, but August could hear the static in his father's chest, the tick of time slipping, its unsteady rhythm like a faulty clock.

But Henry wouldn't look at him, and his hands were covered in a soldier's blood, so August left, leaned back against the wall outside, and let himself slide down until he was sitting on the floor.

Water dripped from his hair, and every time he breathed, he felt the remains of the river in his lungs.

How long can Sunai hold their breath?

There had been a moment under the surface, before

Soro reached him, when Leo's voice had surged to the front of his mind, and told him to *fall*, to unleash that dark self, the one that slept within his skin.

And he hadn't.

The August I knew would rather die.

You make it worth the pain.

You don't let go.

His body had screamed, the pressure turning to pain in his lungs. He'd heard that drowning wasn't a bad way to die, that at some point it even became peaceful, but it hadn't been peaceful for him.

Would he have given in, if Soro hadn't come?

The lights came back up, the emergency blue replaced by steady white, and August heard a nervous cheer go through the building.

The technicians had contained the damage at the power station and rerouted what power they could back into the Compound, but to do so they'd had to cut the supply from most of the FTF structures. Beyond the front doors, the light strip glowed at half strength. Beyond that, the night was dangerously dark.

Too dark to assess the damage.

Too dark to collect the dead.

They'd have to wait until dawn and hope there were bodies left to burn. Meanwhile, people kept streaming into the Compound, the population of several blocks crammed into a handful of buildings. The lobby was packed, as was the training hall, and every apartment—even the Flynn's home—was being divvied up between Soro's and August's squads, so he stayed there, on the floor outside the infirmary and slicked damp hair off his face as a familiar set of steps came toward him down the hall.

Everyone was made of sounds, and August had learned hers the first day they met.

Kate slumped against the opposite wall.

She hadn't said anything since they'd left the tunnel. Dust and debris streaked her fatigues, she didn't look well—her skin was beaded with sweat, and the silver was threading out across both eyes.

"I keep waiting for someone to arrest me again," she said. "Everyone seems to be busy."

There was no humor in the words. Her tone was cool, her gaze flat, and August guessed why.

Alice.

August rose to his feet. "Come with me," he said, reaching for her hand.

She let him lead her, but her shoulders were tense, her body coiled. "Where are we going?"

"Somewhere private."

She raised an eyebrow, as if such a place didn't exist anymore. There was a line for the elevators, so they took the stairs, climbing floor after floor in silence. Not a comfortable silence, but the kind that grew stiffer with every step. August didn't know what to say and if Kate did, she didn't plan on saying it, not yet.

When they reached the top, he led her not to the apartment, but up the hidden stairs to the flat stretch of the Compound's roof.

For months, he'd imagined showing her this view. In his mind, Kate sat beside him, shoulder to shoulder on the sun-warmed stone, and they looked out at the city. In his mind, the war was over, and there was no North and South, no monster and human, only Verity, and a blanket of stars shining through the dark.

In his mind, it didn't go like this.

The moment they were alone, the levy broke.

Kate turned on him. "Did you know?"

He could have deflected the question. After all, it hadn't been explicit, but he knew exactly what she was asking about.

"Did you *know*?"

August let the truth rise up. "Yes. About a week after Sloan took control. We were on a rescue mission . . ."

"All this time," she whispered, "you knew she was here and you didn't tell me."

His eyes flicked to Kate's shadow, the thin shape twitching like a tail behind her. "All actions have costs. On some level, you had to know."

"No." She shook her head. "I knew what would happen, but I thought—I hoped—whatever it was—it was somewhere *out there*, haunting the Waste. It wasn't supposed to be *here*."

"Well, it is," said August. "It came back. With Sloan."

Kate wrapped her arms around her ribs. "It—it *looks* like me, August. That *thing*—"

"Alice is *nothing* like you."

Kate's head shot up. "Alice?"

"That's what she calls herself."

Something gave way inside Kate. He could *feel* it. "Of course." She looked up at the sky in a way that said she simply couldn't look at *him*. "My father told me that Malchai take their names from our shadows. Our ghosts. Whatever haunts us most. Sloan was his right-hand man—not his first kill, but the first one to leave a mark."

"And Alice?"

Kate closed her eyes. "Alice was my mother. I pulled the trigger in that house, I shot that stranger, but Alice Harker was my first murder. I'm the reason we ran away. I'm the reason Callum sent his monster after us. I'm the reason she's dead."

Two tears escaped down Kate's face, but before August could reach out, she was scrubbing them away. "I'm the reason that monster is here."

August swallowed. He couldn't lie, but the truth was cruel. He took a careful step toward Kate, and when she didn't pull away, he wrapped his arms around her. She didn't soften against him but held on tight.

"We'll stop her," said August.

"She's *my* shadow," said Kate, pressing her face into his collar.

And when she spoke again, the words were so quiet, a human would never have heard them.

"I'll stop her myself."

╫╫╫

Sloan peeled off the gloves and examined his hands, the blistered, oozing surface of his palms.

"Sacrifice," he mused to the shrouded cage. "Callum used to say that sacrifice is a cornerstone of success. Of course, Callum preferred sacrificing *others*. . . ."

He trailed off when he heard Alice coming.

That in and of itself was odd—she usually had an uncanny ability to appear and disappear without warning, but tonight her steps echoed through the basement. They came not from the stairs but from the subway tunnel on the other side. During Harker's reign, the Malchai had been forced to come and go that way, so as not to frighten the building's human tenants.

In the months since Sloan's ascent, and until his newest project, the tunnel had become the realm of the Corsai, and the Corsai alone. But here she was, dusted with ash.

"How was our little diversion?" he asked. "I heard the blasts from—"

"She's here," cut in Alice.

"Who?"

"Kate Harker," she said, eyes burning bright. "She's *here.*"

The words sent a perfect shiver down Sloan's spine. Not fear, oh no, but something sweet. The taste of fresh blood spilling over his tongue, the tang of hate, and the thought of life going out of those blue eyes. Callum's eyes set into his daughter's face. Eyes that no stand-in, no surrogate, no sacrifice could replace.

"You saw her?"

"She looks like me, but wrong, all squishy and human, and she's with the *Sunai*. When did she get here? Did you know?" Alice couldn't contain her excitement. She began to pace. "I wanted to tear her throat out right then and there, but there would have been nothing to savor, and I was caught off guard, but next time—"

"You will not kill her," said Sloan.

Alice's red eyes widened. "But she's *mine.*"

"She was mine first."

"You can have whoever you want—"

"I *know.*"

Alice let out a low snarl before his fingers wrapped around her narrow throat. Pain flared across his ruined palms, and Alice bared her teeth and drove her nails into his arm, but he didn't let go.

Alice had obviously *forgotten*. Forgotten what she was, what *he* was, forgotten that she was not predator to him, but prey.

Drops of black blood slid down her neck where his fingers cut in. He lifted her thin body off the ground.

"Listen to me," he said smoothly, "and listen well. We are not equals, you and I. We are not family. We are not blood. You are a whelp. A shadow. Your strength is the barest echo of my strength. You continue to exist because I let you. But the scales of my favor are delicate, and if you tip them any more, I will rip your fangs out with my bare hands one by one, and leave you to starve. Do you understand?"

Alice let out a low feral sound before answering.

"Yes—"

He saw her start to form the word *Father* and tightened his grip.

And then he let go, and Alice slumped to her knees, breathing heavily. When she brought her hand to her throat, Sloan was pleased to see her fingers tremble.

He knelt before her. "Now, now," he cooed, drawing his gloves back on. "Katherine belongs to me, but if you're useful, I will share."

Slowly Alice looked up, her red eyes blazing and her voice hoarse.

"What do you want me to do?"

ﬀﬀ
|

"How are you feeling?"

Kate peeled her head up from August's shoulder. She knew from his tone—so cautious, so careful—that he wasn't talking about Alice anymore.

"I'm still me," she said, because that was as close to the truth as she could get.

"If Sloan has the Chaos Eater—"

"He *does.*"

"Then we know where to find it. We'll get a team together and—"

August's comm went off in a short shower of static. Kate pulled away as Henry's voice came over the line.

"I could use some steady hands down here."

She took a step toward the edge of the roof. Months ago, the city had blazed with light. Now it sprawled in varying degrees of shadow, dotted by patches of solid black.

"I'm on my way," August said into the comm, starting toward the rooftop door.

"I thought you hated blood," said Kate.

"I do," said August. "But life can't always be pleasant." He hesitated by the door, obviously waiting for her to follow, but Kate couldn't bear the claustrophobic Compound. Not yet.

"If it's all right, I'll stay up here a little longer."

August looked uncertain, but she waved her hand at the vast expanse of nothing. "Where am I going to go?" she teased. "Besides"—she cracked a tired smile— "Soro's less likely to find me up here."

And I'm less likely to hurt someone.

August relented. "Okay," he said. "Just—don't get too close to the edge."

The door swung shut, and Kate was alone. She didn't realize she was fraying until she began to unravel.

She sank into a crouch on the rooftop and wrapped her arms around her knees, the image of the monster— of *Alice*—ghosted behind her eyes. The casualty report, its gruesome murders all marked with an *A*.

What had she done?

She'd spent the last six months trying to save another city while hers burned, six months hunting monsters while her own hunted here.

Something chimed in the pocket of her gear.

Kate dragged her head up. She'd grabbed the vest off the sublevel wall, and never had a chance to check the pockets. Rooting around, she came up with a palm-sized tablet, standard issue for all the FTFs. Someone must have left theirs in the gear and—

Kate's thoughts broke apart when she saw the message on the screen.

It was titled *KOH*, the kind of acronym you wouldn't know, unless it belonged to you.

Katherine Olivia Harker.

And when she tapped the screen, she saw that the message hadn't been sent to this one tablet. It had been sent to all of them. A blanket broadcast across the FTF feed.

The message was only one line.

Are you afraid of your own shadow?

A.

Kate forgot to breathe.

She was back in the tunnel, watching her shadow escape into the dark and wanting to follow, and this time there was no Soro, no August, nothing to distract her, and she was already on her feet, heading for the door, the stairs, the way down, out. The need burned through her veins like fever, and even without the voiceless presence in her skull pushing her on, she knew that Alice was her making, her monster.

And it was her job to kill it.

Before it killed anyone else.

It turned out Henry didn't want August to scrub in.

He wanted him to *play.*

"To the wounded," he explained, gesturing at the infirmary and the FTFs who'd been caught in the power station
blasts, two dozen men and women laid out on cots. The
Compound was running low on sedatives. Injuries had
grown fairly rare in the FTF—when it came to missions,
most either got out in one piece or didn't get out at all.

"The room isn't soundproofed," said August.

"Then play softly," countered his father. "It's worth
some dazed bystanders, if it helps with their pain."

August fetched his violin. Henry stepped outside,
and August closed the door behind him and drew up a
chair, bow hesitating over the strings.

He thought of the soldier in the cell.

Soro snapping the man's neck.

Leo saying it was a waste.

But he also thought of the relief washing over the soldier, the struggle going out of his limbs.

Maybe there is more to us than murder.

He started to play, softly, and within seconds the
muffled sounds of pain fell away. The tension in the
patients' limbs slackened, their breathing eased, and

their souls began to surface, filling the infirmary with pale but steady light.

August exhaled, his own body loosening with the music, and for the first time in four years, the song itself felt like a kind of nourishment, filling him like light, like life, like a soul, and—

Tablets began to chime. They went off at once, all over the Compound, and August faltered, losing the melody. A broadcast? Across the entire task force?

He set the instrument aside, drawing his own device from his pocket.

He read the message once, then again and again, and then he was on his feet, the violin abandoned as he ran.

The doors banged open, revealing an empty roof, an open sky.

And no Kate.

August backtracked to the apartment, trying to stay calm, telling himself she wouldn't do this, wouldn't walk straight into a trap, not alone, that Kate was smarter than that—

But he also heard the words she'd whispered into his collar and saw the silver dancing in her eyes, a demon twisting her thoughts toward violence.

Harris and Ani were playing cards on the couch, Allegro between them.

Ani looked up. "I didn't know you had a cat."

Jackson was making coffee, his tablet in his hand.

"Hey, August, any idea what this means?"

He didn't answer.

The bedroom was empty.

The bathroom was empty.

Harris was on his feet now. "What's going on?"

I'll kill her myself.

He should never have left her alone.

"It's Kate, isn't it?" said Ani, shoving on her boots. "I can tell by your face."

Jackson blocked his path, coffee in hand. August was taller, but Jackson was broader by far. "Get out of my way," ordered August.

"Where are we going, captain?"

"*You* aren't going anywhere," said August.

Ani *tsked*. "No solo missions."

"I'd never ask—"

"You don't have to," said Harris, zipping up his vest. "You go, we go."

August shook his head. "You don't even care about her."

"No," said Ani, holstering a blade. "But you do. And that's a first."

Jackson downed the last of his coffee. "Where's she headed?"

"The tower," said August.

"Odds of catching her before she hits the Seam?"

"Depends if she's on foot . . ."

Ani was on the comm. "Alpha squad here; we need a jeep."

Just like that, they'd fallen into form. As if this were any other mission. "Thank you."

"Don't thank us, boss. Not until we bring her back."

Kate was many things, but she wasn't stupid.

She knew it was a trap. Of course she did. But the way she saw it, either Alice would be waiting for her, or Sloan would, and either way, she had a debt to pay.

She didn't look back, couldn't afford to second-guess.

The Seam rose ahead of her, and the line of light that traced its spine must have been on a different trans-former, because it was still up, soldiers pacing on top. Kate secured her helmet and started up the ladder, reminding herself over and over that she was one of them—or rather, still suited up from the attack at the power station, she *looked* like one of them.

She crested the edge and stepped onto the Seam's spine, thankful she'd never been afraid of heights. North City sprawled out below her—from this position she could see down the main thoroughfare, straight to Harker Hall.

"What are you doing here?" demanded an FTF with the bearing of a squad leader.

Kate didn't hesitate. Pauses give a lie away. "Here to relieve someone, sir."

The soldier held out a hand, as if to shake, but when Kate took it, he pulled her close.

"Relief units arrived ten minutes ago," he said, squeezing her fingers. "Try again."

Kate let out an exasperated breath. She really didn't have time for this. One hand still pinned in the FTF's grip, she drew her gun with the other, leveling it at his chest.

"I'm going over this wall," she said quietly. "One way or another."

The dark sang through her: the weight of the steel in her hand, the shock on his face, the dizzying relief of being in control. It would be so easy—but she kept the safety on and her finger away from the trigger, and the sight of the weapon—or maybe her willingness to use it—was enough to make the man let go.

Kate took a step toward the nearest ladder.

"I'll call it in," he said, "the second you're gone."

"Go ahead," said Kate, swinging her leg over the lip.

If August didn't know, he would soon.

The jeep was waiting at the edge of the light strip.

And so was Soro.

The Sunai stood between August and the idling vehicle.

Sometimes, when Leo had been in a righteous mood, the energy had practically wicked off him, like heat. Ilsa, too, seemed to create her own cloud whenever her thoughts began to spiral, and she had told August more than once that when he was sad, she could feel it in the air around him, like a cold front.

If it was true—that a Sunai could alter the space around them—then the air around Soro was a storm. August signaled for his squad to stay put and started forward across the grid.

"You're going after her," said Soro. It wasn't a question.

"I am."

Soro didn't move, and August had to. Kate was getting farther away by the second.

"If you intend to stop me—"

Soro's gray eyes hardened. "You would risk these lives, and yours, for a sinner."

"No," said August, "I would risk them for a friend."

The Sunai let out a low breath and marched toward him, and August braced himself for a fight, but it didn't come. Soro just kept walking, back toward the Compound.

"You should go, then," they said. "Before it's too late."

ⅦⅡ

The jeep skidded to a stop at the base of the Seam.

Word had come over the comms a minute before—a young female soldier had forced her way through at gunpoint.

Jackson flashed the high beams, but the gate didn't open, and August and Harris climbed out as an FTF started toward them.

"We're on lockdown, sir. No one crosses—"

"But you've already *let* someone through."

"She pulled a gun—"

"Is that all it takes?" asked Harris, freeing his sidearm. August caught his wrist. Somewhere nearby, tires skidded over asphalt. Another vehicle was headed their way.

"We need to get through," he said to the soldier. "*Now.*"

The FTF shook his head. "I'm under strict orders."

"And I'm August Flynn."

"With respect," he said, "my orders come from the top."

Lights flared against the side of the Seam as the second jeep swung to a stop, and Henry got out. Had Soro told him, or had he seen the message for himself?

"Henry, I have to—"

"Sir," said the soldier at the same time. "I was just—"

"Open the gate," ordered Henry.

This time the soldier didn't hesitate. He radioed the order and the gate began to grind open. August turned toward his father. "You're letting us go?"

"No," said Henry, moving toward August's jeep. "I'm coming with you."

"No offense, sir," said Harris, "but I don't think that's a good idea."

Henry laughed softly as he opened the door. "Well, then, it's a good thing I outrank you."

"We can handle it from here," insisted Ani.

But August only stared at his father, his sickly pallor, his too-thin form. It made no sense. Henry was in no shape to fight. "Why?"

Henry put a hand on his shoulder. "I am a man, not a movement," he said. "But if a movement is what it takes to end this war, then I will play my part. Now"— his hand tightened and then was gone—"let's go find Miss Harker."

◆

North City had gotten darker.

That was Kate's first thought as she moved through the streets, HUV in one hand and gun in the other. The Corsai murmured from the shadows, flashing teeth and claws.

harkerharkeritsaharker

Her FTF gear was traced with metal, but there was a difference between *deterring* monsters and *stopping* them, and she tried to stay in the light, what little there was.

Her father's tower rose ahead of her.

Or rather, a hulking shadow loomed in its place.

Kate's steps slowed. She stopped beneath a single low-wattage streetlight, its flickering bulb the only thing standing between her and a blackout zone.

It carved a lightless circle around the base of Harker Hall, a dark inversion of the moat that surrounded the Compound. It felt like a physical thing, that darkness, something more than air and night.

A wall of black.

And, embedded in that wall, a pair of red eyes.

The Malchai stepped out of the shadows, and Kate saw not her own shadow, but her father's.

Sloan.

She'd seen him in dreams, in memories, but they paled compared to the truth. In her visions, he'd been reduced to a shape in a dark suit. Reduced to fangs and blood and malice. But now he stood before her, gray flesh pulled tight over blackened bones, fingers ending in silver points. Fear slammed through Kate's chest, and Sloan smiled as if he could *hear* the traitorous thing raging in her pulse.

When he spoke, his voice grazed her skin like a knife. Metal across skin.

"Katherine."

The sound of her name on his lips, sweet and taunting.

"Sloan," she said, fighting to keep her tone dry. "What a surprise."

He spread his hands. "You didn't think I'd let Alice keep you to herself. Not when we have such *history.*"

Her fingers tightened on the gun. The night rustled around her, dotted with red as shadows emerged from the darkness. Malchai. Not one or two, but a half dozen forming a loose circle around them.

"Not exactly a fair fight."

Sloan clicked his tongue. "What place does fair have in a world like ours? *Fair* is a white flag. A word for cowards." He gestured to her clothing. "You've traded sides. Your father would be disappointed."

"My father is dead." She kept her head high. She wanted to look Sloan in the eyes when she killed him.

Slid the knife under his skin and up into his heart, savoring the delicious warmth.

The Chaos Eater whispered through her, hungry for Sloan's blood; her fear replaced by hatred, cold and steady; but she held the monster at bay. Not yet, not yet. There would be no going back. She would let it out, if she had to. When she had to.

But it would be on her terms.

"You've changed," observed Sloan. His lips parted, revealing pointed teeth. "But I can still taste your—"

"Down, dog," she snarled, firing the gun.

But Sloan moved like light, like smoke, like nothing, and by the time the shot rang out, he was behind her, an arm around her shoulders as he pulled her back against him.

His breath was ice against her neck. "I've waited for this."

"Keep waiting," she growled, slamming her elbow back and up into the side of his head. Sloan was fast but Kate had learned to fight dirty. He fell back a single step, but it was enough for her to get free and put two paces, three, between them.

Sloan laughed: a horrible sound, too high. "You are even more stubborn than I remember."

The other Malchai shifted and stirred, bloodlust heavy in the air, but Sloan had obviously told them this was *his* kill. How long would they listen? Her father had tried to keep the Malchai on a leash—it hadn't gone well.

Kate drew a knife as Sloan came at her again.

She slashed, expecting him to retreat, or at least to dodge. He didn't. Instead the Malchai shifted the slightest step left and let the knife plunge right into his arm as he continued forward, closing the distance between them. Black blood welled up, staining the sleeve of Sloan's suit, but neither surprise nor pain registered on his face. Kate didn't even have time to draw the blade back, to retreat. He was inside her guard.

His hand closed around her neck, his shoe caught her heel, and for a terrible second, when she hit the pavement, they were back in the gravel outside the house in the Waste, Sloan pressing her body down into broken rock, fingers tight around her throat.

She forced her mind back to the present.

Sloan was on top of her, the hilt of the knife pinned between them so she couldn't free the blade. The gun was still in her other hand but when she tried to bring it up, his fingers closed around it, forcing her wrist against the pavement.

He bore down on her. He didn't smell like death. He never had. No, he smelled like violence. Like leather and blood and pain.

His sharpened teeth flashed as he sank them into her

arm, and a scream tore from Kate's throat.

The darkness began to fold around her mind, the monster rising, but Sloan drew back sharply. His mouth was painted with her blood, but he wasn't smiling.

His hand raked through her hair, forcing her head back, not to bare her throat, she realized, but to see her *eyes*.

A snarl of anger escaped his lips. "What have you done?" he demanded, right before a pair of high beams sliced through the dark. Sloan was halfway to his feet when a gunshot tore the air, and a shatter shell hit him in the chest.

The jeep screeched to a halt, Harris and his gun still hanging out the window.

Sloan staggered backward, and the other monsters surged through the dark in a frenzy of nails and teeth.

August was already out of the jeep, drawing a knife, as Harris lunged into the fray. Ani detonated a series of light grenades, a blinding strobe effect that left the Malchai dazed and gave Jackson and Henry time to get to Kate, who was already up. Blood dripped from her fingers but she had a gore-slicked knife in one hand and a gun in the other.

Sloan, too, was on his feet—the shell had hit him in the chest, tearing through suit and skin, but it clearly hadn't reached his heart. His red eyes found August, and August lunged toward him, only to be cut off by two other Malchai. He didn't stop—he slit one's throat and drove the blade up under the other's ribs, Leo's voice weaving through his head.

This is your purpose. And doesn't it feel good?

He twisted, searching for Sloan, as Harris let out a strangled cry. A Malchai had its fangs in his shoulder, but then Ani was there, driving a knife through its neck. It went down, and Harris yowled, and stomped on the Malchai's chest until it cracked, splintered, gave.

"I think it's dead," called Jackson, wiping a streak of gore from his cheek. "They're all dead."

August turned, searching.

Kate clutched her arm as Ani put pressure on Harris's shoulder, and August realized with a sick dread that none of the bodies on the ground belonged to Sloan.

The Malchai was gone.

And so was Henry Flynn.

||||| |||

"Gone? What do you mean *gone?*"

Emily Flynn was not a shouter. The few times August had seen her angry—truly angry—her voice lost all its volume, all its warmth. She went cold and quiet. The rest of the FTF Council wasn't nearly as composed, their questions ricocheting through the command center.

Ilsa stood in the doorway, a faraway look in her eyes, and August wished she still had her voice, even though he knew that if she tried to speak right now, what came out would be only wondering, wandering, lost.

Soro had their voice, but they stood silently against the wall, their expression level in every way but one. Their eyes.

Soro's eyes, the color of stone, asked a silent question.

Was she worth it?

Emily held up a hand, calling for silence as she leaned across the table and met August's gaze. "Explain it to me."

He opened his mouth, but it was Kate who spoke. She pulled free of the medic bandaging her arm. "It's my fault."

"I believe you," said Em. "But that doesn't answer my question."

"He insisted," said August.

I'm going with you.

Marcon shook his head. "Why would he do that?"

"Why would you *let* him?" added Emily, her attention still on August.

Why *had* he?

Because Henry Flynn was in charge of the FTF?

Because he believed in something greater than himself?

Because August believed he had a plan?

"Because he's dying."

August heard the words come out of his mouth. The room went quiet. Emily's face darkened.

Henry had never said the words, not to August, and August had never asked. He hadn't needed to, hadn't wanted to, not in the months of watching Henry grow thin, of listening to his cough, and not in the moments after they crossed the Seam. There was a strange place, between knowing and not knowing. A place where things could live in the back of your head without weighing down your heart.

"That doesn't explain—" started Paris.

"Doesn't it?" challenged Kate. "Maybe he wanted his death to mean something."

"You have no right to talk," said Marcon.

"If you hadn't gone," added Shia, "Henry wouldn't—"

"If I hadn't gone," said Kate, "Henry Flynn would have found another excuse to get himself killed."

The air grew brittle, and August felt Ilsa and Soro stiffen.

"We don't know that he's dead," said Emily tightly.

"What do we tell the task force?" asked Marcon.

"We *can't* tell them," argued Shia.

"You *have* to," said Kate and Bennett at the same time.

Emily straightened. "Henry would want them to know."

Ilsa tapped on the doorframe. August and Soro glanced toward her—no one else seemed to hear. He watched as his sister produced a tablet, fingers dancing on the screen.

"The last thing we need," said Marcon, "is an uprising."

"Actually," said Paris. "I think that's exactly what we need."

Ilsa's fingers gave a flourish and every screen in the room burst to life, showing feeds, not of the city outside, but of the Compound itself, the training-hall-turned-barracks, the lobby, the canteen—room after room filled with people, all of them talking. Sound spilled into the room, a cacophony of voices as cadets and captains, soldiers and night squads, spoke up and over and around one another.

"They've got Commander Flynn."

"We can't just sit here."

"We should be out there."

"What are we waiting for?"

"Well," said Kate, "it looks like they already know."

August remembered Henry's last words. "He's a man, not a movement," he said echoing his father. "But if a movement is what it takes to end this war . . ."

Emily met his gaze across the table. "*If* Henry is alive," she said slowly, "then we will fight to get him back."

Marcon crossed his arms. "And what if he's not?"

Sloan pried the shards of metal from his skin with a pair of tweezers, dropping the slivers into the dish one by one, each coated in viscous black blood.

His suit was ruined, his shirt cast aside, his bare chest a mess of torn flesh. The shards were silver, and his skin sizzled as he dug them out, but the sensation was shallow and fleeting, and it was not so very different from pleasure. He told himself to relish it, though his hand trembled as he worked.

The two engineers lay slumped against the table, their throats torn open.

He hadn't had time to savor the kills, but the meal had helped with the wound, helped rinse away the rancid taste of Kate's blood in his mouth.

Across the room, Flynn's head lolled forward, a thin ribbon of blood tracing a line from the man's temple to his chin before dripping to the floor. Sloan had always imagined Henry Flynn as the flip side of a coin, Callum Harker's equal but opposite force.

He was wrong.

Up close, Flynn was nothing but a too-thin human with graying temples and sallow skin. He smelled— *sickly.* So disappointing. Still, Sloan couldn't help but marvel at the fortune of it, having the head of the FTF dropped in his lap. He'd lost Katherine and gained an idol—even it was a false one.

Sloan straightened, wiping the last of the blood from his shoulder.

"Why isn't he dead?" asked Alice, storming in. "And what happened to *you?*" Her gaze flicked to the engineers. "You didn't save me any."

Sloan slid on a fresh black shirt. "You're supposed to be watching our pet."

"Where is Kate?" she demanded. "You promised—"

"Katherine will return to us," said Sloan. "And when she does," he added, "you can *have* her." Alice beamed at that.

"Did you evacuate the Malchai?" asked Sloan.

"Most of them," she said, hopping onto the counter. She looked down at the bowl of shrapnel and crinkled her nose. "There's a few in the lobby, but they were sound asleep. I didn't want to wake them." Her attention flicked to Flynn. "Speaking of . . ."

Sloan turned in time to see Flynn's eyelids flutter open. He tried to move, but Sloan had bound him to the chair with wire, and he watched as Flynn struggled, winced, and then went still, realizing where he was.

"I have to admit," said Sloan, buttoning his shirt, "I expected more."

Flynn coughed, a deep rattle in his chest. "Sorry to disappoint."

"You didn't put up much of a fight," he mused. "One might almost think you *wanted* to end up in this position. Hoping to rally the troops?" The man looked up at that, and Sloan saw that he was right. "That was quite a gamble, Mr. Flynn."

"Unlike you," he said, a hitch in his voice, "I care about more—than my own life. The task force—will finally—bring the fight here—to me—to you."

Sloan reached out and spun Flynn's chair toward the windows. They were still two hours from dawn, and the night was at its thickest. He pointed toward the beacon of light that was the FTF Compound and lowered his head to whisper in the man's ear. "That," he said, "is exactly what I'm counting on."

Flynn tensed.

Alice, now cross-legged on the counter, only chuckled. "Time to lay out the cards, and see who has the better hand."

Flynn shook his head. "Kate knew you'd see it as a game."

Alice's eyes brightened at the mention of her maker, but Sloan held up a hand.

"Do you believe in fate? Callum did not. Neither do I. And yet, here you are."

Alice began toying with a circle of metal. It was a collar, the kind worn by the Fangs. Sloan plucked it from her hands.

"Make yourself useful," he told her, flicking his fingers toward a camera on a stand. Alice sighed and hopped off the counter. Sloan returned to Flynn's side and fastened the collar around the man's throat, relishing the visible shiver that ran through Flynn at the metal's touch. Sloan swung the chair back around and considered his work. Something was missing. He took up a roll of tape.

"When I first met Leo, he asked me if I believed in God." The tape made a ripping sound as he pulled a length free. "I think he expected me to say no, but if *we*

are not proof of a higher power, what is?" He tore the
strip with his teeth. "I like to think that we are simply
what you humans have sowed and reaped. You have
earned us. Leo and I saw eye to eye on that."

Flynn's gaze hardened. "He drove a metal bar into
your back."

Sloan flicked his hand dismissively. "I would have
done the same to him. Monstrous acts, I can respect.
Besides, he *did* miss."

Flynn looked at him with fire in his eyes. So there
was still a spark left.

"If you're going to kill me—"

"Oh, I don't plan on doing that, much as I would enjoy
it." Sloan leaned in. "Dead, you are a martyr."

He pressed the tape over Flynn's mouth.

"Alive, you're simply *bait*."

They were all idiots, thought Kate.

Henry Flynn had handed the FTF a cause, a reason
to fight. And the Council couldn't get out of their own
damn way.

"It doesn't *matter* if he's alive," she said, a remark that
earned her August's wide eyes and Soro's cold glare and
a whole lot of judgment from the rest of the room. She
pressed on. "You've always been divided into North
and South, us and them. You keep talking about safety,

about defense; but these people, your soldiers, they *want* to fight, and now they have something—someone—to fight for. So for God's sake, don't *waste* it."

Just then the screens throughout the room crackled and went dark. Everyone looked to Ilsa, but Ilsa was staring at her own tablet in a way that made it clear this wasn't her doing.

The signal came back up, but instead of broadcasting from the various Compound rooms, every single screen showed the same image.

Henry Flynn.

Bloody, half-conscious, but alive.

There was no sound on the feed, and even if there had been, his mouth was taped shut, some kind of steel contraption around his neck. It took her a second to process the wires, the small timer ticking down.

59:57

59:56

59:55

59:54

And just like that, the room burst into motion. Chairs pushed back and people rose. The signal was being broadcast across the entire feed, to every screen and every tablet, not just in the command center but across the whole Compound.

It was a gift. A point of no return. The FTFs, already

gunning for their fight, had just been given their target—
the tower—and even if the Council members *wanted* to
argue, they'd never be able to stop the soldiers now.

59:42

59:41

59:40

Ilsa spread her hands across the largest screen, fingers
splayed over Henry Flynn's gray face, while August and
Emily and Soro spoke into their comms, relaying orders
through the ranks.

". . . assemble squads One through Thirty-six . . ."

". . . authorizing arms clearance . . ."

". . . lockdown procedure . . ."

Kate was still staring at the feed, not at Flynn, but
at the room around him. She recognized the floor-to-
ceiling windows at his back, the chair he was tied to,
the steel and glass and wood, all those cold surfaces and
sharp edges that marked her father's taste.

The penthouse.

58:28

58:27

58:26

"I know exactly where he is."

‖‖‖ ‖‖‖

For six months, August had watched the FTF slowly break apart.

Now, in a single breath, it came together.

It was like a symphony, he thought. Every instrument in tune.

Team after team of FTF cadets fell into rank across the Compound, tasked with guarding the structure and the ten thousand civilians now sheltering inside while the Night Squads prepared to take the tower. He spotted Colin among them, and the boy offered August a smile and a small salute as he passed, violin in hand.

Kate walked at August's side, her gaze steady, her face blank. He'd grown used to seeing her shifting expressions, her varying moods, and it was unnerving to remember how good she was at hiding them.

Could he have convinced her to stay behind?

No.

This was her fight as much as his.

Perhaps even more.

He was almost to the doors when Ilsa caught his wrist and pulled him back.

"What is it?" he asked, and she threw her arms around his neck, her grip so strong, it startled him.

Don't go, her arms seemed to say. Or maybe, simply, *Come back.*

And he wondered if she'd known all along that *this* was where they were headed. If this was what she'd seen in the city she'd made on the kitchen counter, the one reduced to grains of sugar that tasted like ash.

August pulled away, or Ilsa pushed him, he wasn't sure, only knew that the weight of her arms was gone.

The heart of the Night Squads had assembled on the light grid, more than three hundred soldiers armed and ready for war, and August swung the violin case onto his shoulder as they made their way to the jeep at the front of the convoy. Harris, Jackson, and Ani were already inside; Em was at the wheel.

A bandage dotted with blood shone beneath Harris's collar, but he was wide-eyed, and gunning for a fight. He made room, and August was halfway into the jeep when Soro strode over from another vehicle and held out a bag. Not to him, but to Kate.

When she hesitated, clearly suspicious, Soro dropped

the bag at her feet and walked back toward their own squad. It landed with a metallic clang, and Kate knelt and retrieved a pair of iron spikes.

"You shouldn't have," she called after the Sunai before stepping up into the jeep.

August laid the violin across his lap, and Kate sat beside him, turning a spike between her fingers, and as the jeep pulled out, he glanced back at the Compound and saw his sister standing at the front doors, one hand pressed against the glass, but he was too far away to read her face.

Sloan approached the gold shroud.

The shadow in the cage was growing restless. Its silence had changed from a hand to a fist, from a fist to a leaden weight, its displeasure like a cold snap in the basement.

chaoschaoschaoschaos whispered the Corsai from their corners.

The truck idled nearby. A Malchai opened the back and lowered a ramp, and Sloan watched as four more took up wooden poles and slipped them beneath the covered cage and lifted. The monster inside weighed nothing, but the cage was steel, and the Malchai struggled under its weight.

"Mind the gold," advised Sloan, adjusting his gloves.

The sheet shifted, nearly brushing a Malchai's skin, and he snarled, almost dropping his end, but Sloan was there to catch it. He would have torn out the monster's throat, but they were on a schedule.

At last, the cage was loaded onto the truck, and Sloan stepped up beside it, the closeness of the gold a pain he tried to savor. He could feel the shadow beneath the shroud, like an ache in his teeth, a thirst in his throat, and knew that it was hungry.

"Soon, my pet."

39:08

39:07

39:06

The convoy tore through the night, Emily Flynn's voice carrying in the car and across the comms at the same time.

"Every squad has been assigned a floor to clear. You will move systematically through the tower. Malchai are to be eliminated on sight. Fangs are to be incapacitated. As you've been informed, there is another kind of monster somewhere in the building, one with the ability to alter minds. If you encounter it, you are to close your eyes. If any members of your team are affected, you are to incapacitate them. . . ."

They reached the Seam.

The gates were open.

They didn't stop.

Time ticked away inside Kate's head as the jeep barreled toward the wall of darkness at the tower's base. Her arm throbbed from the jagged wound Sloan's teeth had made earlier that night, but she held on to the pain like a tether, the blood seeping through the bandage a reminder that she was still human.

The jeeps hit the blackout zone and plunged in, their high beams scattering the creatures in the dark. August leaned over and spoke into her good ear.

"What's wrong?"

Nothing. Something. Everything.

She wasn't sure.

She *had* been, until she'd seen Henry Flynn on that feed, bound up like a prize, like a *present*. It was too simple. Too obvious. Too easy.

Was it a taunt? Was it a trap? What was waiting for them in that tower? Sloan? Alice? The Chaos Eater? Were they all playing by Sloan's rules? Did they have a choice?

She was missing something—they were all missing something—and it was right there, just out of focus, a glance out of sight.

"Kate?" pressed August.

"What if we're wrong?" she murmured softly, so that only he could hear. "What if this is a mistake?"

August's brow furrowed. "This is what Henry wanted," he said. "What we needed. A reason to attack."

And he was right.

Everything was going exactly to plan.

And that was *exactly* why she didn't trust it.

The jeeps came to a stop at the base of the tower.

August strained to hear as they cut the engines, but there were too many soldiers, too much static.

They kept the lights up, blocking out the darkness, and the Corsai shifting hungrily within it. Claws scraped against the sides of the jeeps wherever the light failed to reach, a high-pitched whine of nails on metal.

The Night Squads gathered at the base of the stairs. Most had guns, but Kate gripped an iron spike, August had his bow out like a sword, and Soro held their flute-knife in a fighter's grip. They climbed the tower steps as if every one of the six stairs might be rigged, but nothing happened. No wires tripped. No sudden blasts.

August and Soro took the lead, stopping before the tower doors. The space beyond was dark and August spread his hands against the glass, listening for the tick of a bomb, the rattle and hiss of Corsai waiting to be unleashed—but all he heard were the racing hearts of the FTF at his back, and a soft, almost imperceptible breathing somewhere inside. He nodded at Soro, and together they threw open the tower doors.

Light grenades rolled across the lobby floor, the bounce of metal on stone followed a second later by waves of glaring white as the FTF poured in, their weapons raised. A dozen Malchai sprang up, hissing in surprise before lunging at the nearest soldiers, their teeth bared.

August turned and slashed a monster's throat as Kate drove her spike through another's chest, and Harris made a triumphant sound as he cut down a third. Soro dispatched two more, clearing a path, and they sprinted across the lobby to the bank of elevators on the other side. Emily got there first, calling the car as the rest reached the doors and spun back to face whatever was coming for them.

But nothing came.

The dozen Malchai were dead, and the other Night Squads were already peeling off, heading for the other floors.

Too easy, thought August as the doors slid open behind them.

"Too easy," whispered Kate as they stepped inside. She punched the button for the penthouse with the familiarity of someone returning home. She seemed to realize it, too, her hand hovering in the air.

"Don't jinx us," warned Ani as the elevator rose.

"Yeah," said Jackson. "We can fall to our death at any second."

They all went quiet then, the only sounds in the steel box their heartbeats and the almost-inaudible murmur of Emily marking time.

August had never been afraid of dying, for all he thought about it. It bothered him, of course, the idea of being unmade, but his own death was a concept he couldn't grasp, no matter how hard he tried.

But *loss*—that was a thing that scared him.

The loss of those he cared for.

The loss of himself.

The absence left by both.

Leo would have scorned such a thing, Soro wouldn't understand the point, and Ilsa was never one to dwell on the inevitable. But to August, that fear was the shadow in his life, the monster he could fight but never kill, the reason he had wanted so badly *not* to feel.

And as he stood there, surrounded by his family, his team, his friends, the fear took hold, because Ilsa was alone and Henry was dying and so much of what he loved could fit within a metal box.

And it could all be lost.

Kate gave his hand a single squeeze before the elevator stopped and the doors slid open.

$\cancel{||||}$
$\cancel{||||}$

The penthouse stretched before them, quiet and dark, and the first thing August heard was the sound of stifled breath. He barreled forward without thinking, down the hall and into the living room, and there he was.

Henry.

Bound to the chair, dazed and pale, but alive.

The red numbers flashed on the collar at his throat.

24:52

24:51

24:50

"Ani," ordered Emily, but the tech was already there at Henry's side, and Jackson, too, checking his vitals as Harris and Soro moved through the apartment.

Em knelt before her husband. "I'm here," she said. "We're here. You're an absolute fool, and I'm going to kill you after we save you, but we're here."

Henry tried to speak, but his mouth was taped shut,

and when Em reached to pull the tape free, Ani stopped her. "Don't touch anything," she warned, "not until I defuse this."

Henry's head lolled forward as the comm crackled at August's collar. *Second floor: we've got nothing.*

"There are two dead bodies over here," said Kate. "Both human."

Harris reappeared. "Rooms are clear."

"There's no one else here," said Soro.

It didn't make sense.

"Third floor: empty," said another voice on the comm.

August looked around. Where were the Malchai? Where were the *Fangs*? Where were all the monsters? He saw the same questions written on Kate's face as she drew a tablet out from beneath one of the corpses.

"This doesn't make any sense," said Ani, tugging at the device.

"Wait—" started Em, but Ani was already pulling the collar away from Henry's throat, prying the pieces apart with a force that no one should use when handling a live bomb.

But then August realized, it *wasn't* live.

It wasn't a bomb at all. Just a collar, like the ones worn by the Fangs, with a few added pieces of colored wire, a timer.

"What the hell?" said Harris.

"Fourth floor: nothing here."

With the collar free, Ani eased the tape from Henry's mouth. He was hoarse, his breath rasping, but his words echoed through the penthouse. "It's a—trap."

Everyone stiffened as the reports continued on the comms.

"Fifth floor: we haven't found a thing."

"If it's a trap," said Em, "then why haven't we been attacked?"

"Because," said Kate, holding up the tablet, "we're not the target."

Through a streak of blood on the screen, August saw a map of the city, a too-familiar building drawn over a grid. The Compound.

Kate was already moving back toward the elevator. "We need to go. Now."

Soro issued a string of orders on their comm as Jackson and Ani got Henry on his feet. His legs nearly buckled, the air wheezing in his chest. His skin was gray.

"Stay with me," said Em.

Kate called the elevator, and August thought of Ilsa, standing at the Compound doors, of Colin in the lobby, of ten thousand innocent people crammed into a building meant for fifteen hundred.

The elevator chimed, but when doors opened, it wasn't empty.

Alice stood in the pool of light.

"Going somewhere?"

The truck jerked and jarred over the uneven ground as it barreled through the tunnels beneath the city, its twin beams of light carving a path through the solid black. Beyond the vehicle the Corsai hissed, but Sloan would make it up to them. After all, there would be plenty of corpses soon.

At last the hole came into sight.

Alice had done her job well—a large crater had been opened between the new tunnel and the old, the debris cleared away to make a kind of road. The truck crawled through, and emerged into an abandoned subway station. A broad set of stairs had once dead-ended in a section of ceiling where the subway had been closed up, built over, but a blast had opened that, too.

The Malchai unloaded the cage from the truck as Sloan made his way up the stairs and stepped into the space above. He spread his arms in triumph.

He was standing inside the Compound.

It was a simple concrete hall, *S3* stenciled on the walls, a set of open steel doors leading on to cell-like rooms. They would be perfect, he thought, for the Sunai, Soro in this one and August in that. It would be simple enough, starving them until they went dark.

The Malchai hoisted the shrouded cage into the hall and Sloan's gloved hands came to rest above the golden sheet. His skin prickled with pain but also delicious anticipation. It was like the moment before a hunt, those precious seconds after his prey had been released, when he let the tension build inside him, let his senses heighten, until everything went sharp, went clear.

"Can you feel them, up above?" he murmured. "They are my offering to you."

Sloan wrapped his fingers in the gold sheet, savoring the scorching heat as he pulled it free. He imagined himself a magician performing a trick, only instead of hoping to render the cage empty, he hoped it was still full.

And it was.

Silver eyes hung in a cloud of shadow, meeting his gaze just before a siren began to blare.

Sloan looked up and saw the single red eye of a security camera and smiled, because the alarms were far, *far* too late.

The cage was empty.

The shadow was gone.

The power around him flickered, dimmed, and seconds later, from somewhere above, Sloan was rewarded by the sound of screams.

11

It finds
death
waiting
in ten thousand
beating hearts
ten thousand
restless bodies
tuned like
instruments
ready
to be played
and together
they will
make
such
wonderful
music.

||||
||||
||

Alice stepped out of the elevator.

Kate's stomach turned at the sight of her. The Malchai was dressed in Kate's old clothes, the sleeves stained with dried blood. She'd even pulled her white hair back into a ponytail, her red eyes glowing beneath pale bangs.

August was already raising his violin and Soro's flute was halfway to their mouth, but before either of them could play, Alice opened her hand, revealing a detonator.

"Uh-uh," she said. "You may be fast, but I'll be faster."

Soro glared and August clenched his teeth as he lowered the instrument a fraction. It could be a bluff, thought Kate, but the gleam in Alice's red eyes said it wasn't.

"Leaving so soon? You just got here." The words could have been meant for everyone, but Kate knew they were directed at *her.*

And she understood.

This wasn't about North and South, or the war between Sloan and Flynn.

This was between *them.*

"Alice," started August, but Kate cut him off.

"If I stay," she asked the Malchai, "will you let them go?"

Alice's smiled widened. "I won't even try to stop them." She stepped to the side and gestured toward the elevator. "Freedom, all yours for the low, low price of a single sinner."

"No," snarled August, but Kate kept her eyes on Alice.

"I've got this," she said. "Take Henry and get back to the Compound. They need you."

"We go together."

She glanced his way and saw pain in his eyes, and fear, and it gave her hope. That he hadn't given up. That he was still in there.

"August," she said. "People are going to die if you don't leave."

"Oh," said Alice cheerfully, "I imagine they're already dying."

As if on cue, static tore through the comms, followed by a distress signal, not from the Night Squads, but from the Compound.

"*Mayday . . . mayday . . . we're under attack . . .*"

"Tick-tock," mused Alice.

Flynn tried to straighten, to speak, but nothing came out, the air whistling through his lungs as he fought for breath.

"Oh dear," said Alice. "He doesn't sound so good."

"*Go*," snapped Kate.

Soro was the first to move, casting an unreadable look her way as they stepped into the elevator, followed by Jackson and Ani supporting Flynn, Emily providing cover in case the Malchai changed her mind. August was the last one to go, his jaw clenched, and Kate forced herself to look at him. Even managed a grim smile, suddenly grateful that a hope didn't count as a lie.

"I'll meet you back there," she said, before the doors shut.

The jeep tore through the night.

The distress signals kept coming in, filling the channel with panicked reports of a shadow and FTFs gone mad. August knew what it meant—the Chaos Eater was inside the Compound.

Soro sped up as the voices on the comms gave way to static, or gunfire; in the backseat Henry lay sprawled out, and Em said "stay with me" over and over while Jackson monitored Henry's vitals and August put his head in his hands and closed his eyes and saw Kate, and the look on her face as he left her behind, and he told himself he didn't have a choice—but it was a lie. He always had a choice. Wasn't the point of being alive that you could choose?

"Kate chose." The words came from Soro. The look on their face told him he'd been talking out loud. "She chose to stay and fight. Now," said the Sunai, "what are *we* going to do?"

August straightened, because Soro was right. Kate was fighting. Henry was fighting. It was their turn. His grip tightened on the violin. He didn't know how to stop the Chaos Eater, but he knew how to keep the FTFs from killing one another.

They just had to get inside.

"When we get back to the Compound," he said, "you and I will go in through the back. The Night Squads will stay on the strip."

"Like hell," muttered Harris from the backseat.

"That's an order," said August. "The Compound is now a quarantine zone. Send it out on the comms—*no one* goes past the light grid. Use the jeeps to make a barrier, and stop *anything* that comes out. Soro and I will handle the rest."

Sloan couldn't help himself.

He wanted to enjoy the view. The alarms had cut off, but the power continued to flicker and dim as he ascended the stairs, the sounds of slaughter drawing nearer with every step. A body came crashing down the steps, its uniform torn as if by nails.

Humans could be truly monstrous, he mused, stepping over the corpse.

As he reached the Compound's main level, he was struck by the sweet scent of fresh blood. It streaked the pale lobby floor, and brushed the walls, rose from the bodies; everywhere he looked, the living were at each other's throats.

A man thrust a blade into another's gut, and a woman wrapped her hands around a young boy's neck, and Sloan moved among them like a ghost, unnoticed, their eyes fogged silver by the monster's hold.

The shadow itself stood in the center of the lobby, growing solid as it fed on so much violence, and the Sunai, the FTF's only hope, were across the Seam, attacking an empty tower. By the time they got here, it would be over. By the time they—

The whistle of steel sang through the air, and Sloan turned just in time to dodge a blade as it slashed upward, slicing his shirt and grazing the skin beneath.

He found himself face to face with a ghost.

A ghost with a cloud of red curls and a ragged scar across her throat.

"Ilsa."

◈

The jeep rounded the Compound and skidded to a halt, the rest of the convoy close behind. August and Soro lunged from the vehicle and onto the light strip.

A back door stood ajar, propped open by the corpse of a soldier who'd obviously tried to escape and failed, a pattern of gunfire dappling his back. There was no time to tend the dead. August closed his eyes for an instant as he stepped over the body, and Soro's fingers tightened on their flute-knife as they followed.

Inside, the Compound was in chaos. The power flickered, and in the unsteady light, August saw the corpses littering the hall, most of them in green-and-gray fatigues.

An FTF was slumped on the ground, his back against the training-hall doors, and August's chest lurched when he recognized warm brown eyes in an open face. Colin was bleeding, he couldn't tell where, but when he stepped closer, the boy's head drifted up, and he actually smiled.

"They're safe," he said. "I got the doors closed before"—he coughed—"before it saw—before they saw . . ."

He trailed off, eyes drifting shut, and August went to check for a pulse, but Soro's hand was already on his shoulder, urging him up. They had to keep moving.

Every second was a life, and he straightened just as a voice reached him from the lobby.

A voice that reminded him of fevers and cold steel and falling.

But it wasn't just the Malchai's voice. It was the single word he said.

"Ilsa."

August turned to Soro. "Get to the command center," he said, "hit the intercom and start playing."

Understanding lit the Sunai's eyes, and they took off toward the stairs as August sprinted for the lobby, and his sister, and Sloan.

⊩⊩⊩ ⊩⊩⊩ ⊩⊩⊩

"You got blood on my clothes," said Kate as she took in the room, trying to carve a mental path.

The Malchai looked down at her shirt. "Hmm, I wonder who that was." She smiled, flashing teeth. "You know what I keep asking myself?"

Kate cheated a step to the side, within reach of the sofa. "Why your hair isn't as good as mine?"

Alice's red eyes narrowed. "What it will feel like to take your life." The Malchai crouched, setting the detonator upright on the floor. "There's a beauty in it, don't you think? A kind of poetry. What happens when the effect kills the cause?" She straightened. "I've spent the last six months watching Sloan kill you. Wondering if I would enjoy it half as much. I think I will."

Kate's grip tightened on the spike as the shadow in her head longed to be let in, to be let *out*. "Are you done?"

Alice pouted. "Not one for talking, are you? All right, then."

She lunged, so fast she seemed to blur, to disappear, but Kate was already moving, too, cutting sideways. She got one foot up on the couch and pushed off, driving her spike down into the blurring shape beneath her.

An instant too late.

The weapon scraped against the floor and Kate rolled and came up, twisting just in time to block Alice's shoe as it slammed into her front. Pain exploded down her arm as the blow connected, and the spike went skidding across the floor.

Kate gasped and drew the second spike as she tried to swerve out of the Malchai's path, but Alice was already there. Nails raked across Kate's face, fine lines of blood welling on her cheek.

Alice smiled at the red on her fingers. "You don't honestly think you're a match for me," she said, flicking the blood away. "I am you but better, Kate. You don't stand a chance."

Kate shifted her grip on the spike. "You're probably right."

She ran a hand through her hair, pushing the bangs out of her face, the silver cracks on full display. Alice's eyes flickered with surprise, then suspicion, and it was Kate's turn to smile.

"So it's a good thing," she said, "that I'm not entirely myself anymore."

Ever since that moment in Prosperity, she'd wanted to fight, to hurt, to kill, and she'd resisted, and resisted, and resisted, had run from the shadow, knowing it was only a matter of time before it caught her.

And now, at last, she could stop running.

All she had to do was let the darkness in.

All she had to do was let the monster out.

And so she did.

Kate's resistance crumbled, and the world went quiet as the shadow stole over her.

There was no fear here.

There was nothing but this room.

This moment.

The iron singing in her hands.

The monster in her way.

Alice's eyes narrowed, as if she could *see* the change in Kate.

"What are you?" she snarled.

And Kate laughed. "I'm not sure," she said. "Let's find out."

August reached the lobby just in time to see Sloan slam Ilsa back into the far wall, a knife tumbling from her fingers. Her hair was matted with sweat, the collar of her shirt torn, exposing a swathe of stars along her shoulder.

Sloan kicked the knife away and leaned in close.

"What's that?" he hissed. "I can't hear you."

"Sloan!" shouted August, and the monster sighed and let Ilsa drop to the ground.

"August," crooned the Malchai. "It's been so long."

The last time he'd faced Sloan, August had been starving, feverish—edging toward mortal. Strung up in a warehouse and beaten to the point of turning.

But he had changed.

He was still changing.

Sloan swept a hand over the chaos. "Have you met my pet?"

The Compound was a battlefield. Soldiers wrestled on the blood-slick floor, trapped in their violent spell.

Hurry, Soro, he thought.

Many of the soldiers were still alive, but they were killing one another, and there, in the center of the lobby, still as the eye of a storm, stood the Chaos Eater, its head tipped back and its arms wide, as if to receive them all.

As August watched, he felt it again, that horrible, hollow space, like hunger, in his chest. He forced his gaze back to Sloan.

"Still holding on to that human shell, I see." The Malchai clicked his tongue. "Leo would have faced me in his true form, monster-to-monster, one-on-one."

"I'm not Leo," said August. "And it's not one-on-one."

Ilsa was on her feet, and the air around her had gone ice cold. He had seen his sister lost, and kind, and dreaming, but he had never seen her angry.

Until now.

She had the knife in her hand, and he had the bow in his, and Sloan must have sensed the scales tipping, because he took a single step back but was blocked by the body of a fallen cadet and, in that instant of imbalance, August and Ilsa struck.

Sloan had to choose. And he chose August. But as the Malchai knocked away the bow, Ilsa moved behind him with a dancer's grace and slid her knife along the back of his knees. The Malchai snarled and staggered, one leg threatening to fold, but August caught him by the collar.

Sloan slashed at August's eyes and leaped back, but Ilsa was there. She kicked out his other leg, and his knees hit the floor. She brought her knife to Sloan's throat as August fetched up his fallen bow.

The Malchai bared his teeth. "Tell me, August, where is Katherine? Surely you didn't *leave* her with Alice."

"Shut up."

Sloan laughed. "She doesn't stand a chance."

Surprise flickered across Ilsa's face, and her grip must have loosened, because Sloan lunged to his feet in a last, desperate attempt at freedom. Ilsa's knife carved a shallow line along his throat, and August stepped into the Malchai's path.

"You're *wrong*," snarled August, driving the steel bow straight up into Sloan's heart.

The Malchai swayed on his feet, but unlike Leo, August hadn't missed, and a moment later Sloan fell, his red eyes widening for an instant before their light went out.

It stands
at the center
of a sun
burning
brighter
and brighter
with every
stolen life.

Kate dived for the knife block.

Her fingers skimmed the nearest handle before Alice swept the whole thing off the counter. The knives came free, skittering across the kitchen floor, and Kate rolled, taking one as Alice grabbed another.

"How does it feel," asked Alice, twirling the blade, "to know that I'm only here because of you?"

The knife came sailing through the air and Kate narrowly dodged, the blade burying itself in the cabinets. She tried to drive her own knife into Alice's side, but the Malchai had the block in her hands now, and she caught the blade's tip in the wood, ripping it from Kate's grip before slamming the block itself into her ribs.

Pain splintered across her chest, there and then gone, a burst of light quickly swallowed up by the shadow. She swept up a cleaver, blood singing.

"To know that all the people I've killed—and I've killed a lot of people," added Alice with manic glee, "are dead because of *you*?"

The words were meant to hurt.

"That everything I do, I get to do because of you?"

But Kate felt nothing.

"Can you feel it," goaded Alice, "when I kill them?"

Nothing but the cool weight of the weapons in her hands.

"Does it send a shiver through you?"

"Do you ever shut *up?*" said Kate, feinting with the knife and then driving the spike down into Alice's hand, pinning her to the kitchen counter. Alice let out a snarl of pain, but even as Kate moved to cut the Malchai's throat, Alice tore free.

They collided, again and again.

Came apart, again and again.

Until blood dotted the floor, red and black.

Dripped from hands and jaws like sweat.

Alice laughed.

And Kate growled.

And they crashed together.

every scream
like thread
like muscle
drawing it
together
until
at last—

August pulled the bow free, and let Sloan's body—what was left of it—collapse to the floor just as Ilsa drew in a sharp breath. It was the closest thing to a sound she'd made in months, and August turned, following her gaze.

The Chaos Eater was still there, but it was no longer a silver-eyed shadow.

It was a thing of flesh and bone. August could hear lungs filling with air, and something like a heart beating in the hollow of its chest as a mouth carved its way across its face, and the lips split into a smile, and the smile parted to reveal a voice and—

I
am
real.

Its voice tore through August like a storm, forcing its way through his head, his chest. It stoked the coal that burned at his core, the darkness waiting to be released, and August clutched at his heart as it flared, the tallies on his skin glowing red.

He fought

and lost

and began to fall—

toward that darker self—

away from his body—

away from—

Music poured through the speakers, the steady notes of Soro's song spilled across the lobby.

They washed over August like a balm, putting out the fire before it spread. He struggled up to his hands and knees and saw Ilsa folded on the floor nearby, the light fading from her stars as the fever left her. To every side, the fighting stopped.

Weapons slid from fingers, and hands fell away from skin, and assaults dissolved into tableaus before collapsing entirely.

Light rose to the surface of skin, white at first, and then streaked with red, the crimson glow bleeding through the edges of their souls, staining each and every one.

The music couldn't resurrect the dead, but every living soul went calm, enveloped by the Sunai's spell.

Only the Chaos Eater moved.

It shuddered and twitched, struggling to hold its shape, trying to open a mouth that dissolved and reappeared and dissolved again, sealing its voice away. But as it strained against the music, it began to *win*. Its edges hardened, and the line of its mouth grew firm, and August knew there wasn't much time.

The air around the monster cracked and split, dark lines thrown out like shards, the *absence* of a soul, cold and empty.

August rose to his feet, forcing himself forward.

He had reaped a Malchai's soul, and it had nearly killed him.

He had reaped his brother's, and it still fought inside him.

And as his fingers brushed the nearest shard, he wondered what would become of—

Something darted past him, quick as air.

A cloud of curls and a cluster of stars, swallowed up by smoke as Ilsa *transformed*.

Between one step and the next, she disappeared, replaced by a Sunai with curved horns and burning wings. A blue light, like the very center of a flame, glowed through Ilsa's skin as she threw her arms around the Chaos Eater, and the room *exploded* in silver and shadow, two forces colliding in a way that shook the world.

August staggered, shielding his eyes.

When he looked again, the Chaos Eater was gone, and Ilsa stood alone in the center of the lobby floor.

Our sister has two sides, Leo had said. *They never meet.*

August had always imagined Ilsa's true form as the opposite of her human one, cruel where she was kind, but as he stared into the Sunai's black eyes, all he saw was his sister.

And as he watched, the smoke withdrew and her wings burned away, horns returning to red curls.

But her skin, which should have been smooth and starless, was cracking. Dark lines like deep fissures started on her hands and spread, up her arms and over her shoulders and across her face.

Ilsa looked up at August, and he saw the sadness in his sister's eyes right before she broke apart and shattered on the floor.

卌
卌
卌

Kate stumbled, her vision suddenly blurring, and when it came back into focus, the world was heavy and dull, the sharpness lost. Her limbs trembled, and her body ached, and the shadow in her head was *gone.*

And Alice was on her.

The Malchai caught Kate by the throat and slammed her back into the floor-to-ceiling windows. The glass cracked against her spine, the splinters spreading dangerously.

"What's the matter?" taunted Alice. "Losing steam?"

Instead of trying to break free, Kate grabbed her by the collar and twisted hard, tipping the Malchai off-balance.

It bought her only an instant, just enough time to draw a breath and put what was left of the coffee table— a pile of shattered glass and broken wood—between them. Alice stepped over it with exaggerated care, and Kate retreated one pace, and then another.

She was running away.

And Alice knew it.

Her mind reeled as she tried to piece together a plan with the last of her strength.

A knife, slick with blood, sat on the counter.

Alice *tsked*. "Boring."

But Kate lunged for it.

She almost made it.

Her fingers skimmed the metal before Alice caught her leg, nails sinking deep into her calf. Kate gasped in pain, an animal sound that seemed to stoke the Malchai's bloodlust as she dragged her down to the floor. Kate twisted, rolling onto her back and swinging her boot across Alice's face. The Malchai recoiled, and Kate scrambled up. She tried to ignore the blood running into her eyes, tried to ignore the mounting pain, tried to ignore everything but Alice's red eyes glowing in the low light.

She flexed her fingers, too aware that her hands were empty. Halfway between them, an iron spike glinted on the floor, and Alice grinned, daring her to try to get there first.

Kate knew she wouldn't—she was too slow without the monster in her head, and she was losing blood, losing strength, *losing.*

"I give up," she said. "You win."

The words caught Alice by surprise, which was exactly what Kate needed. She dove for the weapon. Alice moved a second later, but Kate's hand had already closed around the spike and she turned, meeting the monster as the monster met her.

Kate drove the spike up into the Alice's heart.

And Alice drove her hand into Kate's chest.

|||| |||| |||| |

August sank to his knees on the lobby floor.

There was nothing left of Ilsa, nothing but a small white pile of dust in a world of red, and he heard himself say her name over and over until the word lost meaning, until his voice faltered and broke. He reached out and drew his fingers through the ash.

Then he forced his hand to his comm, forced the words from his throat, forced his body to its feet as the music stopped playing and Soro reappeared, dark eyes going wide at the sight of so many stained souls. And moments later, the Night Squads poured in, and the living returned to themselves, and the Compound plunged into shock, and sorrow, and noise.

August started to retreat, and felt something crack beneath his heel. An abandoned tablet. He knelt to retrieve it, and saw it was still transmitting from the penthouse. The screen was dark, and the shot was empty. There was no sign of Alice. No sign of Kate.

No sign of life at all.

The tablet fell from his fingers.

He ran.

The elevator doors opened and August sprinted into the Harker penthouse.

It was a mess of toppled furniture and broken glass, weapons glinting and one window a violent spiderweb of cracks. Blood slicked almost every surface, some of it red and some of it black, and a mound of ash and gore was heaped on the floor, and he barely noticed any of it, because all he saw was Kate.

Kate, sitting in darkness at the kitchen counter, one arm in her lap and the other resting on the countertop, fingers wrapped around her iron spike.

She looked up when August came in. The silver was gone from her eyes, replaced by that steady blue, made bluer by the blood on her face.

"Did we win?" she asked.

A sound escaped his throat, half laugh, half sob, because he didn't know how to answer. It seemed so wrong to call it winning when so many were dead, when Ilsa was ash, and Henry was dying, and the Compound was awash in red. But the Chaos Eater was gone, and Sloan was dead, and so he said, "Yes."

Kate let out a trembling breath and closed her eyes. "Good."

She let the spike roll from her fingers, and he frowned at the sight of her palm, coated with blood. It dripped to the floor beneath her stool.

"You need a medic."

But Kate only shot him a tired smile. "I'm tougher than I look," she said. "I just want to go . . ." She pushed herself upright, the shadow of pain crossing her face as she started toward him.

She never made it.

August was already there when her legs gave way, and he caught her, sinking with her to the floor, and even in the low light, he could see the blood staining the front of her shirt, the way it had when they'd been trapped in the subway car, when the lights had come on and the world had gone from black and white to vicious red.

"Stay with me," he said.

They were her words once—said when he was sick, when he was on fire, when she took his burning hand and dragged him to his feet, and he got up, and he held on—and so she had to now. "Stay with me, Kate."

"Do they stay with you?" she murmured, and August didn't know what she meant because all he could see, all he could think of, was the blood.

There was so much of it.

It soaked through her clothes from a jagged, too-dark tear in her shirt, but when August pressed his hands to the wound, Kate shuddered, red light rising on her skin.

"No." He tried to pull away, but Kate caught his hand, holding it in place. "Kate, please, let me—"

"The souls you take—" Her fingers tightened on his. "Do they—stay?"

And he knew what she asking, and he knew why, but he didn't know how to answer. He thought of Leo, his brother's voice in his head, thought of all the other voices he never heard. "I don't know, Kate." His voice trembled. "I don't *know.*"

"Sometimes—"she said through gritted teeth, "I wish you could lie."

"I'm sorry." Tears were running down his face.

"I'm not." Kate pressed her hand down over his, and he bowed his head, trying to put pressure on the wound even as the red light grew brighter and began to pour through his skin.

He didn't want it—didn't want anything except to give it back, to hold her together the way she'd held him. But he couldn't. He didn't know how. He closed his eyes as the light of Kate's soul flowed through him, strong and bright.

"I don't know," he whispered. "I don't know if the souls stay with me. But I hope they do."

There was no answer.

August opened his eyes. "Kate?"

But the room was dark and quiet, and she was gone.

ELEGY

He found Allegro pawing at Ilsa's door.

It had been three days, and the cat still didn't seem to realize his sister was gone.

August knelt down. "I know." He reached out gingerly to pet the cat. "I miss her, too."

Allegro looked at him with sad green eyes, before climbing into his arms and nuzzling beneath his chin. August had clearly been forgiven.

He carried the cat into his own room, and set him on the bed beside Kate's tablet. The rest of her things—the iron spikes, the silver lighter—lay in a bag beneath the bed, but it was the tablet he kept returning to.

It wasn't locked, and when he first booted the screen, he'd found an inbox filled with unsent messages. Half-formed notes to people August had never met, people Kate would never see again.

Kate—the name echoed through him like a single,

plucked string. There was no voice in his head, no way to know if she was with him. No way to know, but he could hope.

August sank onto the edge of the bed, the tablet in his hands, scrolling through the messages until he found the one from Ilsa, the one that read only AUGUST.

His chest ached.

He missed them both, in different ways, marveled even through the pain at how different people left such different holes.

Someone knocked, and August looked up and saw Henry standing in the doorway, one hand braced against the frame. He moved like he was made of glass, expecting with every step to break. But he had not broken yet.

"It's time," said Henry.

August nodded, and rose to his feet.

The FTFs gathered at the base of the Seam, black bands circling their sleeves.

A marker of the dead.

They were standing before the central gate, Henry leaning on Emily, the Council beside them—Henry said it was important for the FTFs to see the faces of the future as well as those of the past.

August stood at Henry's side, and Soro at his, Ilsa's absence marked by a space between them. August's violin hung from his fingers—he wanted to play for the bodies on the wall, for the dead and for the lost, for Ilsa and for Kate, and for everyone stolen by monstrous acts; but he would wait until the service was over, and the sun went down, and if the living wanted to listen, to lose themselves for a moment in the music, they were welcome to.

But for now, no one spoke, no speeches were made, and that was all right. Mourning was its own kind of music—the sound of so many hearts, of so many breaths, of so many standing together.

The crowd stretched from the Seam to the Compound, a sea of faces turned up toward the wall where the bodies were laid out, two hundred and ninety-eight members of the FTF wrapped in black, like tallies.

It was a warm day for early spring, the sun cutting through the clouds, and August had his sleeves rolled up, his own tallies scrawled across his skin.

One hundred and eighty-seven.

He wouldn't lose count again.

Colin stood near the front of the crowd. Despite his injuries, he still wanted to join the Night Squad. He had always been full of stubborn hope.

Stubborn hope—that's how he put it.

August liked the phrase.

Kate would probably say that she was the stubborn

and he was the hope, and he didn't know if she'd be right, but he held on to that idea—to hope—as Henry bowed his head, and so did August and Soro and Emily and the Council and the crowd, the gesture spreading row by row as the soldiers on the Seam lit the fire, and the bodies on the wall began to burn.

August stood on the roof of the Compound as the sun sank and the fire died to embers on the Seam.

Steps sounded behind him, and a moment later he sensed Soro's arrival, their presence a thing solid enough to lean against.

Even now, he was amazed by the weight of their will, the steadiness of their resolve, unwavering in a way he'd never known. August was full of questions, of doubts, of wants and hopes, fears and flaws. He did not know if they were weaknesses or strengths, only that he didn't want to live without them.

For a long time, they stood in silence, but for once, Soro was the one to break it.

"I saw their souls," said the Sunai. "All those humans, streaked with red. How are we supposed to judge them now?"

August looked their way. "Maybe we aren't."

He expected a fight, but Soro went quiet again, twirling their flute-knife between their fingers as they looked out at the jagged skyline, and August followed their gaze, past the Seam and the smoke to the northern side of the city.

Once, in his first month, August had dropped an empty glass jar.

It had slipped through his fingers and shattered on the kitchen floor, throwing a hundred shards, some big enough to cup in his palm and others like flecks of dust, impossible to see unless they caught the light. It had taken a maddening amount of time to retrieve all the pieces, and even when he thought the task was done, he would still catch the glint of glass hours, days, weeks later.

The monsters of Verity were like that jar.

Sloan and Alice, the two largest shards, were gone, but so many smaller pieces remained. The Corsai, they could only hope to starve with time and light, while some of the Malchai had fled into the Waste, and the rest were scattering across the city, determined to survive. The Fangs were largely gone, but any stragglers would find themselves prey. To monsters. Or to him.

The whole city glinted in the aftermath, the shards thrown wide, and August didn't know how long it would take to find them all, to take them up and make Verity safe again.

As for the humans, they were still divided—by anger,

and loss, fear, and hope. Progress was being made, but August was coming to realize that there would always be cracks in the surface, shadows in the light, a hundred degrees of grays between black and white.

People were messy. They were defined not only by what they'd done, but by what they *would* have done, under different circumstances, molded as much by their regrets as their actions, choices they stood by and those they wished they could undo. Of course, there was no going back—time only moved forward—but people could change.

For worse.

And for better.

It wasn't easy. The world was complicated. Life was hard. And so often, living hurt.

So make it worth the pain.

Kate's voice whispered through him, sudden and welcome, and he drew a deep breath. Darkness was sweeping over the city, and there was still so much work to be done.

"Are you ready, brother?" asked Soro.

And August lifted his violin and stepped to the edge of the roof.

"I am."

ACKNOWLEDGMENTS

This book nearly killed me.

I always say that, but I swear, this time I mean it. It's not a sign I didn't love the work—after all, books can't hurt you unless you care about them.

That's how they get in—through the cracks that caring makes in us.

This book nearly killed me because I cared. I cared so much about Kate and August, and telling their story. I knew from the start it wouldn't be a happy one. Hopeful, yes, but in a world with places like Verity, even hopeful endings come at a cost.

This book cost me something, but it didn't kill me, because of those I had at my side.

My agent, Holly Root, who reminded me to breathe.

My editor, Martha Mihalick, who helped me up every time I fell (and then kept me on my feet).

My team at Greenwillow, who never lost faith.

My mother and father, who assured me I'd been down this road before.

My friends, who had the emails and texts and memories to prove it.

We say it takes a village, and never has it been more true.

Thank you.